ZARA DUSK

A Court of Whimsy and Ruin

Contents

The story so far...

This book is about Lexi and Dominic.

But it's also about the five heirs of Verda, the realms of Caprice and Fen, the Shadow Walkers, and their epic battles for supremacy.

As a quick recap, the five heirs of Verda are:

Neela Flora

Heir to the Floran throne. Her big brother and parents died a year before she was summoned to the realm and discovered she was fae.

She Ascended into a powerful Grower, so she can always whip up a chamomile plant for a nice cup of tea, or kill you with a vine. She and Ronan have been an item ever since he stopped trying to kill her. Pixie-like, pale skin, with spiky sky-blue hair.

Ronan Mentium

Heir to the Mentium throne. His Dad, Malachi Mentium, is the highest-ranked among the current crop of kings and queens.

Ronan is a kickass Mentium, which influences mood. Great

at a party. Tall and brooding with tan skin, black hair and eyes, wears a lot of black.

Leif Caro

Heir to the Caro throne, which is all about sex and lust. Also great at a party, but only for over-eighteens. It gets really awkward otherwise.

His mom, Stella, ruled until she was killed by a Shadow Walker and Leif was thrust into the position of Alpha of Alphas, leader of all wolf packs in Verda. Tall, pale skin, slimly muscled, with long silver hair, usually seen wearing track pants and bouncing a tennis ball.

His mate is orange-haired **Alara Everly**, who is now the sole beneficiary of all his sexual attentions. Lucky her.

Gabrelle Allura

Heir to the Allura throne, which is all about beauty. She has Lure and can get inside your mind and make you do whatever she wants, so *she* certainly has fun at parties.

Gabrelle used to think masking her feelings to mimic her ice-queen mom, Chantelle, was a top idea, but she's since softened and is now super emotional. Deep brown skin with dusty pink hair and eyes.

She's partnered up with black-eyed **Thorne Sanctus**, who gave up his reign of the Realm of Fen to be with her. Fen is where you have to tell the truth, so he's very direct. Not so good at a party, but he'll let you know if you've got spinach stuck between your teeth.

Dion Dionysus

Heir to the Dionysus throne. He's a kickass chef. He can

make you taste sunsets or memories, like that time you pashed an unwashed Metallica fan out of desperation to experience your first kiss. Hmm, maybe skip that dish. His Dad, also Dion Dionysus, is one of the kings. Rugged features with hair and eyes that match whatever he last ate.

The other important players are in the Realm of Caprice, where the land itself is almost sentient. **Delph Athar** (pale skin, silver eyes, long black hair) and **Darzan Davin** (onyx skin, hair like liquid gold, silver eyes) are the newly crowned King and Queen. Delph is half-fae with Lightning magic, and Darzan is a glowering asshole with Lightning and War. They make a cute couple.

There's something else important... oh yes, the **Shadow King**. He has an army of Shadow Walkers, creatures made from darkness who breed and multiply by feeding on shifters. And any fae who dies by their hand will rise again to fight as an undead soldier. Not recommended for parties.

The only weapon against the Walkers is the Stone of Veritas, which the heirs of Verda possess, but honestly, it's just one little rock against an army of shadows and zombies so, you know, good luck, guys.

Lexi

"I am a badass. I am competent."

I repeated my mantra in different ways, but it wasn't working today. My words weren't filling me with pride and confidence, and they weren't stopping my legs from shaking. And what was with the sweat prickling my forehead?

Maybe something to do with the fact that a three-hundred-pound man with a red beard and leather armor was shouting in my face. Maybe something to do with the heavy sword he held above his head, ready to strike.

Or maybe because I was mumbling my mantra instead of really shouting it. Yeah, that was it.

I threw back my shoulders and tried again, this time really selling the words, upping my tone from a murmur to a roar. "I am a competent badass!"

The field was filled with warriors stomping the grass into mud and yelling and swearing. I remembered finding the thunk of swords against leather very disappointing during my first battle—I'd expected clanging and ringing of steel, but most people missed their targets, and sword fights were usually clumsy. A far cry from the elegant parrying you saw in movies, and with none of the special sound effects.

Some folks slowed down their attacks and made it orchestrated, almost like a dance. But if I wanted that, I'd go to the damn ballet. No, it was real fighting for me, or it was nothing.

With a primal scream and a final bellow of "competent," I rushed my red-bearded enemy, plunging my sword right through his belly. Well, except he jumped aside, moving faster than I gave him credit for. Panting, I went over my mantra again, my wide eyes still on the massive man.

Something in my face must have terrified the poor bastard because he put down his sword and looked at me with worry. "Are you okay, luv?"

Sweat and mud drowned my senses, and I couldn't tell if it was mine or everyone else's. The crowd around the perimeter was cheering wildly, and the occasional judge darted through the fight, trying to avoid being hit.

There was even a tang of fresh blood, which made me think somebody was wearing blood-scented perfume. I narrowed my eyes and looked at Redbeard. "Are you wearing blood?"

He preened and a smile fluttered on his lips. "Yeah. I got it online."

Anger swept through me at the idiocy of this conversation. Here I was in the middle of a battle I'd driven two hours to attend, and this guy was making it feel fake.

"Stay in character," I snarled and launched an elbow at his gut. It landed, jolting pain up my arm, but the pity in the man's face only deepened. "Look, I might go and fight someone my own size. No offense, yeah?"

I roared after his retreating back. "Yellow belly!"

He just shrugged those massive shoulders and kept walking away.

Snarling, I surveyed the battle for another opponent. I ducked around a guy wearing black jeans, narrowing my eyes at him. I tried on a growl, but I felt stupid so I stopped. But come on. Black fucking jeans. He shouldn't have been allowed in.

I'd spent hundreds of bucks on my fighting leathers. Chocolate leather pants, a hand-sewn cream linen shirt, which was a bastard to clean. Plus my pride and joy, a thick leather jerkin with metal studding that deflected body blows and had the added bonus of looking totally badass.

A loose strand of black curly hair popped free of my pony tail as I leaped over a fallen soldier. I pushed it behind my ear impatiently and scanned the field, looking for an opponent.

Today was the most important day on the LARPers calendar. It was the day that determined who would be crowned champion of the tournament. After months of hard work and training, I had a chance to win glorious metal armor. Not leather, metal. Tension laced the air as each warrior thirsted for victory.

I'd already aced the battle strategy written exam. Tactics were where I shone—I actually was a competent badass in that department, no ego-boosting required. For example, I saw a massive woman with a thick forehead that looked like a battering ram, and I strategically headed in the other direction.

All I had to do today was stay on my feet and fight a few opponents, and I'd win my division—the "Young Female Warriors" class. They used to call it the "Young Ladies" division, but we'd kicked up a stink until they changed it. In reality, only a minority of LARPers were women, and only a handful were under twenty-five, but I still wanted that trophy. Metal armor cost a fortune.

I fished my dagger from my boot and stabbed up at a passing 12th-century guard wearing striped livery, aiming for his heart.

Sadly, my thumb hooked painfully into my leather jerkin and I stabbed thin air instead of organ. The bloke didn't even notice my attack, so I sauntered past as if nothing had happened. Hopefully the judges weren't looking.

All I had to do was beat Lisa Munroe, my bitter rival and mortal enemy. She wasn't as good at strategy, but had biceps the size of elephants and was a killer on the field. Lisa Munroe had won the YFW division two years running, and it was time someone knocked her off her pedestal. She dripped with bloody superiority and needed a good kick to the ego.

Happy to oblige. I just had to stay on my feet and maybe have one more skirmish. I scanned the battle field, looking through the stomping limbs and flattened grass, searching for someone I could beat. I must have earned a few points defeating that red-bearded mountain, but I might as well seal the deal.

Then I saw her. Lying on the ground with her face twisted in agony. She was holding her knee like it was a fae glass vase, which could shatter under a heavy breath. Lisa Munroe.

Good. She was out of contention. My bitter rival, my mortal enemy, the woman I wanted to knock off her throne, was out of the competition. From the look of the way she was rocking back and forth, she wasn't getting up any time soon. If she didn't finish the battle on her feet, she was ineligible to win.

Excellent. I was glad. I'd look fucking spectacular in the silver armor, my black hair contrasting against the killer breastplate. I deserved it too. I'd worked harder than anybody and had aced that strategy exam.

Thank God I couldn't hear her crying because that might make me feel bad for her. From her screwed-up face, she was definitely weeping. Sobbing, even. Which, I had to admit, was unusual for her. A cry-baby sobbing was one thing, but Lisa Munroe showing emotion? Unheard of.

Her face was red, but her eyes looked glazed over like the pain was deadening her soul. She kept holding that knee and rocking back and forth, her forehead scrunched up and crumply.

A trio of chunky men were battling behind her where she couldn't see, too focused on their opponents to notice the small woman crouched on the ground, about to be trampled underfoot.

Damn. This shit was about to go sideways. Those chunky fuckers were about to trample an injured woman. And Lisa Munroe was crying. The world was upside down.

"Fuck it," I mumbled, then plunged into the fray, dodging around an older woman's massive backswing and ducking between two skirmishes.

When I reached Lisa, her eyes hardened into pips. "Fuck off, Lexi," she snarled, and I tried not to take it personally. But I kicked her short sword out of her reach, just as a precaution.

"Do you want my help or not?" I hissed. I couldn't believe I was offering my aid to the woman I hated most in the universe. I felt bad about it, but I'd feel even worse if I watched her skull get stomped in.

"Not," she spat. "Definitely not. I don't need help from a pipsqueak like you."

I stared at her for a long moment. "Pipsqueak? Really? Just cos I don't have watermelons hanging off my upper arms."

Lisa scowled and wiped the sweat off her forehead, leaving a muddy streak that leached into her blond hair. "They're not watermelons. They're biceps. You should consider growing some, they're really handy in battle."

How dare she? I never should have come to help her. "I've got muscles, bitch," I retorted. My natural instinct was, of course, to flex, but my muscles were more internal than external, and they never looked as big to other people as they did to me, so I held myself back.

"Good comeback," she mocked.

I eyed the trio of chunksters who were clomping closer and closer, their backswings and movements growing wilder as they tired. "Come on," I muttered. My thick leather jerkin cut into my belly as I bent down to yank Lisa to her feet. "Good battle," I said snidely. "Pity about the knee. And the fact you lost the competition."

She limped beside me, putting a lot of weight on my shoulder. She was a big, heavy bitch with too many muscles for her own good.

When we made it through the crowd, which was thinning out due to "dead" people littering the ground, I helped Lisa to the medic tent. One of the nurses wore long black robes and a beaked bird mask, and I gave him a massive smile. The other one wore a stupid modern white outfit that made me want to puke. So out of character.

Lisa hobbled over to the bird doctor, which made my estimation of her grow. I might hate her as a bitter rival on the field, but I couldn't fault her authenticity. Her blond hair was pulled back in plaits, and her fighting leathers were as realistic as mine but in black.

I looked back at the battlefield, drawn to the thuds and cries. Just one more decent skirmish would assure my victory. If I took home the trophy, my father and sisters would have to respect me, at least for a few days. Wouldn't they? All the teasing and poking fun would take a backseat. But then I looked at Lisa's slumped shoulders and pained face, and with a dramatic sigh, I crossed to her side and placed a soft hand on her shoulder.

The bird doctor removed his mask to look at Lisa's knee, which was a shame. Behind the mask, I could imagine him as young and gorgeous, but the reality was a graying old dude with a bulbous nose. Typical LARPer, really. This was not the place to pick up.

While the bird doctor prodded at Lisa's knee, she turned to me. "Why'd you help me? You finished off the field, so you can't win. You forfeited."

I slumped onto the mattress beside her. "I know."

"So why'd you do it?"

The glimmering silver armor that I'd given up hovered above me like a vision while I considered my answer. Truthfully, I couldn't let anybody's skull get smashed in, not even Lisa Munroe's. But I couldn't tell her that.

"Because I'm a fucking idiot," I said lamely.

The doctor wrapped support around Lisa's knee, gave her some painkillers, and told her to get an x-ray.

"No such thing," Lisa said grandly before hobbling out of the tent and into the fading sunshine. Back in Hebes there were x-rays, but not here. Not today.

I had to admire that woman. Hate her, of course, but admire her too.

"Drink?" she asked, looking up at me as she plonked herself heavily onto a battle-side bench and propped her injured leg along its length.

"Sure," I said, holding out an empty palm. "But you're paying, since I saved your ass. And you cost me the prize."

My best friend snorted, but she fished some copper coins

out of her tunic. I stalked through the mud to the tavern tent and returned with two frothing mugs of ale. I joined her on a bench beside the field, where we watched the rest of the battle play out.

Outside of LARPing, Lisa was my bestie. Inside, she was my enemy. It worked well. Now it was all over, I felt extra bad about her injury.

"You know," I said, wiping froth off my upper lip. "In Arathay, you'd be Healed instantly. Some fae specialize in Healing, and they lay hands on you and mumble a spell or something, and you're magically better."

"Sounds hocus," Lisa said, knocking back her ale in one massive, impressive, ugly gulp. Her throat bobbed while she downed the whole thing, then she turned and asked me for another.

"It's not hocus," I grumbled. "It's magic."

She waggled her mug in front of my face, urging me to take it. "Are you listening to yourself? You sound like a lunatic. Fae are just, I don't know…"

An elderly couple of women were battling nearest to us, barely tapping each other with each attack. I was pretty sure the fight would only end when one of them fell down from exhaustion.

"Fae are just what?" I snapped. "Fake? Made up? Do you think my cousin's a liar? She's been over there for months. She's got Lightning magic, for fuck's sake."

Lisa waved away my annoyance. "I know, I know, it's just hard to believe. Like, how quickly I finished my ale and how I'm injured and can't get myself another one." She shook her head sadly. "So hard to believe."

She had a nerve. Trust her to use her injury to get out of an argument.

"Fine," I grumbled, scooping up her empty mug. "I'll get you another one."

"Good." Lisa nodded seriously. "It's medicinal, you know."

"Sure," I said, groaning to my feet. As I went to fetch some more drinks—and finished off my own so I didn't get left behind—I thought about Delph and all the adventures she was having in the fae realm.

She didn't need to fake adventure like I did, she lived it every day. Jealousy swept through me as I thought of how she had everything I wanted in life. A hot fae prince and a life of magic and adventure. But I brushed it aside and watched one old lady finally get in the killing blow on her opponent—a weak jab to the upper arm that might have hurt a fly.

A smile twitched at my mouth.

"Two ales please," I said when I reached the bar. Then, considering how far the tavern was from Lisa's bench and how thirsty she was, I amended that. "Actually, make it four."

No need to make more trips than necessary. My muscles— which definitely did exist—were burning after a long day of fighting and adventure.

Pity it was all fake.

Lexi

I had a sneaky little drunk-drive home. Not the sort of thing I endorsed, obviously, but it was far more convenient than taking an uber two hours back to Hebes and then back again tomorrow to collect my Mazda. Cheaper too.

And more adventurous. Not that I wanted to have a car crash, but it felt like I was living on the edge—even if I was only making twenty miles an hour.

Lisa grumbled about the whole plan, but she didn't fork up the cash for a taxi, and she got into the passenger seat.

"I'll do my seatbelt up twice," she said, like that would help.

"What the hell does that mean?"

Lisa was buzzed on painkillers and way-too-many ales, so she was off with the faeries. She plugged her belt in, then unplugged it, plugged it in again, and looked up at me triumphantly.

By the time we got back to town, she was snoring lightly with her head thrown back and her tongue hanging out. Good thing I didn't love her for her grace and elegance.

Pulling up outside her house, I nudged her awake. When that didn't work, I shouted her awake. Her eyes didn't even flicker until I leaned across the handbrake and shoulder-charged her awake.

She scowled, wiping a trail of saliva off her chin. "Fuckoff."

Lisa was always cranky when she first woke up. The first time she slept over at my house, I'd waited until she fell asleep, then I dipped her hand in a glass of cold water to see if it would make her wet the bed. It didn't.

But it made her wake up and lunge at me, growling like a feral bear. She almost killed me before she woke up properly and remembered that I was her brand-new friend from middle school. We'd been besties ever since.

"We're home, nasty lady," I said sweetly. "I'll help you inside."

I parked illegally outside her front door, then hobbled on my overused muscles to the passenger door and helped her out. With her busted knee, she needed the assistance.

When she was safely inside and plonked on a sofa, she nodded over at her home bar and winked at me. "Night cap, babe?"

Usually, that was an automatic yes. But I was in a drank-too-many-beers-two-hours-ago-then-drove-morosely-while-contemplating-my-life-decisions funk, so I wasn't in the mood.

"Pass," I said. "You need to sleep, and I'd better get home." The thought of going back to my dreary house wasn't at all appetizing, but Lisa really did need to rest.

"Boooo," she said while toppling sideways onto the sofa and closing her eyes.

Closing Lisa's front door softly behind me, I glanced down the street and saw a parking nazi working his way toward my illegally parked car.

"Shit." I patted my hips and butt, searching for my car key, but of course, my fighting leathers didn't have any pockets. "Fuck." Where had I put my car key?

I hobbled down the front stairs, not sure if I should try to talk my way out of the ticket or hide my head in shame and pretend the car wasn't mine. I looked like a fucking lunatic, covered in fake blood and real mud, but I couldn't afford the ticket.

At the last moment, I felt the small sharp key lodged in my bra and fished it out, yelled "Huzzah!" triumphantly at the parking guy, then slid into the driver's seat and started the engine.

The parking inspector looked up at me with a weary expression, not realizing he'd just lost an important battle with me. I flipped him the bird as I drove past him, and he only nodded like he got that a lot. Damn, now I felt bad.

Still, I didn't have a parking ticket, so that was a win. Who said I never got any adventure?

It was only a few blocks to my place, and reality sank in as I drove them. I still lived with Dad and my little twin sisters, and they were fine. Lovely. I loved them, and they loved me.

Boring. If I could afford it, I'd travel the lands and seas and explore the whole world. There was something mind-numbing about waking up in the same bed every morning and going to the same job at the same delicatessen, then coming home to the same conversations. *How was your day? What's for dinner? Is Ginny and Georgia on your Netflix profile or mine?*

My cousin's life must be so different from mine. She grew up in Hebes, just like me, and now she lived in a fae realm with hedges that caught you if you tripped over and stopped you from skinning your knee.

When I found a (legal) park and staggered to my front porch,

I tumbled through the front door and stumbled a few paces down the hallway, eyeing the floorboards menacingly before I righted myself and smirked at them. Who needed magical plants?

"I'm home," I called out, then went into the formal lounge room and slumped onto a second-hand sofa that Dad found outside a rich person's house.

Our home was grand, inherited from some great-somebody, and our furniture definitely didn't match. But I kinda liked it that way. It was unexpected, and I always appreciated the unexpected.

Dad strolled through the door, beaming. "Hey, Lex. Did you win?" He wore a black turtleneck and black pants, wearing his ancient-history-professor outfit. He was a quirky dresser, and you never knew from one day to the next if he'd go tie-dyed hippy or alligator-polo preppy.

"Nope. I totally, completely failed to win. Fucking Lisa got injured, and—"

"Language," Dad warned.

I looked up. "Sorry. Fucking Lisa got *hurt*, and I had to help her, so I finished off the battlefield. Got disqualified."

Dad tried to look annoyed by my cursing, but his lips twitched. At twenty years old, I was way too old to be censured for the odd shit or fuck, and he knew it. Even if he didn't like it.

"That's a shame, Lex. Are you hurt?"

I shook my head, but I undercut the message by groaning dramatically and wriggling into the sofa. "No, but I could use a glass of water?" I said hopefully, making it a question.

Dad took pity and went and fetched me a long tall glass of ice-cold water. The twins, Kayla and Razelle, trailed into the lounge room behind him.

I repeated the whole bit about how fucking Lisa Munroe cost me the tournament and then explained how poor Lisa Munroe got injured but she'd be okay.

"Still manufacturing adventure," Kayla said with a maturity beyond her years. Honestly, she sounded like an old matron from ye olde times, lacing her tone with world-weariness. With her shining straight blond hair and her gorgeous twin, she saw the world differently from me. They were tall and glamorous and popular and, most irritatingly of all, they were content with their lives in Hebes.

I was the opposite in every way. Short, with curly black hair past my shoulders, very few friends under sixty, invisible muscles, and an itch to see the world that burned so hard I should probably find a cream for it.

The fae scrying amulet thingy on the mantel pulsed a vibrant silver and sang out a beautiful note, alerting us to an incoming call.

I sat up straighter on the sofa, though I was still slightly tilted. I'd forgotten we were due for our weekly call with our cousin Delph—that explained why Dad and the twins were hanging around.

Apparently fae phones were rare, and it was only because Delph's boyfriend was a fae prince that she'd found one for us. It was basically Skype, but it worked between realms.

Razelle squeaked excitedly, "Accept," and Delph materialized like she was in the room with us. It was only a hologram or something, but it looked so damn lifelike. A faint hum buzzed through the air, sending a tingle across my skin, and the ethereal light of Caprice filtered into our dingy lounge room, with a large spired building seeming to appear just behind the TV.

My routine was to swipe a finger through Delph to check she wasn't real, but I was too tired to get up so I just kicked out a foot instead. It didn't even reach the hologram and only made my sweaty body jerk. Smooth.

Delph looked magnificent. Some days, I still struggled to reconcile the regal woman in our weekly calls with the scrappy street-wise badass I grew up with. Before the twins were born, she lived with me and Dad, but I was so young I barely remembered those days—just a vague sense of her being older than me and awesome in every way. Then she went off to live with Grandma, and I'd never lost the sense of awe at her older-and-badasser-ness.

"You look like a princess," I said dreamily.

"Well, I am a queen," Delph replied. "The clothes come with the gig."

"I know," I said, righting myself on the lounge. "I'm just saying you look as good as a princess."

"Um... thank you?"

Delph's long black hair was loose around her shoulders, but she wore some kind of frock that was very different from the black leather jacket and black jeans she used to wear so much she probably slept in them.

Weirdest of all were her eyes, which had turned from green to shining, piercing silver.

She greeted each of us warmly. When it was my turn, her smile deepened as she took in my state. "Been LARPing again, Lex?"

Before I could share my tragic tale of heroism on the battle-field that cost me my silver armor, Kayla butted in. "Yes, she's still seeking adventure in fantasy," she said dismissively.

"Yes, thank you, wise toddler, I can answer for myself," I said. Honestly, teenagers these days. I hadn't been one in months, and I was over their brattiness. I turned to Delph. "Yep," I said grandly, popping the p. "And I almost won."

Delph grinned, looking more like her old self. "Well then, almost congratulations!" Her silver eyes penetrated right through me, and that pang of jealousy I often felt about her life surged through me. But I wouldn't hold it against her. Never. She was awesome and badass and I missed the hell out of her.

Delph's smile split the room. "I have some news," she said. "And a massive favor." She looked around to make sure we were all listening. I was practically falling off my seat with anticipation—news from the fae world. Most people still didn't believe humans could survive crossing the barrier to the fae realm, since nobody ever went then came back. And here I was, with a hotline straight to the Realm of Caprice. Which, I happened to know, was one of six fae realms.

"Spit it out," I said, my leg jiggling and threatening to topple me off the sofa.

Delph threw her arms wide. "I'm getting married."

Razelle squeaked and clapped her hands together. "To the prince?"

"Yes," Delph nodded. "Of course to Darzan. He's the king, by the way." Joy surged through me, but it was outshone by what she said next. "And here's the favor: I'd like you to come to my wedding."

My leg jiggled me all the way to the floor, and I thumped onto the floorboards with my jaw tickling the rug. "In Arathay?" My voice rose in a squeak.

"Yes," Delph said, still beaming. "Will you come?"

"Of course," I yelled, scrambling to my feet and launching myself to hug her, but of course tumbling straight through the hologram.

My cousin grinned and hugged herself, so I made do with hugging myself too and pretending it was her. This was the adventure I needed. The trip I'd been waiting for my whole life. My whole body vibrated with the need to travel to the fae realm like I was fulfilling some kind of destiny.

Finally, this was the opportunity I needed to prove myself. The gentle teasing from my family was a small symptom of how pathetic my life was, and I longed for more than just the fake adventure I manufactured. I wanted a real challenge. A chance to live up to my own potential. This felt like the first step into a new life, and I was ready for it.

There was no time to monitor Dad's reaction or the twins'. Honestly, it didn't matter. I was a grown-ass woman and I would go to my cousin's wedding even if my father forbade it and I had to rob a bank to get there.

Fate had finally looked me up and called, and I was definitely answering.

Arathay, look out. I was coming.

Lexi

I liked to think of myself as a patient person—even though I wasn't—but watching my twin sisters get ready that morning like they had centuries to burn had me screaming with frustration.

Kayla flipped her long golden-blond hair and looked at me in exasperation. "Honestly, Lex, do you have to keep making that squeaking noise? You sound like an over-excited mouse."

I scowled at my younger sister and cocked out a hip. I was not a mouse, I was a freaking dragon. "Roar," I said, to make the point, and she shook her head then went back to folding her underwear and sliding it into her suitcase.

"Nobody will check the creases have been ironed into your panties," I hissed. "Here, let me do it for you." I flung open the nearest drawer and scooped all the clothing out, then dumped it into her bag. "You won't want to wear this human stuff anyway," I told her as I flipped the lid on her suitcase and sat on top so I could zip it closed. "Delph will give us fae gowns and stuff."

Our cousin, Delphinium, had lived in the fae realm for months, and she had already handed in her dodgy black jeans for stunning outfits that defied the light, reflecting photons in every direction and making my mouth water in jealousy.

As I struggled to close her suitcase, Kayla shared a knowing look with her twin. Without a word being said, I knew she was waiting for me to finish my little performance and leave the room so she could unpack her case and start all over again.

I let out a loud harrumph to make my position clear, then turned on my heel and stalked away, deciding to wait for them by the front door where I couldn't hear the moss growing on their slow-moving limbs. With every passing minute, it was getting harder and harder to convince myself that I was a patient person, until eventually I slumped over my bag with my head in my hands, counting down from a thousand. For the second time.

Three years later, the twins and I were finally down at the Docklands with our cases, searching for the boat Delph had promised would meet us. Naturally, I expected a ship with a high prow, garlanded by flowers, since it was a vessel from the fae realm. But nothing like that was anywhere to be seen.

The air was thick with the smell of brine and diesel, and the uneven planks of the pier creaked as I dropped my black suitcase.

"The boat's gone. It left without us because we were late."

Kayla and Razelle shared that infuriating twin look again—the one that said, 'Lexi's being dramatic' without uttering a word.

"Lex, we're ten minutes early. Be patient," Kayla said.

Razelle chuckled at the word patient, as though it couldn't possibly apply to me, and I couldn't help smiling a little too. "Fine," I conceded, my eye catching on a tiny fishing boat that was more carbuncle than wood and looked anything but seaworthy. Its bow was splintered and chipping, the paint peeling away in strips, revealing layers of different colors underneath.

The boat's name, The Sea Witch, was scrawled in faded red letters on the side, barely legible. Seaweed and shells clung to its sides, and the deck was littered with ropes and nets in need of repair.

"I'll go talk to that guy," I said, nodding at the gnarly seadog who stood on the little vessel with a scowl etched into his deep brown face like crevices on a treasure map.

Razelle grabbed my wrist. "Lexi, that man looks dangerous. Don't talk to him."

Looking the captain over, I could see her point. Tattoos covered the man's arms, his beard and hair a wild tangle of grey and brown. He was exactly the sort of person Delph had spent years telling us to avoid. He was the reason I wasn't allowed down in the Docklands.

Determination squared my shoulders as the promise of adventure carried to me on the salty sea spray. "I'll be fine," I insisted then before I could change my mind, I picked my way along the pier, past the more respectable-looking boats out to where the fishing boat somehow managed to stay afloat, holding my black suitcase in one hand.

When he realized I was headed for him, the seadog's scowl deepened until his eyes sank right into his face.

"Hi," I said brightly, reminding myself that I was badass and forcing the words out fast and strong. "ImLexiandmysist ersandIneedaridetoArathay."

The man's voice was a scratchy as his beard. "What?" he barked.

Hm, maybe my words were too fast and strong. There I was being too badass again. I repeated myself, forcing myself to slow down and enunciate clearly.

The man jerked his head toward the boat. "Get aboard," he

said.

I stared at him, twisting my lips and breathing in a wash of salt spray. I brushed a black curl from my face and tried to figure out what was happening. Was this man offering me a lift to Arathay, as prearranged by my cousin, or was he up to no good?

Honestly, it was impossible to tell. I ran over our brief conversation and was none the wiser. Ordinarily I'd be up for any escapade, even a good ransom situation, but today I had a fae wedding to attend.

The man had already turned his back and was untying a hefty rope from the pier, and I had to raise my voice to get his attention.

"Excuse me." I cleared my throat and tried again. "Excuse me." He finally cocked an ear my way, and I raised my voice again. "Are you kidnapping me?"

He turned his bushy head until those deep eyes were staring at me again. "No," he said.

He seemed to mean it. And although I knew that asking a would-be villain if they were villainous didn't always produce trustworthy results, I couldn't come up with a better question.

This was probably a terrible idea, but I turned and beckoned my sisters to join me. Even from this distance I could read their hesitation in their body language, but they started toward me anyway.

At the thought of putting my little sisters in danger, I figured I'd better have another stab at figuring this seadog out. I cocked out a hip and folded my arms across my chest. "Hey, Mister Seadog, did Delph Smith send you to collect us?"

He continued working on his knots, ignoring me completely. By the time he deigned to turn his bulky frame around and rest his seagrass eyes on me, my sisters had arrived and were glancing around warily.

"Athar," the man eventually said, which I figured must be fae for 'yes.'

I turned to Kayla and Razelle and said brightly, "See, there you go, here's our lift."

The man grunted and gestured for us to get aboard the boat. We scrambled onto the rough wooden planks, Kayla clutching her oversized bag and Razelle grasping my hand tightly. The seadog followed us on, his movements surprisingly agile for someone of his size.

Once we were all settled, the seadog pushed off from the pier and started up the engine, steering us out into the open water. I looked back at the Docklands with a twinge of nostalgia. It was chaotic and grimy, but it was also familiar and full of memories.

But now we were headed toward an unknown adventure, and I practically vibrated in excitement. Thrill-seeking was in my DNA, although my father, who had declined to join us on the trip, claimed I didn't get it from him.

We headed directly toward the shimmering barrier that dropped across the ocean, a magical boundary between our world and the fae world. It hovered just above the water's surface, glimmering and iridescent, like the whole sea sat beneath a curtain made out of the inside of oyster shells, only the oyster shells were invisible. You get it.

The colors shifted and swirled, creating an ever-changing kaleidoscope of purples, blues, and greens. I had spent so many hours staring at the shimmering curtain, imagining what lay beyond, and today I would finally find out.

As we approached the barrier, a sweet, floral scent filled the air, the smell of freshly bloomed flowers on a warm spring day, and an electric charge prickled my skin. The nerves in my belly rose to meet it, punching inside my stomach and blooming into nausea.

Beside me, Razelle had gone as white as death. "I need to go home," she said. "This doesn't feel right. I feel like I'm going to…"

I opened my mouth to disagree with her, to tell her not to be silly and that we were having a wonderful adventure, but the word that escaped from my lips to finish her sentence was… "die."

She nodded and curled into Kayla's side, clutching her like she used to cling to our father during thunderstorms. Her twin didn't look any better, her face bloodless, almost lifeless, and fear clutched my heart. I couldn't lose them. Not like this.

We were going to die. This wasn't a grand adventure or a fucking day trip, this was real and I was going to lose my life. My fingers curled around the edge of my wooden seat.

"Stop," I commanded the seadog. "Turn back this vessel immediately."

His head snapped to me instantly, but his face was grim and determined, though I could see the fear behind his seagrass eyes. "We keep going," he said, then turned back to look at the imposing curtain of magic that grew and grew as we got closer.

"Swim!" I yelled to my cousins, but as my muscles clenched to leap overboard and swim back toward Hebes, my body didn't obey. Magic kept me firmly in my seat, and magic would kill us if we entered that shimmering barrier, I knew that fact as well as I knew my name.

I wrenched my gaze from the barrier, which was almost

upon us, to my sisters, huddled in fear and clutching at each other. They held each other, but they stared at me, and I knew I was responsible for their deaths.

"I'm sorry," I told them as we entered the barrier, and my entire body erupted in a tingling sensation. A thousand pinpricks pierced all over my skin, and probing magic pulsed through every cell in my body. Fear and regret consumed me as we hurtled deeper and farther.

I tried to focus on something else, anything else, but the glittering curtain of magic stretched on forever. I closed my eyes and took deep breaths, trying to calm myself down.

For one terrifying moment, I felt my heart stop, like the barrier had reached inside me and yanked it out. Then warmth rushed in, like sunlight on frozen skin. The tingling sensation faded, replaced by warmth and a sense of comfort, as if the magic was welcoming us instead of trying to harm us.

I cautiously opened my eyes and gasped. The sense of dread had evaporated, and the ocean itself had taken on a new vibrancy, with deeper blues and greens than on the human side.

Kayla and Razelle flashed smiles that shone as brightly as the sun above us, and eagles circled in the clouds above, casting dark shadows over the boat.

"We made it," Razelle said.

"We aren't dead," I agreed enthusiastically.

"Thank God," Kayla said, and the three of us pulled into a tight hug that set the small boat wobbling beneath us.

Even the seadog seemed calmer, his muscles unwinding like frayed rope and his expression softening, as he glanced up at the circling eagles.

"You didn't kidnap us," I praised him, and he grunted in

reply.

But my joy evaporated when I realized that the circling creatures above us weren't eagles at all, but some kind of predatory magical creatures. Half a dozen of them. My stomach sank as the creatures dived, their shrieks cutting through the air like the whistle of a blade.

Kayla caught the direction of my gaze and looked up. "Yay, more adventure," she deadpanned.

VFA

I strode into the clearing, the stiff collar of my formal attire chafing at my neck. Lurlin Forest loomed before me, ancient trees pulsing with magic that made my skin prickle. All around, fae scurried about in a frenzy of activity–hanging garlands, erecting pavilions, their chatter grating on my nerves.

"Watch where you're stepping," a winged faery squeaked as she darted past, nearly colliding with my boot.

I bit back a snarl. This frippery and fuss were no longer to my taste. Give me the raw power of the wild any day over these preening court peacocks.

I scanned the tree line, searching for any hint of movement in the shadows. Old habits died hard. Even here, in the heart of the fae realm, I couldn't let my guard down.

"You there!" I barked at a nearby guard. "Report on the perimeter defenses."

The young fae jumped, eyes wide as he stammered out a response. "A-all secure, my lord. Triple patrols as ordered."

I grunted, unconvinced. These fools wouldn't spot real danger if it danced naked before them. My presence here was proof enough of that.

As I prowled the edge of the clearing, my thoughts turned to the task at hand. A royal wedding. The perfect cover for an assassination attempt. Or something far worse.

My fingers twitched, longing for the familiar weight of my blade. But no weapons were permitted at this farce of a celebration.

A flicker of movement caught my eye—there, in the deep shadows beneath an ancient oak. I tensed, ready to spring into action. But it was only a faeling, giggling as she wove flowers into her hair.

I exhaled slowly, forcing the tension from my shoulders. Perhaps I was getting paranoid in my old age. But then again, paranoia had kept me alive this long.

As I resumed my patrol, I couldn't shake the feeling of wrongness that clung to me. I didn't belong here, among the glittering throngs of fae nobility. I was a creature of darker realms, more at home in blood and shadow than silk and champagne.

But duty called. And I would see it done, no matter the cost.

A sudden impact against my chest jolted me from my brooding. Cold liquid seeped through my formal attire, clinging uncomfortably to my skin. I looked down to see a young female stumbling back, her now-empty glass clutched in her hand.

"Oh! Shitburgers!" she exclaimed, her cheeks flushing. "I wasn't watching where I was going. I am so sorry."

I studied her, my eyes narrowing. Most fae would be cowering by now, sensing the danger that radiated from me like heat from a forge. But this girl met my gaze without flinching, a smile playing at the corners of her mouth.

I was here for business, not distractions, but despite knowing better, I engaged with her. "No harm done," I growled, more curious than annoyed. "Though I cannot say the same for this ridiculous outfit."

I siphoned the worst of the spill off my tunic with a wave of my hands, but a dark red stain remained. I looked around for a serving fae to fix it, so I could resume patrolling the perimeter without looking such a fool.

The female laughed, a bright, carefree sound that seemed out of place. "I'm Lexi." She offered her hand. "And you are?"

I ignored the question, focusing instead on her features. The rounded ears, the slight imperfections in her skin—she was human. That explained her lack of fear. She was clueless and out of her depth.

"You are new here," I stated, watching her reaction carefully.

Lexi's eyes lit up. "Is it that obvious? I arrived yesterday. This place is...would it be absurd to say this place is magical? I mean, because it literally is. But also, it's fucking magical, you know?"

I grunted, amused by her enthusiasm. One moment longer in conversation wouldn't derail my plans. "The fae realm can be intoxicating to mortals. But it is not without its dangers."

She leaned in, lowering her voice conspiratorially. "That's what makes it exciting, don't you think? The hint of danger, the promise of adventure around every corner. I'm actually a war champion back home, hardened by battle and all that, so I should be fine."

I raised an eyebrow, both impressed and concerned by her boldness. "You would do well to be more cautious, human. Not every shiny thing is worth collecting." But even as I said the words, I wondered whether this particularly shiny girl might make an excellent addition to my own collection.

Lexi grinned, undeterred. "Maybe. But isn't that half the fun? Besides, I have a feeling you could teach me a thing or two about staying alive in this place."

A sound that many would describe as a chuckle bubbled out of me, but I knew better. I didn't chuckle. I snorted. It had been a long time since anyone had spoken to me so freely. Her audacity was refreshing.

"Perhaps," I conceded. "Though I am not sure you would like all the lessons I have to teach."

Lexi's eyes sparkled with mischief. "Well, why don't you give me an overview of the syllabus while I get you out of those clothes."

That comment was so unexpected I made another almost-chuckle-like noise, but it was more of a splutter. "I beg your pardon?"

The woman flushed deeply and spoke so fast it was like she was trying to speak over herself. "I mean, because of the tunic and the spill and how I just barreled right into you, and you said you didn't like those clothes anyway, but I mean I can clean them or something."

Lexi was delightful, a pure beam of joy, and I wanted nothing to do with her. I had my own plans for this wedding, and they didn't include becoming distracted by this mortal.

"No," I began, but she cut me off. Nobody had cut me off in decades, and I was dumbfounded for a few moments while she spoke.

"Oh please say yes. I'm just over in the Spike, so it isn't too far away, and—"

"The Spike?" I asked sharply. That was the strategic and literal center of the realm, where the throne room was situated and only royals could enter freely. It was surrounded by a ring of mounted guards, day and night, and fae never spoke so casually of it. "Who did you say you were?"

"Lexi Smith," she said proudly. "Battle-hardened LARPer and cousin to Delph Smith, I mean Delphinium Athar, and daughter of Jackson and older sister of Razelle and Kayla, resident of the town of Hebes."

I tilted my head and studied this unusual woman.

The fabric of her strapless dress was woven with shimmering blue and golden threads, twinkling with the light of magic. It clung to her figure and exuded a faint scent of wildflowers as if it had been spun with the essence of nature itself. Mixed with the earthly smell of the town, it was a pleasant combination. Despite wearing clearly fae-woven clothing of high quality, it was clear from her every movement that she was human. Black curls cascaded below her shoulders like waves of ink, reminding me of shadow magic. The blue of her eyes was startling, made even more so by not matching her hair.

As she moved, her dress rustled softly, like leaves dancing in the forest, and, being human, she moved constantly. Even as she stood regarding me with a fixed blue gaze, she twitched in micro-motions that I couldn't look away from, the tic of a cheek, the squint of an eyelid. An odd instinct had me wanting to reach out a hand to smooth her furrowed brow or trace the line of her cheekbone or press a thumb to her full lips.

"Do all humans speak in such tortured sentences?" I finally asked.

She narrowed her sapphire eyes. My gaze kept switching between her black hair and bright eyes like my brain couldn't reconcile that the two didn't match, as all fae's did. "I was being extremely royal and elegant," she snarled. "That's how we royals speak, you know."

A smile touched my lips but didn't land, of course. I didn't do smiles.

This human woman was something else. She was funny, only I didn't know if it was intentional, and she was distracting, which I didn't need right now. But she also had access to the royal grounds so the decision was clear.

I held out my arm for her to take. "The Spike is not so close, you know," I said in a low rumble.

She curled her two little white hands around my arm, snuggling close against me. "Actually, I don't have a clue where it is," she said with a lilt, "I figured you'd know how to get there. I'm new here, remember."

As we walked, I observed our surroundings with a predatory focus. Mounted guards patrolled in precise patterns, and magical wards shimmered faintly in doorways. I filed away every detail, constructing a mental map of the Spike's defenses but finding nothing I didn't already know.

As we crossed the Spike forecourt, the flagstones ringing beneath my heels, the female stumbled and, without thinking, I caught her, allowing myself to hold her soft arm for a moment too long before releasing her.

"Take care where you step, human."

Lexi looked up at me and deepened her voice in a mimicry of mine. "Good advice, fae."

I grunted, then resumed my observations of the castle defenses. Lexi was oblivious to my scrutiny.

"I should mention that I don't actually have access to clean tunics. Or a dryer. Or anything at all helpful for you," she said lightly. She leaned in close and spoke into my ear, enveloping me in an earthy scent, but her human-volume whisper was loud enough that every fae nearby would be able to hear. "I'm in it for the adventure. This is a once-in-a-lifetime situation. Fae realm, am I right?"

We reached the Spike itself at the center of the castle grounds, and I followed Lexi up the winding stairs, noting the magical wards and rooms that were brightly lit against the threat of Shadow Walkers.

To enter Lexi's chambers, I had to make physical contact with her so the wards would let me through. She looked up at me through her long lashes and held out a hand.

"Ready for an adventure?" she asked with a daring smile.

I took her hand, so soft and small and pulsing with life, and allowed her to pull me through the wards. Her bedroom smelled of her, floral and earthy like springtime. Still holding her hand, I tugged her closer and bent down to sniff her neck, confirming it.

She looked up at me for a moment with a tilted head, before tugging her hand free. She crossed the small room and flopped onto a plush settee beneath the round window, grinning up at me. "So, mysterious stranger, what hidden wonders of the fae realm will you reveal to me first?"

Like in every other room we had passed, this was filled with lights so bright they made my eyes hurt. Light was a successful defense against Shadow Walkers, but they made the room seem clinical and unwelcoming. My first move was to extinguish the lights, restoring the room to the darkness I preferred.

With a flick of my fingers, I set two globes of faelight hovering in the space above us, bobbing and glowing with a pale-yellow light. Shadows played along the stone walls, and the magic in the air felt tangible without the distraction of bright lights. The thick silver rug underfoot glowed more brightly, and the bedsheets looked softer and silkier.

Lexi watched my simple spell with wide eyes, seeming to

think that was the wonder I wanted to show her. "Can I learn how to do that?" she asked.

I stood motionless, assessing her. She was a moth drawn to flame, eager to dance with fire without understanding the burn. Part of me admired her spirit, even as I recognized the danger it posed–to her, and potentially to my plans.

Her audacity was like a spark igniting the tinder of my restraint. I shouldn't be here, I should be patrolling outside and overseeing the wedding preparations, not observing one female in her bedchambers. I had no wish to become entangled with her or anyone, and I no longer allowed myself to become close to anyone.

"You would invite a stranger into your warded room, mortal?" I growled softly. "Are you sure you made the right decision?" At every moment, I expected her to recognize my danger and run away screaming, but she just kept coming closer.

I shouldn't be here, but one more moment wouldn't hurt. I had met very few humans, and they intrigued me. Lexi rose from the settee and stepped closer, her pulse thrumming visibly at the base of her neck, her breath quickening as she looked up into my eyes. I could see the fine hairs on her arms stand on end.

"Not even a little bit," she whispered, her hand tentatively reaching out, brushing against the fabric over my chest, tracing the tension of muscle beneath. Her touch was light, but it sent a surge of power through me, potent and raw.

I caught her wrist gently, feeling the delicate bones and the soft skin that gave way under my grip. "Careful, Lexi," I murmured, "you do not know who I am. I am more dangerous than you could ever understand."

Her other hand dared to graze my jawline, and I leaned into the contact. "You don't know me either," she countered, and a heat of desire pulsed through me at her bold words.

I spun her around, my hands finding the curve of her waist, drawing her back flush against me. She tilted her head, offering her neck, and I obliged, my lips grazing the sensitive skin there. The shiver that ran through her body echoed within me.

The strength she'd seen in me, the power she had yet to fully comprehend, it was all there for her—if she dared to take it. And she did, boldly turning in my embrace to face me once more.

I was not used to such potent arousal, especially not from the mere act of foreplay. But there was something about Lexi— the vibrancy of her mortal essence, the way her unusual beauty stood starkly different from the fae. She was all warm blood, fierce heart, and curious mind.

And she responded to me with a bravery that felt like a challenge. Every time I touched her, she met my gaze squarely, unafraid, almost defiant. It was exhilarating, watching her boldness match my every move. I felt an intoxicating sense of control as if I held the reins to this wild creature.

I ran a slow finger down her side, past the swell of her breast and into the dip of her waist. She sighed under my touch, and I sensed her awareness of my every movement.

The sensation of having power over such a spirit—it was addictive. Her response to my touch, to the pressing of my chest against hers, to my hand on her hip, was hypnotic. For once, the shadows that always played at the edges of my thoughts were banished by the heat of our connection.

In the flickering faelight of her chamber in the Spike, with the softness of her pressed against the length of me, I allowed myself to indulge in the sensations, the primitive joy of curves against planes, the wispy fabric of her dress barely enough to contain her. Forbidden, dangerous, intoxicating—I was drawn to her, consumed by the same adventure she craved.

My hands found the hem of her gown. With a singular, fluid motion, I peeled the fabric up and over her head, revealing the pale canvas of her skin. As the material whispered through the air then landed on the stones, her form was bared before me, every curve and dip illuminated by the soft glow of faelight. Her nipples were small and brown, pert against the afternoon chill. Her little belly button poked out instead of in, and the small mound of her belly was framed by the points of her hipbones.

"Beautiful," I murmured, the word slipping past my defenses as my gaze traced the lines of her body. She probably thought she was standing still, but her movements were unrefined and constant, showing an eagerness that fae grace could never replicate. She was all raw sensuality and living flesh.

I pressed a finger against the fine hairs at her nape, watching them dance at my touch. She shivered, a gasp slipping from her lips, and I reveled in her intense reaction. Every spot I touched sang under my fingertips. The arch of her back, the soft swell of her breasts, the line of her thigh.

"Your skin is like fire," I said, my voice rough with desire as I leaned down to trace the path of my fingers with my tongue, savoring the salt of her skin. I dropped to lick her belly button, then across to her hip, feeling the shape of the bone beneath the skin. She stood impatiently while I tasted her skin, wriggling under my caress.

When I finally made my way past those fine hairs on her neck and up to her mouth, she sighed into my lips as she took her fill of me, almost as though we were taking turns. Her hands, small but insistent, fumbled with the fastenings of my pants, releasing my cock with a boldness that stoked the fire within me. I watched her eyes widen—part surprise, part delight—as she wrapped her fingers around me. Her touch was tentative at first but grew confident as she learned the weight and heat of me.

I stepped out of my pants and reached around to the back of my neck, hooking a finger into my shirt and pulling it off over my head. Standing face to face with a naked woman, I wondered how long it had been since I'd last shared myself with someone. Years uncountable.

"Tell me what you want," I commanded, not willing to relinquish control even as I stood bare before her.

"Everything," she breathed out, her voice rough and insistent.

"Then everything you shall have."

I guided her onto the bed, positioning myself between her thighs, my eyes never leaving hers. Her gaze was an odd mix of innocence and seduction, those blue pools vibrant and alive, and I couldn't look away.

Her fingers threaded through my hair. Her body was so warm beneath me, every curve and crevice of her seeped with heat. I growled low in my throat as she moved her hips invitingly, the heat of her center pressing against my hardness. The desire curling in my gut was almost primal.

"Wait," she said, placing one hand on my chest, not pushing but holding me at bay.

I pulled back a fraction. "What?" I asked, wondering who

had control now and suspecting it was no longer me.

"If we have sex, will you have some kind of fae power over me or something?"

I huffed out a laugh, and the movement made my cock jump against her soft inner thigh. "No."

"Promise?"

"Solemnly."

"Well, alright." She ran her hand across my chest, tweaking my nipple on the way past. I didn't move, so she skimmed my hip and pushed my lower back down toward her. "Carry on then."

I took hold of her wrists, pinning them above her head against the plush bedding. I dipped my head to kiss her deeply. Our tongues competed for dominance and I lost myself in her taste, in the softness and heat of her mouth. She was so lacking in composure, so raw, so human, and the sounds she made were like liquid fire.

Her hands wriggled free of my grip and found their way to my back, tracing flames down my spine that made me shiver. She moaned into our kiss when I pressed against her, the hardness of my arousal pressing against her softness, teasing her entrance.

"Mortal," I murmured against her lips, pleasure coursing through me at the whimper that escaped her.

"Lexi," she corrected with a giggle. "Pleased to meet you. Again." Then she pushed herself up with her arms, seeming to levitate so she could press her breasts against my chest. She pulled back for a moment and snagged my gaze. "And you are?" she asked, hoping to get my name. The way she looked up at me, the honesty in her eyes, it was utterly disarming. Her touch of breasts squashed against my chest was electric, unlike anything a fae had ever made me feel.

"Very fucking aroused," I replied.

She whimpered and fell back to the bed, then hooked her legs around my waist and tried to tug me into her depths. I was done with restraint, and so I yielded, pressing my tip against her hot, wet entrance. As I slid into her, our bodies melded together and I leaned down to feel her breasts against my chest again. Her pussy was warm and inviting, clasping around me and shattering any remaining restraint.

Her hips rose to meet mine in a steady rhythm. Our sighs and moans filled the room, and I was beyond caring about the attention we might attract. The sensations were overwhelming, the slick heat of her, the way her inner walls gripped me, drawing me deeper.

"Look at me," I demanded, needing to see the play of emotions across her face. In the throes of passion, her features were unguarded, wild, and it was intoxicating. She turned those sapphire eyes on me and trapped me in them.

I lost myself in her, each movement deliberate, seeking to draw out the exquisite pleasure for us both. My cock drove into her with a purpose, feeding my hunger. Even the lurking shadows, those ever-present watchers, couldn't tear my attention away from Lexi. Her body writhed beneath me, and in that moment, nothing else existed, just the sweat on our skin, the smell of her arousal, and those damn sounds she kept making.

My hands trailed down her body, tangling in the long strands of her hair and following the arch of her spine. She was so responsive, each caress drawing a gasp, each thrust eliciting a whimper that filled the room.

"Let go," I found myself urging her, my voice a low growl

against the shell of her ear. "Surrender to me."

The words ignited something within her. Her eyes fluttered open, meeting mine with an intensity that shook me to my core. Without a word, she nodded, her grip on my shoulders tightening as she braced herself.

The climax rocked through her like a dam had broken inside her. Her back arched off the bed and she let out a strangled cry, her nails digging into my skin as waves of pleasure radiated from her core. I followed shortly after, my body shaking with the force of my own release.

I pulled out slowly, my body humming with satisfaction. Gently, I swept away the damp hair from her forehead. The sight of her sated and flushed was more compelling than any fae beauty I'd ever seen.

As I sat on the edge of the bed, a strange kind of peace settled over me as if every shadow had been chased away by the warmth radiating from this woman beneath me.

Lying there, spent and breathless, Lexi curled into herself on the bed, totally relaxed. Nobody was ever relaxed around me. Ever. Her skin glistened faintly with sweat, and her chest rose and fell with languid breaths. "Stay," she murmured, patting the bed with a delicate hand, inviting me in.

For a moment, I was tempted. The air was heavy with the scent of sex, and her hair spread around her like a dark halo against the pillow. She reminded me of times long past when afternoons were lazy and filled with pleasure, before my world had become a battleground of power and revenge. I hadn't allowed myself such indulgence in years.

But Lexi didn't know me—not really. She didn't understand the danger that clung to my skin like a second layer, or the weight of the bloodied past that I carried on my shoulders. She was human, wild and unfettered by the games of my kind. To linger in the softness of her bed would be to invite weakness, and that was something I could not afford.

"No," I replied, the word more growl than speech, pulling on my clothes with swift, practiced movements. My muscles ached pleasantly, but I pushed aside the sensation. Vulnerability had no place in my world.

As I fastened the last button of my shirt, which was definitely not dry, Lexi propped herself up on one elbow. "At least tell me your name," she asked, a playful lilt to her voice that scratched at my defenses.

I met her gaze, drawing out the moment. "Some things are better left unknown," I said, dodging the question as I always did. Names held power, and mine was a weapon I couldn't afford to have turned against me.

"Fine," she huffed, though the smile never left her lips. "I'll call you 'VFA' then."

"VFA?"

"Very fucking aroused."

A chuckle escaped me unbidden, a sound so rare it felt foreign coming from my throat. "Whatever keeps you from asking more questions," I said flatly, but my laughter had already given me away. I'd lingered too long already, and I couldn't afford to stay a moment more.

Turning on my heel, I strode out of the room, leaving behind the temptation of her warmth, her fearless search for adventure, and the sense of lightness I hadn't known in far too long.

Lexi

I'd never given my own wedding much thought. I wasn't one of those girls who dreamed about the big white gown and all the smiling guests. Whenever I pictured my future, it was usually holding a big LARPer trophy over my head, or making my way through bustling markets on the far side of the world. But, if I'd ever imagined my wedding, it was a small affair in a park with a big party afterward.

Here in Caprice, they did things differently. Apparently for royal weddings, the realm itself, as in the land beneath our feet, determined the nature and even the exact timing of the ceremony. It might decide Delph and Darzan should tie the knot at the top of the nearest mountain at sunrise tomorrow, or inside one of the massive caves that burrowed into the surrounding mountains in, say, five minutes time. As a result, we were supposed to be ready to go any time. The twins insisted on sleeping in their fancy gowns, but I was pretty sure Delph was pulling our leg with the whole 'the realm decides' business, so I snuggled into my superbly comfortable bed in my usual yellow cotton nightie with the tiny white squirrels.

A cold breeze lifted the hairs on my arms, but I was too tired to close the window, so I snuggled deeper under my blankets. VFA filled my thoughts as I drifted off to sleep, looking almost as good in my memory as he had in real life. Hard cheekbones and a strong jawline, accented by a hint of stubble, with black hair styled messily. Even before I'd kissed him, my mouth had watered, wondering if he would taste of the hint of mint I caught on his breath. As I fell asleep, I also tumbled into his deep black eyes that held the weight of the world.

I'd only been here one night and I was already having marvelous adventures. And, despite his warnings about how dangerous he was, that mystery man seemed like a big gooey marshmallow to me. He'd brushed me so tenderly, taken care to protect my head as he pulled me to the bed, and gifted me the best orgasm I'd ever had. He'd even murmured compliments in my ear that made my toes curl, and he'd treated me with a mixture of tenderness and awe. Then, when it was all over, I could see he was tempted to cuddle me. He was a heartbeat away from diving beneath the sheets and spooning, but instead he put on his lethal-fae act and slunk off into the shadows. If that was fae danger, then I was here for it. Sign me the hell up.

I woke up shivering, my covers strewn on the floor, but as I leaned over to tug them back onto the bed, they resisted. They must be caught on something. Sleepily, I swung my legs over the side and bent double, trying to feel for the snag, but whenever I gathered more blankets into my arms, they tugged farther away.

"The hell?"

Crouching down, I spotted two little yellow eyes, and, blinking, I made out a furry face that looked like an adorable kitten but with oversized paws and opposable thumbs. It was reeling in my blanket like fishing wire.

"Hi, little guy. You cold, huh? The thing is, I am too. Maybe we can share?" I held out my hand to show the creature I meant no harm, but it just rolled its eyes at me and bounded across the stone floor, its little butt wiggling in the air and the blanket trailing after as it leaped out the window and scurried down the side of the tower.

"Or not," I sighed. Crossing to the closet, I flung it open searching for another blanket. The glorious midnight-blue gown that Delph had given me to wear to the wedding fell out onto a crumpled pool at my feet, and I carefully picked it up and re-hung it. Leaning down to tug open the drawers, the damn dress fell on me again. In my sleepy state, I must have hung it wrong, so again, I laced the hanger through the sleeves and placed it over the rail. I watched it for a few seconds to make sure it was secure, then closed the closet doors and scanned the room for another blanket. Maybe I could use the rug? I knelt down and felt its plush softness, so thick and warm I rested my cheek for a moment against it, drifting back to sleep on the floor.

A scuffle of paws across stone had me flicking open my eyes. The little kitten guy with the weird paws was back but he didn't have my blanket. He looked between me, prone on the rug, and the closed closet, and I swear disappointment flickered across his gaze.

"Well you're the one who stole my blanket," I complained.

Kitten-guy prowled across the rug, and I clenched it tight in my fist in case he tried to steal it, although he'd have to get it out from under the heavy four-poster bed so I didn't like his chances. He crossed to my face and put his nose to mine, assessing me, then put a paw on my cheek. It was soft and just about the cutest thing I'd ever seen. I scooped him up into my arms for a cuddle, but the snarl that came from him was so loud that I dropped him like a hot coal. He trotted to the door and waited for me to follow.

"No way, little guy. I'm bushed."

I crawled back into bed and leaned down to tug the edge of the soft rug up over me. It was still caught under all the furniture, but a small corner reached me, which I put across my middle.

I patted the mattress beside me. "Come snuggle, little guy. We'll adventure in the morning."

The kitten let loose a horrific noise that sounded like a baby strangling a hyena, loud and fearsome enough to make me sit bolt upright.

"Okay," I said, getting to my feet and crossing to the door. "Adventure now."

It was only when I made it down to the Spike forecourt that I realized my mistake. Despite the middle-of-the-nightness, the cobblestones were littered with fae dressed in their wedding finery. Layers of chiffon and lace and gravity-defying jewelry that hovered above fancy hairdos filled the space, along with the lithe bodies and perfect complexions in every color that marked the fae.

Kayla wore her cream-and-gold gown, which was slightly rumpled from sleep, but it was a damn sight better than my yellow cotton nightgown with the white squirrels. Her expression was anxious, and she only relaxed when she saw me through the thinning crowd.

"Lexi, you fucking idiot," she said by way of greeting, looking me up and down.

Razelle, in a teal gown with gossamer sleeves, huffed a laugh.

I chewed my lip. No way was I turning up to my cousin's

royal wedding wearing my old mortal nightie. "Be right back, wait here," I said, turning to race across the cobblestones to go and change into my stunning midnight-blue gown with all the frothy fae silk. But before I made it a single step, my little kitten-guy nipped the hem of my nightgown and yanked me to a stop.

Now, I'd never been an ace at physics in school, but my hundred-and-forty pounds should win over this three-pound kitten in a tug-of-war. But somehow, the rogue cutester tugged me in the opposite direction, trailing the crowd of fae in their finery who were all headed in the same direction.

Razelle shrugged with a wicked grin. "No time to change, I guess," she said. "Cute catler," she added, bending down to pat my kitten-guy, who arched into her hand like it was made of cashmere.

I hinged at the waist to pat him too, but he let loose another weird, loud noise, this one like a steam train mating with a goose, and I jumped back before he bit me.

"The fuck?"

Kitten-guy didn't like me, and I didn't like him. But there wasn't much I could do about it. He used his superior strength and wiles to force me along the path after the last of the fae, with Kayla tutting and Razelle chuckling unhelpfully beside me. The cobblestones were cold and bumpy under my bare feet, but we soon turned down a street that was actually a forest, with lovely soft grass underfoot.

Capricia, the capital of Caprice, was a small city with forested avenues intersected by cobblestone ones. Standard stone buildings were interspersed with houses made entirely from wildflowers, and one particularly noticeable abode that was carved into a giant toadstool. We alternated between street-

street and forest-street, going at a trot until we caught up with the main pack, by which time my feet were numb from the cold.

"You should have worn shoes," Kayla said unhelpfully when I commented on it.

"Now, why didn't I think of that," I retorted sourly.

But my bad mood couldn't last when I saw what Gaia had manifested for Delph and Darzan. As we approached the wedding spot, the murmurs of fae grew louder, and the air prickled with excitement.

We arrived at a meadow of wildflowers, many of which had reared up to form an arch. The sky was lit with stationary lightning bolts, massive zigzags of light that stayed lit, casting the meadow in an eerie glow.

Kitten-guy ushered me and the twins to a group of the handsomest and hottest beings I'd ever laid eyes on, right near the front of the flower arch. It was humiliating enough to be wearing my nightgown, with my bare legs and feet poking out from the knees down, but to be tugged by a tiny kitten who clearly didn't trust me to make my own decisions was just shameful. He even stayed beside me while I took my seat, keeping one large, adorable eye on me at all times.

The fae in the seat next to mine had a cute freckled pixie face with spiky blue hair and, of course, matching blue eyes. She tossed me a massive grin when she saw my outfit. "Nice," she said appreciatively. "I'm not into all this pomp and ceremony either. If I could get away with wearing my pajamas I definitely would."

"We can swap outfits if you like," I offered hopefully, although she was a least a size smaller than me. Still, I bet the clothes here would adapt, they were much more helpful than human clothes.

She considered my offer while she casually stroked a flower that preened into her touch, but a large fae with black hair and terrifying black eyes loomed around her from the other side. "Neela," he said with a gravelly voice, "Try to remember you're a damn princess."

A princess? A weird yip came out of me, which I hoped nobody noticed, but then a row of gorgeous and perfectly made-up faces turned to peer at me from the rest of the front row, indicating they had. Right beside me was Neela, then her boyfriend with the black eyes and the possessive hand on her thigh. Past him was a male with intense silver eyes that held a glint of amusement and long silver hair, although in his dark gray suit and pressed white shirt, he looked like he could eat me for breakfast. He squeezed a tennis ball in one hand and had the other resting lightly on the thigh of a stunning female with bright orange hair.

"Nobody said we could wear our PJs," the silver male whined. "Not fair."

"You can't wear your damn pajamas, Leif," the terrifying black-eyed dude said. He seemed to be the only sensible one out of the lot of them, and so I felt immediately drawn to the others.

I figured I should explain myself. "It was the middle of the night, and my kitten-guy didn't wake me in time," I began, but my catler interrupted my excellent stream of excuses with a loud growl, so I had to raise my voice to continue, "and I decided this would be more comfortable."

Neela grinned. "You totally didn't believe the bit about the realm deciding the timing of the ceremony," she said, accurately. "You must be one of the human cousins."

"Lexi," I said, nodding, feeling extremely out of place. I had never been referred to as a 'human cousin' before, and it was quite disconcerting. "And this is Razelle and Kayla. They're twins. Actually, apart from our hair, and our height, and our presence and general demeanor, and how elegant and beautiful they are, all of our faces are really similar, but you can tell us apart by—"

"By the fact you're wearing pajamas," Leif interrupted with a smirk.

"Well, yes, and I have a freckle right here by my nose," I added.

"Okay," Leif conceded, "If all your clothes fall off and your hair falls out, I'll inspect your nose to tell you apart."

I smoothed down my cotton nightdress and hooked my legs at the ankles. "Good," I said, trying to sound sensible but quite sure I'd lost control of the conversation. "The realm really should know better than to have this wedding in the middle of the night," I added.

"Actually that's true," terrifying-black-haired-guy said, with a tone of concern in his voice. "Light is our major defense against the Shadow Walkers, I'd hate to think what would happen if they came here."

"They haven't been seen this far West," Neela said. "Plus we have lots of guards around ready to produce light."

"Hmm," the man said, "but a lot can happen in a few seconds."

I let those comments sit for a while, trying to parse them. What were Shadow Walkers? And why weren't they invited to the wedding? I'd already had my dose of danger with my super adventurous sex with VFA, and I'd nailed it, so I wasn't too worried.

Razelle and Kayla talked in low voices about the magnificent outfits all around us and the stationary lightning bolts in the sky, and I let it all soak over me while I kept an eye on my catler, who kept an even closer eye on me. This was the epitome of all my life goals. Adventure, meeting new people from new places, and seeing my badass cousin finally get the happy ending she deserved after a frankly difficult life.

My new pal Neela crossed her legs and looked at me frankly, so I gave up trying to see her outfit through the corner of my eye and just looked. She wore a pale-blue sheath dress with a stunning diamond necklace and diamonds studded through her blue hair. I tilted forward to inspect her shoes, which were also covered in diamonds.

She smiled at me. "I used to be human," she said conversationally.

The terrifying black-haired man, who was dressed head-to-toe in equally terrifying black, snorted. "No you didn't, tomcat. You were always fae, you just didn't know it."

My hands clutched the edges of my seat. I had never heard of somebody believing they were human but actually turning out to be fae, and the prospect opened up a whole world of possibilities. I mean, Delph turned out to be half-fae, but maybe she wasn't the only magical being in the family.

"Do you think I could be fae?" I asked.

Neela twisted her lips. "Umm..."

"Do you know your parents?" Her scary boyfriend asked.

"Yes," I admitted.

"Are they fae?"

"Well..."

"Then no, sorry babe," Neela said, squeezing my bare knee. "Probs not."

She went on to introduce me to the other heirs from her realm, Verda, which she described as the Realm of Greed and Excess. Scary-boyfriend was Ronan, then the silver man with the smirk was Leif, and the orange-haired beauty beside him was his mate Alara.

"They're still in their honeymoon phase," Neela said quietly. "Longest honeymoon ever."

"Aw, cute," Razelle said, leaning out around me to look at the couple, but Neela's eyes widened and she shook her head vigorously.

"Not cute," Neela hissed. "It makes them dangerously possessive of each other. I suggest you don't spend long talking to either of them and definitely not alone."

"Or...?"

"If you talk to Leif, Alara will transform into a wolf and gut you. She will rip out your innards and feed them to Leif."

The blood left my face. "I don't suppose you're joking?" I asked hopefully, and Neela shook her head.

"Right, no talking to Leif," Razelle said.

"Or Alara," Leif growled from beside Ronan, and every bloody hair on the back of my neck rose to salute the dominance in his voice. I didn't know I had that many hairs back there, but every one of them was Leif's bitch.

"Yes sir," I said, and the row of heirs laughed at my instant obedience.

Embarrassment flooded me, bringing all that blood back to my cheeks and making me hot.

"Don't worry, babe," Neela said, patting my knee. "He used his Alpha voice. Noone can resist that." She turned to her friend and added, "Naughty wolf."

He growled at her in a way that made me want to sprint out

of his presence, and if KG hadn't leaned against my ankle at just that moment, I might have done so.

But Neela was clearly used to it, and she simply laughed at the werewolf.

Did I mention? Werewolf.

"Up next is Gabrelle," Neela continued, "our beau—"

Her introduction was interrupted by a quiet throat clearing from the far end of the line of heirs, and Neela's sentence changed direction.

"Our wonderful and powerful Lure friend," she finished.

I had no idea what a Lure was, but when I caught sight of the female named Gabrelle, my heart ratcheted up to a million beats a minute. She had stunning deep brown skin, as smooth as porcelain, pink hair that cascaded around her face and shoulders, and eyes the color of candy floss.

She was the most exquisite creature I'd ever seen, and it was only when I reached out a hand to touch her flawless cheek that I realized I'd left my chair, marched along the line of heirs, and bent down to make physical contact with this captivating fae. Still, I couldn't help myself from stroking her face, and a bolt of joy fizzed up my arm at her touch.

"Knock it off, Gabrelle," Ronan said.

Razelle was beside me, and she knocked me out of the way and perched on Gabrelle's lap, then cuddled against her. Fury rose through me that my little sister dared to snuggle with the fae I needed to be with, so I tugged at her and pulled her onto the grass.

"I'm not doing anything, I swear," Gabrelle said, and even her voice was like ecstasy and silk.

"Can't you like, anti-Lure or something?" Leif asked, as Razelle and I wrestled on the grass, trying to get closer to the source of our delight.

"I've never tried," Gabrelle said. "Hang on."

I watched in awe as she screwed up her face, but even in intense concentration, she was an unparalleled beauty, the epitome of everything I wanted in life. She—

A wave of metaphorical water doused me, and my intense attraction to the Lure princess evaporated. Now I was just a mortal woman in a nightgown, wrestling with my sister on the grass beneath a floral arch, while thousands of perfectly-dressed fae looked on, including all the princes and princesses of all the fae realms.

Razelle and I fell still instantly. I climbed to my feet, brushed stray blades of grass off my cotton squirrel nightie, and stalked back to my seat with as much dignity as I could muster.

"Fuuuuck," I whispered to Razelle once we were back in our seats, speaking quietly so nobody else could possibly hear. We were so out of our depth here. Maybe VFA was right, and this realm held more dangers than I realized. First, mention of the ominous-sounding Shadow Walkers, and now some kind of mind control. "These guys are fucked up," I said.

Razelle nodded in agreement and we shared a small smile, but it dropped at the next words.

"We can hear you," the male on the far side of Gabrelle mentioned matter-of-factly.

Neela chuckled. "That's Thorne," she said. "He has a bad habit of telling the truth even when it would be kinder not to."

From the corner of my eye, I saw the dark-haired fae balk. "Oh, sorry, I didn't realize this was one of those situations," he said mildly.

"And last but not least, up the end is Dion," Neela said, and a male with corn-colored curls waved back at me down the line. She smirked at me. "You can call him Double D."

"No," the curly-haired fae said, "you cannot."

Neela winked at me and mouthed, "Double D."

At that moment, every wildflower in the field turned to look South, and the solid, stationary strobes of Lightning in the sky exploded into a million fragments of light that rained down in the same direction, illuminating Delph and Darzan who appeared in the distance.

Every moment of embarrassment and growing concern about my safety in this realm was forgotten as I turned to watch my cousin marry a fae king.

Lexi

As Delph floated over the field of wildflowers, beneath the static Lightning bolt, she was the definition of surreal beauty. I could have sworn that her dress was woven from threads of pure moonlight, shimmering and almost translucent. She wore a crown that twinkled with stars like the night sky above us, and her piercing silver eyes would put galaxies to shame. Her long black hair was swept up in a complicated arrangement that I could spend a lifetime trying and failing to replicate.

She was already a queen and looked it from head to toe, but now she would become a wife.

Darzan, on the other hand, was a grandeur in his own right. He looked like my cousin's opposite, onyx skin against her pale, hair that glowed like liquid gold against her river of black, tall and broadly muscled, against her slim figure. Even their clothes were opposites. Instead of her flowing gown of moonlight, he wore a suit made of shadows and night, dark and intimidating but full of regal charm.

The thing that tied them together was their eyes, glowing with the power of Lightning bestowed on them by Gaia herself when she chose them to lead the realm. And the glowing joy on each of their faces was identical.

Silence swept through the field like a wave, and every orchid, marigold, and lily bowed down as they passed by. Even the princes and princesses of fae realms held their breath as they watched the pair approach the altar of thorny brambles beneath the wildflower arch. The world fell silent. Every creature, every blade of grass, even the wind fell still.

As they took their places by the altar, Delph looked at Darzan with a love so raw and pure that my heart clenched. Her eyes were wet, shimmering with her inner Lightning, while Darzan gazed at her with flat-out devotion. Someday, someone would look at me that way.

The ritual began with an ancient fae song that echoed through the quiet night. The melody wove through the meadow, delicate yet haunting, but as it lingered, a subtle unease prickled at the edges of my senses. The flowers seemed to shiver, and the air grew dense. I glanced at Razelle, who clutched my arm, her brow furrowing. Something felt off.

I shook off the feeling of unease as Delph prepared to speak. This part I knew. It was when the vows were spoken, the words that would unite Delph and her lover together under Gaia. But first, the shadows at the edges of the night, from the deepest black that surrounded the meadow, gathered into solid forms.

"Cool," I breathed, looking at the new part of the ceremony, although something about the shadows sent tingles down my spine.

The night itself solidified, clumps of midnight that became corporeal, and as I swiveled my head, I saw they were everywhere, closing in on all sides and approaching across the meadow fast.

"Pretty," I said with a tight smile, hoping the chill wind and thickening darkness were part of the ceremony. And then the screaming started.

The temperature dropped, and every hair on my skin stood on end. A blood-curdling shriek started my pulse racing as pure darkness covered the stars and static Lightning, enveloping us completely. The only points of light were from Delph's and Darzan's wide Lightning-filled eyes, then a body smashed across my lap, toppling me to the grass, and I landed heavily on my wrists in absolute dark.

I tried climbing to my feet, but another body crashed into me, and I stumbled into a chair, barking my shin.

I recognized the werewolf prince's voice as he shouted, "Don't shift!"

Other screams and yells flew across the dark meadow like arrows, and I felt like I was in a LARP battle. But without my fighting leathers or sword, I felt utterly useless, and of course, I knew I'd be helpless even with them. All my years of training were worth absolutely zero in the fae realm, and a cold fear swept through me.

Bubbles of faelight flared into existence around the meadow, and I realized that was what many fae were shouting about. Light, light, make light. Don't shift, make light. And screaming, so much screaming.

I was in a patch of dark but I could see now from the distant bubbles of faelight, and I watched in horror as one corporeal patch of night hugged a nearby fae, coating her gorgeous green silk in a layer of night, and then gashes appeared across her belly, cutting the gorgeous green silk in two and letting black-red liquid fall out, the blood splashing against my ankles. The fae dropped with an anguished cry, crumpling at my feet in a pool of gorgeous gown and gore.

Staring at her, I backed away, my numb feet moving slowly

as I struggled to make sense of what was happening. This wasn't supposed to happen, this was Delph's wedding day and my big adventure, and now it was a massacre.

The shadow around the fallen fae dissipated and then reformed into a new solid being, turning its attention to me. The temperature plummeted, and my chest squeezed so tight I had to gasp air in small sips as I backed away, but I couldn't make my feet move fast enough, and the shadow was upon me. It coated my skin, cold and slick like oil, sliding down my arms and around my belly, passing right through my nightgown as though it wasn't there, settling me in a shiver.

Dread made my pulse spike, and my gaze locked onto the fae in the green silk who lay on the grass a few steps away. As I watched, her dead eyes opened, soulless and flat.

Still coated in the oily shadow, I broke into a run, sprinting over dead bodies, heading for the nearest bubble of faelight. I dived into it, panting hard. The pool of darkness slunk off me and I was free, somehow still alive and able to breathe again. The tang of blood made the scent from the wildflowers smell sickly, and I retched.

Lightning strobed overhead, casting fierce bolts of light that made the shadows shrink away, as the realm itself joined the fight against the darkness. Wildflowers grew tall and wound around the ankles of the risen dead, anchoring them in place.

I looked around desperately for Delph, and a wave of relief washed over me when I spotted her amongst a group of fae. She cast a bolt of pure Lightning into a shadow monster, which held it at bay.

The Verdan heirs held up small stones which pulsed with luminescent blue light, and the nearest shadow creature let out a screech that soured my blood and then rained onto the ground in ashes, not dissipating into the darkness but dying on the grass as small flecks of nightmares made real.

Lightning couldn't kill the creatures, but these glowing stones could. It was enough to turn the tide of the battle, and the remaining Shadow Walkers fled into the darkness of light, leaving behind the meadow in shambles.

I scanned the battlefield, now lit brightly with hundreds of faelights and more static Lightning in the sky. I looked for the twins amidst the fallen bodies. There was no sign of them. I ran around, my heart pounding so hard it threatened to escape from my chest. I had to find them, they couldn't be...

A rustle behind me made me freeze. From the darkness emerged Razelle, her clothes torn and body speckled with droplets of blood that were not her own.

"Are you okay?" I asked, rushing across the crushed wildflowers slick with blood. She nodded, clutching her side where a dark stain was spreading through her dress. "You're hurt."

"No," she said, but pain was etched on her face. "One of them tried to kill me but..."

Nausea swelled in my belly at the memory of being coated in the oily Shadow Walker. But it hadn't killed me, and I suspected that was because I was human. Clearly, being human had saved Razelle's life too.

"I know," I said, since Razelle couldn't finish her sentence. "Me too."

She pulled me into a hug, or I pulled her, I didn't know and it didn't matter, I just needed to hold onto her, to know that she was okay, that we were both okay. She clung to me fiercely, her body trembling as she buried her face in my shoulder.

Something warm enclosed me from behind and I turned my

head to see Kayla hugging us too, and a sob of relief bubbled up from inside me as I held my little sisters close.

Still clutching each other, we looked around at the scene of the battle. The meadow was now littered with bodies, their bright gowns like oversized wildflowers that instead of sweetness smelled of blood.

"The darkness," Kayla began, her voice hoarse, "It came from the forest. The shadows." She shivered against me and I tightened my grip around her.

"Did you see where they went? The remaining ones?" I asked, my gaze scanning the edges of the clearing where the trees began.

She shook her head. "They vanished. Like smoke."

I wanted to ask more but a pitiful moan caught our attention. A fae woman lay beside us, clutching a deep wound in her side. Her eyes fluttered as she attempted to focus on us.

A bubbling panic gripped me but I wrestled it down, forcing a calm that I didn't feel. I did my best to look confident as I knelt beside the fae woman, gripping her hand gently. "It's going to be okay," I told her, though I had no idea if that was true. Her eyes flickered up to meet mine and I tried to project a sense of serenity.

Razelle's eyes were wide as she looked at me, then down at the woman. "What should we do?" she whispered.

"I don't know," I admitted, "but we can't just leave her here."

It wasn't only about this woman. It was about all of them. All the fallen fae who needed help, who were injured or worse.

With shaky hands, I reached out and pulled away the tattered edges of the fae woman's gown to expose the wound. It was deep, too deep for me to do much except press Razelle's hands to the wound to staunch the bleeding while I ran for help.

Ducking and weaving through the battlefield, I finally found Delph kneeling beside a family of small winged faeries. "Delph," I cried, and she turned and hugged me fiercely.

"The twins?" she asked.

"They're okay. But there's a fae woman who's bad. We need bandages and penicillin and hot water and towels. Yes, towels." I was reciting a list I'd seen in emergency medical situations in movies, but now I wondered if those items were just for giving birth. "She's not pregnant," I added, in case Delph needed to know.

My cousin looked so calm and collected, and, well, queenly. She placed a warm hand on my shoulder. "Breathe, Lexi. I'll send a Healer. They have Healing magic and will be able to mend all the injured fae. You're sure Kayla and Raz are ok?" I nodded. "Now, the three of you need to head back to the Spike. I'll send two guards with you to light the path."

I grabbed her hand, my fingers closing around her cold wrist. "Delph, I—I'm so sorry this happened."

My cousin's face was grim, and I saw a universe of pain in her eerie silver eyes. It wasn't just her wedding that had been ruined, but her city, dozens of her guests and subjects slain in the most horrific way imaginable.

She held my gaze for a moment without uttering a word, then turned to summon guards, and I obediently let her pack me and the twins off to the Spike. There was nothing I could do out in the meadow, not even my basic first-aid-slash-maternity skills were useful compared to fae with Healing magic. And my sword was not only useless against darkness but it was back in Hebes. The twins and I walked in silence, jumping at shadows, though the guards kept us bathed in bright light.

Back at the Spike, I changed out of my blood-splattered nightgown and into an oversized sweater I found in a closet, then the twins and I huddled together in a common room waiting for the others to get back.

Eventually, Delph and Darzan filed into the lounge room where the twins and I sat sipping on some dark alcohol a nice serving fae had brought us. Delph's eyes looked haunted, and when I pulled her into a hug, she collapsed against me for a moment. I settled her onto a couch beside Darzan and pressed a glass of the dark liquid into each of their hands.

We sat in silence until the Verdan heirs joined us, a bedraggled crew. Leif, the silver wolf, pulled Alara, his orange-haired mate onto his lap. Leif's silver eyes were dark with despair, and I suddenly saw the depths of pain beneath their bright exterior. He was a male who had experienced a lot of loss and far too much death. Alara nuzzled close against him as though her touch might heal some of his pain, and perhaps for wolves that was true. I didn't have a lot of experience with werewolves.

Ronan and Neela sat on a fourth sofa, the elfin female sitting close beside her large partner. Serving fae appeared and provided glasses of the dark liqueur to everyone, and left the bottles on a side table.

Darzan waited until everyone was settled. "All salted and burned?" he asked with a tight voice. Even his golden hair seemed to glow less than usual.

Ronan nodded, his movements sluggish and weary. "The dead won't be rising again tonight," he confirmed.

I sipped my much-yummier-than-but-looked-like whiskey, clinking the glass against my teeth, letting the weight of the room settle into my bones.

The spiky-blue-haired princess tilted her head and asked softly, "Did you get a body count?"

Darzan sighed deeply and wiped a hand across his mouth.

Delph placed a white hand over his black one. "One-hundred and fifteen," she said quietly. "Jayke and the other Healers were able to save dozens, but... not the ones who had already gone."

A shudder ran through me that seemed to bristle through the entire room. So many dead, all in one evening. I knew Delph would blame herself in part, because it was her wedding, and I would make sure to tell her tomorrow that it wasn't her fault. Tomorrow, and every day after, if need be. But right now we all needed to wade our way through the shock and settle into the sadness.

I didn't know much about fae, but I knew births were extremely rare and lifespans were supposed to be long, like hundreds of years long. So an early death was a cruel blow here, and a massacre of this size could impact the city for centuries to come.

Silence settled like a cloak, and the warm liquid in my belly pulled my eyelids closed. You couldn't pay me a million dollars to leave this room and these powerful fae and head back to my room alone, so I let myself fall into sleep beneath the bright faelights.

Hours later, I woke to quiet murmurs. I listened sleepily for several long breaths as the heirs discussed tactics. Apparently, Gabrelle and Thorne were off somewhere using Delph's scrying amulet to communicate with Realm of Fen, where Thorne was from, to see how they fared with the Shadow Walkers. Nobody had expected the Walkers to have made it as far West as Caprice, so Fen, which lay East of here, was definitely at risk.

Dion had returned home to Verda City to update the monarchs on the wedding massacre. The heirs had sent something called a Spellbird last night to inform their parents, the current rulers of Verda, but they were expecting an in-person update too.

Delph and Darzan were no longer in the room, probably off checking on the cleanup and recovery.

That left Neela, Ronan, and Leif, plus Alara who never went anywhere without her mate. They were arguing in whispers about whether to try negotiating with the Shadow Walker King.

"He is a monster who kills indiscriminately," Ronan argued. "There's no point trying to talk to him. That's a fucking suicide mission, and I won't let any of you go. As the highest ranked among us, I absolutely forbid it."

"The rankings aren't final," Leif hissed. "You can't forbid shit."

"We have to at least try to talk," Neela said. "We don't even know why he's doing this. Or who he is. Or anything about him. We need more information so we can plan our defense."

Their voices were creeping well above secret-whisper volume, and I risked peeking open one eye. Neela stood with her hands on her hips, and if I didn't know she was a freaking powerful magical princess, I would say she looked kinda cute.

Ronan scoffed, rolling his piercing black eyes. "Yeah, 'cos we might find out he just wants a back massage, then we can have a lovely massage train and he'll piss off back to the Shadow Isles."

Neela scowled at her boyfriend, and power rolled off her in waves. I quickly revised my opinion of her being cute and decided dangerous was a much better word for her. "You think we should put all our eggs in one basket, and only rely on the Stone of Veritas?"

The heirs exchanged curious looks. Leif and Alara tilted their heads at precisely the same angle.

"Eggs?" Alara asked.

"Basket?" Leif asked.

Neela waved her hands. "It's a human saying, idiots. Anyway, we need to diversify our strategy. If the Stones fail, we need something else that might work, no matter how far-fetched."

Ronan got to his feet and started pacing. He'd dumped his black jacket during the night and now wore black pants and an oh-so-very-fitted black shirt that pulled beautifully across his chest as his arms swung. "Fine, I'll bite. But what about the fact it's a damn suicide mission. Nobody can get within two feet of a Shadow Walker without either producing light and scaring them off or dying. So how do you propose to get to the Shadow Isles for a chit-chat with the Shadow King?"

My lips were moving before I'd run it past my half-awake brain. "I can," I said.

It was very satisfying to watch four fae heads snap in my direction looking surprised because it wasn't every day a bumbling human could be awake without them noticing. Fae senses schmenses.

"What are you talking about?" Alara asked.

"Those Shadow Walker things can't kill humans. One of them coated me last night and tried, but it gave up and slunk away. I guess you could say I have a human superpower." I rolled over elegantly to punctuate my point, and rolled onto the floor with a thud.

Ronan looked down at me, and I swear he made his pecs dance just to mesmerize me. "You're going to represent the fae realm and talk to the Shadow King to save the world?"

I tugged my oversized sweater down, trying to ignore how ridiculous I must look. "Yep," I said, forcing a confidence I didn't quite feel. The room fell silent, their skepticism heavy in the air. My heart raced, but I squared my shoulders. "I'm not saying it's a perfect plan, but if no one else can go near him, what choice do we have?"

I waited for the round of applause and all the outpouring of gratitude, but Ronan only scowled at me, said, "Nope," and turned his back on me.

Neela whacked her boyfriend with the back of her hand as he paced past her. "Arrogant asshole," she said. Then she crossed over and pulled me to my feet with surprising strength given her size. "Sorry about him," she said as I popped up in front of her. "But he's right, you're not going. I'm not sure you have the right...skills." She picked a leaf out of my hair and gave me a smile.

Well, thank God for that. For a moment there, I thought they might take me up on my offer. I mean, adventure was one thing, but leading negotiations with someone called the Shadow King was something else. No, that was better left to the professionals.

"Send a Negotiator," I said, really leaning on the N of negotiator so that is sounded like a magical profession.

"No such thing, babe," Leif said, and Alara growled at me as soon as he called me that.

The feral, possessive she-wolf didn't look like she was about to attack me, but I backed up a few paces, just in case. Alarmingly, Neela stepped between us as though she expected her pal to dismember me, which was less comforting than she probably thought.

"Okay, go find a negotiator from Hebes to help. Or some human kung fu spy. Someone with my human superpower and also skills," I said, and I was pleased to see their eyes light up at the idea.

Although, deep down, I knew I really *did* have the skills. I was a battle-hardened Live Action Role Player with a head for strategy, and I'd been spending my life looking for adventure.

Just not quite that much adventure.

Lexi

Breakfast the next morning was a subdued affair. Fae were mourning, Delph and Darzan hadn't been officially married, and the royalty from across the five Seelie realms was strategizing and planning, trying to figure out the next steps against the Shadow Walkers.

The dining room had high arched ceilings with silver woven through, and the air felt fresh and inviting. I plonked myself down at a long marble table among the Verdan heirs, choosing an inconspicuous spot between Neela Flora and Thorne Sanctus, keeping as far from the mated wolves as possible for my own safety, and far from the Princess of Lure, for hers.

"Skipping the nightgown today, I, see?" Leif teased, his voice carrying down the table and drawing every eye to my not-so-inconspicuous-after-all arrival. Thankfully I was decently clad in a pair of jeans made from some fae material that was both soft and durable, plus a white shirt I'd found in my closet that was flattering but modest.

"And your ass is covered," Ronan added, referring to the minor wardrobe mishap when I'd rolled onto the floor to declare my noble intentions to negotiate with the Shadow King and my sweater had ridden up.

"Can't wear my finest every day," I retorted, earning some

giggles from everyone and a particularly loud snort from Neela.

Delph and Darzan arrived in the dining room with great fanfare from the serving fae, but Delph waved them away and took a seat across from me. She greeted the heirs and then asked what their plans were regarding the Shadow Walkers. It was exactly the question I wanted answered too, but it carried more weight coming from a queen, so I made do with craning to hear their answers.

"The Walkers multiply by feeding off shifters, but their breeding phase appears to be complete," Ronan said, putting down his fork and folding his arms across his chest. "They now have sufficient numbers for full-scale attack, if the wedding is anything to go by. I'm afraid this means we must consider ourselves at war."

My eyes slid to Darzan, the War Wielder, and I wasn't the only one. He seemed the best placed to comment on War, given his innate power. With a flick of his fingers, he could slice a fae in half.

He cleared his throat. "My War is no use against the Shadows," he said, his voice low and rough. "Thorne told me as much after Delph's Ascension Rite, and now, after trying and failing to use it against our enemies last night, I'm forced to admit it's true. War is useless against the Shadow Walkers, like trying to cut the night with a sword."

Delph sat with a regal air and looked so much like my cousin playing dress-ups that I had to stifle a smile. But her every word dripped with gravitas and the smile slipped from my face as she spoke, replaced by awe. "Our Lightning was useful in repelling the Shadows, in the same way as sunlight or faelight, but it did not kill the Walkers. The only items capable of killing them are the fragments of the Stone of Veritas."

Heads nodded solemnly, and pride bubbled through me at my cousin holding court with these royal fae. She had clearly dressed quickly and without fanfare, but she still exuded an aura of majesty and power as she sat at the dining table. Her black hair was like a crown atop her head, pulled up in a loose bun that framed her regal features and highlighted her striking silver eyes. Her outfit, a flowing gown in shades of deep purple and gold, added to the effect.

Delph's voice echoed through the throne room, powerful and commanding like a royal decree. "As you are aware, my king and I divided the Stone of Veritas into a dozen pieces, effectively creating twelve weapons instead of one." She paused, her piercing gaze scanning each heir before finally resting on Neela. "Princess Flora, you once swore to be forever in our debt. Now is the time to fulfill that promise."

Neela's hands went straight to her thighs as she took a deep breath, her fingers clenching into fists. The atmosphere became tense as everyone in the room could sense what was coming: Delph was going to ask for something big, something the heirs were not eager to provide. But if they owed a debt to both Delph and Darzan, and it was also true that their arsenal had expanded by twelve times due to splitting the Stone, then surely, they were obligated to fulfill whatever request was asked of them.

Delph waited for the weight of her words to settle, and Ronan was the first to speak. "I have just said we are at war, and our resources will soon be stretched to their limits. This is not the time to call in favors."

My cousin's tone was icy. "This is precisely that time. I request merely one twelfth of what I gave to you, and I do not ask it for myself but for all the fae of Verda. You have seen how unsafe we are, how the Shadows have pierced our core. We have our greatest Cleavers analyzing the ashen remains of the felled Shadow Walkers, but I know as well as you that we will not discover a new method of killing them. There is only one."

This was a conversation unlike any I'd ever participated in. Even the strategy sessions at LARPing were more relaxed than this, and I took a mental note of the exact tilt of Delph's head so I could reproduce it during the next tournament.

Gabrelle leaned forward, her dusty pink hair spilling over her shoulder. The sight was intoxicating, and I automatically began to rise from my chair to get closer to her, but Neela put a firm hand on my thigh and made me settle back in my seat. I focused on the hard chair beneath me to distract myself while Gabrelle spoke, her voice as smooth as honey. "You want a piece of the Stone?" she asked.

"Nope," Dion said, "That's not possible. Sorry, but we need all twelve pieces. One for each of our Verdan Houses, that's five, plus four more to line along the eastern coast that fronts the Shadow Isles, where all the damn Walkers are coming from. We need one piece for the Unseelie to barter for their support, one for the Realm of Fen, and one for the mortals. It's already planned out."

"We need to send them to the most vulnerable positions," Ronan added. "We've discussed it at length and concluded that's the best strategic response. It leaves the Western realms open, but they'll have to get through us first."

Darzan, the Warrior King with the sharpened steel gaze, who would be very fucking terrifying if he wasn't my cousin's fiancé and, frankly, still was, cleared his throat, and all eyes snapped to him. I knew he was a fae of few words, and more used to communicating with sharp barbs or fists than with diplomacy, so every word of his stung. "A debt is a debt," he growled, and as his eyes roved the group, each fae bristled under his gaze.

Neela's restraining hand on my thigh got too firm, her fingernails digging into my flesh. "We will honor it," she said. "I told you I owed you, and I meant it. But know that it comes at the expense of lives elsewhere."

Delph and Darzan exchanged a quick look, laden with meaning.

"We must look to Caprice first, then to the rest of Arathay," Delph said. I had the odd urge to duck under the table to peek, and I was sure I'd see Darzan squeezing his Queen's thigh in support. But I kept myself seated like a normal adult while my cousin kept speaking. "Please believe that we would risk much to see the other realms succeed, but we cannot risk our own fae."

Honestly, I wanted to applaud. My cousin was nothing short of impressive, and if I had a placard handy, I'd wave it around for her while I hooted and cheered. She was taking these lifelong royal fae head-on, and she was winning. But I kept it to a massive grin and double thumbs up.

Surprisingly, Leif was the first to get to his feet and lean across the table to shake my cousin's hand. "I respect that," he said, his voice as pure as moonlight. "I would make the same call for my wolves, any day of the week." Even Alara didn't seem to begrudge her mate's physical contact, she just nodded approvingly.

Thorne was next to his feet. He chucked a napkin onto his plate and scraped out his chair. "I will take one piece of the Stone to Fen. That is the realm where we found the weapon, and I promised King Erevan Reissan to return with the Stone to defend the realm when it became necessary. I have my own oath to fulfill, and I will not be found wanting." He turned to Gabrelle. "Will you join me?"

The dark-skinned beauty rose with the grace of smooth-flowing water to join her partner, and moments later they disappeared from view. They were quickly followed by Leif and Alara, who took five pieces of the Stone of Veritas to Verda—a decision that met with unanimous agreement. After all, they were mostly heirs of Verda themselves, and Leif had not only a realm to protect but also every pack within it to lead. He could not afford to delay his return.

It was agreed that every realm should have at least one fragment to defend themselves, including the Unseelie realm, plus Hebes. A troop of guards left to take the stone to the mortals and stay there to wield it if need be.

"We should send one to the Barbed City of Ourea," Ronan said. "They run independently of the rest of Ourea."

"They are too far West and South to be of concern," Dion grumbled. With five pieces in Verda, plus one in each of the other five realms and one in Hebes, only one fragment remained to be allocated, and our conversation shifted to how best to utilize it.

I savored some heavenly breakfast meringues—nutritious, or so they claimed—which felt like a testament to the existence of God given how delightful they tasted. When Delph and Darzan excused themselves from our discussion, I watched them go regretfully, wishing I was a Queen of a fucking fae realm so I could leave whenever I wanted. Not that my lack of royal blood was the biggest problem we faced right now, what with the declaration of war, but some autonomy would be nice.

Then I realized I was an adult, so I could do as I damn pleased. I seized the moment to follow my cousin into the next room, strolling extremely elegantly and powerfully as I did.

As soon as we entered, I flung my arms around Delph, overwhelmed by admiration for her. "You were amazing in there."

"I was shaking like a leaf," she admitted, although she looked as still as a statue to me. "I'm just some mortal girl who's playing at Queen," her voice softened, losing its earlier authority.

"You *are* a Queen," Darzan roared fiercely, and though I cowered beneath his intensity, Delph looked up at him with a smile that seemed to draw strength from his power.

"Keep pretending if that's what it takes," I encouraged her. "Whatever you're doing is working—you're kicking royal butt." I squeezed her hands tightly. "What's your next move?"

She smiled back at me, taking a deep breath. "You and the twins need to get home safe. Go pack. I'll arrange some Fliers to take you back to Hebes. You leave in one hour."

A pang of reluctance gripped me at the thought of leaving. Despite the danger and drama surrounding us, I felt more alive than ever and wasn't ready to relinquish this adventure just yet. Perhaps if the Shadow Walkers could kill humans, I'd be scrambling for safety, but realistically, I knew I was in less peril than everyone else.

"But you guys aren't even married yet," I protested weakly, grasping for any reason that might convince them to let me stay.

Darzan's gaze locked onto mine like cold steel pressing against my throat. "The marriage won't happen anytime soon," he said firmly. "You and your sisters need to get home so Delph can concentrate on protecting the realm. She can't think straight with you here."

"At least let us travel across the country to the Requin Sea, and then we can fly or sail from there. I want to see more of the land before I leave," I pleaded, my voice filled with urgency.

Delph shook her head firmly. "We're in the middle of a fucking war, Lexi. Don't be an idiot."

"The Walkers can't kill me," I insisted, meeting her gaze with determination. "And, in case you forgot, I've grown up a lot since you left Hebes. It might have only been a few months for you, but it's been four years for me, and I'm not a child anymore. I've survived without your help. All I'm asking for is a small taste of the adventure you get to live day in and day out. Just have some guards escort me and the twins to the Sea, and I promise I'll go straight home to Hebes. Otherwise, I'll have to..."

I let my sentence trail off deliberately. I didn't want to resort to threats about running away; that sounded childish. Yet deep down, the desire to escape was strong. If she made me leave this marvelous place in one hour without seeing any more of it, I would pack my bag and head for the hills—perhaps VFA would even help me make my getaway.

Delph crossed her arms over her chest and regarded me like a disobedient child. "There is no way in hell I'm sending my little cousins, who I've spent a lifetime protecting, by the way, home through Brume. Just drop it, Lex. It's not happening."

I clenched my fists, frustration running through me. I was an adult, and I was sick of being treated like a child. Dad and the twins always teased me about LARPing—well, them and everyone else—and made fun of my desire to do something with my life other than sit around watching TV and slicing meat for customers at the deli.

Well, I wouldn't be dismissed anymore. "I don't actually need your permission." My hands flew to my hips, and I sucked in a breath, waiting to see how she would reply.

Surprisingly, it was Darzan who came to my defense. "It might be safer to travel light and fast across the land. Caprice could look after her as far as the border, and—"

"What about the mist in Brume? She isn't a fighter. You and I almost died in there," Delph shot back sharply.

"We'd send guards," Darzan countered confidently.

"Please, Delph," I begged, unable to hide the pleading tone in my voice.

"Plus, it would free up our Fliers for the war," Darzan added persuasively. I was really starting to like this guy.

After long moments of watching Delph twist her lips and scowl hard at our arguments, she finally relented with a resigned sigh. "Fine, but you leave in an hour. You take the most direct route possible, and you don't try to lose the guards."

Without thinking twice, I pulled her into a massive hug and spun her around enthusiastically, squeezing a squeak out of her before rushing off to share the good news with Kayla and Razelle.

* * *

Kayla and Razelle didn't agree that it was good news. Kayla grumbled about blisters and sore muscles and muddy feet until I had to bribe her with my favorite dress so she quit the whining and didn't make Delph change her mind, promising to give her the pale-yellow A-line as soon as we got back home.

"Remind me why we aren't flying?" she asked for the seventeenth time as we waved goodbye to Capricia.

"Adventure," I said firmly.

In any case, when we entered the moonway, Kayla was as smitten as I was, and Razelle was positively euphoric. The pathway was invisible to the naked eye, or to the human eye at least, but when you stepped on, it was like walking on a travelator on steroids. Every step was dozens of paces, the fields blurring beside us and standing still again as soon as we stopped.

"Now, this is what I call a vacation," I called as I sprinted, covering hundreds of yards in seconds. At one point, I veered off the path and was suddenly standing in the middle of a field of purple and gold flowers, and all I could see of the path was a slight blur of color as the six guards and my sisters walked past. The flowers and grass flattened out before me, gently guiding me back to the moonway, and once I was back on, I took more care where I was walking.

The moonway ended in a completely different realm called Brume. As soon as I stepped off, a shiver wracked my body and I pulled my borrowed cloak tight around me. It wasn't cold so much as empty feeling, like all the warmth and joy had been sucked out of the atmosphere. It felt like we were leaving more than just the realm of Caprice—we were stepping away from safety.

The thrill of the moonway began to fade as the creeping mist of Brume loomed ahead, its edges curling like sinister fingers.

"What's Brume known for?" I asked the nearest guard, one of six assigned to protect us. He had white hair and pure white eyes with no visible ring around the pupil, making it hard to meet his gaze without flinching.

"Mist," he said, indicating the rolling rivers of fog on both sides of us.

Delph's last words to us had been *Stay out of the mist*, and I didn't need to be told twice to avoid those sinister-looking mountains of white.

I took a step closer to the nearest one and reached out a hand, wondering if it felt cold to the touch.

"Stay out of the mist, milady," white-eyes said, pulling me closer.

Okay, apparently, I did need to be told twice.

"Jesus, who died and made this the land of the cemeteries?" Razelle asked as she tugged her cloak tight and looked around. She plopped to the ground and leaned back on her wrists. "Rest time," she said in response to the eight sets of eyes that landed on her.

"No, milady," white-eyes said, "We have to keep moving. We need to make Port Lonsdale before dark. I can carry you if you like."

Razelle threw me a this-sucks look, then scrambled to her feet and kept trudging.

Caprice had been a picture-book magical place, with helpful plants and a sweet atmosphere of joy. Even after the horrific events at the wedding, the realm itself had seemed calm and serene. But Brume was a completely different place. I had no idea air could have a feeling, but it did, and here it was dread and anxiety. Not adrenaline-producing fear, but a permeating layer of unease. Walking through it was like trudging through a thick layer of fear.

After we'd hiked long enough that my calves were beginning to regret the adventure, I glanced around to see if any more adventure was happening without me noticing. Something was off. "Didn't we used to have six guards?" I asked Kayla, having counted only five. As she turned around to scan them, the sixth guard popped out from behind another.

Kayla shoved me. "Quit fooling around, I'm scared enough already."

The mist slithered along the ground like living tendrils that recoiled slightly at our presence only to close in tighter behind us.

"Wuss," I muttered, my voice shaky despite the attempt at bravado. My hand brushed Kayla's arm, more for my own reassurance than hers, as my heart pounded louder with every silent step. I noticed she and Razelle were connected firmly at the elbow.

Every footstep was swallowed into the mist, making no noise at all. When I started up a merry hum to brighten the mood, white-eyes shushed me without even calling me milady, which ratcheted my anxiety up to a whole new level.

"We don't know what's in the mist," he whispered when I glared at him. "Don't want to call attention to ourselves."

"Well, that's comforting," I hissed, shuffling a micro-step closer to Kayla, like she'd be able to do anything other than scowl at any monsters who leaped at us from the white gloom.

A faint rustling reached my ears, and I froze mid-step, my breath caught in my throat. The mist shifted unnaturally, coiling and uncoiling like something alive. The guards exchanged uneasy glances, and white-eyes placed a hand on his sword. 'Keep moving,' he murmured, his voice a strained whisper.

I started a habit of counting the guards every few minutes, reassuring myself each time I made it to six. Until the time I only counted five, when I completely failed to feel reassured.

"A guard's missing," I hissed, and Kayla reached for me, her fingers digging into my forearm.

"Lexi, I swear, if you—"

"Shhh," I said, counting again.

As I watched, a fae was yanked into the mist in absolute silence, and then a scream poured from me like boiling water from a kettle.

The world turned dark, like the world's biggest cloud was crossing the sun, and shadows poured from the mist, a merging of swirling white and dark that coated the fae.

The mist hit me like a wave, icy tendrils wrapping around my arms and legs, pulling me into the suffocating dark. My screams were swallowed by the void, leaving nothing but the frantic thud of my heartbeat in my ears. I reached out blindly, but Kayla and Razelle were gone, their warmth replaced by a bone-deep cold that froze my breath. My mind raced, grasping for logic, for escape, but all I found was an endless, soul-crushing fear.

Lexi

I woke in a dungeon. Solid rock below, above, and on three sides, broken only by a chunky metal door. Where the fourth wall should be was a long, fatal drop to a churning ocean far below. Waves crashed loudly, and the air tasted of salt and spray. I scowled at the sea, but it just kept thrashing as though I was nothing more than a speck which, it occurred to me in a moment of horrible clarity, was true.

It was a starless, moonless night, and darkness clung to me like a second skin, pressing down on my bones and suffocating me with cold. The air tasted of salt and metal as if I'd been sucking on an old coin. Just to be sure, I poked a finger in my mouth, but it contained no currency, fae or otherwise. As I sat up, the roughness of the stone floor bit into my hands. Shadows danced and shifted in the occasional glimpse of starlight that broke through the clouds, and I shivered.

The memory of the ambush in Brume came flooding back, and I called Kayla and Razelle, screaming until my voice was hoarse, but the only reply was the crashing of waves at the cliff's base.

The metal door clanged open, and in the doorway, a dark figure materialized, shrouded in shadows. Intimidation emanated from him, his tall, broad stature and menacing aura filling the room.

"How do you resist my Creatures?" he bellowed, his words thundering around the cave.

I rose to my feet, assessing my options. Fear coursed through me, my palms clammy against my jeans. But I was a totally competent badass, and I would get through this. Strategy was my strength, and I had already figured out that my identity was the only ace I held, and I wouldn't play it early.

Squaring my shoulders and lifting my voice to a shout to overcome my nerves, I managed to form a complete sentence. "Who are you?" I demanded although it was pretty damn clear who he was. The only thing I really wanted to know was where my sisters were, but I didn't expect a straight answer, and I didn't want him to know what really mattered to me. I had to play this hand carefully.

If I thought this male was roaring earlier, he upped his tone to a veritable thunderclap. "You dare to question the Shadow King, imp?"

"Who are you calling an imp, monster? I've seen better costumes at a Halloween party and heard better insults from a preschooler, so how about you shut the fuck up and either bring me a blanket or leave me the hell alone?"

My words were bold, but inside, I was trembling.

As the king crossed the space, shadows swirled around him. I could only make out the darkness covering his face and the glint of black eyes, with no hint of any other features, like he was made out of blackness. A wisp of smoke flowed out behind him as he crossed toward me, his movements eerily silent as if he was floating. He emitted a faint scent of ash that curdled my stomach.

"Such bravery, imp," he cooed. "I wonder how long that

will last."

A shadow wisp separated from those swirling around him and reached toward me, stroking my neck like a feather. But it didn't penetrate me or immobilize me or stop me from breathing, the way I knew he hoped it would.

"Stop it," I said, trying to sound calm although my heart was galloping and my breathing unsteady. "You're tickling me."

The Shadow King tilted his head and lowered his arm, the shadow wisp curling around his fingers and then disappearing back into his form. "Tickling you," he repeated as if the concept amused him. "Interesting."

The king's face remained hidden in shadow, but I sensed a slight shift. As if my words aroused his curiosity rather than anger. His dark essence quivered slightly as if electrified.

"Indeed," he mused, then the shadow tendrils retreated back into his form. "I think I shall enjoy breaking you."

For a moment, my heart stilled at his threat. But bravado was my only armor, so I forced myself to meet his gaze squarely. "You'll have a hard time breaking what's already been broken," I replied, my voice steady even though my insides twisted. At least that sounded badass.

The Shadow King considered me for a long moment. I could feel his eyes on me, piercing through the darkness and into my soul. It was as if he was trying to unravel me, peeling back the layers of skin and muscle with his black gaze.

"Indeed," he said, his voice dripping with amusement. "I admire your courage, imp. But let me assure you, you've not yet experienced the depths of despair that dwell within the Shadow Isles."

With a wave of his hand, shadows surged forward, wrapping

around me like chains, encircling my wrists and ankles and pinning me to the rock wall behind me. I fought against them but they were too strong, cold and hard like steel.

Turning his back on me, it was clear that he was about to leave me, no longer with the option of jumping into the sea and taking my chances.

Desperate for something to keep him there, I blurted out a random thought.

"Two," I shouted, my voice shaky but defiant and only just audible above the crashing waves.

The monster turned, the full glare of his attention back on me. "Two what, imp?"

"Two to zero," I replied with a hint of smugness.

Another shadow slithered toward me, increasing my fear of what was to come. "Explain," he demanded.

Watching the snaking darkness cross toward me, I forced myself to speak slowly. All I had left were my identity and my bravado, and I didn't want to give either away easily. "Two pieces of information you gave me," I clarified. "Your identity and our location in the Shadow Isles. And you learned fuck all from me. So, you know, sucked in."

The dark snake paused before my face, all shadow and nothingness, and I figured I had just uttered my last sentence. The Shadow King didn't have a good reputation, to be honest, and I was provoking him. But my strategic side wanted to keep him here, to keep him talking, so I could squeeze him for as much information as possible. I wouldn't learn much by staring over the ocean.

The wisp reared back like a cobra about to strike.

Frankly, I wasn't happy with "sucked in" as a final sentence, so I tried for something more profound. "Wait," I yelled, "I want to add that..." My mind raced for good parting words. "Leather armor is better than the plastic stuff, even if it's more expensive."

The shadow snake dispersed into the air, and I took some deep breaths of relief. Clearly the King found my wisdom as keen as I did.

"You are no Warrior," the King growled, his words rumbling around the room as a large wave crashed far beneath.

"Is that a question?" I asked, "Or just an incorrect statement? Because actually I am. I'm a certified LARPer and victor of numerous battles. Only last week I came second in a tournament for...oh, never mind." It occurred to me, somewhat belatedly, that I was sharing detailed information about myself and he hadn't even asked a question. Let's hope the tally stopped counting at two-zero because I was pretty sure I was losing now.

The monster king cocked his head, seeming almost confused by my words. "Larper?" He enquired, the word foreign on his tongue.

"Ah," I responded, an awkward chuckle escaping me. "It stands for Live Action Role Play, and it takes strategy, courage, and skill."

The Shadow King's chuckle resonated like a bass drum in the cavernous cell. Did he think he was at a damn comedy show? "A Larper you say?" Apparently, that was hilarious, and his laughter echoed through the chamber. "So your battles are mere games?"

I clenched my jaw in frustration. Clearly, he thought the idea of me battling in real life was ludicrous, just like everybody else did. My pride burned at being made to look foolish. "Not games, exactly," I muttered, but it was hard to explain how very non-gamelike the games were, so I didn't expand on that thought.

Eventually, his amusement died down, and he moved closer to me once more. The shadows that swirled around him condensed as he approached, creating an almost tangible darkness that made it difficult to breathe, and the temperature plummeted.

"Tell me this Larper, do you believe that you have what it takes to survive here? On my isles?"

"As much as anyone can in this hellscape," I retorted, the words slipping out before I could reign them in.

"Interesting choice of words." His voice was eerily calm, devoid of any discernible emotion. Nonetheless, a shiver ran down my spine at his tone. "You would compare my kingdom to Mortia's realm?"

"Well, isn't it?" I snapped back recklessly. My nerves were fraying, my careful control slipping, and the salt in the air was tinged with ash. "Isn't that why they call you the Shadow King? Because you rule over a kingdom of darkness? A kingdom of despair? I mean, it's dark, cold, and filled with shadows. It isn't exactly heaven."

For a moment, the chamber was silent, save for the echoes of my words bouncing off the stone walls. The king was still, his shadowy form radiating a cold, intimidating power.

"You presume much about me, Larper," he finally responded, his voice low and dangerous. "And yet, you know nothing."

He raised a hand and the shadows around him shifted, swirling in a chaotic dance. They moved faster and faster until they were a tornado of darkness. I squeezed my eyes shut and braced myself for whatever was to come.

But instead of pain, I felt release. The icy chains binding me to the wall disappeared. I sagged against the wall, gasping in surprise.

"Sometimes things are not as they appear," he said.

"What is that supposed to mean?" I asked, my tongue rattling off words despite my brain wanting it to shut up.

In response, the Shadow King extended a hand toward me, summoning another tendril of shadow that reached toward me hesitantly. I concentrated on staying still, my heart pounding as the wisp brushed against my cheek. It was cold but not uncomfortable, like frost on bare skin.

The shadow began to trace lines over my face, not unlike a lover's touch. It ran over my eyelids, down my nose, and across my lips, making me shiver.

"You speak of despair and darkness," the Shadow King began, his voice so low it was barely a whisper in the shadow-filled room. "Yet I see none of that in your eyes."

He stared at me with an intensity that made my breath hitch.

"I see defiance," he continued, as though he were reading the lines written on my face. "I see courage that burns when it should not. I see a mind and heart that will be sweet to break." He gestured vaguely toward my chest with his other hand. "I see ignorance and bias that willfully misread my kingdom."

I frowned at him, not understanding the point he was trying to make. The shadow against my cheek traced a line down to my chin, before retreating back into the form of the King. I stepped backward, away from the intimate brush of his icy smoke, stumbling over the uneven stone.

His gentle touch made me angrier than any of his threats had, and my voice rose dangerously. "You murder shifters, you tear apart families, you turn fae into the living dead, walking around like fucking zombies," I yelled, my chest rising fast. "I've seen what you've done. And you want me to believe that I'm misinterpreting things? What, that you're actually some poor misunderstood fae who deserves a second chance?" I pooled moisture into my mouth and then spat directly onto his evil, shrouded face. "Fuck no. You're a monster."

The King didn't flinch, even as my spit landed on his face and evaporated into smoke. Instead, he stared at me with what could have been curiosity. Or amusement. His aura seemed to relax, the shadows around him becoming less oppressive. He was silent for a moment before he spoke.

"Monster?" His voice bounced back from the stone walls eerily. "That's what you believe? That because of the harshness of my reign I am a heartless creature?"

His words hung in the air. The shadows swirled around him and he was silent for a moment. "Perhaps it is true that I have done unspeakable things," he said, his voice barely more than a whisper. "The fae would rather see themselves as victims than stare at their own savagery in the mirror."

He paced slowly around the room, his dark form casting eerie shadows on the ground, his feet making no sound against the rock. "Do you think my kingdom is born out of love and light? Or birthed from the ashes of ills done to me?"

The Shadow King stepped back from me, his form giving off an aura of chilled command even as his words echoed in the silence. His hands dropped to his sides, shadow tendrils retreating into him. His countenance shifted again.

"And you are so certain," he remarked, his tone nonchalant, as if he found my anger amusing. "You see only what is on the surface and judge accordingly. You believe you understand my actions, judge me by your standards, yet know nothing of my purpose."

I clenched my fists at my sides, my anger burning hotter than ever at his dismissive attitude. A loud crash of waves pounded below.

"Your purpose?" I spat out the word wishing I could spit venom instead. "Your purpose is destruction. What kind of purpose is that? Death and destruction isn't purpose, it's the opposite. It's, it's anti-purpose." Dammit, that sounded stupid out loud.

He hummed, a low, haunting sound that bounced off the stone walls and echoed until it drifted off over the pounding ocean. "Ah yes," he said, pacing toward me slowly, his shadow jerking along the rough cave floor. "That's what you think because that's what you've chosen to see."

I shook my head, backing away until my spine was pressed against the cold stone wall. "There's no other way to see it," I argued, fighting to keep my voice steady.

His expression remained impassive, his dark eyes watching me intently. "And you, Larper," he replied smoothly, the corners of his lips curling up slightly in an expression that was more mockery than smile. "You who have played at battles in a world far removed from the harsh realities of this one. Do you genuinely believe you understand the complexities of my realm?"

My heart pounded. He had a point. I didn't understand this world, I'd only been here a few days, but nothing could excuse his actions.

"It doesn't take a genius to know what you're doing is wrong," I retorted, my fists clenching at my sides. "Murder is pretty universal."

"Are you a warrior who fights for justice? For peace? Or do

you merely LARP for glory?" The king's voice was laced with iron that scratched against my resolve as he managed to nail me in one short breath, and I pushed aside the image of that silver armor I'd wanted so badly. "You seem to forget that in darkness there is also solace. In shadows, there is safety." He reached out toward me again but this time, I didn't flinch away.

I held his gaze as his shadows curled around me gently, an embrace of velvet darkness.

The Shadow King paused at the doorway, his form blending with the darkness. "You'll learn, imp," he said, his voice like distant thunder. "When despair takes root, you'll beg to understand. In shadows, there is also pain." And then he was gone.

Lexi

Sleeping on a rock floor while shivering to the tune of crashing waves didn't make for a good night's sleep. Go figure. Since there was nobody to hear me apart from the seagulls over the ocean, I didn't bother internalizing my chant "Cold, very cold, cold, very cold," but just said it loud and proud while I hugged myself and watched the moon travel across the sky.

But when I stopped chanting, I could still hear my words echoing around the cave. It seemed too early to be going crazy—I'd leave that until next month, I reckoned—so that meant somebody else was saying the words.

"Cold?" I called out in a questioning tone.

"Very cold," somebody replied in a deep voice that did not sound like me, not even like me on an echo.

I jumped to my feet and dashed to the opening over the ocean, crashing far below. The sound hadn't come through the solid rock walls, so it was emanating from out here. Creeping as close to the slippery edge as I dared, I saw nothing but black sky and even blacker sea, with just the foamy tops glinting in the moonlight.

"Cold?" I asked again, worrying that I'd stepped up my timeline and was doing the crazy thing now. I mean, why wait a whole month when you could get in early and go full postal before the first night was through?

The echo of my own voice faded, leaving only the rhythmic crash of waves below.

"Are you cold?" the deep voice asked, and I jumped. I mean, that was a break from the traditional chant, and my brain never could have come up with something so radical, so this must be somebody else. Right?

"I'm Lexi," I answered, as though we were at a tea party and he'd asked my name. "Who are you?"

The beats of silence stretched so long that I worried I'd scared my new friend off. Even if he was only imaginary, and an early onset figment of my madness, I still felt like a chat. Anything was better than the never-ending darkness and cold and aloneness.

But finally, he answered. "I believe you would call me an acronym."

It took me too long to figure out what was going on. First, I had to convince my brain off the loop of me being mad— either I was or I wasn't, and there was no point dwelling on it, I just had to move forward. Then I had to wonder how the hell this prisoner knew that I tended to call fae strangers by odd acronyms. Then I was able to get on with the part where I realized this was the same guy.

"VFA?" I asked, incredulous. "Really? My VFA?"

"I would not say I am yours, exactly," he said, but I recognized his voice now. Deep and husky, it sent shivers down my spine as he spoke. Or maybe that was the freezing-to-death thing. Still, his voice might have been smooth and confident but had a hint of vulnerability to it. It was the fae from Delph's not-really-a-wedding. The guy I'd slept with.

"What the hell are you doing here?" I blurted out, but before he had a chance to answer I barreled on. "You weren't one of the guards in the group crossing Brume, were you? I don't remember you—"

"You do not remember me?" he asked, and I was pleased to detect surprise in his tone. After all, he'd been more than a little alpha in his actions and words, and I didn't mind bringing him down a peg or two by pretending I'd barely noticed him.

But the words were spewing forth before I could stop them. "Yeah, I don't remember the hottest guy I've ever slept with, who I banged the one time I left the mortal realm. The fae with the black eyes and the black hair and those abs and the trick with his hips that made him hit me in just the perfect spot. Nope. No idea who that might be."

His dark chuckle ran straight down my spine and settled in my core. It was like a stroke of dark velvet against my skin.

"So I suppose you are not the vibrant human woman who never stops moving or thinking or analyzing? The one with the unusual beauty, the startling eyes, who stands out among these dull fae like a horse among asses. The mortal with the fierce heart and the curiosity that might get her killed? That is not you?"

I spluttered for a few moments, saving up my elegance for later. "Well, um..."

"The woman drawn to adventure and either stupid or brave enough to give me sass?" He continued. His voice was gently teasing, so I couldn't help smiling.

"It *is* starting to sound a little bit like me," I admitted. "Although I don't know why you're comparing me to fae's asses..." Obviously, he was referring to donkeys, and it was one helluva compliment to be told I was a horse among a sea of fae donkeys, but now I couldn't get the image out of my head of my face in a police lineup with a bunch of fae backsides.

"That answers the question," he said, speaking loudly so I could hear him over the sea, which was going through a noisy crashing phase.

"What question?"

"Whether you are brave or stupid," he replied. "Clearly, you are—"

"Hilarious," I interrupted before he forgot about all the lovely compliments he was paying me and started insulting me instead. "I'm extremely hilarious and clever. Also funny."

"You are certainly something," he conceded, and I decided to take that as a win.

The ocean reared up before me as I tilted toward it, and I decided I'd better sit down before I fell. Sliding down the rock wall until my ass hit the rough ground, I pulled my knees in tight and hugged them, trying to capture every speck of body warmth before it floated out to sea.

"Why are you here?" I asked once I was settled. "Last I saw you, you were in Capricia and, um..."

Really, now my face went red from embarrassment? Now? At least VFA couldn't see, but I was sure he could hear it in my voice. I was thankful when he didn't tease me but just pressed on with the conversation.

"Same with you, Lexi," he said on a sigh. "Why are any of us here?"

I let out a humph. "Either you're getting philosophical on me, or you were also kidnapped by that Shadow King asshole and dumped here." I wriggled my butt off a particularly sharp section of rock and onto a more standard cold-numbing bit. "I'm guessing you don't know what he wants with us, then?"

A loud set of waves came through, crashing noisily below,

and VFA waited until they'd passed before speaking into the relative quiet. "I do not think he even knows," he said. "He is so focused on his plan I am surprised he has any time for prisoners."

"His populate-the-world-with-zombies-and-fuck-it-up-for-everyone plan?" I asked.

I waited for a small laugh. After all, I was hilarious. And funny. But my mystery guy wasn't known for his sense of humor, so I didn't get the chuckle I deserved. VFA was more abs and brooding and hot, hot sex than joking around, so I let him off the hook.

"I suppose there is more to it than that," he eventually said. "He must have his reasons, assuming he is not simply a psychopath."

I raised a hand like he was counting votes. "Complete psycho," I said. "Definitely."

"Perhaps you are right," he conceded after a few moments. "He has little regard for others. Most others, at least."

I rubbed my hands up and down my arms to try to bring some warmth into them. I'd definitely heard that was either a really good idea because it kept your blood circulating, or a terrible idea because it brought your blood to the skin and let the heat escape. Oh well. At least it was something to do. Salt was so thick in the air from the sea below that I could not only taste it but also feel it on my skin.

"Is anyone coming for you?" the man asked.

"You did," I blurted out, then reddened so hard that he might be able to see the blush through the thick stone wall that separated us.

A pause, then a clarification. "I mean coming to find you. At the wedding, you seemed rather close to the royal heirs from the various realms. Do you expect them to launch a rescue mission on your behalf?"

I huffed a small laugh and watched the fog of my breath dissipate. The problem with craving adventure as fervently as I did was that it led me to make stupid decisions. Like convincing Delph to let me and my baby sisters travel overland in the middle of a damn war, and having no way to contact her if things went sideways. Like they did. Oh, so sideways. As far as Delph knew, I was already back in Hebes.

The only people who would notice me missing were Kayla and Razelle. My wonderful, sensible twin sisters, who always did as they were told when holidaying in dangerous magical regions in the middle of a war. I wriggled my butt to try to find a comfier bit of poky cold rock and sighed. I was starting to see the upside of being sensible.

Even the twins might not notice I was missing until they got home to Hebes. I was exactly the type of person who'd find my own way home without telling them just for the adventure. And when they got home to Hebes, they had no way of contacting Delph other than waiting around and waiting for a call via the magical stone thingy, which only our cousin could initiate.

I sighed again, more dramatically this time. "Nobody's coming for me."

"Ahh. I get to keep you all to myself then," VFA said.

"Lucky you," I said.

"Lucky," he echoed, and I wondered if my tone sounded as dead and flat as his. "Will your cousin not come for you? She is the Queen of Caprice, is she not?"

I licked the salt off my lips while I came up with a way to avoid answering that question. "Oh, she's very busy," I said lamely.

"Too busy to rescue her human cousin from the Shadow King?"

There was that phrase 'human cousin' again, which felt more disconcerting every time I heard it. I was no longer so sure I could handle myself in the fae realm, and the extra cold prison rock beneath my ass wasn't helping me feel competent. Or badass.

"Well…"

"Tell me, Lex."

"It's a long and complicated business."

He huffed out a breath. "Do you have somewhere else to be?"

I supposed there was no harm in telling him. Apart from the distinct possibility he would think I was an idiot. But after he pressed me several more times, I relented.

"Delph doesn't know I'm here. It's a funny story actually," I added, trying to make it sound amusing rather than pathetic. "I kinda ran away. At least, I convinced her to let me travel overland. She wanted to pack me off home where it was safe because of, you know, the Shadow King and the war and stuff, but I wanted to see more of the fae realms first. To live a little, you know. Take in the sights and sounds, soak up the fae world."

I stared dejectedly over the large expanse of fae world I was soaking up close and personal. It looked very much like a desolate stretch of water and gray sky in the human world, but perhaps I could comfort myself by noticing that the rock I sat on was a little harder and colder than normal rock. Yay me.

"Sounds tragically pathetic," he said, and frankly that was hardy to deny. Still, I wasn't a fan of it being quite so explicitly noted between us. "Lie down," he added, like that was the next logical move.

"Why? Because all I can do now is roll over and die?" I asked, starting to feel huffy and annoyed. I might be a fucking idiot, but I didn't appreciate being told so.

"No, because I am going to pass you something from my cell. If we both lie down and stretch as far as we can, we can probably reach so our fingers touch."

I nodded while I considered that. The addition of anything to my frigid cave would be an improvement, so even if he was planning to pass me a live rat, I'd appreciate it. Wincing when my knobbly knees bit into the cold rock, I maneuvered myself into a prone position and wriggled forward as far as I dared, until my nose poked over the edge of the cliff and I had a straight look down to the sharp rocks far below. I inhaled fast and my skin broke out into goose bumps.

Now was the time to show how brave I was. Time for something eloquent and laissez-faire.

"Ummm," I began.

"Here," VFA said, thankfully cutting me off before I blathered any more. "I will swing it up for you to catch."

"Is it a rat?" I asked in my calmest tone of voice, although out loud it sounded more like a squeal.

"Not a rat," he said, and this time I detected a trace of humor in his voice, making me think it was definitely a rat.

Despite being fairly sure I had to keep my gaze locked on the sea below me to make sure it stayed in place, I risked a glance to my left and saw VFA smirking at my discomfort. His head and shoulders poked out over his bit of sea, and they looked broad and heavy enough that he might topple forward at any moment. His eyes glinted with amusement, and the stubble on his jaw somehow highlighted the sharpness of his cheekbones.

"Here," he said, then swung something brown and furry my way. "You need this more than I do."

I elegantly caught it, with only a small yelp, and flung it into the depths of my cell before looking back at VFA, whose black eyes glinted with amusement. He nodded in the direction of where I'd chucked it, and I found the courage to shimmy backward away from the cliff's edge then go and fetch it. A blanket. A brown, furry, soft, warmth-giving, God-loving blanket.

Wrapping it tight around me, I instantly felt the chill of the air lessen and smiled. I slid back into my groove at the cell's edge and wriggled out far enough to see him. He looked at me with such intensity I was momentarily lost for words. "It's even better than a rat," I finally said, already feeling my body warmth heating the space around me.

My earlier loneliness and panic drifted away as I snuggled into the soft warmth of the blanket and looked into the piercing eyes of my mystery man. Tight-lipped and tight-abbed men weren't my usual source of comfort, but his presence meant I wasn't alone here, and that was worth everything. For the first time in hours, I relaxed completely.

He nodded solemnly. "You are welcome, Larper."

My limbs tensed at that nickname. "Why did you call me that?"

His black eyes were unreadable, but his brows drew together. "You told me when we first met." He nodded toward the ocean. "At the wedding."

"Oh, right." I let my muscles melt again and soaked up the comfort of the blanket and his closeness. "Does ASK do all that weird shadow-caressing stuff with you? Like you think he's about to kill you, then instead he touches you softly. And you think he's all serious, then suddenly he's laughing."

"ASK?" he asked.

"Asshole Shadow King." I was wedged against the wall into a small groove that felt safe, supported at an angle so I could see my new buddy, and, with my hand under my ear, I was relatively comfortable.

VFA huffed out a breath while he considered my question and something wistful passed across his face. "I think he has forgotten I ever existed," he said.

I scoffed. "You can't have been here more than a day or two."

VFA's brow darkened. "The truth is, the Shadow King does not forget his prisoners, Lexi. Not unless he has already taken what he needs. But if he is ever hurting you or scaring you, just know that I am here too, listening. I will always be there, even if you cannot see me."

After long minutes of listening to the crashing waves and staring at the gray sky, he reached out a hand toward me, and I wriggled a hand free of my blanket cocoon to do likewise. The quiet weight of his movements made it clear—this meant something to him. Something bigger than the icy sea or the miles of stone between us, so I reached out to touch his fingers with mine.

We lay that way in silence for a long time.

VFA

I stretched my arm out over the precipice, my fingers inter-lacing with Lexi's cold ones. The Requin Strait churned and roared far below, foam-capped waves crashing against jagged rocks. Gray clouds hung heavy in the sky, pregnant with rain. Salt spray misted my face as I inched forward, more of my chest now suspended over the abyss.

"I have you," I growled, gripping her hand tighter as her arm sagged with fatigue.

Despite the perilous position, a strange sense of calm washed over me. For the first time in centuries, I felt content. Happy, even. The damp air filled my lungs, and I savored each breath.

"You're trembling," Lexi observed, her voice barely audible above the pounding surf.

"It is the cold," I lied.

My mind drifted to her cousin's royal wedding, where I'd first held her in my arms. Her boldness had drawn me in, her fearlessness intoxicating. When we'd finally come together, her warmth had set my blood on fire. She'd writhed beneath me, wild and untamed, awakening parts of me I'd thought long dead.

Now, her fingers were like ice in my grasp.

Lexi's grip loosened, her fingers slipping from mine. Her breathing deepened, becoming slow and steady. Alarm shot through me as I realized she was drifting off to sleep.

"Lexi," I said sharply, giving her hand a firm squeeze. "You need to move back. Now."

Her eyes fluttered open, confusion clouding her brow. "Hmm?"

"It is not safe to sleep here," I commanded, my voice brooking no argument. "Wriggle back into the cave. Immediately."

For a moment, I thought she might resist. But then she nodded, carefully inching away from the precipice. I waited, tensed and ready to grab her if she faltered. When she was safely inside, I inched back into my cave too, my body thrumming with relief and something else.

Power. Control. The thrill of having this wild, untamed creature obey my command sent a jolt of pleasure through me. It was intoxicating.

"You're quite bossy for a fellow prisoner," Lexi mumbled, settling against the cave wall as her voice floated around to me on the sea-spray air.

I smirked. "You surprise me, I suppose. I half expected you to wriggle free and make a run for it. I could mistake you for somebody compliant."

She snorted, but I heard the smile on her lips. "Don't get used to it. I'm just too tired to argue right now."

As I listened to her drift off to sleep, I considered her lack of fear. Most fae cowered in my presence, their terror palpable. But Lexi treated me as an equal. A fae, not a fiend. It was because she was human, I reasoned. Her senses and instincts were dull.

But as I listened to her deepening breaths, I knew it was more than that. Lexi was special. Unique. And my curiosity about her was rapidly evolving into something far more dangerous.

I found myself imagining every detail of her sleeping form so clearly it was like I could see her. The way her nose crinkled slightly as she dreamed. The small, round belly button that peeked out from beneath her rumpled shirt, as unique as her.

The memory of her shiver when I'd traced a finger down her cheek flooded my senses. I longed to do it again, to pull her into my arms and shelter her from the harsh realities of this world.

It was a foolish, impossible desire. I was the harsh reality she needed protection from.

"What are you doing to me, little human?" I whispered, careful not to wake her.

For the first time in centuries, I felt an unfamiliar ache in my chest. A need to protect, to cherish.

The realization should have terrified me. Instead, I found myself moving closer and placing a hand on the cold stone wall that separated us, drawn to her warmth like a moth to the sun.

Once she was deep asleep, I carefully pushed away from the rock wall, my muscles coiled with tension. Lexi's soft breaths echoed in the stillness of the cave. I called out, my voice a low rumble.

"Guards. Open the cell."

The heavy iron door swung open with a groan. I strode through, my shoulders set and jaw clenched. The two fae guards snapped to attention, fear radiating off them in palpable waves.

"My lord," one stammered, bowing low.

I fixed him with a cold stare. "Double the patrol on the

eastern ramparts. And send word to the kitchens–the prisoner is to receive a hot meal when she wakes."

"At once, sire," the other guard replied, scurrying away.

I moved through the fortress like a shadow given form, issuing curt orders as I went. Torches guttered in my wake, and servants pressed themselves against the walls to avoid my path. The fear in their eyes should have pleased me. Instead, I found myself contrasting them with Lexi's fearless gaze.

The war council chamber loomed before me, its obsidian doors etched with inspiring battle scenes. I pushed them open, the room beyond swallowing me in darkness. As I took my seat at the head of the long table, another faelight flared to life, casting an eerie glow over the gathered generals.

"Report," I commanded, my voice filling the cavernous space.

As my lieutenants droned on about troop movements and supply lines, my gaze wandered to the massive map sprawled across the table. The Shadow Isles lay off the Eastern coast of the fae realms, a dark stain beside the vibrant lands. A dark stain that was steadily leaking to the West, through Caprice and beyond. My fingers traced the outline of my domain, pausing over the spot where Lexi now slept.

"My lord?" A tentative voice broke through my reverie.

I looked up, meeting the terrified eyes of Valdor. "What is it?"

"Th—the armies of the dead await your command, Shadow King."

I had spent centuries earning that name, building my army and waiting for my moment. It was finally here. I leaned back in my throne, a mirthless smile twisting my lips.

"Indeed they do," I replied, my voice as cold as the grave.

"And soon, all the realms will tremble at their approach."

I surveyed the sycophants surrounding me, their eyes wide with a mixture of fear and anticipation. General Vex, a gaunt specter of a man, cleared his throat.

"My lord, what of the southern border? Our scouts report increased activity from-"

"Increased activity?" I cut him off, my voice sharp. "And what, pray tell, do you propose we do about this activity?"

Vex stammered, his translucent form flickering. "We could... perhaps... reinforce our defenses?"

I scoffed, my mind drifting to Lexi's unwavering courage in the face of danger. She would have proposed a bold counter-strike, not this cowering nonsense.

"Reinforcements," I muttered. "Is that the extent of your strategic prowess, General?"

The room fell silent, tension thick in the air. I drummed my fingers on the armrest, impatient with their incompetence.

"My lord," another voice piped up. "What of the prisoner? The human girl?"

My jaw clenched. "What of her?"

"Should we not interrogate her? She may have valuable information about—"

"Enough," I growled, rising to my feet. The generals flinched as one. "The prisoner is not your concern. I have her under control. Focus on the task at hand."

As I turned away, my thoughts circled back to Lexi. Her strength, her defiance—so different from these sniveling wretches. She saw me as a fae, not the monster they cowered before. When had I become this creature of darkness?

For centuries, I'd embraced the role thrust upon me, relishing in the fear I inspired. But now, with Lexi's laughter echoing in my memory, I felt a stirring of something long forgotten. A whisper of the fae I used to be before exile and bitterness twisted me into the Shadow King.

I clenched my fist, pushing away such dangerous thoughts. I was what I had to be.

I leaned close to my most trusted advisor, whispering orders to ensure Lexi's comfort and safety. With a curt nod, I dismissed the generals, striding from the war room with purpose. My footsteps echoed through the dark corridors as I made my way to Lexi's chambers.

Outside her door, I paused, steeling myself. With a subtle nod to the guard, I allowed my wrists to be bound in shackles. The cold metal bit into my skin, a reminder of the deception I was about to perform.

I entered, dropping my shadows and letting my true face show. Lexi's bright blue eyes widened as she took in my bound wrists. Her dark curls were unruly like the calligrapher who drew them had spilled his ink. As she climbed to her feet, I saw that her fine fae jeans and shirt were dirty, and I was glad for the decision I'd taken to pamper her and warm her up.

"What's happening?" she asked, her voice concern and curiosity.

I offered a rueful smile. "It seems we are to be bathed. A small luxury in this fortress, I suppose."

Her brow furrowed and that cute shade of pink she liked to pretend didn't exist stained her cheeks. "Both of us? Together? Um, okay."

"Separate baths, I assure you," I replied smoothly, although the speed at which she'd agreed made me wonder if that was necessary. "Shall we?"

As we walked to the bathing chambers, I was acutely aware

of her presence beside me. The warmth radiating from her body, the subtle scent of her skin. Intoxicating.

The bathing chamber was a study in contrasts. Luxurious cream marble tubs stood against the dark, forbidding stone walls and obsidian floor. Steam rose from the water, filling the air with rose and lavender.

Lexi hesitated for a moment before beginning to undress. I tried to avert my eyes, to give her privacy, but found myself transfixed. The curve of her hip, the elegant line of her neck—each revealed inch of skin sent a jolt through me. And there was that outie belly button and the triangle at the top of her legs.

She stepped into her bath with a soft sigh of pleasure. A bead of steam clung to her breast, and my body responded, heat pooling low in my belly.

Swallowing hard, I shed my own clothes and lowered myself into the adjacent tub. The warm water enveloped me but did nothing to quell the fire in my veins. I was achingly, embarrassingly erect, and silently thanked the steam for providing cover.

I watched as Lexi sank deeper into her bath, her eyes closing in bliss. "You seem to be enjoying yourself," I remarked, my voice rougher than I intended.

Her eyes fluttered open, a lazy smile spreading across her face. "A bath is one of life's greatest pleasures, don't you think?"

I grunted noncommittally. "I wouldn't know. Pleasure has not been a priority for quite some time."

She turned to face me, curiosity sparking in her gaze. "Why not?"

The question caught me off guard. I found myself speaking

before I could think better of it. "Life took an unexpected turn. I was accused of a crime I did not commit." My fists clenched beneath the water. "Since then, I have been consumed by anger, by the need for justice."

Lexi's expression softened and I waited for questions about the murder, the crime, all the gory details everyone always sought.

But she said, "That sounds lonely."

"It has been," I admitted, surprised by my own candor. "There has not been much room for pleasure."

She leaned closer, the water lapping at the swell of her breasts. "There's always time for pleasure," she murmured, her voice low and sultry.

My cock twitched in response, and I shifted, trying to hide my body's reaction. "Perhaps," I managed to say.

"Life's too short to deny yourself joy," Lexi continued. "Even in the darkest times, there are pinpricks of light."

Her words stirred something in me, a long-dormant part of myself I'd thought lost forever. I found myself opening up, sharing more of my past than I had with anyone in centuries. It was unsettling, how easily she drew me out.

As I spoke, I gradually relaxed, sinking deeper into the warm embrace of the bath. For the first time in longer than I could remember, I allowed myself to simply enjoy the moment, the soothing heat of the water, the gentle scent of the oils, the quiet intimacy of conversation.

I closed my eyes, savoring the unfamiliar sensation of contentment. It was dangerous, this softening of my guard, and yet I couldn't bring myself to care. In this moment, with Lexi, I felt more like my true self than I had in eons.

"You know," Lexi said, her voice cutting through the steam,

"maybe the Shadow King isn't a total bastard after all."

My muscles tensed instantly, heart hammering. Had she somehow discovered my true identity? I fought to keep my voice steady. "What makes you say that?"

She shrugged, water droplets glistening on her shoulders as I watched for a moment too long. "Well, he's letting us wash up, isn't he? That's almost decent of him."

I exhaled slowly, relief flooding through me. "I suppose so," I murmured, my mind racing.

Was I a bastard, as she so eloquently put it? Everything I'd done–raising my army, plotting my revenge–it was all justified. They'd condemned me, exiled me for a crime I didn't commit, and forced me to spend centuries by myself on this Gaia-forsaken island with nothing but shadows for company. How could I be blamed if I made use of what I had and found a way to forge those shadows into an army? My jaw clenched as the old rage surged through me.

But then I looked at Lexi, so vibrant and alive. She was utterly unlike anyone else in my world–human, wild, unfettered by the constraints of fae society. And she had no idea how dangerous I was.

"You sound almost sympathetic toward him," I probed, curious to learn more.

Lexi's laugh was sharp. "Hardly. But even monsters can have moments of not complete monstrosity, I guess."

She washed her hair, and then I watched her rise from the bath, rivulets of water streaming down her lithe form, her water-straightened hair almost reaching the crack of her bottom. The interplay of vulnerability and strength in her movements was mesmerizing. For a wild moment, I was tempted to confess everything, to pull her into my arms and bare my soul completely.

The ache in my chest deepened, but I couldn't quite make sense of it. Was it her words or her presence that had caused it? Perhaps both. I had spent centuries in this fortress, learning only to control, to suppress. And now, in the heat of this bath, I was tempted to unravel all of it.

But then I imagined the horror that would spread across her face, the way she'd recoil from my touch. When she'd seen me in my Shadow King form, wreathed in shadows, she'd hated me, hurled insults my way, and looked at me with utter disgust. Just the thought of that look etching permanently onto her face made my throat tighten, and I swallowed hard.

Instead of confessing my true identity, I gave a subtle nod to the guard. As he approached with the handcuffs, I kept my eyes fixed on Lexi, drinking in every detail of her as she dressed.

"Time to go," I said, my voice rough.

The warm, soft water had barely dried from my skin before the chill of the stone halls crept into my bones, the torches casting long shadows that seemed to chase me. As the guard led me away, my thoughts remained with her. Her warmth, her laughter, the way she made me feel almost fae again. It was a dangerous weakness, one I couldn't afford. And yet, I couldn't bring myself to regret it.

Gabrelle

"What's up, trickster?" Thorne asked, and I squeezed his hand in reply, looking at the thicket of trees that marked the edge of Caprice. I had asked our Fliers to land here while I gathered my thoughts.

Nature in Caprice was on our side, because we were aligned with the King and Queen, and the land itself mirrored their moods. Fallen leaves on the grass gathered themselves up into little chairs, doing everything they could to be helpful. But neither I nor Thorne sat.

"Nothing," I lied, because I was actually terrified but didn't want to worry my lover.

Beyond the trees, the sun shone brightly in the neighboring realm, where it was always summer. It looked inviting, but only if you didn't know it well enough to be scared.

We were about to return to Fen with one fragment of the Stone of Veritas, hoping to defend Isslia and the rest of the realm from the Shadow Walkers. And there were so many problems with that plan that I couldn't begin to see a way of it actually working.

For starters, we had only the smallest idea of how to wield our fragment, and despite Thorne's reassurances that we'd figure it out, I didn't see how we could use one tiny bit of rock to protect as vast an area as the Realm of Fen.

Secondly, I was nervous about entering the land of truth. Within the borders of Fen, no fae could tell a lie. Last time I'd visited, truth bombs had exploded from my mouth with regularity, and it was only with supreme concentration and a steel throttle on my emotions that I'd been able to control them. And that was back when I though emotions were for the weak and had a lifetime's practice of restraining them. Now, some kind of feelings dam had been broken and they poured from me like never before, so I dreaded to think how little control I'd have over my words in Fen.

And then there was Erevan Reissan. He and Thorne had been bitter enemies, both vying for the throne of Fen in the political vacuum caused by the death of Thorne's mother and sister. In the end, Thorne had given up the crown for me and handed leadership of the realm over to his worst enemy. In exchange, Thorne had walked away with the Stone of Veritas, and here we were returning with a fragment of it.

Plus, I'd slept with Erevan a bunch of times, including a memorable victory of mine during the Wild Hunt. Which was also when my Thorne had first tried to kill me.

All in all, I had a lot of complicated memories associated with Fen, and I was terrified of returning.

"I don't believe you," Thorne said with his usual candor. "Are you thinking about Reissan?"

I swear, sometimes this lover of mine could read my fucking mind. I was the one with Lure, I should be doing all the mind-snooping around here.

"Erevan can go fuck himself," I spat, and Thorne pulled me into a hug.

I crashed into his shoulder, breathing in his minty scent

with those familiar dark undertones, letting the leather of his tunic squish my lips.

"As long as you don't want to fuck him," Thorne said, and I realized this must be just as hard for him. Not only was he returning as a foreigner to the land he'd once expected to rule, but he had to visit with his bitter enemy, whom he'd handed his kingdom to and, to rub salt into the wound, had also slept with me.

"Erevan is an ugly asshole and I want nothing to do with him," I said as tears flowed down my cheeks and wet the leather on Thorne's shoulder. "Damn these emotions," I murmured into the salt pool of my tears on his tunic.

He put a finger under my chin to lift my head. "I love your emotions," he said simply and, because it was coming from him, I knew it was true. We might not yet be in the Realm of Truth, but my lover had a lifelong habit of speaking it, and I could always rely on his honesty. It was one of the things I loved most about him.

I wiped my tears away with a quick dab at my cheeks. "Okay, stop mucking around, and let's get going," I said.

Thorne smiled and kissed me, long and hard, like it might be the last time we ever did it, and for a moment I drowned in his lips, in his strong arms around me, knowing this moment was everything I needed in life, and even if I died the instant I set foot in Fen, it would be worth it for this kiss. The salt of my tears mixed with his familiar taste, and our lips moved in perfect synchrony as a dry wind caressed my dusty pink hair.

Pulling away, I nodded, and we called to our Fliers, who were standing a polite distance away, then headed back into the skies.

I preferred to travel by moonway, but that was impossible in

Fen. The landscape was so unreliable there, always changing and morphing, so moonways tended to swap destinations or disappear entirely, leaving travelers stranded in the harsh forest or plains. Personally, I'd spent more than enough time battling the native creatures of Fen, like pteroclaws and osquips, and I would rather suffer the humiliation and discomfort of dangling from a Flier than face them again. Plus, being in the middle of a war, time was of the essence.

The Fliers soared above a patchwork of shifting landscapes, the verdant forests of Caprice giving way to the stark, glacial plains of Fen. The air shifted subtly as we crossed the border between realms, feeling somehow less mischievous and more somber in Fen.

A cold wind howled past us, carrying whispers of truths unspoken, and the golden glow of eternal summer gave way to a piercing, silvery light. My stomach twisted—not from the flight, but from the growing sense of unease as we neared Isslia.

Blood pooled in my feet as I dangled my way through the sky, finally landing in Isslia, the city of eternal summer that was lined with buildings made from pale blue stone that looked exactly like ice, which probably had Gaia laughing like a banshee.

Gaia liked her paradoxes, especially when it came to Fen. The summer city with streets paved in ice. The realm of truth populated by fae who were experts in deceit. Only truths could be spoken, leaving the local fae expert at weaving lies through implication and inserting artifice into the spaces between words.

Our feet touched the broad stones of the street, which curved and turned like icy rivers winding through the short buildings of bluestone and greywhite stone. The city's protective walls, built to hold off the worst of the infrequent but unpredictable ice storms, were constructed of the same stone, but higher and visible from everywhere in Isslia, a bright blue silver.

I took a deep breath to soak in the new realm, inhaling the scent of summer blossoms and cold stone, but Thorne immediately stopped a passing fae who wore floor-length white robes with a long metal strip down the back to protect against storms.

"Have the Shadow Walkers reached Isslia?" he asked, holding her in place with a raised hand. I knew Thorne loved living in Verda with me but he also missed Fen. But I hadn't realized how worried he was about the safety of his homeland until I heard the urgency in his voice.

"No such thing," she muttered, then moved to go around him, but he stepped to block her path, grabbing her wrist.

"I have seen them," he said simply, letting the words sit in the air between them without further explanation, and I recalled how sparse conversations were in Fen. Nobody needed extra words to convince and cajole, because the truth required far fewer words than guile.

The fae looked him square in the eyes, suddenly giving him her full attention. She had pale eyes and hair with the faintest tint of yellow in them, and her skin was so white she practically disappeared into her robes.

"You have not," she replied, tilting her head.

Thorne's shoulders tensed. "I could not say it more plainly," he said, and I could hear the tightness in his tone. "I have seen Shadow Walkers with my own eyes, while waking. They exist."

She huffed out a breath. "A faeling can say she has seen a human if she believes it so."

"I didn't fucking imagine the Shadow Walkers coating the skin of fae until they died, rising later as walkers of the dead," he hissed, sounding more emotional than usual, and I realized how much he'd changed since leaving his home. Like me, his emotions were closer to the surface than they ever used to be. We had turned each other into walking, talking towers of feelings instead of the bottled-up ice statues we used to be.

The jury was still out on whether that was a good thing.

Those yellow-white eyes narrowed at Thorne. "So says the faeling about the human," she replied, then she yanked her wrist free of Thorne's grip and marched away, shaking her head.

Thorne turned his anguished blue-black gaze to mine, and I held up a hand to halt him. Instead, talking over my shoulder, I dismissed the two Fliers who'd brought us, ordering them to alert the Court of Fen that we were here and asking for accommodation to be prepared. Then I gave my full attention to Thorne.

"At least she answered your question," I said, looking for a silver lining. "The Shadow Walkers haven't reached Isslia, or she'd know about it."

"She didn't believe me," he said, and his eyes burned with horror. "She thought I was fucking imagining things. How can we possibly convince everyone to prepare for battle if they don't believe we're at war."

He walked a few steps up the street, and I started to follow, when he abruptly changed direction and came back, starting up a good old-fashioned fit of pacing, his boots echoing on the stone. While he paced, he rambled about how he'd never truly understood his own land, how he'd acted so superior to fae from other realms because he thought them all liars, when in fact he'd been living among deceivers all along.

I stood in his path to stop him, then grabbed his hands. "Thorne, you're sowing truths like a farmer sows seeds. You've lost your resistance to the realm. Take some deep breaths and count to ten."

His time in Verda had clearly weakened his immunity to the truth-telling effects of the land, because I'd never heard him string so many words together, and he needed to calm down. He clung onto my hands like a lifeline while he sucked in long, slow breaths.

Unfortunately, my own words and thoughts bubbled up inside me, wanting to pour into the silence between us. Finally, I couldn't contain them any longer and I blurted out the one truth I'd been hoping to hide from him.

"I don't think Erevan is an ugly asshole," I began, horrified at the words coming from me but unable to stop them. My body wanted to rid me of the last lie I'd said, just before we entered Fen, when I'd called him that, and my brain didn't seem to have a say in the matter. "I think he's gorgeous," I continued, "like seriously good looking, with those caramel eyes that make my panties melt and that swagger, and, oh, the way he runs his hand through his caramel hair. And his way with words, he's so charming and flirty. Honestly, he's some kind of temptation God wrapped up in a hot package."

Finally, I yanked my hands from Thorne's grip and plastered them over my mouth to dam the flood of words, but it was too late. The damage was done.

Thorne's expression froze, his hands dropping to his sides. A flicker of something—pain, perhaps—crossed his dark eyes, and his jaw tightened. For a moment, he said nothing, the silence between us heavy with unspoken emotions.

Thorne sighed, running a hand through his hair, and forced a smile. "You want to fuck him?" He wasn't angry, but the hurt in his blue-black eyes was never-ending, and the muscles in his forearms bunched out.

"No," I immediately said. "I only want you, for sex or anything else." I should really have left it at that, but my mouth kept running. "Except conversations and stuff, like I will talk to other fae, and maybe joke with them and stuff, but no sex. Sex is just with you."

Thorne thawed a little, but I could see he was still hurting. "Okay, so you only think he's hot, and—"

"Really fucking hot," I interrupted, then I let out a little squeak of apology and bit my lips shut.

Thorne held out his hands in a stop-talking gesture, that I really wished I could obey. "Yes, I got that part," he said tersely.

"But not as hot as you," I said, and a big grin stretched my mouth so wide it hurt.

Thorne looked up at me, setting his shoulders straighter, not quite allowing himself to smile. "Do you mean temperature-wise, like I run like a furnace, or..."

I stood back, folding my arms across my chest and looking over him slowly, from black boots, up his strong black-clad legs, letting my gaze linger on the firm planes of his chest beneath the fine fae silk shirt I'd convinced him to wear.

"I mean," I purred, "that you are the sexiest fae I've ever seen. One look from you can make me weak at the knees, and your body is the most fuckable I've ever touched, your face is stern and sometimes intimidating but oh, so, sexy, and I want to spend forever as your lover."

He looked at me for a few moments. "Well, alright then."

Gabrelle

While the Fliers who'd carried us to Isslia secured us quarters at the Court of Fen, where esteemed visitors were accommodated, Thorne and I headed straight to the Ice Palace in the fading light of dusk.

The palace was intricately carved with patterns of snow, giving the illusion of delicate lace. It was made from the same blue stone as the streets, as if it was made from ice, and the glittering spires reflected deeper blue at their tips.

As Thorne and I approached the palace, the air became colder, carrying a sharp, crisp scent of winter.

"It's spelled to look and feel like ice," Thorne explained. "Until a visitor is welcomed, they become colder and colder until they can no longer move or breathe."

A shiver ran through me at the words. "We better hope we're welcome."

As we stepped across the threshold to the grand foyer, the sound of ice cracking and shifting had me grasping Thorne's forearm. It sounded like the whole place was about to come down on our heads, and the cold was seeping into my skin so it was all I could do to keep the shiver inside.

"It's just part of the illusion," Thorne assured me, but that didn't stop my breath from crystallizing before my face or my skin from jumping into goose bumps.

I looked around at the vast, empty hall, searching for signs of life. "Where's the damn welcome party?" I huffed, starting to shiver.

Thorne kept his silence, but I knew exactly what he was thinking. He couldn't tell a lie within the borders of Fen, so he couldn't assure me that King Erevan would be striding in any moment to welcome us with open arms. My lover's silence told me everything I needed to know: maybe nobody was coming. Maybe we would stay in the foyer until we were nearly frozen and forced to leave. Maybe this whole trip was a fucking waste of time.

I tugged my jacket tighter and made my body as small as possible, wishing I'd worn furs instead of these black leather pants, which welcomed the cold in.

My shivering reached a fever pitch, my whole body shaking uncontrollably, and Thorne squeezed my hand, although the sensation was dim through my numbing fingers. "T-t-time t-to c-c-call it," he said.

I wanted to say no, to demand that we stay until the damn princeling whom we'd handed his kingdom came to greet us, but my eyeballs were starting to crystallize, so all I could do was stumble toward the grandly carved ice doors that would lead us back to warmth.

As I reached out one hand to push on the doors, a scraping of footsteps snared my attention, and I turned slowly as a deep voice rumbled through the entrance chamber.

"Welcome to my palace," Erevan said, and warmth flooded into my body as though I'd stepped into an oven. My sluggish blood started pumping properly, my skin came back to life, and then every cell in my body started screaming with pins and needles.

I dropped to my knees, dimly aware of Thorne doing the same beside me, and cringed through the agony of my body thawing. As soon as possible, I regained my feet and cocked out a hip, trying to get some kind of upper hand here.

Erevan wore a beautifully tailored navy suit that highlighted his broad shoulders and narrow waist and those lovely muscled legs, plus the long ice-blue robes typical of the ruler. And, the ass, he was wearing his fucking crown atop his artfully tousled butterscotch hair while he smirked at us.

"You kept us waiting," I growled. The last time I'd been in Fen, I'd been expert at hiding my emotions and speaking in riddles, but I'd learned a lot about myself since then, like that feelings were valid and masking them was overrated.

I'd also Ascended into Lure and spent hours practicing the subtle art of mind control. With the finest of magical threads, I sent a wisp of energy toward Erevan, letting it dance around his face until it no longer felt foreign to him, then I let it settle around his head, seeping slowly and gently into his mind. The first few times I'd done this, I'd been instantly clocked by my powerful buddies, but now, with patience and care, I could infiltrate even the strongest of minds.

Of course, the other Verdan heirs had insisted on updating our no-sex-among-the-heirs pact. We'd put it in place to avoid future conflicts. Given that we'll hopefully be ruling our realm alongside one another for centuries, we don't want any awkward sexual histories to affect our decisions. Hence the no-sex pact. Only now that we'd all Ascended into our powers, most recently Ronan, who'd finally become a decent Mentium, we'd had to update the pact. It was now a no-fucking-with-each-other-magically pact. I wasn't allowed into anyone's head. Ronan wasn't allowed to influence our emotions. Neela wasn't allowed to attack us with her earth magic, which she had a history of doing, and Dion wasn't allowed to poison us. Leif wasn't allowed to turn us into sex zombies with his sex powers, although, frankly, despite the pact he'd tried a bunch of times and never succeeded.

The heirs had let me practice on them a few times, and I'd gotten good. So, while Thorne and Erevan exchanged barbed pleasantries, I smiled along but focused on gently penetrating Erevan's mind. I needed to convince him to take the Shadow Walker threat seriously, and to accept our offer of help.

"I see you've taken quickly to being king," Thorne said in a veiled jab at Erevan wearing his crown to intimidate us.

"I was always better suited to it than you," Erevan replied smoothly. Their bitter fight for the rule of Fen had ended with Thorne conceding in order to secure the Stone of Veritas, but Erevan had always maintained he would make the better king. And perhaps, given his diplomatic prowess and savage streak, he was right.

"Yes, the robes look marvelous on you," Thorne said, deliberately misunderstanding and bringing the conversation back to fashion.

I snorted, not bothering to hide it, but tuned them out while I focused on my magic. I had to dismantle the thick walls Erevan had constructed around his mind. A lifetime of subterfuge and masking had made his defenses stronger than most, despite having no training in mental blocking. I gently tugged on one brick in the wall, wincing when his gaze flicked to me. And the damn brick didn't budge.

Erevan's butterscotch eyes flicked between us, amusement barely masking the tension in his stance. "You are back sooner than I expected," he said, his voice as smooth as the polished floors beneath us. "Perhaps you'll stay for the Wild Hunt again?"

Thorne stiffened beside me, and I fought the urge to smirk. The jab wasn't subtle, but it still hit its mark. "I'm not interested in prey," I replied, keeping my voice light. "I prefer males who can equal me." I tilted my head toward Thorne, making my point clear.

Erevan's smile faltered, and in that moment, I nudged my magic deeper into his mind, trying a different approach. Instead of battering my way through the thick, rough walls he had erected around his consciousness, I floated above it and tried to drop down inside.

Slowly and gently, lifted on the breeze of my Lure, I eased my tendril of awareness into his inner castle while Thorne distracted him with conversation.

Everybody was different on the inside. Ronan was ordered and neat, except when he thought about Neela, when everything went swirly and messy. Erevan's mind was also ordered and compartmentalized, very similar to Ronan's.

Neela's mind was full of sharp edges and cliffs, and I was always wary of wandering around in there in case I got trapped in a hidden corner I couldn't escape. Leif's mind was like a sunny meadow with thoughts flitting through it like butterflies, and if it wasn't for the frequent alarms and howls, it would be a great place to meditate. I'd never been inside his mate Alara's mind, because Leif threatened to disembowel me with a straw if I tried, and I believed him. Dion's mind was categorized by color and smell, and he stored hay with butterscotch because they looked similar, but kept the concept of fate alongside hairdressers because they both, apparently, smelled like mint.

I'd never made it inside Thorne's mind, despite hours and hours of trying. He swore blue he wasn't doing anything to keep me out, it was just a natural defense. And it was also one of the things I loved about him.

I nodded to Thorne, and he took the cue, turning the conversation to the Shadow Walkers so I could follow the trail inside Erevan's mind.

"There have been reports of Shadow Walker activity in the West," he said, and I followed the path that lit up in his mind, winding between sky-high bookshelves to a tiny alcove devoted to the zombies right beside a tower of human tales in a section labeled "Bullshit".

"It's not bullshit," I blurted out before I could stop myself.

Erevan arched a golden brow. "You've made that abundantly clear." But the bullshit sign in his mind flashed neon, while his eyes narrowed suspiciously at me. I eased off his mind, letting myself float above it, while he returned his attention to Thorne.

Before I could push further, a sound like a thousand mirrors shattering filled the air. The walls trembled violently, and a section of the ceiling collapsed with a deafening crash. Guards poured down the stairs behind us, filling the entry foyer within moments, their ice-blue livery dancing among the settling dust.

And then they came. Shadows surged through the breach, dark and formless, blocking out the stars. Behind them shuffled the dead, their hollow eyes fixed on us.

Gabrelle

The ravaged look on Erevan's face made it clear he was in shock. The Shadow Walkers made a terrifying image as they launched themselves into the hall, pouring in through the crumbled eastern wall and shattering the silence with creaking stone.

"Attack!" bellowed the king. His power exploded outward from him and I felt it spark along my skin, a physical force. He flung out his hands and a wave of force erupted from him, but it passed through the Shadows without touching them.

The guards squared, their ice-blue livery shimmering against the ring of blades unsheathing and the muted roar of spells.

Dread filled my hollow bones as I watched the shadows creep closer, pooling onto the cold stone floor.

"Spells won't work," Thorne yelled beside me. "Cast light." But Erevan was focused on the seething mass of shadows.

Erevan unsheathed his sword. "Turn them back," he yelled, his voice barely audible over the screeching of the Shadow Walkers. He yelled over his shoulder to a battalion of wolves. "Shift!"

"No." Thorne summoned a globe of faelight. "Shifting doesn't help. Make light," he roared, but his voice was lost over the din of battle, the screams of fae, and the pounding of spells against stone.

I focused inside Erevan's mind, now fracturing into disorder as his perfectly constructed system was washed away in a wave of chaos. "Light," I implored inside his mind, willing him to listen. I abandoned subtlety and used a damn sledgehammer in his brain. "Summon light."

A Shadow Walker slithered over a fallen guard and lunged at us. Thorne was fast, his power surging forth to repel the creature, his muscles coiled for combat. But it was like trying to fight smoke with a sword—the shadow simply flowed around him.

"Light!" I screamed again, both out loud and in Erevan's mind. The king stumbled back, his sword falling from numbed fingers as his eyes locked with mine.

"Summon light!" he roared, the order echoing through the vast hall.

The guards reacted without question, throwing their hands high to create a surge of blinding white light that washed over the battlefield. The Shadow Walkers recoiled, flitting into the shadows around the edges of the foyer and back out into the night. The guards roared as they pressed their advantage, advancing toward the crumbled eastern wall.

But the Shadow Walkers weren't our only enemy. Fallen fae stumbled forward through the breached wall, unaffected by the light, a horde of the dead. As they attacked individual guards, pockets of darkness appeared through the chamber and Shadow Walkers seeped back in.

"No!" Thorne bellowed, lunging for me as a Shadow Walker swept toward us, its form rippling like liquid darkness. But he was too late. The shadow collapsed onto me, wrapping around my body like a shroud. Cold seeped into my skin and I gasped, my breath jarring as my eyelashes frosted over.

I fell to the hard floor, unable to move, even to expand my lungs for air. The creature coated my skin, stilling my heart, my breath, my lifeforce.

Then Thorne was standing above us, his shard of the Stone of Veritas a brilliant blue in his outstretched hand, and the shadow that clung to me screeched then solidified and shattered into particles that floated to the ice-blue floor in a sprinkle of black dust.

My lungs seared for air, but it took me a few gasping breaths before I could suck any in. My eyes flicked open at Thorne's touch, a lifeline in the madness. "Stay with me," he said, his voice a tether pulling me from the brink.

"More light!" Erevan bellowed. The fae guards responded with fury, releasing another surge of blinding light. The Shadow Walkers recoiled, their dark forms melting away like frost under the morning sun.

But more Walkers slithered through the breach in the castle wall and hid in pockets of darkness behind the soaring blue pillars. Every victory was met with a fresh wave of dread as I watched more dead fae soldiers rise into the shadow army.

Thorne placed me down while he turned to fight. A dead guard, with a slash of crimson across his ice-blue livery, turned on me and, staggering, his gaze pulsing with venom. I was empty of magic, but Thorne moved swiftly, his blade a blur as he stepped in to fell the undead fae, leaving him twitching on the blue stone floor.

Yet even as one fell, another three rose in its stead.

"Thorne," I gasped out, struggling to my feet though my body felt weighted by stones. The three undead fae inched closer, but Thorne's attention was elsewhere. His gaze was fixed on a battalion of shadows heading our way, his power undulating around him like a physical cloak.

My years of battle training made my limbs dance even though they were weighted with lead. I cast a carving spell to remove the head of one of the approaching guards and spun around and kicked the second in the belly, buying myself time while he fell to the floor. I didn't have my bow and arrow with me, and it would be of little use in these close quarters, so I had to make do with quickly cast spells.

I threw up an air shield as the third undead guard launched himself at me. That Shadow Walker had sucked most of my life force from me, and I couldn't keep this up much longer, so I glanced around for help.

Thorne was directing the beam from the Stone of Veritas fragment to the corners of the shattered room, killing any Walkers that lingered in the shadows, although they still lurked behind pillars and just beyond the breach. Living guards were casting fae light, although the coverage was patchy now as some of them fell beneath the hordes of the undead. Into the new pockets of darkness, the Walkers crept and slithered, and Thorne couldn't keep them all at bay.

"More light," Erevan roared, and the fae obeyed, another wave of blinding light washing over us. As it had before, the wave hit the Shadow Walkers and they recoiled like nothing more than smoke in the wind.

But it wasn't enough. The fae light only delayed them, and the Veritas fragment was just one weapon against a horde.

More Walkers swarmed from the shattered eastern wall, forcing us back toward the towering oak doors. Light from our spells dimmed as the breach widened, plunging us into pockets of deepening shadow.

"Move!" Thorne snapped, pulling me closer to him. His grip tightened around me and moved me backward. His black eyes were aflame, and I could feel his urgency in the pressure of his hold as he shielded me with his body.

As Erevan retreated from the frontlines with an injured guard in his arms, Thorne and I found ourselves pressed further into a corner. A team of fae guards formed a protective barrier around us while others continued to ward off the rising tide of Shadow Walkers and staggering undead.

It was like fighting against a tsunami with a bucket. We were tiring, our energy dwindling, while the Shadow Walkers gained strength with every fae we lost.

Thorne edged us along the wall toward the castle's massive oak doors, hacking and slashing through the undead. We were almost at the exit when the heavy oak door swung open.

Outlined against the harsh whiteness of buildings beyond it, was a figure cloaked entirely in black. Even from this distance, the dread was overwhelming as I came face to face with the Shadow King.

"He's here," I whispered. Thorne didn't need to ask who I meant.

The Shadow King's presence felt like a death curse, a void that sucked away all warmth and light. His cloak moved like ink, tendrils extending before him and merging with the shadows in the room, bringing more undead fae back to their feet.

The Shadow King advanced slowly, his presence washing over us like a tidal wave of despair. The light from our spells dimmed slightly at his approach and the fae soldiers faltered, their movements sluggish and hesitant.

I fought back the cold dread crawling up my spine, focused my magic, and managed to erect a protective shield around us. The effort was staggering, but we needed time to regroup. The fae soldiers could barely hold their ground against the relentless onslaught of the Shadow Walkers, and I feared what would happen once the Shadow King joined the melee.

Thorne released a barrage of energy bolts, trying to keep our immediate surroundings clear. Sweat poured down my face, soaking into my already-drenched collar. My hands shook with fatigue, but I drew on the last of my power to maintain the shield and keep the undead at bay.

Suddenly, a shriek echoed across the room as another guard fell. Her light died with her, and a mass of Shadow Walkers surged forward into the space she had occupied. I gasped and poured more energy into my magic, trying to expand the shield to protect the vulnerable gap. But I was nearly spent, and I could feel my strength wavering.

"Thorne!" I screamed again, desperate.

He reached out, placing one hand on mine where it rested in midair sustaining the shield spell. His touch sent a jolt of much-needed energy into my body, and I was able to stay on my feet a few moments longer.

The Shadow King came closer, and the world dimmed. The screams of combat around us faded, and the air grew heavier. We were trapped in a nightmare.

Suddenly, a brilliant beam of light cut through the gathering darkness. Thorne stood tall, his blade glowing with an almost divine light from the energy he was channeling from the Stone of Veritas fragment directly into the sword. His gaze met the approaching Shadow King's, and in his eyes blazed a defiance so fierce it made my heart pound louder than the chaos surrounding us.

"Stand down!" Thorne's voice echoed through the ruined hall.

But the Shadow King only laughed. "You think to stop me with a glowing toy?" he asked. "I have paid for my vengeance with centuries. I have forced death itself to its knees, subject to my command, and you think a pretty sword will scare me?" He stalked closer. "I do not scare easily, faeling."

"You don't have to do this," Thorne retorted, his voice cool as ice despite the draining battle. "This is not the way."

The Shadow King paused, regarding Thorne with a dismissive glance. "I disagree," he said simply. His voice was soft, almost bored, and it sent shivers down my spine.

"But why?" I spluttered. "You're a living, breathing fae, just like us. Why destroy the lands and turn everything to ruin? You won't have a kingdom left to rule after you've desecrated every inch of it. So why are you doing this?"

My words reverberated through the silent hall, and I heard the plea in the dying echo.

The Shadow King considered my question for a moment before replying. "Ask a mosquito why he bites, or a lion why she roars," he said. "I was made for this, Gabrelle Allura, just as your dear Mommy fashioned you into a beauty queen. You Ascended into Lure, as fate foretold. I shall Ascend into a God."

He knew my name—and somehow, I knew I couldn't let him speak it again.

Thorne snorted. "The God of nothing," he said, gesturing around to the broken room and all the fallen fae. "This is what you want? To be the ruler of a wreckage? Captain of a shipwreck?"

"What I want, Thorne Sanctus," the Shadow King said, his

shadows swirling around him, and his voice deepening to thunder, "is for you and your kind to have nothing. To be nothing." He smiled cruelly. "To have and to be exactly what you deserve."

One of the shadows wreathing his body darted out and swept Thorne from his feet, eliciting a dark chuckle from the Shadow King as my lover tumbled onto his face.

"Gaia will never allow it," Erevan called from across the room, standing tall and looking every inch a king as all eyes whipped to him. "She will never allow you to be anything more than a hiccup in history. The earth goddess will restore Arathay and send you straight to hell."

The Shadow King slowly turned his head to the King of Fen, and his tone darkened, all trace of humor gone. "I have made Mortia my bitch," he sneered, referring to the God of Death. "I will do the same for your precious Gaia. I will beat her down, keep her in a kennel, and only let her out for walks. I will destroy her precious realms and she will pant my name. Do not rely on her." He stalked closer and whispered in Erevan's face. "I am your God now."

With that, he thrust out his arm, and a bolt of pure darkness shot from his palm and blasted Erevan, sending the King of Fen flying backward, crashing into the castle walls. The room fell silent as the realm's ruler slid down the wall and landed in a puddle of broken bones and flowing blood.

A guard dashed forward to heal him but stopped when the Shadow King called out. "Leave him. He is already mine." Then Erevan's lifeless butterscotch eyes flicked open.

I felt Thorne beside me, staggering onto his feet again ready to defend us. His once divine-looking sword only held a dim light left now—the brutal battle had drained most of its energy.

"Time to go," he muttered to me.

We stumbled to the nearest doorway, holding each other up and maintaining a small fae light around us through sheer force of will. We waited while a dozen surviving guards rushed through the door, fleeing the disastrous scene. As we were poised to follow, dark shadows snaked around my feet, locking me in place, and I saw Thorne caught beside me.

The Shadow King's mirthless laughter mocked us as we writhed in place, unable to move our feet which were as good as melded to the stone floor. "No escape for the wicked, I'm afraid," he drawled.

"Let Gabrelle go," Thorne said, throwing a protective arm across my chest. "Kill me, but leave her alive to tell the others what happened here."

The Shadow King smiled, thinking it over. "What an interesting idea." He turned his black gaze on me, and I stilled under it. "You'll have a new tale to tell your friends, and I do so like to be the hero."

"Hold on," Thorne muttered, his hand steady on mine, a spark of his energy surging into me. His strength kept me standing, but my resolve was fraying.

The Shadow King's gaze found me, and my knees buckled. "Gabrelle Allura," he said, his voice a whisper that cut through the chaos. "You'll be my messenger."

Before I could speak, Thorne held his sword aloft, the blade glowing with the last dregs of the Veritas fragment's light. His defiance blazed like a beacon.

"We won't bow to you," Thorne said, his voice calm but edged with steel. "Not today. Not ever."

The Shadow King smiled—a cruel, hollow thing. "Oh, you already have."

Then he unleashed a blast of shadow as dark as space, and a scream tore from my throat.

Shadow King

I strode through the obsidian gates of my fortress, the taste of victory still fresh on my tongue. The tepid warmth of Fen was a distant memory now, replaced by the familiar gloom of the Shadow Isles. My footsteps echoed through the cavernous halls.

"Take the prisoner to the dungeons," I barked at a cowering servant, shoving my captive from Fen roughly, pleased to see one so high and mighty brought to a stumbling low. "And prepare the war room. I want my generals assembled immediately."

As I marched toward my chambers, a smirk played at the corners of my mouth. My strategy had been flawless–Shadow Walkers leading the charge, undead fae cannon fodder clearing the way, and me claiming my victory. Centuries of meticulous planning were finally bearing fruit.

In the privacy of my chambers, I paused before a towering mirror, studying my reflection. The Shadow King gazed back at me, a figure of nightmares and legends. Pride swelled in my chest, a dull ache that had become as familiar as breathing.

I had done it. The first domino had fallen.

But as I stared into my own eyes, another image flickered across my mind. The faces of the fae at the Ice Palace, the moment I materialized on the battlefield. The clash of steel had ceased, replaced by a deafening silence. Every face–friend and foe alike–had been etched with pure, unadulterated terror.

A low chuckle rumbled in my throat. Fear was the most potent weapon of all.

I turned from the mirror, pacing the length of my chambers, picturing the horror on the Verdan heir's pretty brown face at the death of Erevan Reissan. I had brought her with me and left her pathetic lover alive to spread tales of the Shadow King's might. Fear was like wildfire–it would consume their armies from within.

I clenched my fist, savoring the surge of power that coursed through me. I was the puppet master, and all of Arathay danced on my strings. Let them tremble. Let them cower in the dark, awaiting my next move.

For a moment, I allowed myself to bask in the glory of my impending victory. But even as I did, a nagging thought tugged at the edges of my mind–a pair of defiant blue eyes that refused to look upon me with fear.

I shook my head, banishing the image. There would be time for such thoughts later. For now, I had a war to win.

Two hours later, I strode out of the war room, my footsteps echoing like thunderclaps. Servants scurried away, pressing themselves against the walls, their eyes downcast. The scent of their fear was palpable, intoxicating. Terror could win wars, and if I could just infect my opponents with it, I'd...

My thoughts trailed off. Unbidden, an image of Lexi flashed through my mind. Her fierce gaze, her unwavering spirit. She alone stood tall in my presence, unafraid.

I growled in frustration. Even now, basking in the glow of victory, I couldn't shake thoughts of her. My steps faltered as I pictured her shivering in that dank cell, her fire slowly dimming.

My fists clenched at the image. The idea of her suffering gnawed at me, an unfamiliar ache in my chest. I needed her safe, comfortable. Protected.

But how? She believed me a fellow prisoner. If she knew my true identity...

I pictured the revulsion that would twist her beautiful features, the horror that would cloud those mesmerizing eyes. The thought was like a dagger to my gut.

A plan began to form. "Guard," I bellowed. A shadow materialized before me, awaiting command. "Prepare new quarters. Luxurious ones. For two."

The guard bowed and vanished. I allowed myself a small, satisfied smile. Lexi would have her comfort, and I... I would have her close. All without revealing my true nature.

Soon she would learn that not all shadows contained monsters.

I strode toward Lexi's cell, shadows coiling around me like living armor. The salty tang of the ocean air assaulted my senses as I opened the door to her cell. My heart hammered against my ribs, an unfamiliar nervousness taking hold.

As I entered her line of sight, Lexi's head snapped up. The transformation that came over her features was immediate and visceral. Her lips curled in disgust, her blue eyes blazing with a hatred so pure it staggered me. Gone was the warmth, the spirit I'd come to crave. In its place stood a stranger, regarding me in my Shadow King form as one might regard a venomous serpent.

"What do you want?" she spat, her voice dripping with venom.

I steeled myself, forcing my voice to remain cold and commanding. "Your accommodations are being upgraded."

Lexi's eyes narrowed suspiciously. "Why? What sick game are you playing now?"

"Game?" I snarled, frustration building. "I offer you comfort, and you accuse me of trickery?"

"Everything you do is a trick," she shot back. "A manipulation. Why should this be any different?"

Her words cut deeper than she could know. I took a menacing step forward, shadows writhing around me. "You would do well to show some gratitude, imp. My patience has limits."

Lexi flinched but held her ground. "I'd rather rot here than accept anything from you."

Something snapped inside me. "Guards!" I roared, whirling to face the cowering sentries. "Take her to bathe then escort her to the new quarters. Now."

As they scrambled to obey, I stormed from the cell, my chest tight with unfamiliar emotions I couldn't begin to untangle. One thing was painfully clear: Lexi could never know the truth. The Shadow King would forever remain her enemy, no matter how much I longed for her to see beyond the darkness.

Back in my old chambers, I scrubbed the blood from my skin with savage intensity, watching crimson-tinged water swirl down the drain. The stench of battle clung to me, a reminder of the carnage I'd left behind in Fen. I shed the trappings of the Shadow King and donned the simple garb of a prisoner. The transformation complete, I strode toward the new quarters I'd commanded to be prepared.

The opulent room stood in stark contrast to the fortress's grim hallways. Plush carpets muffled my footsteps as I entered, my gaze sweeping over ornate furnishings and richly embroidered tapestries. A feast for the senses, carefully curated to please her.

My thoughts circled back to Lexi, as they inevitably did. Her defiance was a thorn lodged deep in my side, painful yet impossible to remove. I hated it. I needed it.

I ran my fingers along the spine of a leather-bound book, one of many I'd selected for her reading pleasure. She didn't see the Shadow King, the terror that haunted Arathay's nightmares. Just me. How long had it been since anyone looked at me without revulsion or terror?

I clenched my fists. This obsession was dangerous, a weakness I couldn't afford. And yet the thought of her smile, of her treating me as an equal, sent a thrill through me that rivaled any battlefield victory.

The door creaked open, and Lexi's gasp of astonishment filled the room. I turned, drinking in her wide-eyed wonder as she took in her new surroundings, turning a full circle and ending on the massive fireplace adorned with carvings of twisted, thorny vines.

"Holy labradoodles," Lexi breathed, her fingers trailing over the mantle. "This is incredible."

A smile lit me up to see her so happy. "It is a step up from those cells, is it not?"

She spun, her eyes alight with excitement. When she was happy, she glowed like the damn sun, and I never wanted to be shielded from her light. Even her freshly washed and dried hair seemed to curl around her face and shoulders contentedly. "But how? Why would the Shadow King—"

I cut her off, the lie I'd prepared falling easily from my lips. "I did him a favor. This is my reward." I gestured around the room. "Our reward. I insisted you be moved here as well."

Lexi's brow furrowed. "A favor? What could you possibly—"

"Does it matter?" I interrupted, not wanting to delve too deeply into that fabrication. "We are here now. Safe. Comfortable."

Her gaze fell on the single, luxurious bed, and a hint of color rose in her cheeks. "There's only one—"

"We shall manage," I said, my voice rougher than I intended.

Suddenly, Lexi crossed the room and threw her arms around me. "Thank you," she whispered, her breath warm against my neck. "For thinking of me, for getting me out of that awful place."

I froze, overwhelmed by her closeness, the scent of her hair like sun-warmed grass and wild honey. My arms moved of their own accord, wrapping around her slender frame. She fit perfectly against me, as if we were two halves of a whole.

Lexi pulled back slightly, her sapphire eyes searching mine. Our faces were mere inches apart, and I found myself leaning in, drawn by an invisible force. Her lips parted, a soft sigh escaping them.

I wanted to crush my mouth to hers, to claim her as I had claimed victory on the battlefield. But this wasn't a conquest. This was Lexi—brave, fierce, beautiful Lexi—who saw me as a fae, not a fiend.

She danced out of my arms, and I reached into my pocket to fish out the final present, hoping to lure her back with a bribe, I supposed. I pulled out a delicate silver chain with a small iridescent crystal dangling from its end.

"It's beautiful," she murmured, coming closer. "What is it?"

"A Dream Weaver," I explained. "It allows the wearer to experience different fae realms while dreaming." Crafted in the Twilight Forge by the Lightfae centuries ago, the Dream Weaver was a relic of peace—ironic, now that it lay in my hands.

Lexi's hand brushed against mine and her eyes lit up with excitement. "The actual realms of Arathay?" she asked.

I pressed the necklace into her hands. "Yes."

My breath caught as she took the gift. Seeing her joy as she held it aloft made my chest tighten in an unfamiliar way.

Lexi's eyes sparkled. "Yes! Oh, VFA, can you imagine? All of Arathay, open to explore without ever leaving this room." She pressed the necklace to her throat, and the crystal glowed faintly against her skin.

"Turn around," I said, and she complied, brushing her hair aside so I could connect the necklace's clasp. Her skin was cold against my warm fingers, and I longed to press them against her flesh to heat her up.

"It is perfect for you," I said, my voice low and intense. "You have always craved adventure. Now you can have it safely, beyond the reach of... of the Shadow King." The words tasted bitter on my tongue.

"How does it work?" Lexi asked, fingering the crystal as she turned around to face me.

I cleared my throat. "A skilled magic Weaver imbued the crystal with perfect replications of every realm in Arathay. When you sleep, your consciousness can travel freely through those realms."

What I didn't tell her was that the Dream Weaver showed only Arathay's most idyllic aspects–no war, no suffering, no hint of the devastation I'd wrought. It was a beautiful lie, but a lie nonetheless.

Lexi's face glowed with such pure delight that I felt a sharp pang in my chest. "This is perfect. Thank you."

I watched her, drinking in her happiness. For the first time in centuries, a flicker of warmth settled through me that had nothing to do with conquest or revenge. I'd given her this gift, this moment of joy. It felt good.

The realization unsettled me. I grasped for my usual cold logic, trying to remind myself that this was all part of my plan. Keeping her close, under my watchful eye—that was the true purpose. And yet…

"I am glad you are pleased," I said gruffly, turning away to hide the conflict on my face. "You deserve some happiness, even in this place."

But as I moved to the window, gazing out over the sea, I knew I was only fooling myself. The warmth in my chest, the lightness I felt at her smile—it had nothing to do with strategy. For the first time in an age, I'd done something purely for another's benefit.

And Mortia help me, I wanted to do it again.

But first, I needed sleep. The battle at Fen flashed through my mind—the clash of steel, the screams of the dying, the taste of victory. Yet as fatigue washed over me, I found myself craving not the thrill of conquest, but the quiet comfort of Lexi's presence. It was a heady feeling, more intoxicating than even the fulfillment of my centuries-long vendetta against Arathay.

I moved to the single bed, my muscles aching from the day's exertions. "Come," I commanded, patting the space beside me. "You must be tired as well."

Lexi hesitated, and I sensed the conflict within her—the desire to obey warring with her innate rebelliousness. I admired that fire, even as I longed to feel her warmth against me.

Her gaze fell on the single, luxurious bed, and a hint of color rose in her cheeks. "There's only one–"

The corner of my mouth quirked upward, though I quickly suppressed it. "We are both adults," I replied evenly, my voice betraying none of the tension coiled within me. "We shall manage."

After a moment's pause, she relented, sliding under the covers beside me. I immediately pulled her close, my arm curling protectively around her waist. She let out a soft moan of pleasure at the bed's softness and the warmth of the blankets.

"This is nice," she murmured, her body relaxing against mine.

My cock hardened instantly at the feel of her curves pressed against me and inhaling her faint sunshine scent. I'd deliberately chosen a small bed, engineering this closeness, and for a moment, I wondered if I should feel guilty for the deception. But then Lexi wiggled her ass, grinding back against my erection, and all coherent thought fled.

I sucked in a sharp breath, captivated by the perfect roundness of her ass and the small, breathy sound she made. "Lexi," I growled, my voice rough with desire.

She turned her head slightly, her lips mere inches from mine. "Yes?" she whispered, and I could hear the rapid beat of her heart.

Lexi

I could not believe my luck. My cell had been upgraded to a luxury suite, and I was being forced to share a single bed with the hottest fae in the universe. I mean, I could think of worse ways to spend an evening. I hadn't even begged him to sleep with him, he'd practically insisted on it.

Sure, he didn't insist on the sex part, but I mean, that was a given, wasn't it? Judging by the rod of steel pressing into my back, he wasn't opposed to the idea, and neither was I.

Seriously, the bed itself was almost enough to make me orgasm. After countless nights sleeping on a cold rock floor exposed to the elements, a soft mattress and warm blankets were like a piece of heaven on earth. The silky sheets brushed against my bare skin, causing goosebumps to erupt all over, a sensation that I had forgotten could be pleasurable after those nights in the cell.

He shifted slightly, his breath hot and ragged against my earlobe. My heart hammered and a warm flush spread across my cheeks as he traced his fingers lightly over my hip. Tension knotted in my belly, a familiar and welcome sensation that had been absent for so long.

Turning slowly, I rolled in place until I was facing him. His eyes were black and unreadable in the dim moonlight that filtered through the curtains. Emboldened by the darkness, I ran a finger across his full lips, and the soft gasp of surprise he gave out made heat pool between my thighs.

"You dare to touch me?" he asked, and I laughed in reply.

"I've touched more than just your lips," I teased. "Or have you already forgotten?"

His breath grew ragged, and his chest expanded, pressing against my forearm. "I will never forget you."

He said it as though we were already over, done, our relationship a thing of the past and we were saying goodbye, but to me, it felt as though we were taking the first steps across a bridge to a wonderful new land.

"You won't have to," I murmured, trying to let him know that I had no intention of leaving him. He was so strong and pretended to be so dangerous, making big proclamations about how I should be scared of him, but I sensed a vulnerability within him that he was covering up, like a little kid with no mom.

Not that I had any intention of being his mother figure. Holy hell, that was a big no.

Slowly, he leaned toward me, his breath ghosting across my lips as he drew closer. The anticipation was electric, running like fire beneath my skin, igniting every nerve ending in my body. The muscles between my thighs clenched instinctively at his closeness, a wave of anticipation washing over me. I wanted him, needed him in a way that was raw and primal.

His lips finally met mine in a searing kiss that set the room alight. It wasn't tentative or shy, it was as if a dam had been released, and our bottled-up passion flooded out, no longer manageable or containable. His hand slid down my back, cupping the curve of my ass, pulling me closer into his body.

The hardness of his arousal pressing against my core sent shockwaves of desire through me.

"Do you trust me?" he whispered against my lips, his deep voice vibrating through my veins. His arms were toned and defined, the epitome of strength and power. His hands were rough but gentle, and I shivered as he brushed a strand of hair behind my ear.

Trust? Was that even a question right now? I trusted him enough to let him touch me in ways no one else ever had. I trusted him enough to bare not only my body but my soul as well. After our time in the cells together, he had redefined trust for me. So I nodded, not sure I could speak.

The heat of his body against mine was an exquisite torment. His fingers moved downward, making a tantalizing path across my stomach, circling my outie. His eyes, those beautiful dark orbs, searched mine for a moment before he buried his face into my neck and trailed hot kisses along my collarbone.

"Are you sure?" he murmured again, an edge of concern in his husky voice that did nothing but ignite my desire even more. I nodded again, not trusting myself to speak out loud. This was what I wanted. What we both wanted.

I should have been wary, maybe even scared, but in his arms, I felt something I hadn't in years. Safe. Valued. Respected. And that was terrifying in its own right.

His fingers continued their descent, now exploring the sensitive skin of my inner thighs. A gasp escaped me as he brushed against my wet center, teasing me with feather-light touches. His thumb found the hard knot of nerves and circled it slowly, and I gasped, my hips lifting off the bed in response. He chuckled softly at my reaction, a sound that sent warmth spreading through me.

His eyes, dark with desire, met mine as he slid a finger inside me. I bit my lip to hold back the moan that threatened to spill from my lips.

His eyes never left mine as he added a second finger, stretching and filling me. The rhythm was slow and torturous, driving me crazy. Unable to hold it back any longer, I let out a soft moan, my body writhing under his touch. He smirked against my neck, nibbling gently on my skin before finding my lips again.

"I love hearing your sounds," he murmured against my mouth, his fingers quickening their pace as they stroked my inner walls. "So beautiful. All for me."

My words came out long and slow as I struggled to form them between the sliding of his fingers and the bucking of my hips. "I...love..." His fingers tensed and stilled inside me, and I realized he was panicking at what he thought I was saying, so I rushed on to finish them sentence before he left me hanging. "Your fingers," I rushed, grabbing his free hand and placing it over my nipple, just to be clear I meant it only in a physical way.

But fuck, the way I was feeling, all the emotions were spiraling through me, a swirling storm that threatened to carry me away, and it didn't feel like it was only physical. It was emotional too, his warmth and his bottomless, fathomless gaze and that expression on his face as important as his fingers. I grasped the Dream Weaver hanging around my neck, wondering if I was dreaming, but I knew it was all real. Nothing had ever felt as real, like we were two birds flying through the clouds, ducking and rising, dancing higher and higher.

I was spiraling out of control, falling deeper into ecstasy with every stroke. My body arched off the bed, strains of pleasure echoing through me. He was relentless, his fingers moving in a rhythm that had my toes curling and breath quickening.

"Look at you," he murmured. His voice was a soothing balm against the raw waves of pleasure that washed over me again and again, soothing yet teasing all at once. "So beautiful."

My chest heaved and I squeezed my eyes shut, unable to bear the intensity of his gaze anymore, of his words that held as much power as his touch. I had been with men before, but none had ever made me feel like this—loved, cherished, adored.

But it wasn't over yet. His free hand slipped from my breast, tracing a path to join its partner between my thighs. My core clenched around him involuntarily as he added another finger, stretching me further than ever before and curling slightly inside me.

But I didn't feel any discomfort, only overwhelming pleasure that intensified with every thrust of his skilled fingers.

"Open your eyes," he commanded softly, his voice hoarse with desire. I complied, my heavy lids fluttering open to meet his intense gaze. There was a spark of something wild in his eyes, an animalistic hunger that sent shivers along my arms.

I cried out again, arching against him as the pleasure spiked to another level. He watched me intently, drinking in every moan and gasp, every shift and roll of my body under his hands.

"Not yet," he whispered against my lips as if sensing how close I was to the edge. "I want to be inside you when you come."

His words were a promise and a command, a voice rich with desire and layered with intimacy.

My breath hitched at his words, my mind spinning with anticipation. He removed his fingers and the loss of contact made me whimper softly. But he was quick to soothe my complaint, pressing a soft kiss on my forehead before moving down my body.

I watched as he discarded his clothes effortlessly, revealing his finely toned muscles and the throbbing monster between his thighs. His confidence was intoxicating, seeping from him in waves that left me breathless.

With a swift movement, he positioned himself between my legs, our bodies lining up perfectly. His heated gaze burned into mine as he held himself still, the tip of his erection teasing my entrance.

"Do you want this?" he asked, his voice sounding strained. I could see the effort it took for him to hold back, to give me one last chance to change my mind. But I had no intention of denying either of us.

"Yes," I breathed out the word that sealed our fate. This didn't feel like last time. At Delph's wedding, I'd craved a new experience, and he'd provided it. It had been wonderful, and just the adventure I'd wanted. But this time, I craved him, purely and utterly him.

The sensation of his hardness pressing against me was both thrilling and terrifying. My body reacted instinctively, the muscles in my thighs quivering with anticipation. He paused, looking down at me with an expression that held a hint of vulnerability. I reached up to cup his face, offering him comfort and assurance as I pulled him closer.

"Please," the word was a soft plea that caressed his lips before our mouths met in another searing kiss. Then, he entered me. A gasp tore from my throat as he filled me, the sensation overwhelming yet perfect.

He stilled inside me, allowing me to adjust to his size. It was an act of control that spoke volumes about the man he was. Even in his own pleasure, he ensured I was comfortable, that I was ready for him. I tightened my hold on him, pressing my chest against his as if trying to meld our bodies into one.

Then he began to move again, starting with slow, shallow thrusts that soon turned deeper and faster. Every angle, every movement seemed calculated to drive me crazy with pleasure. His fingers trailed over my body, setting my skin aflame wherever they touched.

His lips found mine in a heated, passionate kiss that echoed the rhythm of our bodies.

His groan vibrated deep within me, sending tendrils of pleasure curling through my body. He pulled back slowly and then drove into me again, setting a maddening pace that had my head spinning and my body writhing beneath his. Each thrust made me gasp, each withdrawal left me aching for more.

"My beautiful girl," he murmured in my ear, his voice thick with desire. "So perfect." His praise was another kind of intimacy we shared, and I loved it.

A low moan escaped from deep within me as he hit a particularly sensitive spot. A cry fell from my lips like a sweet mantra, as he pushed deeper and harder. The coiled tension in my body built with each thrust, each stroke that brought me closer to the edge. I was on fire, my body pulsating and begging for more.

"N-Near," I managed to gasp out, clutching at his shoulders.

"I know," he growled back, the sound feral and raw. The teasing gentleness was gone now, replaced by an intensity, a ferocity. His rhythm quickened, driving into me with a fervor that edged out everything else.

My body tightened around him, pulling him deeper into me. With one final powerful thrust, he pushed me over the edge. A cry ripped through me as wave after wave of pleasure cascaded through my body. My vision blurred and I clung to him as my world shattered into a million pieces.

His movements faltered as he followed me over the edge, his own release claiming him with a hoarse shout. His body tensed and then convulsed with his release. He burrowed his face into my neck, muffling his cries as he rode out the aftershocks.

We stayed intertwined, panting heavily. His fingers lazily traced patterns on my sweat-slick skin, and I shivered at the ticklish sensation.

Finally, he pulled away gently, rolling onto his back while pulling me into his arms. I nestled my head against his chest, listening to the steady rhythm of his heart. His fingers danced over my back in a gentle caress.

His voice broke the silence, low and tinged with emotion. "Can you ever forgive me?" he asked.

My serenity shattered, and I pulled away from him. "What the hell do you mean? My consent was pretty clear. I'm not some virginal child you need to take care of, buster, I'm a grown-ass woman and I make my own decisions."

He pulled me closer, completely ignoring my very sensible points. "I'm not talking about the sex," he murmured. "These fingers don't need forgiveness." He waggled them, and I chuckled.

"True. Your penis is quite forgiven too," I added.

He laughed, a full-throated roar that rumbled through him and made my head wobble where it rested on his chest. "Penis," he said, and I figured he was laughing at my word choice. "You are rather cute."

"Am not," I retorted. "I'm sexy and brave and—"

He flipped me over onto the mattress and caged me beneath him, and I let out a squeal. "You are all of those things, Lexi," he said intensely. "I'll never doubt it again."

Well, that shut me up. I was so used to asserting my bravery, and all my other excellent qualities that most people failed to see, that I didn't know what to do when somebody acknowledged it. "Oh," I said eloquently.

He flipped us around again, so he was lying on the mattress and my head was back on his chest, and I was starting to get seasick. "Less flipping, please," I said, waiting patiently for the room to stop spinning.

"Yes, milady," he said, and I got the distinct impression he was teasing me again.

I traced a finger on his chest, feeling the hard muscles beneath the soft skin. "Why do you always pretend to be dangerous?" I asked.

A hardness entered his tone when he replied. "I don't pretend to be anything," he said flatly, his body tensing beneath my hand. "I *am* dangerous." He made to get out of bed, but I tugged him down and he finally relented.

"Yeah, and I'm a battle-hardened general," I agreed, "but really. Why do you push people away?"

He placed a hand over my fingers, stilling their exploration of the planes and dips in his chest. "I don't push anyone," he said. "They run."

"Bullshit," I said, freeing my fingers and slapping him lightly on the back of his hand. I wiped away a small droplet of drool that was threatening to land on his chest and ruin my elegance, and he stilled my hand with a firm grip around my wrist.

"You don't know me, Larper," he said, his grip on my wrist tightening as his voice faltered. "I've done some...bad things."

I shrugged and nuzzled into his chest, letting a fresh wave of post-coital bliss wash over me. I was exhausted from nights of bad sleep in the hell-cave, and this bed, this warm body beside me, this soft mattress, were conspiring to lure me to sleep.

"Ivedunbadthinzztoo," I murmured as my eyes closed.

The last thing I heard was his sigh, and then he pulled me around the waist, tucking me tight into his body, filling me with the knowledge that I was exactly where I needed to be.

Dominic

"Dominic Branco," I whispered into Lexi's ear as she finally stirred from her slumber. She blinked at me sleepily, wiping a dark curl from her cheek, and the soft smile that lit up her face at seeing me melted my heart. Her brows pulled together in confusion, and I pressed my lips to them as I explained. "You asked my name."

Her full lips parted and my name spilled from them, whispered almost reverently. I hadn't heard my name on another's lips in centuries, and my soul trembled at the sound. In truth, it took me long moments to dredge the name from my memory because I had cast it so deep inside me.

She pulled herself up onto my chest, laying her ear against it and drawing lazy circles on my belly. "You're shuddering," she said.

"I have not heard my name in a long time," I said, balling my hand into a fist behind her back.

She kissed my chest, tracing a finger along the scar that ran beneath my ribs. "Is it something to do with this scar?"

"I keep that as a reminder, yes. So I'll never forget my purpose."

"Tell me about it?" At her touch and the softness in her tone, at the lingering memory of making love with this human, at the intimacy we were sharing, something inside me thawed, and the words came pouring out.

"I told you how I was convicted of a crime I did not commit, a long time ago. That crime was murdering the king."

Lexi gasped. "Murder?" Her hand on my chest stilled, and my fist behind her back squeezed tighter.

I rushed to explain my innocence, caring too much about her opinion of me. "I did not do it, Larper. I laid no hand on that bastard, but I wish I had. They found me guilty of his murder and, according to the laws of the day, they ostracized me."

"Kicked you out of the city?" Her hand resumed roaming my chest, and the concern in her voice kept me talking. "You and your whole family?"

I scoffed. "My mama, who had loved me as much as any mother ever loved her child, turned her back on me when the verdict was chimed though the town square. Regicide. Every fae cast me out. Especially my family."

"I'm so sorry," Lexi said, peppering my chest with kisses. "And for what it's worth, I never would have cast you out."

"They had to. They believed me to have disrespected Gaia herself, who chose the kings and queens."

"Fuck Gaia," my little human spat with venom, and my fist at her back relaxed into an open palm, which I used to squeeze her tighter.

"Indeed," I agreed, a smile on my lips. "But at the time I knew no better. I spent years groveling for forgiveness, following my mama around town and proclaiming my innocence. She never once met my gaze or acknowledged me in any way." I chuckled darkly. "I must have made her life hell."

"She deserved it," Lexi said darkly, and my dick twitched at her tone. Maybe this human was more my equal than I realized, even down to the depths of her soul. A depraved queen to match the Shadow King. "I don't care how much society blamed you, a mother should defend her child with her fucking life. Her fucking soul. She was the one who deserved to be chucked out of the town. Her, and all the assholes who found you guilty in the first place."

Lexi was still speaking into my chest, and with one movement, I dragged her up my body so her lips were level with mine, and I slammed my mouth against hers, devouring every spark of her anger, tasting the anger she felt on my behalf.

Her hips pressed down over my hard cock, which twitched uncomfortably beneath her weight, wanting to be inside her, surrounded by her, part of her.

"In the end, I left," I said, feeling more understood by this woman than I ever thought possible. She recognized the hurt and betrayal I'd suffered, and she didn't forgive the perpetrators any more than I did. "I clung to my name like a lifeline, as though it tethered me to the past before being named a king killer," I continued. "And then, one day, I stopped caring. I realized I no longer wished to be that fae. I deserved more."

"Too fucking right," my depraved queen agreed, and my heart swelled at the ferocity in her tone. I pressed my palms over her breasts, just holding them, feeling their perfect weight in each of my hands. She moaned, and a sound erupted from me, a primal growl that made her nipples harden between my fingers, and I squeezed them gently, increasing the pressure as I drew more delicious noises from her throat.

"They didn't deserve you," she said, pressing her hands into the mattress beside my head and easing her hips over my cock. She rested her entrance at my tip, and her wet heat made me quiver and jump for her. Her breasts jiggled in my hands at her movement, and I massaged them gently, suddenly needing them in my mouth.

But when she eased herself slowly down my cock, every other thought in my head disappeared.

"I deserve you, Dominic," she said as our bodies locked together, her clit pressing against my pubic bone, her gaze fierce. My name on her lips made pre-cum roll from me and into her beautiful flesh.

"Yes, you do, human," I ground out, moving my hands to grab her ass and hold on.

"Tell me more," she said, rolling her hips agonizingly slowly.

"Anything," I said, struggling to concentrate on her words instead of her body. I wanted all of her, her mind and her body and her depraved fucking soul, and I wanted it now.

She tucked a dark curl behind her ear, pushing her chest forward as she danced on my dick. "Did you get your revenge?" she asked, each word a siren's song.

"I am working on it," I gritted out, watching the way her hips gyrated, her breasts jiggling slowly, and her lips parted sensually.

She giggled, and her usual cheekiness entered those blue eyes. "Why is this so hot?" she murmured. "I think I have a revenge fetish."

"I have a *you* fetish," I replied, mesmerized by her movements. I'd bedded many fae women, and they all had grace and elegance and style, but none of them had this human's perfection. Lexi was wild and unfiltered, an uncaged animal who moved like she meant it and whose face showed everything she was feeling. I could come just from watching her, let alone from the slick tightness of her pussy.

"You are unbearably sexy," I said, my voice hoarse with desire. I clutched the sheet beneath me, my knuckles white as I held back, craving the control that was slipping from my fingers with every movement she made.

Lexi's cheeks flushed a pretty pink, and her movements became more erratic, grinding into me with an abandon that made my toes curl. "I always wanted a dangerous lover," she murmured, her blue eyes meeting mine.

Her words hit my chest like a sledgehammer. "And you are the most dangerous thing to me," I admitted in between ragged breaths, feeling her clenching around me. Every inch of my body was focused on her, on the way she moved above me, the taste of her mouth against mine, even the way our breaths echoed in sync in the room.

"I want more," she confessed in a whisper so soft I almost didn't hear it above our mingling breaths. I wanted to ask what that meant, to shake her until she admitted she was as obsessed with me as I was with her, but I didn't get the chance. She leaned forward so her hair caged us. "Tell me more about your revenge," she said, distracting me again and making this moment even hotter.

She had a damn revenge fetish, and I was the literal king of vengeance. I could make her come harder than she ever had before, just by telling her the truth. A truth I'd kept bottled inside me, separated from my old fae self, from Dominic, and now, in one fell swoop, she was combining my two halves, my two identities, and she was getting off on it.

The words escaped me as a growl as I tried to keep a measure of control. "I am building an army," I said, "and I will kill them all."

Her pussy clenched around me, and she threw her head back with a scream as she came all over my cock. The sight of her, writhing above me in pure pleasure, sent me over the edge, and I roared my own release, my seed painting her insides as I rode out my climax.

She collapsed on top of me, her heart pounding against mine. I held her tight, my arms wrapped around her back. I was the Shadow King and she was my depraved queen.

"That would be nice," she eventually said, running a hand up my sweat-slicked bicep. "To have your own personal army, I mean. To take down whoever you wanted."

I brushed a strand of damp hair from her face. "You do not believe me?"

She rested her chin on my nipple and looked up at me through her lashes. "Should I? Do you really have the nice army?"

She took some deep breaths, her chest rising and falling against my own, while I considered my answer. This was the perfect time to admit my true identity, and she was the right woman to tell.

"Nice is not exactly the right word," I began, not exactly sure how to discuss this. My two personalities did not always mesh. I stared at the carved wooden ceilings, searching for the words.

"I guess not. But if you really had an army, you'd have been able to stop the Shadow King from capturing you, right? That fucker would be in the ground."

My gaze snapped back to her, her black curls flaring across my chest as anger and revulsion lined her face. I couldn't tell her the truth about me after all. Not yet. Not if it risked her turning that disgusted look on me.

I twisted my lips, pulling the silk sheets into my fist. "He did not capture me in the way you think," I said. No point denying that Dominic was, in some ways, the Shadow King's captive, but only in the sense that time and careful planning had morphed one into the other. I might not be ready to share my full truth with her, but I didn't wish to lie to her either.

She rolled off me, and I resisted the temptation to stop her. My queen deserved some autonomy, after all. She rose from the bed, gifting me a lovely view of her round ass, then she pulled on a silk dressing gown and threw me a sly wink. "I figured. Not all prisoners get silk clothes and soft beds," she said. "What are these favors you're doing for him?"

I rolled out of bed and pulled on a second dressing gown, then cast a quick spell to summon guards with breakfast. I had come dangerously close to telling her the truth, and I couldn't risk talking about my past any longer. "I have been talking about myself all morning," I said. "Tell me about you. What were you really doing in the fae realm, and how did you end up here in the Shadow Fortress?"

Obviously, I'd orchestrated her capture since I'd been so fascinated by her at the wedding, but I was curious to hear her take on it. I settled down at a small round table made from black marble, and she sat in the other chair. "As you know, I came for Delph's wedding, but the Shadow King and his shadow minions messed that all up."

A guard arrived bearing juice, coffee, and breakfast meringues, which he laid on the marble table before swiftly leaving.

"And how did you end up crossing through Brume on foot?"

Lexi sipped her juice and moaned at the flavor, making my eyes dip to the low neckline of her dressing gown, seeking flesh. It was a supremely sexual sound, and I adjusted my dick as she answered.

"After the wedding disaster, all the heirs had a strategy talk about how to deal with the Shadow King."

I had to school my features into neutrality while I absorbed that nugget of gold. Lexi had been present while my most powerful enemies discussed their plans for my downfall. This information was so delicious I almost laughed. "And what did they decide?" I asked.

"They have this Stone of Veritas, which is the only thing that can kill the Shadow Walkers. They cleaved it into twelve parts, and they're sharing them out among the realms, so every ruler has a way to defend their land. They even sent one to Dust to try to get the Unseelie to fight with them."

I squeezed my glass so tight that it shattered, spilling juice all over me and across the blood-red rug. They had a weapon that could kill my Walkers? That was bad news. The worst news. And if the Unseelie entered the fight, I could find my side of the war going badly. I had to find a way to make sure the Unseelie stayed out of this war.

"Mortia damn it," I hissed, and with a quick water spell, I siphoned the spilled liquid away, lifting the droplets of juice from the rug and my robe, leaving them both clean and dry.

"You're bleeding," Lexi said, staring at my palm. Crimson poured from two deep gashes across my hand, dripping onto my knee.

My Healing skills were limited because my magic was more practiced in death and destruction, but I knew enough to staunch the blood. "It's nothing," I said, hiding my hand beneath the table so it didn't distract her. "Tell me more about this Stone of Veritas."

"The Walkers can be held back by light but not killed by it. They consume shifters to multiply and breed, and they consume other fae to turn them into zombies, like an undead army," she explained, before taking a bite of the breakfast meringue. "This is fucking delicious, by the way."

I tapped my fingernail on the marble table, tap-tap-tapping. "They know so much," I said. Clearly, I'd been underestimating my enemies, imagining them to be ignorant of how my creatures operated. But it hardly mattered, because regardless of how much information they gathered, they still couldn't stop me.

"Yes. But the Veritas Stone thingy is the best of all. With that, they can actually kill the Shadow Walkers."

I needed this information to win the war I'd planned for centuries, but probing Lexi for it, using her in such a calculated manner, felt wrong. But how could I justify throwing my life goals away just to keep our relationship honest? Just to keep one human woman happy?

I couldn't. Plain and simple. This was too important. I placed my hands on my lap, making sure I was holding nothing sharp or fragile.

"Can the Stone of Veritas kill the Shadow King?" I asked, keeping my voice even and avoiding looking into her trusting blue eyes, instead keeping my gaze fixed on the flickering flames in the fireplace.

She shrugged. "They don't know. But they were talking about sending a delegation here to talk with His Assholiness himself. Peace talks, I guess."

I laughed hollowly. "Peace is not possible."

"Anyhoo," Lexi continued, dismissing my comment with a wave. "I volunteered to come here and lead the talks since humans aren't affected by the Shadow Walkers. So I'd be safe."

I rose to my feet, clenching my fists so tight that I reopened the wound on my palm and drew more blood. "You fucking idiot, Lexi. It is not safe for you anywhere except by my side."

She regarded my outburst through narrowed eyes. "Calm down, buddy. I was just explaining how the Shadow Walkers don't work on humans. Besides, the heirs and rulers didn't think I was the best person for the job, for some reason, so I was in that group crossing Brume on my way home."

I crossed to the window that overlooked the Omber Strait, trying to get my breathing under control. I couldn't believe she would endanger herself like that by volunteering to discuss strategy with the Shadow King. With me. She was right about one thing—I needed to calm down. My obsession with this woman was putting my whole plan at risk.

I took some deep breaths and replied to her comment about humans. "Yes, I noticed. That is what makes you stronger than fae." Her humanity was what separated her from the monster fae, made her immune to my Walkers, and made her stronger, more resilient. More my equal, and deserving to be my queen. "But your cousin should not have—"

"Oh, piss off, Dominic. You don't get to should me. I'm a grown-ass woman and I make my own decisions." I turned to look at her. With her dark hair curling around her shoulders, and those maddening blue eyes, the sass in her voice and written plainly across her face, I couldn't deny her anything.

"Sorry, Larper," I said, issuing my first genuine apology in centuries, and it felt surprisingly good. "You are right. I said I would never underestimate you again, and I shan't. Your decisions and skills have proven their worth. Forgive me."

She grinned at me instantly. "Forgiven." She flew across the room and into my arms, and as I pulled her close and rested my chin on her head, I began plotting how to use the information she'd shared with me to win the war against her friends.

Dominic

I stood at the window, my gaze sweeping over the churning sea below. The war raged on, demanding my attention, but my mind refused to obey. Instead, it fixated on the human creature curled up in the armchair by the roaring fire.

Lexi.

Her presence consumed me, more potent than any battle high. I turned from the window, drinking in the sight of her. Black curls cascaded over her shoulders as she pored over a tome detailing Arathay's history. Her fingers traced the lines of text, and her face was a constant display of frowns, smiles, and gasps.

"Did you know Arathay once had flying ships?" she exclaimed, eyes wide with wonder.

I chuckled, a low rumble in my chest. "Indeed. The mages of old were quite inventive."

"I mean, humans have flying planes, so it's not that impressive."

My gaze never left her as she returned to the book, utterly engrossed. I cataloged every minute detail, the slight furrow of her brow as she concentrated, the way her breath would catch when she read an interesting passage. She wasn't just beautiful—she was maddeningly unpredictable, her human perspectives poking holes in the ancient logic I had built my empire upon.

I clenched my fists, fighting the urge to cross the room and claim those lips for my own. This obsession was maddening, unlike anything I'd experienced in centuries of existence. I, who would bring empires to their knees, found myself utterly captivated by this mere human.

"Lexi," I growled, my voice rough with desire.

She looked up, a question in those impossibly blue eyes. "Yes, Dominic Branco?"

At the sound of my name on her lips, I froze. I recovered quickly, straightening my shoulders. "What fascinates you so much about Arathay's past?"

Lexi's face lit up with enthusiasm. "Everything! The magic, the cultures, the way they built their society. I grew up in the world's most boring place with school and work and cell phones, and even in my wildest dreams I never imagined the fae realms would be so exciting."

I moved closer, drawn by her passion. "You are lying to me," I said. She frowned, and I rushed on to erase that crease from her forehead. "You have the imagination of a Goddess, I am sure you imagined all this and more."

She bit her lip, smiling. "Well, I used to picture these flying highways, air currents where you could duck in from the side and then tumble along at top speed until you popped out and somersaulted through the air at your destination. Kind of like the current in Finding Nemo, you know?"

"Who is this Nemo?"

"Oh, just a movie. I can't believe you have actual, literal magic, and you've never even seen a TV."

"Human technology interferes with our powers."

"I know, I know. But you're missing out on talking fish, that's all."

I sat on the edge of her armchair. "What a shame," I said drily, and she giggled.

I felt so fae around this woman, like the male I used to be, the one I'd spent centuries telling myself was weak and useless. I'd fashioned myself into a weapon since then, a monster capable of terrible deeds, all in the name of erasing that weak male. But suddenly love and emotion didn't feel weak at all.

A sharp knock at the door shattered the intimate quiet like a blade slicing through silk. I whirled, instinctively positioning myself between Lexi and the potential threat.

A guard, clad in the obsidian armor of my elite forces, strode in. "You," he said, jabbing a hand in my direction. "Come with me." I could see the effort it cost him to speak so rudely to me, but it was necessary to keep up the illusion that I was a prisoner.

Even so, I wanted to slap that arrogance right off his face.

I clenched my jaw but restrained my impulse, acting the part of a prisoner. With a growl of frustration, I turned and cupped Lexi's face in my hands. I crushed my lips to hers, pouring all my longing into that fierce kiss. When I pulled away, her cheeks were flushed, her eyes wide.

"I shall not be long," I promised, my thumb tracing her lower lip.

I strode from the room, not daring to look back. As soon as the door closed behind me, the mantle of the Shadow King settled over me like a cloak of darkness. The warmth of Lexi's presence evaporated as the air turned cold, my instincts snapping back into their ruthless rhythm. I dismissed the guard with a curt nod and began my descent into the bowels of my fortress.

The Shadow Fortress loomed around me, a monument to my ambition. Walls of polished obsidian reflected my distorted image as I passed, a reminder of the monster I was. Shadows writhed at my feet, eager to do my bidding. I breathed in the fear that hung in the air, drawing strength from it.

As I descended the winding staircase to the dungeons, the temperature dropped. Icy fingers of dread clawed at the edges of my consciousness—remnants of the emotions I'd stripped from my victims down here. I reveled in their despair, letting it fuel my resolve.

But even as I embraced the darkness, a small part of me ached for the warmth of Lexi's presence. I pushed the feeling aside, burying it beneath centuries of calculated cruelty. There would be time for softness later.

I wrapped myself in shadows, obscuring my identity as I entered the dungeon. The stench of fear and decay assaulted my nostrils, a perfume I once savored but now found oddly unsatisfying. My gaze locked onto the figure chained to the far wall. Gabrelle, the Verdan heir to House Allura.

Even in captivity, her beauty was undeniable. Stunning dark brown skin gleamed in the dim torchlight, contrasting with pale pink hair that cascaded past her shoulders in soft waves. Those matching pale pink eyes glowed with hatred. Her poise and grace remained intact, despite the shackles that bound her.

I found myself comparing her to Lexi. Where Gabrelle's beauty seemed meticulously crafted, Lexi's was wild and untamed. Gabrelle was a polished gem, Lexi, a force of nature.

"Come to gloat, Shadow King?" Gabrelle's voice dripped with venom.

I chuckled, the sound echoing off the stone walls. "Merely checking on my guest."

"Where's Thorne?" she demanded, straining at the iron chains that kept her magic bound and her wrists against the damp stone wall.

"How cute. Your first thought is of your loyal hound. Did he not give up an entire kingdom just to suckle on your nipples? To follow you like a spineless worm instead of ruling in his family's name. How disappointed his dead mother and sister must be in him. Especially since they hated you so much."

I wouldn't give her the pleasure of knowing I'd allowed her toy safe passage out of Fen so he could relay the story of the battle. I preferred my prisoners to be roiling in uncertainty, it made their torture so much sweeter.

Gabrelle's face contorted with rage. Before I could react, she spat at me, a glob of saliva hurtling toward my face. With a flick of my wrist, I caught it mid-air with my shadows, suspending it inches from my cheek.

"Now, now," I tsked, "is that any way to treat your host?"

With a cruel smirk, I reversed the trajectory, sending her own spittle back into her face. It splattered across her cheek, a small victory that felt strangely hollow.

I circled her like a shark my shadows writhing around me. "Tell me, Princess. What grand schemes are you and your little friends concocting to overthrow me?"

Gabrelle's jaw clenched. Her silence was a fortress, each word she withheld a brick in the wall of her defiance. It was almost admirable. Almost.

I leaned in close, my breath hot on her ear. "Your resistance is commendable but futile. Isslia has fallen."

A flicker of pain crossed her face, quickly masked.

"Oh yes," I continued, relishing each word. "The capital of Fen is mine. My creatures, with my army of undead fae, have taken the whole city. And do you know what the most delicious part is?" I paused, savoring her tension. "The 'decent' fae are literally dying to join us."

I laughed at my little joke. Because, of course, any fae who died became part of my undead army. I was unstoppable.

"You're lying," Gabrelle hissed, but doubt clouded her eyes.

I felt a tendril of her power probe the edges of my mind, like a baby snake seeking entry to a fortress. But I was prepared for her brand of magic, her Lure powers, and used my shadows to dispel her snake into nothingness.

I smiled at the shock on her face, summoning visible tendrils of shadow. They coiled around her arms, cold and biting. "You seek to test me, princess? Perhaps you'd like a demonstration of my power."

The shadows tightened, and Gabrelle gasped, her composure finally cracking. I watched as pain etched itself across her features, fascinated by her struggle to maintain control.

"Last chance, Princess. Tell me your plans."

"I'd rather die," she said, her dusty pink eyes blazing with defiance.

I released her, disappointed our games were ending so soon. "That can be arranged." A cruel smile twisted my lips as I stepped back, surveying her defiant posture. "In any case, I know everything."

She dared to scoff. Fucking scoff.

"Let me guess," I drawled, my voice dripping with mock contemplation. "You have found the Stone of Veritas, split it into twelve pieces so each of your little friends can have one, and are using it to kill my Walkers." I paused, watching her eyes widen in shock. "And you are trying to determine if you can use it to kill me. You cannot, by the way," I bluffed, having no damn idea if it could.

The look on Gabrelle's face was priceless. Her carefully cultivated mask of indifference shattered, revealing raw shock beneath. I drank in her reaction, savoring every nuance of her disbelief.

"How...?" she whispered, her voice hoarse.

I chuckled darkly. "Oh, faeling. I know everything."

As I studied her, I mused on the rumors I'd heard of the Verdan heir. They called her an ice queen, emotionless and untouchable. Yet here she was, her failure written plainly across her face for anyone to see. It was almost disappointing.

As I circled Gabrelle, her raw defiance reminded me of another face—bright, open, and utterly undeserving of my lies. A sour taste coated my tongue, and for a moment, my grip on the shadows wavered.

I scowled, pushing the sensation aside. Lexi was meant to be a tool, nothing more. And yet the thought of using her left a bitter taste in my mouth. I wanted more from her. I wanted her by my side, not just as a source of information, but as my queen. My depraved queen.

Dammit. That could unravel centuries of carefully laid plans. But as I stood there, facing my captive, I knew with absolute certainty that Lexi had become more than just a means to an end. She had become my weakness—and my greatest desire.

I clenched my fist, shadows coiling around my arm like tendrils of smoke. "Guard." My voice echoed through the dank dungeon, commanding and cold.

Heavy footsteps approached, and a burly guard materialized from the gloom. He saluted, awaiting my order.

"Execute the prisoner," I growled, my gaze fixed on Gabrelle's defiant face. "Make it slow."

The guard nodded, unsheathing his blade with a metallic hiss. As he advanced on Gabrelle, her dusty pink eyes widened, fear finally breaking through her mask of contempt.

Suddenly, unbidden, Lexi's face flashed in my mind. Her soft smile, the warmth in her eyes when she looked at me. I remembered her speaking of Gabrelle–not with the reverence most showed the Verdan heir, but with genuine delight.

"Stop." The word tore from my throat before I could stop it.

The guard froze, confusion evident even through the face-plate obscuring his features. "My lord?"

I hesitated, shocked by my own actions. Never, in all my years of conquest, had I rescinded a kill order. Was I growing soft? Weak?

But as I pictured the look of horror that would cross Lexi's face if she learned of Gabrelle's fate, I knew I couldn't do it. The thought of seeing hatred in those eyes that had only ever looked at me with trust and affection was unbearable.

"Leave her," I commanded, my voice rough. "She lives. For now."

The guard's surprise was palpable, but he bowed and re-treated without question. As he left, I turned back to Gabrelle, who was staring at me with wide eyes.

"Consider this your lucky day, Princess," I sneered, masking my own confusion with contempt. "I may find a use for you yet."

With that, I swept from the dungeon, my mind tumbling. What was happening to me? Had Lexi really changed me so fundamentally in such a short time? And what would I do about it?

My footsteps echoed through the cavernous obsidian halls. The shadows clinging to me were a comforting shroud that concealed my confusion. As I climbed the spiraling staircase, my battle general materialized from the gloom.

"My lord," he said, dropping to one knee. "Word from the front lines. The fighting in Caprice has intensified. The king and queen are mounting a stronger defense than anticipated."

I clenched my jaw, the taste of ash momentarily bitter on my tongue. "Keep a close watch on the situation. I want hourly updates on their movements, their strategies. If they so much as sneeze, I want to know about it."

"Of course, my lord. Shall I prepare for your immediate departure to Capricia?"

The question hung in the air, heavy with expectation. Centuries of meticulous planning, countless lives sacrificed on the altar of my ambition—all of it culminating in this pivotal moment. They needed me on the front line, that was where I should be. And yet...

Lexi's face swam before my eyes, her smile as radiant as the dawn. The pull of her was stronger than any battle cry, more intoxicating than the sweetest conquest. Wars could be fought and won without my presence, but Lexi's hold on my soul was a far greater threat—and perhaps, my only salvation.

"No," I said, the word tearing from my throat like a confession. "I shall remain here for now."

My general's surprise was evident in a quick tightening of his brow, but he knew better than to question me. As he departed, I found myself walking back toward my chambers. Toward her.

Lexi. My weakness, my strength. She called to me like a siren's song, drowning out the clash of steel and the screams of the dying. In her presence, the war that I had planned for centuries felt like a distant storm, while she was the eye of the hurricane—a moment of calm amid chaos.

I had thought myself as immovable as the mountains, as relentless as the tide. But Lexi was gravity itself, bending the fabric of my existence around her. And I found, to my shock, that I no longer wished to resist.

Lexi

I flopped back onto the plush armchair, a dopey grin plastered across my face. My lips still tingled from Dominic's kisses, and my body hummed with the afterglow of all that sex. Three times in less than twenty-four hours—the man had stamina, I'd give him that.

"Yes," I boasted, smirking at the stone fireplace. "I had more hot fae sex." It looked very impressed. I picked up the dusty tome on Arathayan history I'd been reading and flipped to a random page, deciding I should probably focus on something other than Dominic's hard abs and magic hands.

"The Third Age of Arathay was marked by…" I read aloud, my voice trailing off as my eyes glazed over. Even the history of a magical realm couldn't keep my attention while the image of Dominic's biceps floated around my brain.

I tossed the book aside with a dramatic sigh and sat up, stretching like a cat. I looked around at the opulent furnishings, the silken robes, the four-poster bed, which was all very nice, but it was still a prison cell. It was all smoke and mirrors, fancy trappings to distract from the cold, hard truth.

I ran my hand along the smooth stone wall, searching for any hint of weakness. Nothing. The ASK might be a bastard, but he knew how to build a fortress.

I paced the room, picking up trinkets at random. A delicate crystal vase here, an ornate silver mirror there. Each one probably worth more than I'd ever seen in my life. Sure, we lived in the nice part of Hebes, far from the grimy Docklands, but we never owned anything as nice as this.

"As prisons go, I approve," I announced to a jewel-encrusted paperweight, tossing it from hand to hand. But it didn't explain what I was doing here.

The Shadow King had barely said two words to me since I'd arrived. He'd swanned in a couple of times and thrown his shadows around, but he hadn't exactly interrogated me. So what was his game? Kidnap me, stuff me in a gilded cage, and what? Hope I'd develop Stockholm syndrome?

"Fat chance, buddy," I snorted, setting the paperweight down with a satisfying thunk.

My thoughts drifted to Dominic. My mystery man. He'd mentioned doing "favors" for the Shadow King, but the whole situation reeked of fish left out in the sun too long on the Docklands wharves. Either he was a prisoner or a colleague, it simply couldn't be both.

"So which is it, VFA?" I flopped dramatically onto the bed.

I was truly asking myself some excellent questions. So insightful. No wonder they called me a strategic genius back home... or was that just me? Anyway, the question remained. Why was Dominic in the seaside cell beside mine? How did he score this upgrade? And how did he convince the Shadow King to let me come too? What exactly were these favors he was doing for ASK?

A chill ran down my spine as I remembered spilling my guts about the Stone of Veritas. Had I been too trusting? Too eager to confide in a handsome face?

No. Dominic wouldn't betray me. He couldn't.

But even as I thought the words, a tiny seed of doubt took root in my mind. What did I really know about this man? Apart from those eyes, those damn eyes. And those magic hands. And the excellent penis.

I shrugged off my silk robe, letting it pool at my feet as I padded over to the ornate wardrobe. Swinging open the doors, I whistled low. My fingers danced over impossibly soft fabrics in a rainbow of jewel tones. I pulled out a sapphire blue tunic and matching leggings.

A chill prickled the back of my neck as I tugged on the sapphire tunic. The shadows in the corners of the room seemed darker than before, shifting when I looked away. And as I twirled in front of the mirror, admiring how the fabric shimmered, my thoughts drifted back to the night of the wedding, and I stopped mid-twirl. I had to stop playing dress-ups and use my badassery and my battle brain.

It all started and ended with Dominic. He was my key to figuring out what was going on. He'd been so open, so vulnerable when he'd told me about his past. The pain in his eyes when he spoke of being cast out by his family and town had been raw, real.

But he had more sway around here than he wanted me to know, and there was only one way to figure out just how far his influence went.

I injected my voice with as much authority as I could and called for the guards. To my shock, they heeded my call. The door swung open almost immediately, and a stern-faced guard in obsidian armor stood at attention.

I plastered on my most innocent smile. "Oh good, you're here. Dominic said I simply must get some fresh air today.

A promenade by the ocean. You wouldn't want to go against Dominic's wishes, would you?"

The guard didn't seem to notice I'd started talking like a Jane Austen heroine. His eyes widened slightly, but he nodded. "Follow me."

I should have been elated that I'd been granted freedom so easily, but the emotion that trickled through me was disappointment. Dominic had been holding out on me, after all.

I sauntered after the guard, my footsteps echoing off the obsidian walls of the Shadow Fortress. The place was a maze of darkness, all sleek black surfaces that absorbed light. As we walked, the temperature dropped, and I couldn't suppress a shiver.

"So, big guy," I chirped, trying to sound nonchalant, "you been working here long? Get many prisoners? I mean, guests?" I played the fool, but the underlying plan was to probe him for information. Everybody underestimated the joker.

Silence. The guard's armor clinked softly as he marched on, and I clenched my fists in frustration.

We rounded a corner, and I nearly stumbled as my eyes fell on a spiral staircase winding down into inky blackness. The air wafting up from below carried a damp, moldy scent that made my skin crawl. I imagined a poor prisoner down there, probably chained up and filthy and, the hairs on my arms stood on end. To my dismay, my instinct wasn't to save them but to get as far away as I could.

"Oookay, definitely not the spa," I quipped, quickening my pace to catch up with my silent escort.

Finally, we emerged into the open air, and I gasped. The sky was a roiling mass of storm clouds, tinged with an eerie green glow. Salty sea spray stung my face as wind whipped my hair. Before us stretched a grassy plain leading to a cliff's edge, beyond which churned a tempestuous ocean.

As I gazed out over the turbulent waters, my heart clenched. Kayla's and Razelle's faces flashed in my mind, their eyes wide with fear as we'd been ambushed in the fog. They'd better be fucking okay.

I'd forced the twins to travel home overland through the dangerous mists of Brume, seeking adventure like a damn child. I should have insisted on being flown straight home to make sure they were safe. Delph was right. Dad was right. Everyone was right—I was an immature loser who needed to pay more attention to my life. Following my own instincts had got me locked up in a Shadow Fortress in the middle of a fae war. I should definitely follow someone else's instincts from now on.

Glancing around for someone who might have good instincts I could follow, I saw only my chatless guard standing at attention at one side, and I decided to postpone the switching until later.

My eyes stung, and I told myself it was just the salt in the air. I thought of Delph, my kickass royal cousin, last seen amid the chaotic aftermath of her ruined wedding. The Asshole Shadow King's handiwork. My fists clenched.

My mind raced through a montage of worried faces–Gabrelle and Thorne in Fen, Neela and the others in Caprice. All in danger because of the damn Shadow King, and I wasn't doing a thing about it.

I squared my shoulders, forcing a grim smile. "Alright, Lexi," I told myself. "Pity party's over. Time to figure out how the hell to get out of here and save their collective asses."

I turned back to face the looming obsidian fortress, my mind made up. This little vacation in the Shadow Isles was officially over. At first, I'd had the notion of negotiating with the Shadow King, but he was just a big pile of black steam and I'd barely laid eyes on him. Now it was time to leave.

But that meant leaving Dominic. I pictured his harsh jawline and those soulful eyes, and my heart did a painful little flip-flop. But my family needed me more.

Maybe I could convince him to come along. He'd make a great sidekick. Plus, those abs would be a crime to leave behind.

I counted the boats bobbing in a hidden cove—one, two, three rickety-looking dinghies. Not exactly five-star transportation, but better than a stab to the belly from an oversized redhead who smelled of fake blood.

"Time to go, prisoner," the guard's gravelly voice interrupted my escape planning.

I held back my snippy retort. I would have come up with something witty and cutting if I wasn't trying to stay on his good side. Something like, "Time for YOU to go," or maybe even something better.

As we trudged back, I mapped out my escape. Night time would be best. The thought of those creepy Shadow Walkers sent a shiver down my spine. They would be lurking in the darkness, and even though they couldn't hurt humans, they did a good job of terrifying us. But the night provided better cover, and with some luck and good winds, I'd sail away and be over the horizon before morning. With or without Dominic.

I swung open the bedroom door, a smile still lingering on my lips from the salty sea air, only to find Dominic standing there like a storm cloud about to burst. A lock of black hair flopped across his forehead and his eyes flashed dangerously as they locked onto mine. Even his cheekbones looked harder than usual.

"Where the hell have you been?" he growled, advancing on me.

I raised an eyebrow, my smile fading. "Out exploring. Didn't realize I needed your permission for that."

"You cannot wander around here, Lexi. It is not safe." His voice was more gravel than velvet today, and his black eyes had a tinge of mania.

"Oh, please. The guard was perfectly happy to escort me. What's the big deal?"

Dominic's jaw clenched, and I hoped I hadn't just condemned the guard. "The big deal is that you are supposed to stay here. In this room."

"Right, because I'm a prisoner," I spat, anger flaring in my chest. "You lied to me, Dominic. This whole time, you've been lying."

Dominic's jaw clenched. "Lying? I've never..."

"Oh really?" I laughed, but it was hollow. "Then explain to me how a fellow 'prisoner' suddenly has the run of this place. How you can come and go as you please while I'm stuck here playing damsel in distress."

He ran a hand through his black hair, frustration evident in every line of his body right down to the stubbled jawline and the tense, high shoulders. "It is...complicated."

"Then un-complicate it for me," I challenged, crossing my arms. "What's really going on here?"

Dominic paced the room, tension radiating off him in waves. I watched him, my heart pounding. Anger boiled my blood and made mush of my brain. I was falling for this lying ass and if he didn't come clean, I'd never believe anything he said again. "Tell me the truth or I'll jump into the fucking ocean, Dominic, and swim back to Hebes."

He whirled on me, and I saw the panic in his face. He grabbed my wrist. "You would die."

That was an excellent point, and I'd probably revise the plan and take a boat instead. But he didn't need to know that.

"Humans die really fucking easily," I spat, twisting my wrist free of him. "Tell me the damn truth. You do favors for the King? You're his prisoner yet you come and go as you please? And now you're trying to lord it over me and monitor my movements. Tell me the truth."

Dominic's eyes darkened, shadows curling at the edges of the room like creeping vines. His voice dropped, colder than the wind outside. "You want the truth, Lexi? Fine. Here it is."

I froze, my heart pounding as the temperature in the room plummeted. The shadows moved as if alive, coalescing around him, swallowing the man I thought I knew. When the darkness cleared, he stood taller, colder, more commanding, and I found myself face-to-face with the asshole I'd been running from all along.

The Shadow King.

"Hello, Lexi," he said, his voice echoing from the cloud of darkness that obscured his features, deeper and more menacing than Dominic's.

His presence was unbearable. My mind raced, cycling through every touch, every whispered word. How had I let myself fall for this? My chest ached, but I shoved the hurt down and let fury rise in its place.

Anger exploded in my chest like a supernova. Without a second thought, I launched myself at him, a primal scream tearing from my throat. My arms locked around his neck as we crashed to the ground, toppling over a nearby stool with a resounding clatter.

I straddled him, one hand squeezing his throat, glad to find something solid to grab beneath all those shadows. "Have you killed Delph or Razelle or Kayla?" I snarled, my face inches from his.

"Lexi, stop," he rasped, shadows curling protectively around his throat as I tightened my grip. "You don't understand—there's more at stake than you know."

"Have you killed them?" I roared.

"No," he choked out.

"Have you killed any of my friends?" I demanded, tightening my grip, listening to his breathing begin to bubble. "Neela? Ronan? Gabrelle? Leif and Alara?"

His silence was deafening. He could stop me in an instant, rein me in with his shadows, but he let my fury play out, and so did I. In a flash, my free hand shot down, grabbing a fistful of his family jewels. I twisted, relishing his pained gasp.

"I don't care who the fuck you are, buddy," I hissed, channeling all my rage into each word. "So help me God, if you don't answer me, I will twist your ball sac off and juggle the tiny shriveled peas I find inside. Have. You. Killed. My. Friends?"

He wheezed, "Do you know Erevan Reissan?"

"No," I spat.

"Then I haven't," he managed, and his voice sounded softer, more like Dominic's, giving me fucking whiplash.

I released his throat but kept my grip down south. "If you're lying to me, Dominic Branco, or whatever the hell your real name is, I swear I'll make you regret the day you were born."

Standing up, I ground the ball of my foot into his Adam's

apple, savoring his gurgle. "And just so we're clear, if you hurt any of them, I'll necromancer the fuck out of your mother so she can come back and ignore you for the rest of your miserable life."

He winced at my words, and I enjoyed it.

I leaned in close, my lips curled in disgust. "Don't test me, Dominic," I spat, pleased to see him flinch as I used his name in hatred instead of love. "You have no idea what I'm capable of."

Dominic

I was no stranger to facing anger. I'd faced the scalding disappointment in my mother's eyes when they named me King Killer, those long moments when she'd stared at me with disbelief and fury until my sentence was handed down and she never looked at me again.

In the centuries since then, anger had been my constant companion. It lived in my breast and in the eyes of every creature who looked upon me, and I reveled in it, stoked it, drank it in.

But nothing could have prepared me for the raw, unbridled rage that blazed in Lexi's eyes now. Her cheeks were flushed red and her dark hair curled around her pale face like Medusa's snakes.

I climbed to my feet, the opulence of our shared bedroom suddenly suffocating. The silk curtains mocked me. My injured throat constricted as I struggled to form words, to explain.

"Lexi, I-"

"Don't." She recoiled as if my breath was poison. "How could you? All those innocent people. The war, the deaths. It was you?"

Her revulsion hit me like a physical blow. I, who had

reveled in hatred for so long, now drowning in an ocean of unfamiliar emotion. Guilt. Shame. A desperate need for her understanding.

"You do not know the whole story," I growled, my fists clenching at my sides. "What they did to me—"

"I don't care." Lexi's scream shattered the air between us. "Nothing justifies this. You're a monster."

The word echoed in the cavernous chamber of my chest, stirring something I thought long dead. Pain. Rejection. A longing so fierce it threatened to bring me to my knees.

I advanced, reaching for her, needing to make her see. "Lexi, please—"

Rage narrowed her eyes. "Stay away from me."

I froze, my hand suspended in the air between us as realization struck me. I'd lost her. Lost her trust. And lost the possibility of redemption I hadn't even known I craved.

The door burst open with a thunderous crack, shattering the charged silence between us. My war general, Valdor, stormed in, his face lined with urgency.

"Prisoner," he barked at me, "Come outside."

"Speak freely," I snarled. "She knows I am the Shadow King."

Valdor dropped instantly to one knee. "My lord," he said, barely sparing a glance for Lexi. "Capricia's frontlines are overrun. We're losing ground fast."

I clenched my jaw. I was needed on that battlefield, I should have been there hours ago, but I'd waged my own war right here with Lexi. Well, it was time to take my responsibilities seriously.

With a sharp nod to Valdor, I turned to Lexi one last time.

"This is not over," I growled, more to myself than to her.

Lexi's face crumpled as I turned to leave. "Don't go."

For one long, stupid moment, I thought she wanted me to stay by her side. I whirled to look at her, but her eyes glowed with a hatred that rivaled my own centuries-old rage. "Don't go to Caprice," she said, clarifying her request. "No more war. No more deaths. Just stop," she pleaded. But her expression burned with disgust. I committed that look to memory, another wound to fuel my resolve.

I strode from the room, my cloak billowing behind me like a storm cloud as she screamed my name in rage. Outside, I grabbed the guard by his collar, yanking him close.

"She does not leave this room," I snarled. "Under any circumstances. Understood?"

The guard's eyes widened. "Y-yes, my lord. But she usually bathes in the afternoons—"

"Not anymore," I cut him off. She couldn't leave this room, it wasn't safe. The image of Lexi's fragile form plummeting from the cliffs into the churning sea below seized me with a terror I'd never known. Her threat to end her life if I didn't reveal the truth still echoed in my ears. "She stays here. No exceptions."

I began to walk away, then turned back, my voice low and dangerous. "If any harm comes to her—by her own hand or another's—your suffering will be legendary."

The guard swallowed hard and nodded.

As I strode down the corridor, my hands shook. The thought of Lexi's body disappearing beneath the waves, lost to me forever, sent ice through my veins. I'd faced countless battles, endured centuries of isolation, but nothing had prepared me for this visceral fear.

I'd keep her safe, even if it meant becoming her jailer. Even if it meant she'd despise me until her last breath.

It was a price I'd willingly pay.

Most fae traveled by moonway. I sneered at the thought as I prepared for my journey. Such delicate, luminous paths, woven from strands of moonlight by skilled Weavers. Elegant. Pristine. Utterly useless for my purposes.

It hadn't taken much to pervert their magic, to twist it into something darker, more potent. Where they drew from the moon's gentle glow, I harnessed the raw power of shadow and void. My darkways sliced through the realms like obsidian blades, undetectable, unstoppable.

I stepped into the inky blackness, which closed around me like a second skin. The familiar chill settled in my bones as I traversed the impossible distance between my fortress and Capricia. With each stride, a piece of myself calcified, another fragment of my soul hardening to stone.

Once, I'd reveled in this sensation. I'd craved the numbness, the gradual excision of all feeling. Now, as Lexi's face flashed in my mind, I mourned each lost shard. Would this make me less worthy of her love? Less capable of earning her forgiveness?

I emerged from the darkway onto Caprician soil, cloaked in shadow. The stench of blood and magic assaulted me immediately. My Shadow Walkers, relentless and brutal, clashed with the living fae in a maelstrom of violence.

Spells crackled through the air, leaving ozone and char in their wake. The ring of steel on steel raised the hairs on my arms, punctuated by screams of agony and triumph. Blood-slick grass squelched beneath my feet as I surveyed the carnage.

A fae soldier, his armor gleaming despite the gore, cleaved

through one of my undead pawns. The corpse crumpled, its usefulness spent. Nearby, a Shadow Walker's claws raked across a living fae's face, tearing flesh from bone.

The air tasted of copper and fear, tinged with the acrid burn of expended magic. I inhaled deeply, savoring the familiar bouquet of battle. Yet something was missing–the thrill, the satisfaction I'd always derived from such chaos.

Instead, I found myself wondering what Lexi would think of this slaughter. Would she see the necessity, the justice in my actions? Or would her eyes fill with that same revulsion I'd seen in our bedchamber?

I pushed the thought aside. There was work to be done.

My gaze swept the battlefield. The ranks of my Shadow Walkers were thinner than they should have been, their obsidian forms less numerous among the swirling melee. Something was amiss.

A blinding flash of light drew my attention. King Darzan stood atop a small rise, golden hair shining like liquid metal, his arm outstretched. In his hand glowed a blue stone, pulsing with power. That must be the damn Veritas fragment. As I watched, he unleashed a blast of pure energy. It struck one of my Shadow Walkers, and in an instant, the creature I'd spent decades perfecting let forth a hackle-raising screech and then simply ceased to exist.

I should have felt rage. Fury at the destruction of my creation. Instead, I felt nothing. A yawning emptiness where my anger should have been.

What was the point of it all? This war, this death, this unending cycle of violence–what did it accomplish? I'd been driven by revenge for so long, it had become my purpose, my essence. But now, all I could see was Lexi's face, twisted in horror as she learned my true identity.

The fae I fought weren't even those who had wronged me. They were descendants, inheritors of an injustice they didn't understand. And what would their deaths bring me? Peace? Satisfaction?

Or just more emptiness?

I teetered on the precipice of doubt. Everything I'd built, everything I'd worked toward for centuries—was it all for naught? And all because of one human woman, her eyes filled with disgust as she looked upon my true self.

What would revenge bring me, in the end? Certainly not Lexi's love. Nor her forgiveness.

My gaze swept across the battlefield, drawn to a flash of crackling energy. Queen Delphinium stood surrounded by a horde of my undead fae, her lithe form a beacon of defiance amidst the chaos. Lightning arced from her fingertips, searing through rotting flesh and ancient bone. But for every undead she felled, two more shambled forward to take its place.

"Is this what you wanted, Shadow King?" Delphinium's voice carried above the din, raw with fury. She had spotted me at last. "To drown us in an endless tide of the dead? Is this the world you want to rule over?"

I watched, unmoved, as she unleashed another barrage of Lightning. The air filled with the stench of ozone and charred flesh. "You fight a losing battle, Queen," I called out, my voice amplified by my shadows. "How long can your power last?"

Her eyes, wild with determination, found mine in the darkness. "As long as it takes to see you fall."

A flicker stirred in my chest. Admiration? Nostalgia for a time when I, too, had believed so fervently in a cause?

My attention was drawn away as King Darzan carved a path

through my forces, the Veritas fragment glowing with sickly light in his grip. Each Shadow Walker that crossed his path shrieked and disintegrated, reduced to wisps of ashy darkness that dissipated on the wind.

"Your abominations have no place in this world, Shadow King!" Darzan roared, his face contorted with righteous fury. "I'll send them back to whatever hell spawned them."

I clenched my fist, shadows coiling around my arm. "And what of me, Darzan?" I taunted. "Will you send me back as well?"

His eyes met mine, filled with a hatred to rival my own. "With pleasure," he snarled, raising the stone.

For a moment, I saw myself reflected in that hatred. Is this what Lexi saw when she looked at me? A creature beyond redemption, worthy only of destruction?

I turned to unleash myself on Darzan when his Queen's voice cut through the chaos, sharp as a blade. "King-killer! Face me, you coward."

The title hit me like a physical blow, dragging me back centuries to that fateful day. My muscles tensed, rage boiling up from the depths of my being.

"You dare?" I snarled, whirling to face her. "You know nothing of what transpired."

Delph's eyes blazed with righteous fury. "I know you murdered King Erevan in cold blood. That's all I need to know, king-killer."

The injustice of it all crashed over me like a tidal wave. Memories I'd long suppressed burst forth—the shock on my mother's face, the disgust of my peers, the crushing weight of exile. All for a crime I didn't commit.

"You were not there," I growled, darkness seeping from my

pores. "None of you were. You do not know the truth."

Delph raised her chin defiantly. "The truth is written in blood. In the devastation you've spread throughout our lands."

Something snapped inside me. The doubt, the second-guessing—it all burned away in an inferno of rage. This was why I fought. This was why they all deserved to suffer as I had suffered.

"Then let me show you real devastation," I roared.

With a savage gesture, I unleashed a torrent of shadows. They surged outward in a deadly wave, engulfing everything in their path. Fae warriors screamed as the darkness consumed them, their life force snuffed out in an instant.

I watched with grim satisfaction as bodies crumpled to the ground. Let them feel a fraction of the pain I'd endured. Let them know the bitter taste of helplessness and despair.

As the last echoes of death faded, I turned my attention back to Delph. Her face was a mask of horror, but her eyes still blazed with defiance. A cruel smile twisted my lips.

"Tell me, Your Majesty," I drawled, my voice dripping with sarcasm, "how fare your dear cousins? Safe and sound in Hebes, I presume?"

Delphinium's brow furrowed, confusion momentarily replacing her anger. "Of course they are," she spat. "They're far from your reach, monster."

I chuckled, the sound dark and hollow. "Oh, I would not be so certain. Perhaps you should double-check your facts."

Her eyes widened, a flicker of fear finally breaking through her bravado. "What have you done?" she whispered.

I said nothing, letting my silence speak volumes. The truth about Lexi's captivity hung between us, an unspoken threat.

I hated myself for using her again, using her to inspire fear in my enemies, but I liked the thought of her echoing in my head.

I stretched out my arm toward Queen Delphinium, almost as though to touch her across the battlefield, but I was gathering my shadows to launch. As I stared at her, preparing to strike her down, Lexi's face flashed in my mind. I saw again the revulsion in her eyes when she'd learned my true identity. The horror that had carved itself into every line of her face. "Have you killed Delph?" she roared in my memory.

I knew, with a certainty that cut to my core, that killing Delph would drive the final wedge between Lexi and me. She would never forgive such an act. But then, how could she hate me more than she already did?

I pushed Lexi's face aside, hardening my heart. This was war. This was vengeance. This was everything I'd worked toward for centuries.

I turned my full attention back to Delph, gathering the shadows around me like a cloak. My power coiled, ready to strike. One more death. One more step toward my ultimate goal.

And yet, as I prepared to deliver the fatal blow, Lexi's eyes haunted me still.

Delph

The Realm of Caprice reflected the mood of its queen, and I was pissed. All around me, chaos reigned as my fae warriors clashed with the Shadow Walkers and their undead minions. The night sky cast the battlefield in a muted gloom, the only light coming from the pockets of faelight and the crackle of magic. I watched in horror as one of my fallen subjects rose again, eyes eerily vacant, to join the ranks of our enemies.

And above me, towering and black as the Spike, was the Shadow King himself. In that moment, I was helpless before him, a rat before a mountain lion. My ears were ringing with his hateful words, and the image of my cousins trapped in his dungeons bounced around inside my skull, while I struggled to pull together another spell, another Lightning bolt, one last stand.

"Your precious cousin," he'd taunted, his voice like oil on water, "is enjoying my hospitality in the Shadow Fortress. Perhaps you'd like to join her?"

The words echoed in my mind, mocking all I'd sacrificed. Memories flashed before me—being cast to the streets to make room when they were born, watching over them in the Docklands, stepping forward to be the Caprician prince's plaything to keep them safe. And now? It had all been for nothing.

The Shadow King's arm rose, dark energy crackling around his fingertips. Time slowed. I locked eyes with him, defiant to the last. If this was it, I'd go out like the queen I was—head high, even if I was trembling.

My mind raced. Darzan's face flashed before me, his rare smile and hair like molten gold, and those fathomless, bottomless eyes. My cousins, their laughter echoing from happier days in Hebes. I'd failed them all.

"Do it, you coward," I spat, bracing for the killing blow.

But then, something flickered in the Shadow King's eyes. Hesitation? Curiosity? I couldn't tell. His arm wavered, then slowly lowered.

"What the hell?" I muttered, genuinely confused.

The Shadow King's lips curled into a sinister smirk. "Oh, Delphinium," he purred, "killing you would be far too simple. I have grander plans for you, little queen."

My skin crawled at his words. "I'm not playing your twisted games," I growled, Lightning sparking at my fingertips.

He chuckled, a sound like bones rattling. "Oh, but you already are."

With that, he stepped back, melting into the shadows. I lunged forward, but my hands grasped only empty air.

"Coward!" I shouted into the darkness. "Come back and fight."

But he was gone, leaving me alive and utterly baffled. The battle raged on, but my mind lingered on his parting words, their implications more chilling than the clash of steel around me. He had me completely at his mercy, and he didn't kill me. What was his game?

As I stood there, processing the Shadow King's cryptic

departure, the earth beneath my feet trembled. Thick, gnarled vines erupted from the ground, wrapping themselves around the legs of nearby undead fae.

A grim smile tugged at my lips. Caprice wasn't going down without a fight. All around me, the realm itself was joining the fray. Fireflies swarmed in glowing clouds, their light burning the shadows that clung to injured fae. A wounded faeling nearby let out a relieved sigh as the insects' glow drove back the creeping darkness.

"Delph!" Darzan's voice cut through the chaos. He appeared at my side, his leather armor dripping with dark ichor. "You okay?"

I nodded, my eyes scanning the battlefield, inhaling the ash and iron of burned grass and spilled blood. "Yeah, I'm fine. Our realm's not going down without a fight."

Shadow Walkers clashed with the living fae, their shadowy forms flickering and flowing. The undead fae shambled forward relentlessly, but now they had to contend with the landscape turning against them.

"Look." I pointed as a group of Shadow Walkers tried to flank our forces. Tree branches whipped out, snagging their shadowy forms and holding them in place.

Darzan whistled low. "Remind me never to piss off the local flora."

As we fought side by side, I caught glimpses of my soldiers and guards fighting for their lives. A team of fae cast light over the battlefield, doing what they could to keep the Shadow Walkers at bay, and it seemed to be working.

But with the Shadow King leaving the battle, the Shadow Walkers' attacks became less coordinated. Darzan and I surged forward, our renewed vigor spreading through our ranks like wildfire. Darzan used his War magic to slow the dead with a flick of his finger, carving them in two so they had to crawl forward using their arms. The fireflies that had been shielding our wounded now swarmed the enemy, their light seeming to burn the shadows away.

As we pushed harder, the Shadow Walkers began to retreat, fleeing into the darkest corners.

"That's right, you creepy bastards," I yelled. "Run back to whatever hellhole you crawled out of."

Darzan chuckled beside me. "You're enjoying this a bit too much, pet."

I shrugged, not taking my eyes off the battle. "Can you blame me? They ruined my fucking wedding." That wasn't exactly what I was trying to say, but somehow it encompassed all the death and chaos they'd caused.

As the sky began to lighten, the retreat turned into a full-on rout. The Shadow Walkers fled en masse, disappearing into the lingering darkness like smoke on the wind, leaving trampled mud and grass and littered bodies.

"Thank God that's over," I said, watching them retreat.

Darzan nodded, wiping his hands on his leathers. "Let's hope they stay gone this time."

I sighed, finally allowing myself to relax a little. "Somehow, I doubt we'll be that lucky. But for now? I'll take the win."

I surveyed the aftermath, my heart sinking at the carnage. Bodies of fae littered the ground like fallen leaves. The air reeked of copper and decay.

"Shit," I muttered, running a hand through my matted hair. "What a mess."

Darzan was already moving, barking orders to our remaining troops. "Gather the dead. We salt and burn immediately."

I watched as he took charge, tension hunching his shoulders. He knelt beside each fallen fae, sprinkling salt over their bodies before setting them ablaze. The flames cast eerie shadows across the battlefield.

As I stood there, feeling pretty useless, I caught sight of an unexpected figure weaving through the injured. Jayke Sansett, my ex and former rival, was moving from fae to fae, his hands glowing with Healing energy. He was a powerful Healer, but he usually kept himself away from mess, and this was very messy.

"Bloody hell," I said, making my way over to him. "Jayke Sansett, actually getting his hands dirty?"

He looked up, lines on his face. "Someone has to clean up this mess, Delph." I watched as he hesitated over a winged faery, her tiny wings torn and bloody, sure he would pass her by to find a noble in need. But he knelt at the faerie's side and pressed gentle hands onto her tiny body.

"You're even helping the lesser fae," I noted, genuinely surprised. "That's new."

Jayke shrugged, not meeting my eyes. "I was never the monster you thought I was, Delph. I was just ambitious."

I snorted. "That's one way of putting it."

He finished with the faerie, who fluttered away with a grateful chirp. "Look," he said, finally facing me. "I know we've had our differences—"

"Understatement of the century," I interjected.

"—but I'm trying here, okay?" He gestured at the chaos around us. "This is bigger than our petty squabbles."

I sighed, and the weight of the day settled on my shoulders. "You're right," I admitted. "And... thanks. For helping. It means a lot."

Jayke nodded, a ghost of our old familiarity passing between us. "Don't mention it. Now, if you'll excuse me, I've got more Healing to do."

As he moved away, a small knot of tension released in my belly. I smoothed down my fighting leathers and tried to find the courage I needed to keep going, forcing my shaking hands into fists. On a deep breath, I squared my shoulders. Time to be the queen these fae needed.

As I walked among my fae, ensuring the wounded were Healed and the dead salted and burned, my thoughts kept returning to that moment when the Shadow King stayed his hand. He could have killed me, but he didn't. I couldn't shake the nagging feeling that his mercy was part of some larger, more sinister plan. Whatever game he was playing, I was determined to come out on top—for Caprice, for my people, and for the cousins I'd sworn to protect.

One thought burned brighter than the rest. I'd get my cousins back, even if I had to tear apart the Shadow Fortress stone by shadow-cursed stone. The fireflies had burned away the darkness here, and I would do the same for them—no matter the cost.

Dominic

I burst from the darkway, shadows suffocating me like a tight cloak. The acrid taste of twisted magic lingered on my tongue as I surveyed the alien landscape before me, feeling a flicker of unease at being here. Dusty red streets stretched in every direction, flanked by squat stone houses with narrow windows like suspicious eyes. The air hung heavy, thick with the scent of brimstone and decay.

My fists clenched, power thrumming through my veins. This was the Unseelie Realm of Dust, as unwelcoming as its name suggested. Yet a part of me felt a twisted kinship with this Gaia-forsaken place.

A tremor ran through me, and Delphinium's face flashed before me, her eyes wide with fear as I loomed over her in Caprice. The shadows had danced at my fingertips, eager to strike.

"Damnation," I growled, my voice rough in the stillness. I was a heartbeat away from ending her. If I had given in to that murderous impulse, if I had let the shadows fly...

Lexi's face appeared in my mind, her features twisted with grief and rage. Her voice, usually so melodic, rang harsh in my imagination. "You killed my cousin. You're a monster."

My chest ached at the mere possibility. Lexi, with her

quicksilver smile and fierce spirit, was the one light in my shadow-shrouded existence. The thought of extinguishing that light with my own hands was unbearable.

"I came too close," I admitted to the empty street, my words carried away by the hot, dusty wind. I had to be more careful. For her sake, if not my own.

With a deep breath, I straightened my shoulders and strode forward. The war still raged, and I had business to attend to in this desolate realm. But Lexi's face lingered in my mind, a reminder of what truly mattered.

A group of lookouts feigned playing chess, their hair dyed violet to match the king's, an odd custom that made their features unmatched to their eyes and gave them an eerie human quality. They watched me from beneath their long, hooded robes, covered in dust, as I shouldered open the heavy stone door and stepped into the cool darkness beyond.

The interior hit me like a wall of ice after the blistering heat outside. My eyes adjusted quickly, shadows coalescing into familiar shapes—rough-hewn furniture, twisted iron sconces flickering with eerie blue flames. The air was thick with the scent of damp stone and something metallic, like old blood.

"Welcome, Shadow King," a voice purred from the depths of the chamber.

I tensed, shadows curling instinctively around my fingers. There, lounging on a chair of twisted charcoal, sat King Mala Draylar. His violet hair cascaded over one shoulder, matching eyes gleaming with interest.

In one fluid motion, he rose and drew a sword that glinted wickedly in the dim light. "I was beginning to think you'd lost your nerve."

I let the shadows writhe between my palms, a clear threat.

"You should know better than that, Draylar."

We stood frozen, neither willing to make the first move. The air crackled with tension and barely restrained power.

"Tell me," Draylar said, his voice deceptively casual, "how fares your little war?"

I narrowed my eyes, weighing my response. "It progresses. The Seelie realms will fall, one by one."

"Ah, but at what cost?" The Unseelie King's smile was razor-sharp. "I hear whispers of a certain female who's caught your eye. Queen Athar's cousin, isn't it?"

My jaw clenched, shadows pulsing dangerously around my hands. "Tread carefully, Draylar. My personal affairs are not your concern." I forced my face into a mask of cold indifference. "My war with the Seelie realms is proceeding exactly as planned. Their defenses crumble before my Shadow Walkers."

Draylar circled me, his violet eyes gleaming. "And yet, you come seeking an accord with the Unseelie. Curious, isn't it?"

"Pragmatism," I growled. "Nothing more."

The Unseelie King's laughter was like shattered glass. "Oh, come now. We both know there's more to it than that."

My shoulders tensed, the shadows around me writhing in response to my agitation. But as I stood there, surrounded by the twisted beauty of the Unseelie realm, a strange sense of belonging washed over me.

"You feel it, don't you?" Draylar's voice was almost gentle now. "The kinship."

I met his gaze, my own reflection staring back at me in those violet depths. "We are both outcasts," I admitted, the words tasting bitter on my tongue. "Rejected by a society that fears what it does not understand."

Draylar nodded, a spark of something like respect in his eyes. "The Seelie cast us out, branded us monsters. But each of us, in the shadows and the dust, we've forged our own kingdoms."

I looked around the chamber, taking in the raw, untamed power that thrummed through every stone. It was so different from the gilded cages of the Seelie realms. "It feels more like home than any Seelie court ever did," I murmured, almost to myself.

Draylar's lips curled into a predatory smile. "And so you wage war against your own kind, Shadow King. Tell me, how do your undead legions compare to my twisted fae? Shall we put it to the test?"

The shadows pulsed around me, eager for conflict. "My Shadow Walkers would tear through your ranks like fingers through mist," I snarled, dark energy crackling at my fingertips.

"Perhaps," Draylar conceded, his own power flaring, causing the eerie blue flames in the wall sconces to flicker and dance. "But my soldiers have a hunger that even death cannot sate. They'd keep coming, no matter how many fell."

As we postured like roosters in a cockfight, I knew I could win a war against Dust, and crush the Unseelie beneath my heel. But to what end?

"It matters not," I said, my voice low. "My war is with the Seelie realms. They are the ones who cast me out, who branded me a monster."

Draylar raised an eyebrow. "And has your revenge brought you peace, Shadow King?"

The question hit me like a blow to the gut. Centuries of rage and battle, and for what? The betrayal still burned, but it was a cold fire now, more habit than passion. And with every realm

I conquered, every life I snuffed out, I pushed myself further from the one thing that mattered.

Lexi's face flashed in my mind, her eyes burning with anger and disappointment. I clenched my fists, feeling suddenly hollow. "That is not your business," I hissed, refusing to answer the question.

"And yet you claim you could destroy my realm," Draylar said, his tone somewhere between a question and a statement.

I locked eyes with Draylar, resolve hardening within me. "Let us end this posturing. We both know a war between us would be mutually destructive."

The Unseelie King nodded slowly, a cunning smile playing on his lips. "Indeed. What do you propose, Shadow King?"

"A pact," I said, my voice firm. "I shall keep my Shadow Walkers out of your Realm of Dust. In return, you stay out of my conflict with the Seelie."

Draylar's violet eyes narrowed, assessing me. "No aid to our mutual enemies?"

"None," I confirmed. "Your twisted fae remain here, my undead army stays in Seelie territory."

A tense moment passed before Draylar nodded. "Agreed. But words are wind. We need something stronger."

I smirked, shadows coiling around my fingers. "Of course. Bring forth your Binder."

At Draylar's gesture, a figure emerged from the shadows. The Binder was a gaunt fae with eyes like swirling vortexes, magic crackling in the air around them. He leaned heavily against the rough wooden table, and I hoped his magic was stronger than his body.

"Your oaths," the Binder said.

I spoke first, choosing my words carefully and allowing my

true name out as a measure of trust. "I, Dominic Branco, Shadow King, swear to keep my forces from the Unseelie Realm of Dust."

Draylar followed suit. "I, Mala Draylar, King of the Unseelie, vow to withhold aid from the Seelie in their conflict with the Shadow King."

The Binder raised his hands, and I felt the magic take hold, twisting around us like invisible chains. The oath settled into my bones, a constant pressure at the edge of my consciousness.

As the magic of the binding settled, my first thought pierced through the haze of power. Lexi would be safe from the Unseelie. But the relief was short-lived, giving way to a gnawing realization. I was the one endangering her. My war, my relentless pursuit of vengeance—it was driving a wedge between us, pushing her further away with each battle I waged against her kin.

"Something troubling you, Shadow King?" Draylar's silky voice cut through my thoughts.

I clenched my fist, shadows dancing between my fingers. "Nothing that concerns you, Unseelie."

He chuckled, a sound like breaking glass. "Ah, but everything about you interests me. Especially your distractions."

My eyes snapped to his, a warning growl building in my throat. "Watch yourself, Draylar."

"Peace," he said, raising a hand. "I merely observe. This war of yours doesn't bring you the satisfaction you seek, does it?"

I turned away, staring at the flickering blue flames in the nearest wall sconce. "My reasons are my own."

"Of course," Draylar murmured. "But consider this—what

if there's something more valuable than revenge?"

His words hit too close to the turmoil in my mind. Lexi's face swam before me again, this time softened by memory–her laugh, her touch, the way she looked at me before she knew what I was.

Lexi wasn't just a fleeting thought; she was the tether holding me back from becoming the monster they claimed I was. More important than my war, more vital than centuries of festering revenge.

I needed to see her. To erase that hatred from her face, to make her understand. To prove I was worthy of her love.

Without another word to Draylar, I summoned the darkness. It swirled around me, a vortex of shadow and night.

"Until we meet again, Shadow King." Draylar's voice echoed as I disappeared into the darkway.

The shadows swirled around me, my usual refuge, but they felt heavier now, burdened with the weight of her name. Lexi. For the first time in centuries, I knew where I truly needed to be.

Lexi

I pressed my forehead against the cool glass, watching frothy waves crash against jagged rocks below. It might be a step up from my last seaside prison, but still just a cage.

The opulent bedroom behind me was all gleaming marble and silken fabrics, but I couldn't shake the feeling of being trapped. My fingers twitched, itching to throw something valuable and breakable.

"Stupid, stupid, stupid," I hissed, thumping my head against the window pane with each word. How could I fall for his act?

Rage bubbled up inside me, making my whole body shake. Dominic—no, the Shadow King—had played me like a game of tiddlywinks. I'd thought we were fellow prisoners, kindred spirits. Ha. More like predator and very gullible prey.

I'd told him all about the heirs' battle plans and the magic rock fragments. I groaned, sliding down the wall to sit on the plush carpet. "Lexi, you absolute moron." I might as well have gift-wrapped the Stone of Veritas and handed it to him on a silver platter.

Not competent. Not badass. Lisa Munroe would not be proud.

My friends and family were in danger because I couldn't

keep my fucking mouth shut.

I stood up, wearing a groove in the carpet as I paced. Next time, I would engage my brain before my hormones.

I marched to the door, pounding on it with both fists. "Hey! Open up."

The door creaked open, and a guard peered in, his face hidden behind that stupid intimidating mask. Impossible to know if it was the same one I'd tricked into taking a walk with yesterday.

Anger rose inside me again at the sight of him. "How do you sleep at night working for the King?" I asked, actually fucking curious. "Is the dental plan really that good?"

The guard just tilted his head, assessing me.

"Seriously?" I threw my hands up. "That's all you've got? A head tilt? What, did the Shadow King cut out your tongue along with your moral compass? You're just as bad as him but without the power."

Another infuriating tilt of the head.

"Oh, for the love of—" I slammed the door in his face, my blood boiling. I couldn't bear having a conversation with one of his minions, let alone face him in person.

What was I going to do? I had to leave and let Delph know that the Shadow King knew about the Stone of Veritas. As soon as night fell, I would sneak out and steal a boat. Despite living on the coast, I hadn't spent much time in the Docklands because Delph had spent most of her life stopping me from going there, but I knew enough that I could sail if the winds were right.

Until then, I should rest, but energy coursed through me, and I paced the room doing my caged lion act, my mind racing faster than my feet. The plush carpet muffled my steps, but it couldn't silence the echo of Dominic's words in my head on the day we first met.

"Careful, Lexi, you do not know who I am. I am more dangerous than you could ever understand."

I snorted, rolling my eyes at my past self. He practically spelled it out for me, and I still missed it. My very competent badassery was starting to feel feeble to the point of nonexistence, just like my muscles.

My stomach churned as I recalled that night. His dark eyes glittering in the hovering faelights in my plush room in the Spike, how his touch had set my skin on fire. I'd felt so clever, so adventurous, so worldly. Such a fucking rebel.

His whole demeanor had changed when I'd casually dropped my relationship with the Queen. The way his eyes had lit up like it was Christmas morning, or whatever they celebrated here in Arathay when I mentioned I was staying at the Spike.

I buried my face in a pillow and let out a muffled scream of frustration. I was officially the Biggest Idiot in the Fae Realm. I wondered if there would be a ceremony.

"Maybe I'll get a prize," I mused aloud. I rolled over, addressing the ceiling this time. "Basketball tickets? A new blanket?"

I hugged a pillow to my chest. The memory of shivering in the dungeons hit me like a tidal wave. The damp chill of the stone walls, the relentless crash of waves outside, and Dominic—no, the Shadow King—giving up his only blanket for me.

"Here," he'd said, his voice softer than I'd ever heard it. "You need this more than I do."

I snorted, burying my face in the pillow. He had hundreds of blankets and a soft warm bed to retreat to, he wasn't doing me any favors at all. He wasn't some misunderstood bad boy in need of redemption. He was a literal monster.

But he had shown me sweetness. How could two such different individuals as kind as Dominic and ruthless as ASK exist within the same body? Hadn't he once said as much? Back in the seaside cells, his voice had cracked when he told me the Shadow King had "forgotten I ever existed." And "If he is ever hurting you or scaring you, know that I am here too, listening. I will always be there, even if you cannot see me." At the time, I'd thought he was speaking metaphorically, but now...

"Holy shit," I gasped, sitting bolt upright. What if Dominic was trapped here just as much as I was? Could it be possible? A good fae, imprisoned within the monster?

I jumped up, pacing again as my thoughts raced. It made sense. Well, as much sense as anything around here. The sweet guy who gave me his blanket, the one who looked at me like I was his whole world, that was the real Dominic, and he was suffocating under centuries of oppression from the vengeful Shadow King.

My heart hit the ceiling. I could save him. A grin spread my mouth wide, and I twirled around the room, caught up in my own excitement. If I rescued him from himself, I'd also be helping my family and friends and ending this war. There was no downside to trying, at least.

Then I paused, a slight frown creasing my brow, remember-ing back to Delph's wedding. But that all happened before he got to know me, and I was sure the real Dominic had emerged a helluva lot since then, and he wouldn't be so cruel now. Already, he was becoming kinder, I was sure of it.

A sharp rap at the door interrupted my heroic daydreams

of saving my guy and ending the war. "Come," a gruff voice barked.

"OK," I chirped, hopping off the bed. The guard's stony expression didn't crack as he led me through a maze of obsidian corridors. I swear, this place was more maze than fortress. It needed an information desk and a few you-are-here signs.

We finally reached a set of towering doors that screamed 'Important Room,' complete with sweet scenes of torture and murder, which dimmed my mood a little. As they swung open, I whistled low. "Well, someone's compensating for something."

The throne room was a cathedral of shadows and sharp edges. Obsidian pillars stretched to a ceiling lost in darkness, while faelights hovered around the walls, casting more shadows than light. The throne itself was a monstrosity of jagged black crystal, looking about as comfortable as a cactus hammock.

As I took it all in, a movement caught my attention, and I spun around, tensing.

"Lexi!" a familiar voice cried out.

My jaw dropped. "Delph?!"

We collided in a tangle of limbs and laughter, hugging fiercely. "Holy crap, you're alive," I exclaimed, pulling back to look at her. "And in one piece. Though your dress is a bit torn. Should've worn your badass leather jeans."

Delph rolled her eyes, but her smile was radiant. "Always with the badass comments. It's so good to see you."

"You too." I squeezed her hands. "But wait—Kayla and Razelle? Are they...?" The thought of my little sisters sent a jolt of worry right into my gut.

Delph's smile tightened. "They're safe, Lex. Made it back to Hebes without a scratch. I spoke to them this morning. They're shaken, but alright."

"Shaken but not stirred," I mused, sagging with relief, though I'd sort of known already. At least, I felt sure I'd know if my sisters were dead. "Thank God," I breathed. "Though I bet Razelle's plotting her dramatic return as we speak. At least, she'll definitely be back for your next wedding. You know how she hates to miss out on a good party."

"No," Delph snapped. "I told them never to come back. It isn't safe for either of them. Or you."

"Is that why you're here? Because I was hoping to be rescued. I mean, my own escape plans were pretty dodgy, if I'm honest, so the rescue is super appreciated. But actually, I think maybe I should stay awhile." She frowned at me like I was crazy, and I opened my mouth, ready to spill my newfound optimism about Dominic's hidden goodness, and how I thought I could end the violence and war, but then I looked at her, really looked at her.

Dark circles ringed her eyes, and her hair was not only matted but lank and lackluster. Her clothes were torn in places, and—

"Is that blood?" I asked, my voice rising at the end.

"I came straight from Capricia," she said, her tone flat. "It was a bloodbath."

My stomach dropped. "What?" That couldn't be right. Dominic was emerging from the shadows, becoming a better fae, and he wouldn't start another battle now, surely. "When?" I demanded.

"Last night," Delph said, her voice shaking. "The Shadow King's forces swept through like a fucking hurricane."

The blood drained from my face. "No, that can't be right. Maybe it was a rogue faction, or—"

"It was him, Lex. The Shadow King led the charge."

I knew Dominic had stormed out on me yesterday to head to Caprice, but I wanted so much for him to be better than this. "No, he can't have."

"Why are you defending him?" Delph's eyes flashed with anger. "Remember Sue Horden, the Grower I introduced you to? They found pieces of her scattered across three different gardens. And the catler who brought you to my wedding? Gone, along with half her herd."

I stumbled backward, my legs suddenly wobbly. "But... but that's not possible. He wouldn't—"

"Oh, it gets worse," Delph continued, her words tumbling out in a frenzied rush even as her hands shook violently. "We had to salt and burn so many bodies, Lex. You remember little Bran? That faeling who kept asking you about cell phones? We had to set his tiny corpse on fire to keep him from rising as one of the Shadow King's undead puppets. He wasn't even supposed to be anywhere near the fighting." Her voice hitched.

A hysterical giggle bubbled up in my throat. "This is a joke, right? Some kind of sick, twisted prank?"

But Delph's haunted eyes told me everything. My knees gave out, and I sank to the cold stone floor.

"Oh God," I whispered, horror hollowing out my chest. "I'm such an idiot."

Delph knelt beside me, her hand digging into my shoulder so hard it hurt. "Lex, what are you talking about?"

I looked up at her, my vision blurry. "I thought... I actually convinced myself I could save him. That underneath it all, there was still good in him." I barked out a laugh that sounded more like a sob. "Turns out, I've just been the world's biggest sucker."

Delph lifted her hand from my shoulder and opened her mouth, whether to console me or berate me I didn't know and I never found out because, in that moment, everything changed.

The massive obsidian doors flew open, slamming against the walls with a thunderous crash that sent my heart leaping into my throat. A chill swept through the room, making the hovering faelights dance and shadows cavort along the walls.

And there he was.

The Shadow King himself, wreathed in tendrils of inky darkness that writhed and coiled around him like living smoke. His eyes gleamed with an unholy light, and that damned half-smile I once found so charming now looked positively demonic.

"Well, well," he purred, his voice like silk over steel with nothing of the warmth I associated with Dominic. "What a touching family reunion."

Delph let out a strangled whimper and scrambled backward. Without thinking, I stepped in front of her, arms spread wide.

"Oh, yay," I drawled, surprising myself with how steady my voice sounded. "You came back."

Inside, my emotions were churning like my body was a washing machine. Fury, betrayal, and confusion swirled together in a cocktail that threatened to make me either vomit or burst into hysterical laughter.

But outwardly? I was the picture of snarky nonchalance.

"What's the matter, Dominic?" I taunted, scanning his face and posture for signs that Dominic was trapped inside. "Ran out of kittens to drown? Because I know you didn't come back for us. There is no us."

His eyes narrowed dangerously, but I saw a brief flicker of humanity in them. Until he spoke. "Careful, little imp. You're not as safe as you think you are."

Dominic

Lexi snorted. "Right. Because I felt so safe when you were slaughtering my friends and family. Tell me, did you think of me while you were burning down Capricia? Or were you too busy getting off on all the screaming?"

The throne room flickered and cavorted as the hovering faelights danced. In the stillness of the room, the air felt charged, as though the entire fortress was holding its breath.

I stepped toward Lexi, but she stepped back, maintaining her distance, dust swirling around her feet. Fire blazed in her sapphire eyes as she glared at me and her cheeks were flushed pink, her dark curls framing her face in the dim light.

She stood between me and the treacherous snake Delphinium with her arms flung out, always responding to me with anger instead of fear. "How could you?" she spat. Attacking Capricia, slaughtering innocent people?"

Delphinium spat at my feet. "Kidnapping Princess Gabrelle Allura and locking her in your dungeons?"

Lexi paled and turned to look at her cousin. "What?"

My jaw clenched. Of course Delphinium had poisoned Lexi against me. "I did what was necessary," I growled. "Your dear cousin fails to mention how she struck first, luring me into her trap and trying to kill me. It was a pathetic attempt."

Delphinium's lips curled in a sneer. "Only to defend my fae from your tyranny, Shadow King."

I longed to crush her where she stood, but Lexi's presence stayed my hand. My gaze was drawn inexorably back to her. Even in her anger, she was breathtaking—a ray of sunlight in my world of darkness. The curve of her cheek, the soft fullness of her lips. I ached to pull her into my arms, to feel her warmth against me.

"Lexi," I said, my voice low and urgent. "You do not understand. Let me explain—"

"There's nothing to explain," she snapped, but I saw the flicker of doubt in her eyes.

My heart thundered. I took a step toward her, my hand outstretched. "Please. I never wanted to fight you."

She hesitated, and for a moment I dared to hope. But then Delphinium's poisonous words slithered between us once more. "Don't listen to him, Lex. He'll say anything to manipulate you."

Lexi's expression hardened, and my fists clenched in frustration. I'd fight Gaia and Mortia for this woman, and yet here she stood, turned against me by my enemies. The urge to lash out, to unleash my power, clawed at me. But I forced it down. I couldn't lose her—not when I'd finally found something worth living for in this cursed existence.

I stalked closer, my gaze locked on Lexi's, my jagged black throne in the corner of my eye. The air between us crackled, thick and heavy as storm clouds as our shadows flickered. Her chest rose and fell rapidly, her blue eyes flashing.

"You feel it too," I growled, my voice rough with emotion. "This connection between us. It is undeniable."

She shook her head, but I saw the tremor in her hands. "It

doesn't matter. What you've done—"

I closed the distance between us in two swift strides. "It is the only thing that matters."

Lexi hesitated, taking a step away from me, but I sensed her softening, opening up to me, so I stepped forward, mirroring her move. I could see the pulse hammering in her throat. Neither of us could deny the pull between us, even if she screamed against it.

Before she could protest further, I cupped her face in my hands and crashed my lips to hers. For a heartbeat, she was rigid against me. Then she melted into my embrace.

Our kiss was a supernova—an explosion of light and heat in the darkness. Her lips were soft, tasting of sunlight and possibility. I drank her in greedily, my fingers tangling in her dark curls as I pulled her flush against me.

My entire body thrummed with energy, and I felt truly alive.

"Lexi," I whispered hoarsely against her lips, "I—"

A blinding flash erupted behind us, the crackle of Lightning splitting the air. The walls groaned with the intensity of the magic crackling in the air, the obsidian floor trembling.

In an instant, Lexi's hands were on my chest, shoving me aside with surprising strength. I stumbled, the scent of ozone filling my nostrils as Delphinium's attack sizzled past, missing me by inches.

My eyes narrowed, rage bubbling up inside me. How dare she attack while my back was turned? I whirled to face Delphinium, shadows coalescing around my fists.

"How can you kiss him?" Delphinium shrieked at Lexi, her face contorted with fury. "You know what he's done. He's killed hundreds of my subjects." Her silver eyes flashed with hatred. "You're a monster."

"And you a fool," I spat back. "Your fae would have been safe if you had bent the knee. Their blood is on your hands, not mine."

I felt Lexi tense behind me. "Stop it, both of you," she cried out, her voice strong. "This solves nothing."

I half-turned, keeping Delphinium in my peripheral vision. "Stay out of this, Lexi," I warned, my tone softening slightly. "I will not let her harm you."

"I'm not the one she needs protection from," Delphinium hissed, electricity crackling around her fingertips.

My lip curled in a sneer. "You have no idea what true power is, little queen. Do not make me show you."

As Delphinium's fingers crackled with electricity once more, I unleashed my shadows. Inky tendrils shot forth, wrapping around her wrists and ankles, immobilizing her in an instant. She struggled against my magic, but it was futile. I was the Shadow King, and my power dwarfed hers like a mountain overshadowed an anthill.

"Enough," I growled, my voice resonating with authority. "You will listen, Delphinium, or you will suffer."

I turned to Lexi, marveling at her composure. Every fae I'd ever encountered cowered before me, yet this human woman stood tall, unflinching. Her blue eyes met mine.

"Are you hurting her?" Lexi demanded, gesturing toward Delphinium.

I shook my head. "She is restrained, nothing more. Are you willing to talk now?"

Lexi's gaze lingered on Delphinium. "Release her first," she hissed.

"No," I said firmly. "She stays bound until we have finished."

Lexi's jaw tightened, but she relented. "Fine. Speak your piece, Dominic."

I took a deep breath, steeling myself. "During the battle of Capricia, I saved Delphinium's life," I said, my eyes locked on Lexi's, watching closely for her reaction. "I did it for you."

A bark of laughter erupted from Delphinium. " Saved me? Or perhaps you just wanted to control the outcome, as you always do, Shadow King. You would have killed me if it suited your purpose. You only saved me from yourself," she spat venomously.

I whirled on her, shadows writhing around me. "I also saved you from my Walkers, you ungrateful wretch. They would have torn you apart."

I turned back to Lexi, my heart pounding with desperate hope. The time for half-measures was over. I would lay everything bare before her.

"Marry me, Lexi," I said, my voice a low, powerful rumble. "Be my queen. Rule by my side. Together, we can reshape this world. You can mold it, improve it, build it up, or tear it down as you see fit. Every realm will bow to your will. You will have the power to right every wrong, to enact justice as you see fit. You will be my queen, and the world will be yours to command."

I reached out, longing to touch her face, to feel her warmth against my skin. But Lexi took a step back, her blue eyes clouding.

"I can't, Dominic," she whispered, her voice barely audible. "I won't rule over a world of shadow and darkness. I can't be the queen of death and destruction."

My breath froze in my lungs, which couldn't expand or contract, and oxygen was suddenly a valuable resource I'd do anything to obtain. Lexi's face was still, suddenly as still as any fae's, and her gaze was unwavering as she stared at me.

"You do not understand," I growled, struggling to force air behind my words from my burning lungs. "With you by my side, it would not have to be that way. We could build something beautiful from the ashes of the old world. Once I have my revenge, there'll be no more deaths, no more war. Whatever you want, Lexi."

But I could see that her heart and mind were closed to me, her ears deaf and her eyes blind. Her rejection was a dagger twisting in my heart, and something within me began to crumble.

"Be Dominic," she said. "Not the Shadow King. Give up this revenge and choose to be the fae I know you can be, not a monster."

Her words hit me like a battering ram, shattering the walls I'd built around my heart. I recoiled, my fists clenching at my sides. "You would ask me to give up my quest for vengeance?" I snarled, my voice raw. "You know my history, Lexi. You know how I have been wronged. You of all people should understand why I must do this."

The dagger in my chest scraped against my organs, my liver my heart. I advanced on her, my shadow magic swirling around me in agitated tendrils. "I'm offering you the world, Lexi," I growled, gesturing expansively with one hand. "And you offer me nothing. No, worse than nothing—you ask me to give up everything I have fought for, to abandon my dreams."

Lexi stood her ground, her chin lifted defiantly. "I'm offering you freedom, Dominic," she countered, her voice trembling but resolute. "Freedom from this awful quest for vengeance. I'm offering you a chance at redemption."

We glared at each other, the air between us crackling with tension. Harsh words flew back and forth, each barb driving us further apart. I could feel my control slipping, the shadows around me growing darker and more menacing with each passing moment.

Lexi's gaze flickered to her cousin, still restrained by my magic. When she looked back at me, she shook her head slightly, biting the inside of her lip. "I can never be with you, Dominic. Not after this."

What had I expected? That she would fall into my arms and accept the darkness in me? Was it too late to change? Should I chase Lexi instead of revenge? My heart clenched at the thought, but the pain was nothing compared to the searing rage that burned at my edges. Her words were the final blow, shattering what remained of my hope. My insides hardened, my heart turning to ice.

The heavy doors of the throne room burst open, and a guard rushed in. "My lord," he panted, dropping to one knee. "News from Verda. Our forces are under attack."

My jaw clenched, shadows coiling around my fists. "Prepare me fresh armor," I commanded, my voice a low rumble. As the guard scrambled to obey, I turned back to Lexi, her blue eyes wide with alarm.

"You're going to fight them, aren't you?" she whispered, a tremor in her voice. "My friends, my family..."

I met her gaze, unflinching. "This is war, Lexi. Did you think your rejection would change that?"

Her face crumpled, and for a moment, I longed to reach out, to comfort her, to smooth out the tic in her cheek and press my thumb to her lip, wipe away her distress. But the ice in my veins held me back. I strode toward the door, my cloak billowing behind me.

"Am I still your prisoner?" Lexi's question halted me in my tracks.

I paused, considering. With a flick of my wrist, I dispelled the shadows holding Delphinium, who tumbled to the floor like a rag doll.

Turning to the guard, I spoke, my voice devoid of emotion. "Lexi is free to leave. She may do as she pleases. She is a queen."

As I swept from the room, I avoided looking at Lexi, not brave enough to see the relief and joy that must be coursing through her at being free.

I dressed in fresh armor and turned again for battle. As I thundered toward Verda, my thoughts turned dark, anger coursing through my veins like poison. The fae who dared to challenge me would soon learn the true meaning of fear. The Shadow King was coming, and mercy was no longer in my vocabulary.

Leif

"Defense alone won't win us this war," I said, after considering King Dionysus' question. Dion's father sat on the heavy golden throne that was studded with way too many bright jewels, in case anybody missed that he was fuck-off rich and a king in the Realm of Greed and Excess. His hair and eyes were mahogany today, making me think he'd just knocked back a bottle of Dionysus red.

The Verdan throne room was difficult to enter and built to intimidate. Visitors popped up in the room's center, encircled by five looming thrones. Beside the Dionysus throne was the elegant Alluran seat with Chantelle Allura perched on top wearing jade green robes and looking stunning, obviously, being the Queen of Beauty. She always looked like she was floating on that chair, all curved, tangled wood that didn't seem to follow the same rules of gravity as the rest of us. On her other side was Ro's dad, Malachi, sneering down at us from his tornado of blue cobalt and yellow gold, which was meant to show contrasting emotions or some shit, but I always thought it looked like he'd just done a spectacular vomit all over his throne. Not that I'd ever mention that to Malachi.

The other two thrones were empty. The twisting wood of the Floran grew directly from the marble floor, and Mom's one, the seat of House Caro, was finer, stronger marble than even the floor, large and solid like the finest den and very, very empty.

A lot had changed since our first visit to this room when the shadows emerged. Back then, we heirs had come on our knees begging for permission to travel to the Realm of Fen to find the Stone of Veritas. We might have told ourselves we didn't need their agreement, but we'd still come here for it and hadn't left until we'd got it. The kings and queens had seemed so mighty, sneering at us from their elevated seats.

But a lot had happened in the three years since the first rumors of Shadow Walkers, the three long years since Mom died. I'd passed through the stages of grief, kicking and screaming all the way, but no matter how hard I fought against it, I couldn't escape the months of darkness, guilt, anger, and then finally, acceptance. Her death catapulted me into the position of Alpha, not only of my pack, but I was Alpha of Alphas of every pack in the Realm of Verda.

I had rallied against that, biting out at my own wolves, sniping and fighting wherever possible. Especially against my mate Alara, who had taken the brunt of my anger during that period, before I recognized who I was.

Part of me wanted to go back and sucker punch the dickhead who'd been so awful to her, but honestly, my treatment of her had lit a fire between us that still burned like the sun. The honeyed moon had mated us, bound our souls together forever, and I had never looked at another wolf since. Alara was it for me. She was my everything.

Even now, three years after our mating, I couldn't go long without her by my side, and one fragment of my soul was with her, at our den finding sleeping quarters for the refugees from her home town, helping her to settle them into their new lives.

Alara grew up in Sylverclyff, a small town of wolves on the Eastern coast of Verda, directly opposite the Shadow Isles. It was the first place overrun by the darkness, the creeping shadows that multiplied by feeding on shifters. Some fae had stayed anyway, hiding in the light, taking turns to keep watch and cast faelight, huddling together like pups.

Alara's father, Rooni, had taken a leadership role. He was old and as sick as a cat, but he had an iron will and had herded the village's wolves along the moonway that led from his den directly to mine, and he had just yesterday cajoled the last wolves to flee to the relative safety of Verda City.

But that safety was under threat. Fen had fallen, King Erevan Reissan slain by the bastard who called himself Shadow King, and Gabrelle taken prisoner. If that fucker hurt one hair on Gabrelle's head, I would gouge out his eyes and stick the eyeballs into the tip of his penis.

But Gabrelle wasn't why we were gathered in the throne room of Verda City, at least she wasn't the only reason. Every sign indicated that Verda would be next on the Shadow King's target list, so we needed to figure out what the hell to do. The three remaining monarchs, Malachi Mentium, Dion Dionysus, and Chantelle Allura were here, plus three of the heirs, me, Ronan, and Dion.

The five noble Houses in Verda shared the rule over the realm. It had been that way for thousands of years and had put a stop to the constant war and bloodshed. Caro, Mentium, Allura, Flora, and Dionysus, the Houses of lust, mood, beauty, nature, and hedonism. All the ingredients needed to make life in the Realm of Greed and Excess perfect.

From the outside, the monarchs appeared to rule as one, but

as heirs to the thrones, my friends and I knew that they ruled according to a hidden hierarchy amongst themselves, which was set by Gaia herself after years of annual trials. The heirs and I had been competing in these trials for years, competing for our future position when our time came to rule, racing and casting and fighting for points from Gaia.

For most of my life, I didn't care about Gaia's trials. I'd joked and laughed my way through them, planning on eating and screwing my way through life and letting Ronan and Gabrelle take care of the serious stuff. But since I'd become Alpha, all that had changed. I'd grown up a hell of a lot, and the closest I got to an orgy was making love to Alara while our betas looked on. I now understood the importance of leadership, and I took my responsibilities seriously.

I glanced up at the marble throne that belonged to House Caro. My mom had sat there, a true Alpha, a strong queen. Although I'd known I'd end up there eventually, I'd never really believed it. But now it felt inevitable and right, and the only question was why I wasn't already on it.

I'd ruled every pack in Verda for three years, I could rule the other fae too.

The monarchy in Verda worked well, and the transition between generations was handled delicately. The five monarchs ruled together. If one died, they kept ruling. If another died, they still had a majority of three and maintained their positions as kings and queens. But if another ruler died, they were all deposed by Gaia—violently—and the next generation of heirs stepped up and took their place.

The rules were clear. I must wait until this generation of kings and queens was finished. I should wait until my peers were ready before I stepped up to claim my throne. But the massive marble seat veined with gold beckoned to me, calling my name, and before I knew what I was doing, I approached it and climbed the stairs behind it, drawing silence around me like a cloak, and when I turned to face the room, every eye was on me. I sat my silvery ass on the throne, and leaned back, watching for everyone's reactions.

No asking permission this time, no waiting around to be told what to do. Today I had claimed my throne, and there was nothing these assholes could do about it.

I swear to fucking Gaia I saw the corner of Queen Allura's mouth twitch. Being the Queen of Beauty aka masks and the original Ice Princess, she quickly covered it, but I was sure that was a damn smile. King Dion Dionysus, who shared a name with his son, and King Malachi Mentium exchanged a glance that looked an awful lot like approval, like they'd been waiting for me to make this move, and I wondered if this was Gaia's Ultimate Test, the one each heir had to pass before becoming the ruler for their House. Maybe it was just growing the balls to take your place.

The throne was warm beneath my butt, as though Mom had just been sitting here, and my gut twisted at the thought that I was stealing her place. But the temperature of the air cooled, alerting me to the importance of this moment and my new role. I leaned back carefully, finding it more comfortable than it looked. The carved silver wolf heads fit perfectly beneath my palms as I rested my forearms along the armrests, then spread my legs and smirked.

I was a King of Verda now, as well as the Alpha of Alphas. I couldn't wait to get home and tell Alara—she would probably fuck me for three days straight.

From up here, sitting on my elevated chair on my raised

dais, I looked down on my friends. Double D gaped up at me, his mouth hanging open and a subtle scent of strawberries crossing to me from his strawberry-colored mop of hair. I smirked back at him, then tossed a wink to Ronan, who gave me a mock bow, and I barked out a laugh, the sound echoing around the silent room.

The others weren't here. Alara was settling in the new wolves from Sylverclyff at our den, and Thorne was in the Library of Whispers figuring out a rescue plan for Gabrelle. Who the hell knew where Neela was, but it was a shame she wasn't here to witness my self-coronation.

"So what do you suggest instead?" King Dionysus asked, following up on my comment that defense wouldn't win us the war. His throne was beside mine, and now that we were at an equal elevation, he didn't look nearly as intimidating. Fatigue lined his eyes, and he looked more like an old fae looking for help than an arrogant king demanding answers.

I rubbed my thumbs over the heads of the silver carved wolves on the arms of my throne. "We have to mount an attack, but we must be deceitful about it. Make it seem as if we are failing, let the Bastard King underestimate us, then corner him and take him down once and for all. I'm sure that once he has fallen, his creatures and walkers will topple like...like wild rhona."

"Which famously don't topple," D said, craning his neck to look up at me. "They're literally the sturdiest animal in the world."

"Quiet, subject," I roared at my friend, and he flipped me the bird, eliciting a very regal smirk from me.

King Dionysus simply stared at me for a moment, unblinking, before he gave a slow nod of approval. The weight of his gaze was heavy, but I didn't shrink under it. I met his eyes confidently, reminding him and myself that this was my place now. I earned it.

"Your plan holds merit," he finally said, tapping his fingers against the arm of his jewel-encrusted throne, "But it is not without risks. The Shadow King is cunning, perhaps more cunning than any of us give him credit for."

"I'm aware," I replied coolly, leaning back into the throne and crossing my legs. "But doing nothing and hiding behind our city walls is no longer an option. Fen has already fallen, and Caprice is on its knees. We cannot allow Verda to follow. We need to act."

Ronan cleared his throat, drawing all attention toward him. "We should be focusing on rescuing Gabrelle. That bastard took her to his Shadow Isles and is probably torturing her for information as we speak. We can't leave her at his mercy. He has none. Once we have her back, we can discuss going on the offensive."

Chantelle Allura tutted quietly, shaking her elegant head. "Gabrelle can take care of herself. She would never want us to derail our efforts simply to rescue her." Gabrelle's mother smiled smoothly as she condemned her daughter to torture.

I shifted uncomfortably on the throne, which suddenly felt harder beneath my ass. How could I weigh up a rescue mission that must surely be suicide against a wild plan to end the war once and for all? It was an impossible decision, but someone had to make it, and I had just made myself a damn king.

"Queen Delph Athar is traveling to the Shadow Fortress to confront the Shadow King and free her cousin," I said. "She will also free Gabrelle." Every fiber in my body wanted to throw everything we had at rescuing my friend but as much as I hated to admit it, Chantelle was right. We couldn't throw away the entire war on a slim chance of rescuing her daughter.

"Fat chance," Ronan hissed, and I kind of agreed. The chance of that mission succeeding was as likely as me growing a potato plant out my ass. "Delph will be tortured too," he said. "We need a proper assault on the Fortress, something that has at least a rat's chance in a lion's den of succeeding."

"If we kill the Shadow King, his prisoners will be freed," King Dionysus said, and his tone brooked no argument. "Our best chance to rescue Gabrelle and Queen Athar is to defeat the King."

"We cannot defeat him," little D argued, and I took a mental note to call him that the next time I spoke to him. "The Shadow King has dark magic we cannot even imagine. He can appear from the darkness, and disappear just as easily. He casts spells I've never seen, and with every death on our side, he recruits another soldier into his undead army. We have to leave. We have to tell everyone in the city to leave, and once we're all safe, we can regroup and think about taking our city back."

I could not abandon my home and instruct every wolf and fae to do likewise. I was an Alpha, and I didn't run from a battle with my tail between my legs. Nor would I be the leader who lost Verda to the dark. I'd worn the mantle of a leader for long enough to know it was never easy, and that the right decision was often the hardest.

"We fight," I said simply, overruling my friend.

A murmur washed over the room, and I held up my hand for quiet. "We have little choice. The Shadow King has already proven he's not above using dirty tactics. It's our survival at stake, and we should scratch and bite and gnaw at that bastard's bones to keep it."

Queen Allura considered this, then nodded slowly. "We've been on the defensive for too long. Perhaps a surprise counterattack is what we need."

King Dionysus leaned forward, his heavy gaze locked with mine. "And where do you propose we make this seemingly weak stand, drawing the enemy in?"

I thought for a moment. We needed somewhere contained but accessible, somewhere nearby. At a location we could disguise as something else, like a party or a celebration. "At the Borogon Arena," I replied firmly. Shocked gasps filled the air. I understood their surprise—Verda was our home, our sanctuary—but it was also our greatest asset, and Borogon Arena lay right at the city's heart.

"Using our city as bait is risky," Dion said. He spoke confidently, drawing the ear of everyone in the room, including his intimidating father. As my friend outlined his concerns, drawing on the Battle at Isslia for examples, which we'd all discussed in detail with Thorne, I watched his father. King Dionysus could teach statues how to hide their emotions, but even so, I detected pride beneath his stern face as he listened to his son.

How odd it must be to rule a realm and know you must die at Gaia's hand so your own child could take your place. Was it any wonder so many of these kings and queens made awful parents? My mom was an exception, always showing me her love through words and showering me with physical affection as only a wolf mom could, but it must have been hard for her. Dion, Malachi, and Chantelle might not win any parenting awards, but they'd certainly raised excellent leaders.

My throne vibrated beneath me and a voice spoke directly into my mind alerting me that Neela Flora was about to arrive in the room. Neat trick. No wonder the kings and queens never looked flustered by my arrival, even when I sneaked in in my sneakiest most sneaksome of ways.

With a flurry of wind, Neela appeared in the central circle, her bright blue hair messed up by the air that had brought her here. She automatically reached out a hand to Ronan, who took it, and then she looked around, counting heads, I supposed. Instantly, she saw me up on my throne, leaving only the Floran one empty.

"What the?"

She dropped Ronan's hand and cast a simple air spell to propel her up onto the wooden throne of House Flora, and she promptly sat her perky ass on it. Without waiting for approval or condemnation, she held out a warning hand to the other three monarchs. "I'm not asking if I can be here," she said firmly. "I'm telling. If he's a king," she yanked a thumb toward me, "then I'm a damn queen."

How odd that the heir the rest of us had once fought tooth and claw to keep from the throne would be the second among us to claim it. She was a friend, now, but her presence at my side was unsettling, another reminder that the realm's leadership was unstable, with three old monarchs and two new.

Ronan grinned up at his lover. "You might need to work on your courtly manners, tomcat," he called, and she silenced him by growing a thin reed straight from her throne and wrapping it around his mouth.

"I have other methods to keep the order," she replied with a smile. The look that passed between the new queen and her lover was heated, and I took a mental note to roleplay kings and serving fae with Alara.

"We were discussing the Shadow King," Ronan's father said sternly, bringing the conversation back to the war and, interestingly, not commenting on Neela claiming her throne. Obviously, the monarchs had been waiting for us to get our acts together and step up. I just hoped Gaia was paying attention to who stepped up first and would give me extra points for it.

"And how we have to go on the offensive," I added, sobering as I recalled that I had just proposed using Verda City as bait.

As King Mentium absorbed my words, his gaze bore into me. "Our city is our heart," he said softly, "But remember, a heart can both sustain life and it can bleed out."

The flashes of memory Thorne had shared of the Battle of Isslia strobed through my mind, the darkness, the terror, the screaming. Capricia had fared little better, although at least Delph and Darzan had survived and were doing their best to rebuild. I didn't want to be the one responsible for bringing Verda City to her knees in the same way those other capitals had been, but nor did I want to be the king who took his throne only to abandon the realm.

Responsibility was heavier than gold.

"Then we bleed only enough to lure the enemy in," I replied, leaning back against the throne and stroking the silver wolf's head under my palm.

Ronan

"Don't. Fucking. Die," were my last encouraging words to Neela before we separated to take our positions around the arena.

"What, so you can inherit my fortune? No bloody way," she'd replied over her shoulder as she strolled away, never taking anything seriously, not even now on the brink of battle.

We'd shared a final kiss, a final embrace, a final squeeze, although neither of us had dared to name it so. I couldn't fathom losing her today, not after I'd only just met her. I needed centuries with her, as long as I could get, and I would do anything to keep her safe.

But, of course, she refused to sit out.

"I don't see you volunteering for canteen duty," she'd replied when I pointed it out. "If you're big and strong enough to fight, then so am I."

"This isn't a competition."

"I know that. But if it was," she added, "I'd win." Fear flashed through her eyes, but she quickly covered it with a smirk.

Honestly, she would never abandon the rest of us to fight alone, I knew that as well as I knew my own name, so I didn't argue for long. And we needed her strength in the battle if we had any hope of winning, so all I could do was pray to every fucking God I could think of that she would survive.

We kept our numbers low since every loss we incurred was another soldier for the enemy. Everybody we brought to the battle could be a body the Shadow King claimed for his own army. So it was only four of us heirs plus Darzan, for his Lightning powers, a few dozen elite Warriors, and King Dionysus.

The discussion about whether the kings and queens should attend had been long and ran in constant circles like a toy train on a very unimaginative track. They shouldn't be here, since if only one more died, their reign would be finished. But they insisted on being present to defend their realm. In the end, we compromised on one of them attending as a kind of negotiator while the others stayed safely behind.

Gabrelle's absence was almost physical, and I pushed down the pang of worry about her safety. We thought she was imprisoned at the Shadow Fortress being tortured for information. Gaia knew Thorne had searched every single body in Isslia and hadn't found her, so we had to assume she was still alive. But I hated that she wasn't here, and not only because we would miss her strength and fighting skills.

Would they call this the Battle of Verda City? Or the Battle of Borogon Amphitheater? Or, hopefully, the Final Battle? History would decide, but it was up to us to make it happen.

When we were all in position, I looked at Neela, standing fierce and ready in her black cargo pants and fitted tee. She looked strong and capable, but I still wished she wasn't here.

I drew my gaze from Neela's and nodded at Leif, who stood across from me. He nodded back, then dropped the faelight from the center of the amphitheater, casting it in shadow and, we hoped, luring the Shadow King to us.

It worked. Before long, the shadows in the center of the open flat ground of the amphitheater solidified and the Shadow King emerged, looking dangerous and wild. The hovering faelights flickered and the temperature of the air fell, making my skin break out into goosebumps.

He arrived. Fell into our trap like an obedient fly.

He turned a full circle, taking in our sparse numbers, each of us up in the stands, high above him.

"I expected more of a welcome party," he drawled. "I've got to admit, I'm a little disappointed." Power rolled off him in waves, a dark tangible force that made the hair on the back of my neck stand up.

Neela gave a low whistle. "Someone's got a superiority complex." Her voice was steady, but I caught the anxious glance she shot in my direction. I nodded at her, promising to myself to protect her at all costs.

Ignoring her, the Shadow King stretched out his arms, summoning shadows to pool around him like a living darkness. A sneer played on his lips as he gestured at us dismissively. "I hope you didn't have any dinner plans."

Shadow Walkers emerged from the shadows by his side, tall and broad, dark and foreboding, stampeding through the portal their master had opened in a never-ending throng.

My hand flew to the sword at my hip, but it would do me no good here. From my peripheral vision, I could see Darzan wielding his Lightning powers, the electric-blue light illuminating his dark face under the shadowy canopy and turning his golden hair silver. King Dionysus stood stoic and silent, a quiet force who emanated wisdom and patience.

As the Walkers swirled around the stadium, dropping the

temperature to the point of discomfort, Dionysus stepped forward and raised his voice. "We would parlay, Shadow King." His tone was measured and strong, and I was suddenly glad he had insisted on coming. He strengthened our position immeasurably.

The King held up a black hand and his creatures stopped in their tracks, waiting like hounds of hell for their next command.

"You want to talk?" The Shadow King sounded amused. "Please, do go on. Get whatever it is off your chest."

With a nod from King Dionysus, I stepped forward, the shadows shifting under my boots as I moved to the edge of our designated area. My heart hammered but I kept my expression neutral. This was not a moment for fear or hesitation.

"We do not seek war with you, Shadow King," I began, meeting his dark gaze with an unwavering stare of my own. "We stand here to find a peaceful resolution, one that benefits both parties."

Laughter erupted from the Shadow King so abruptly and harshly that several Walkers flinched. "A peaceful resolution?" he echoed, his voice twisted with cruel delight. "You are just as dense as your ancestors."

Despite myself, my grip on my sword tightened. "There is no need for unnecessary bloodshed," I continued, ignoring his insult.

"Oh, but who would define what's necessary and what isn't?" He stepped closer, the swirling darkness at his feet pulsating along with his words.

I stepped back, needing to keep him close to the arena's center.

King Dionysus composed his features into a look of determination, setting his shoulders back and raising his chin. "You have taken enough lives," he began, his voice echoing around the cold, empty amphitheater. "You have brought enough darkness. It ends now."

A cruel smile twisted the Shadow King's lips. "You might think so," he said. His eyes flickered to Neela and I could see her stiffen under his gaze. "But I am only getting started."

"And what do you get from this?" asked Dionysus, keeping his tone steady despite the tension crackling in the air. "Power? Dominion? There is more to life than that."

The Shadow King shrugged dismissively, showing his invulnerability by turning his back on Dionysus, before whipping back around to face him. "You wouldn't understand, King. Your kind is too soft, too weak."

"Is it weakness to value life?" Dionysus retorted sharply, his hand twitching near his sword hilt. "Or strength to know that every being has a right to live?"

The Shadow King looked his opponent up and down, taking in the regal posture and fine leather armor that Dion's dad wore. "Do you include me in that? Do I have a right to live?"

Dion's father, the fae I'd always feared and admired in equal measure, drew himself up to his full height. "You have taken more lives than your due, faeling. You do not deserve anything other than death."

A vicious smile crept over the Shadow King's face and his black eyes glittered with malice. "I was hoping you'd say that."

A tingle erupted through the stadium a moment before he struck, and the coldness intensified, as if we had all been plunged into a river of ice water. I swallowed my dread as I watched the Shadow King's hands twist, a small movement that changed the world.

Dionysus began to raise his hands, but it was too late. With a flick of his fingers, the Shadow King cast a bolt of pure darkness right into his rival's chest. For a moment, nothing happened. The Shadow King's cruel chuckle echoed through the amphitheater, and I had to tear my eyes away from him to look at Dion's father, still standing with his arms outstretched and his cream tailored suit unmarked by the attack.

Then red foam appeared around the Verdan King's lips, and a single drop spilled onto his pristine suit. The Magirus's tightly curled hair slowly turned crimson as he swallowed his own blood, and I couldn't tear my gaze away as my friend's father toppled to his knees, then face-planted onto the arena floor, puffing up a plume of dust.

I stared at the prone body of the most distinguished fae I'd ever known, unable to look away from his hair, which was stuck half-transformed between the golden color of whatever he'd eaten for breakfast and the deep red of his own spilled life.

He had always been so strong, unstoppable, immortal. If he could be swept away in the click of a finger, then all of us were vulnerable.

I pulled myself from my horror to look for Dion and found him standing motionless on the far side of the arena, his own curly hair the color of dust, staring at his fallen father. A blink later, he was tearing down the wide stairs and across the amphitheater floor toward his dad, yelling with a cracking voice for a Healer.

But it was too late for Healing. Whatever bolt of darkness the Shadow King had fired from his dark soul had done its job and killed another monarch of Verda. Of the five Houses who ruled the realm, only two were left standing. Not enough to rule in their own right. They no longer had the support of the earth goddess.

The air tingled with unseen power as Gaia herself let out a burst of grief.

Neela

"Now!" Ronan yelled, and my damn fingers fumbled on the damn spell.

Human technology interfered with fae magic, which nobody knew better than I did. I grew up in Hebes as a human ratbag orphan, and it wasn't until weeks after I moved to the fae realms and the effect of human tech wore off that I realized I was actually fae. So, I'd suggested we disarm the Shadow King's dark magic by exposing him to the human magic of technology.

I'd taped a cell phone beneath the stone dais in the center of the amphitheater, the darkest part of the whole area, where we'd planned on the Shadow King arriving. And so far, he was following our plans, lured to the deepest shadows in the middle of the battle. With shaking fingers, I summoned a vine from beneath the hard-packed clay of the arena floor, commanding it to breach the surface right beneath the dais.

I Ascended as one of the strongest Growers ever, and in the four years since my Ascension, I'd practiced every single damn day to improve my range and finesse, and I should be able to flick a switch from twice this distance with my eyes closed. But the adrenaline pumping through my veins made my hands shake, and I couldn't force my liana to turn the cell phone on.

The Shadow King had already killed D's dad, and that vicious sneer on his face promised hell to the rest of us. His eyes were black and reptilian, like his soul had been ripped out of him, and nothing was holding him back from all-out destruction. The Shadow Walkers that filled the arena screeched, sensing the oncoming battle.

With a deep breath, I managed to flick the switch with my vine and turn the cell phone on. From where I stood, at the top tier of seating on the Eastern edge of the space, the effect on my magic was muted, but I still felt my well of power shrink, like an ocean draining until it was a shallow pond. The other heirs and I were equally spaced around the arena, each of us on the top tier, the farthest we could be from the cell phone while still remaining in the amphitheater. At least, we had been before D bolted down to his dying father and was now more vulnerable to the cell phone.

The Shadow King sagged and stumbled forward, clearly disoriented by his magic disappearing.

From my left, Darzan lit up the sky with a kickass display of Lightning, which he cast as a net across the arena, a domed crisscross of shimmering bright light that illuminated every inch of the space beneath it. The Walkers screeched and sought shadows to retreat to, careening around the amphitheater in clear pain.

I dispelled my vine and pulled my fragment of the Stone of Veritas from my pocket, muttering the incantation Alara had found in her hours of research. Around the edges of the arena, the other heirs were doing likewise. Leif was the first to hold his fragment high, and the blue luminescence it cast was intense, probing in every direction as though searching for something, and turning his silver hair a soft turquoise.

As soon as Ronan's spell was complete, he raised his fragment above his head, and the blue light from it joined instantly with Leif's, amplifying and multiplying the luminescence.

It was working. It was fucking working. The Walkers closest to Leif and Ronan shrieked as though their veins were boiling before crumbling into ash, and the other Walkers veered away from them, cawing like a murder of crows.

Dion and I completed our spells in the same instant, and I saw the determination etched on his rugged face, his dust-colored eyes narrowed and fierce beneath his curly mop. When Dion held his Veritas fragment above his head, avoiding looking at his father's corpse, which was now stumbling to its feet to join its shadow master, the light from the four fragments joined in a complete ring.

The moment the ring was complete, a wave of energy pulsed from it, bright, searing, and pure, blasting outward in all directions. A collective gasp rose as every fae present sensed its power.

Then came a shriek, so high-pitched it made my teeth ache. A Walker close to Thorne convulsed violently before turning into a pillar of ash that held form for an instant before scattering across the red clay ground.

From there, it was like a ripple in a pond. Wherever the light touched, Walkers exploded into ash. Their screams were gut-wrenching, echoing around the arena. But these hell spawns didn't deserve our mercy or empathy. They had slaughtered innocent fae across every Seelie realm, devouring the energy from shifters to multiply and cursing all others into bad horror movie extras.

The Shadow King staggered beneath the pulsing blue ring but didn't fall. His black reptilian eyes stared into the brightness. There was no fear in his gaze, only a cold anger that seeped into the clay at his feet and the air he breathed. Sweat poured down my face as I strained to hold the stone aloft while my magic bled away.

Alara burst into the arena, leading a pack of warrior wolves in a wide loop around the edges of the floor, careful not to get too close to the cell phone in the center. They cleaned up any undead fae from our elite warriors who were rising to their feet to serve their new master.

Claws and jaws slashed and ground, ripping heads from bodies and pulling arms and legs from torsos. Several of the weaker wolves turned into their fae forms, the loss of power too much for them to maintain their shifted forms. But even they, naked and unarmed, kicked and beat at the fallen fae. The undead wouldn't stop until they'd been salted and burned, but Alara and her wolves did everything they could to render them useless. We would deal with them properly after the battle.

Every Seelie realm had sent selected fae to our call. Colzan Blunt from Ourea stood by the only exit, cutting down any undead who attempted to leave with wide arcs of his sword.

Healers from Fen were dashing among the fallen fae, looking for any who might be saved rather than salted.

Even the Dread King of Brume had sent a battalion of War fae, and although their ability to slash a fae in half with a flick of a finger was no use against a shadow, they were very effective in keeping innocent fae out of the amphitheater and out of harm's way.

Every fae fighting for us was just a death away from becoming our enemy, so it made sense to limit our numbers and only fight with the elite.

The Unseelie realm was a different matter. We'd explained, visited, cajoled, even begged, and they still refused to send an elite squad to our aid, acting like the spoiled faelings they were.

But it didn't matter because we would damn well do this without them.

As the wolves tore through the fallen, I felt a sudden jerk on my senses. I looked toward the center of the arena. The Shadow King had regained his footing and was standing tall, arms held wide as if challenging the universe. His gaze was locked onto me, and his lips curled into a cruel grin, revealing glinting white teeth.

The rage on the Shadow King's face was palpable. He looked like a fae who had looked his worst fate in the eyes and hadn't blinked. Like a male who had lost everything and had no reason left to fear or stumble. He looked like a monster.

Suddenly, he tossed his head back and howled, an eerie sound that echoed throughout the arena and sent chills prickling up my spine. His black eyes gleamed with an unnatural light, and a heavy sense of foreboding dropped over me as I felt the darkness respond to his call.

Then, from the black depths of his shadows, four monstrous creatures emerged, each clad in armor as dark as the void, standing twice as tall as any fae, their eyes reflecting a cold, otherworldly light. These were not mere Walkers, they were the Shadow King's personal guardians.

These titans didn't burst into flames like the Walkers. They absorbed the light from our stones, their black armor glowing darker than night, and their eyes shone red.

They advanced outward from their master, their swords drawing trails of smoke through the air. I called on the dregs of my magic, summoning vines to entangle their feet, desperate to slow them down. Darzan rained relentless Lightning on them, but the bolts just exploded against their dark armor, leaving no mark. The guardians didn't even flinch.

My heart pounded as Ronan pocketed his Veritas fragment, pulling around the bow and arrow he had slung across his back and falling into a fighting stance like rain into a pool. He wasn't as skilled with this weapon as Gabrelle, preferring the sword, but he was still competent.

Within a moment, he had loosed an arrow that found its mark in one inky eyeball, and one of the four guardians fell. His second arrow went wide, and his third found a tiny chink in the obsidian armor and pierced a guardian's hip, leaving it lame and limping but still alive.

I knocked one of the creatures off its feet with a vine. Alara pounced on the fallen leviathan, shifting into her fae form in mid-air as the effect of the cell phone kicked in, and as Leif screamed, a Fen Warrior tossed Alara a dagger, which she stuck into its eye at the same moment it raked a claw down her naked back.

Both Alara and the guardian fell still in the dust, and Leif howled with such horror that my gut curdled. If she was dead, Leif would lose the plot, and this whole plan would go to shit. We were all as good as dead.

Gaia had prepared us for this too. At trial after trial, she had endangered Leif's mate to drill us all in the importance of protecting her, not just for Leif but for the good of the entire realm.

Dion was the closest, and without a second's thought, he pocketed his fragment of the Stone and darted in, tossing Alara over his shoulder and retreating back from the reach of the two remaining guardians. Dion pulled out a flask and tipped a few drops onto Alara's lips while Leif lost his fucking mind and shifted into a wolf, blurring across the hard-packed dirt in a river of silver fur.

Dion had spent last night in the kitchen, and I'd teased him about skipping the strategy talks just to stuff his face. But he'd cooked up a concoction of healing and hope, and now it had better save Alara's damn life.

With Dion and Leif distracted and Ronan firing arrows at the guardians, only I still held my fragment aloft.

This was everything we'd planned and fought for over the past few years. Ronan, my lover, my soul, the fae who had given up his name and his inheritance so I could stay by his side, the guy who smoothed every jagged edge of me and made me whole, fought beside me now one last time.

His black hair framed his face like a halo, and I sensed the calm motivation pouring from him as he used his mood-altering skills to keep us all focused on the battle.

I squared my shoulders and raised the stone even higher. The veins on my hands bulged with effort as I focused all my energy on maintaining the spell, but my thoughts were stuck on Ronan. If anything happened to him tonight, I couldn't bear it. The prospect of living in Verda without him was unthinkable, untenable. Impossible. We had a future planned, a small house in a field to retreat to when the burden of leadership weighed too heavy, a small rose garden that he wanted to grow without any interference from me, and furtive visits to the Human Towns so I could remember my beginnings.

As I held my fragment higher, it flashed before me as though this perfect future was painted on one side of a coin that was spinning on its thin edge, showing my perfect future interspersed with one where Ronan died today and the world was flat and dead.

A dozen Brume Warriors stepped forward in a coordinated attack, focusing the slashes of their fingers on the weak spots of the devil guardians, the small chinks at their joints and the gashes of their eyes. Of the dozen, seven fell before both Shadow guardians were dead.

"Get the fuck back into position," Ronan yelled.

Within moments, Dion had his Veritas fragment out and high, although his face held a world of pain as he wielded magic beside his father's twitching corpse, which had been bitten and savaged by wolves.

Leif didn't leave Alara's side until her eyes fluttered open and she ordered him to go. Leif's face turned a luminescent lilac from the reflection of his Veritas fragment, his silvery-blue hair standing on end from the magic that charged the air. His eyes glowed with menace to wreak revenge for the injury to his mate, a cold fury that could only end in somebody's death.

As each heir joined, our jagged, wonky circle of light grew stronger.

Ronan and I were still high in the stands, while Dion and Leif were on the hard dirt floor. Ronan's encouraging mood poured from him, keeping my spirits afloat, holding me focused. And as he took a steady step down the steep stair, still holding his fragment aloft, I stuffed my dark thoughts of the danger he was facing into a corner of my mind and stepped forward too.

My magic was drained, and a harsh pain throbbed in my temples, but I didn't stop. Fen was destroyed. Caprice was defeated. If we lost here, every Seelie realm would fall. This might be my last stand, so I would make it bloody count.

As one, each of us heirs tightened the circle of pure blue light around the arena, drawing it like a noose around a neck. Before long, all four of us were on the flat, the red clay hard underfoot, staring down the Shadow King in a perfect circle.

In his arrogance, the Shadow King had summoned most of his Shadow Walkers to the arena to witness what he thought would be his triumph. The creatures were all dead, burned into fire and ash. The flailing limbs of the Shadow King's undead army still twitched around the dusty floor, like a sea of lizard's tails discarded during battle, and the four dead guardians were like hulking wrecks in that sea. Alara's wolves still prowled the perimeter, keeping it clear, while Colzan Blunt guarded the only exit.

The circle of light grew smaller and more intense as we tightened our net. The Shadow King's eyes flashed dangerously, his monstrous form contorting in the blinding luminescence. He roared, the sound vibrating through the ground beneath us, but he made no move to break through our trap.

With each step we took forward, our ring of light pulsed stronger, growing brighter until it was almost blinding. Sweat poured down my face, stinging my eyes, but I didn't dare to wipe it away. My focus was on keeping the stone aloft and maintaining the spell as my magic weakened.

Suddenly, the Shadow King threw back his monstrous head and laughed. The sound echoed in my bones. He was not defeated yet. I could see it in the light dancing in his black eyes, the mocking grin that twisted his face, the set of his shoulders.

Then he bellowed. That sound would haunt my nightmares for years. He lifted his head toward the dome of light, his mouth opening impossibly wide, and began to channel his dark magic into a final spell, using every last drop of power from his nearly dry well.

The spell gathered between his hands, a swirling vortex of pure black energy, and, as he turned his cold, dead face toward Ronan, my heart clenched.

Lexi

Delph was passed out in my bed, exhausted from battle and still spattered in mud and a dark red substance I tried not to think about. As soon as Dominic had released her from his shadowy bonds, she'd collapsed onto the black floor of his throne room and hadn't roused since.

I'd undressed her and washed her arms and legs, and watched over her all night, just nodding off in the armchair by the fire occasionally. Morning light streamed in through the window, and she was still asleep, so I sat waiting very impatiently for her to wake up.

If she didn't, I would kill Dominic. Hey, I might kill him anyway, it was nothing less than he deserved. The only reason I hadn't stormed off to Verda to murder him already was the steady rise and fall of my cousin's chest and her regular heartbeat.

She stirred, and I leaped to her side and clasped her hand, sitting on the edge of the bed. "Delph? Can you hear me?"

Her eyelids fluttered open, those silver beams so bright in the dim room. "Gabrelle?"

"No, stupid, it's me," I said gently.

"Water?" she croaked.

"You're very confused," I told her. "You're not in water, or on a boat. This is a bed. Although it is on the Shadow Isles, so there's a lot of water around."

"Pass me some bloody water," she said, sitting up and pulling the blankets up under her armpits. "Please," she added sternly.

"Good idea." I crossed to the table by the fireplace and poured some fresh water into a pewter mug, which I pressed into her hands. "Drink this, it'll make you feel better."

She grunted ungratefully, but took the water and downed it in one long gulp. "Gabrelle?" she asked, looking straight at me.

"Lexi," I said carefully, sitting on the mattress and looking over my cousin. This was getting concerning. She seemed wide awake now, blinking those sparkly silver eyes at me and waiting for a response. If Dominic had given her brain damage, I would—

"Have you freed Gabrelle from the dungeon?" she hissed.

That rang a bell. When she arrived, Delph mentioned something about the Lure lady being imprisoned here, but with Delph on death's door... "Oh, fuck." I leaped to my feet. "I forgot."

"You forgot there was a princess in your dungeon? One of our closest allies? Jesus, Lex, how is that even possible? I mean, I know you're flakey, but—"

My hands flew to my hips. "I was kind of distracted by you bleeding all over my bed."

Delph was on her feet in an instant, just wearing her panties which I hadn't peeled off her for modesty's sake, although modesty seemed the last thing on her mind now. "Bloody hell. She could be dying, Lex. She might have died overnight while you, what, daydreamed about pashing the Shadow King?"

I definitely hadn't been dreaming about kissing that asshole. At least, not all night. And just because my subconscious was a selfish bitch who hadn't caught up with the fact that Dominic was a murderer and still fed me sex dreams about him, surely that wasn't my fault.

I crossed to the closet and fished out some leggings and a tee. I tossed them at my cousin. "Stop whining, queen, and let's go get Gabrelle."

Five minutes and one nervous guard-escort later, Delph and I were standing outside an underground cell the size of a broom closet that didn't even have enough space to lie down. Which was fine, because Gabrelle was strapped to a stone wall, hanging from her wrists.

The princess' dusty pink hair was coated in dusty and grime, and her clothes hung from her like rags. She stank of blood and piss, and the welts on her wrists were red and smelled infected. She looked like hell, and a pang of nausea throbbed through me.

The Shadow King did this. Dominic did this.

"Free her immediately," I roared, my voice echoing off the damp stones.

The guard, to my surprise, ducked his head and followed my order without question. "Yes, milady."

The guard unbuckled the leather cuffs at Gabrelle's wrists and ankles, and she collapsed into Delph's arms, who held her tenderly and close.

"Carry her upstairs to the king's bathing chamber," I commanded the guard. "Gently. If you hurt her, I hurt you."

Delph looked at me askance at those words, but I meant every one of them. I would happily tear this man's fingernails out if he caused my friend one more moment of pain.

Perhaps revenge was sweeter than I'd credited.

We soaked Gabrelle's filthy body and tended her seeping wounds. I demanded that the King's Healer be brought to her, and he fixed her wounds and restored her energy, although she really needed a decent sleep and a meal.

The princess was silent through the whole process, although her dusty-pink eyes held gratitude. We dressed her, then took her to my bedroom to rest.

"Water," was the first word Gabrelle croaked after we'd settled her onto the soft mattress.

I opened my mouth to check for signs of confusion, but Delph elbowed my ribs and poured a glass of fresh, cool water, which she pressed into her friend's hands and helped her drink.

"Thank you." Gabrelle looked around. "Where am I?"

"This is the Shadow Isles," Delph said, quickly rushing on at the look of alarm on her friend's face. "The Shadow King isn't here, and you're safe. We're all safe for now."

"Thorne?" Gabrelle asked, sitting up and pushing Delph away. "Where is he? I need to get to him."

Delph sat on the mattress and stopped fussing over Gabrelle. "Thorne survived the Battle of Isslia. He's going mad trying to think of a way to rescue you, but he's otherwise fine. You can see him tomorrow after you've rested."

Gabrelle shot Delph a look that would have withered a newborn babe into a wrinkled hag. "Rest? In the Shadow Isles? Are you fucking mad? I'm not staying here a second longer." She tried to get to her feet but tumbled back to the mattress.

"Take it easy, Gabrelle," Delph said, placing a gentle hand on her friend's shoulder. "You need to sleep. The rest of the world will still be there for you to rescue tomorrow."

Gabrelle shook off Delph's hand irritably. "I'm fine," she insisted, but the haggard look in her dusty-pink eyes said otherwise.

More carefully this time, she got to her feet, only swaying a little. Buck ass naked and completely lacking in modesty just like my cousin, she started rummaging through the closet for something to wear.

The Lure princess was healed and clean, and now she was standing before me like a glorious Goddess, and my mind went blank until suddenly my hands were running down Gabrelle's perfect back, her skin smooth and warm without a single imperfection, and the shape of that dip at her waist was—

Delph pulled me off the beautiful princess. "Pull yourself together, Lex," she murmured, although I noticed the way she stared longingly at Gabrelle too.

"Argh, just a minute," Gabrelle said, then screwed up her face in concentration and flicked off her Lure powers.

Embarrassment flooded me, and I glanced away from her body which was, by the way, still fucking phenomenal. "Sorry, I—"

"Don't worry, Lexi, I'm used to it."

"You know my name?" My voice rose in a squeak, and I turned to Delph. "She knows my name." Despite knowing I was falling prey to the princess's Lure magic, apparently I was still excited by any nuggets of her attention.

Gabrelle pulled on a white sheath dress and turned to me with a frown. "The only human I've ever met? The woman who survived a kidnapping by the Shadow King and somehow turned it into a privilege?" She gestured around the opulent room. "The one who just rescued me from certain death at the hands of my enemy? Yes, I think I can remember your name, Lex."

I squealed a little, grabbing Delph's hand, but managed to keep my cool and not say anything else.

"Now," Gabrelle said, marching toward the door. "How do we get out of here?"

* * *

I was no stranger to wrestling with my own thoughts. Half the time, I felt like an unstoppable warrior, a strategic genius, a battle-hardened fighter, and the other half like a fraud. So ignoring my inner dialogue was pretty typical, but even still, I couldn't figure out why the hell I was still here.

Still in the Shadow Isles. Still in the Shadow Fortress. Languishing in the place my jailer brought me.

So what if he'd shown me kindness unlike any I'd felt before? So what if the respect in his eyes when he looked at me made me forget my inner turmoil, the nasty bitch who sat on my shoulder and told me I was a foolish little girl. And that he told me I was the only one who ever stood up to him, who wasn't scared of him, who earned his respect? So what if the only place I'd ever felt truly alive was in his arms, even more than on the LARPer fields? And that my drive for adventure was finally satisfied?

Not me. I cared the least about all that stuff out of anybody I knew. I would rather spend the rest of my life wandering the realms looking for ants to rescue from being stepped on than spend a moment thinking about the way he'd handed me his last blanket, or how he'd trembled when he told me about being ignored by his mother, or even the moment when he'd brought my whole body under his control and I knew I was lost to him forever. That stuff didn't matter at all. Not when the man I loved was an evil fucking monster who killed fae for fun.

I flounced out of my bedchamber, glaring at the guard as I passed. At least Dominic had left word that I was no longer a prisoner.

She's a queen, he'd said, and thinking about those words on his lips sent a shiver down my backbone that set goosebumps along the backs of my thighs.

So why the hell was I still here?

I was free to go. I could go home to Hebes and check that the twins really were safe, check on Dad, and claim my rightful place as heroine of the LARPing fields. But the thought of going back to that world of drudgery, of office cubicles and taxes and traffic, replaced my blood with honey that could barely pump through my body. Just thinking about heading home and never setting foot in the fae realms again made me want to lie down and never get up. A never-ending nap would be preferable to never-ending boring. Maybe I could buy myself a little fluffy toy and a new blanket so I'd be comfy.

As I rounded a corner on the battlements overlooking the raging sea, I sighed. Going back to the human realm wasn't an option. Salt spray hit my face as I swiped a disobedient lock of hair out of my face and faced the ocean. It churned, like it always did around here, as restless for change as its master, the Shadow King. It was wildly beautiful, the foamy caps over the dark water, and the sky a roiling gray above.

The place I really should go was Caprice. Delph and Gabrelle had already left, going home with the same Flier who'd brought Delph here and who, for some reason, Dominic hadn't killed. She had fallen short of imploring me to go with her, because she was far too regal these days to beg, but her eerie silver eyes had borne so far into me that I started worrying she had laser eyes like superman and was trying to kill me.

Instead, she turned away with a sigh and told me to stay safe.

I couldn't leave with her because I needed to check the dungeons and free any more prisoners. Going from cell to cell, I'd come across only one prisoner, and he was a monster twelve feet tall who spat flames at me when I tried to talk to him, so I decided to leave him incarcerated after all.

Dominic had been gone two days. Forty-seven hours, to be precise, not that I was counting. My mind had mastery over time, that was all, so I couldn't help but notice that in just fifty-eight minutes it would be two whole days without him.

Plenty of time for me to escape. Enough time for me to free all the slaves and prisoners and get everyone to safety. But I struggled to find any slaves who wanted liberty, and I didn't fancy traveling with that fire-spitting giant, so here I was, strolling the battlements and wondering why the fuck I was still here.

"Chaos," I muttered to myself, my voice getting lost in the pounding of waves crashing against the fortress walls. "I'm addicted to chaos." That was the only explanation that made sense. A normal life, devoid of magic, monsters, and manic Shadow Kings, sounded as appealing as a plate of wilted greens.

The wind picked up, pulling strands of hair out of my braid and whipping them around my face. It was another turbulent day in the Shadow Isles. Just perfect.

I turned away from the sea and started walking along the

winding stone path that led to the fortress's heart. A serving fae approached and ducked a curtsey. Word must have spread that I was Dominic's queen because over the past two days, everyone seemed to need my opinion.

"My lady," she began, her rose-pink eyes darting around. "The earth sprites, they've gone into a frenzy. They're ransacking the kitchens and tearing up the gardens." She gestured to the chaos behind her where small, vibrant creatures with glowing skin and wild hair were zipping about, drowning flowers in pools of water, uprooting shrubs, and burying kitchen utensils in the soil.

I sighed. What the hell was I supposed to do about that? I was a human, for God's sake, and a fae with actual real-life magic was coming to me for advice on dealing with mischievous creatures. Just two weeks ago I hadn't even heard of earth sprites, and now I was supposed to contain them?

All I knew was that they loved sweet things, so we would have to start there.

"Alright," I said, tucking an insistent lock of hair behind my ear, where it refused to stay and instantly whipped me across the face again. "Bring all the honey from the kitchen into the garden, and let's try to distract them."

The serving fae looked at me with wide rosy eyes. "Thank you, my queen," she said with a small bob, then she hurried away before I could correct her.

Queen. I shook my head at the bizarre title. Everyone around here was in a rush to tie me down to this world, where everything was always at its extreme, whether beauty, menace, or absurdity. Like right now, watching a mob of sprites stuff teaspoons into each other's ears.

But now wasn't the time to dwell on my title, or lack thereof.

The Shadow Fortress needed order, and I was the only one willing to deliver. Then I would leave. Definitely. For sure. No question. Once I had sorted out the place and made sure everybody was happy and settled, then I could, in good conscience, depart forever and never see Dominic again.

Once the sprite tornado was contained, and the little imps were downing honey like there was no tomorrow, I marched toward the fortress, my mind on darker things. I needed to do more than just make the servants happy. I had to take down the Shadow king.

The stone walls, once grim and terrifying, now felt familiar, strong and safe like Dominic's arms. The memory of him made me pause. His image, both the predatory, ice-cold ruler and the man with smoldering eyes that bore into mine with such intensity it made my knees weak, flashed across my mind.

A pang of longing filled me, but I fiercely shoved it down, shaking my head, as if I could physically knock him from my thoughts. And the only thing I would ever do to him again was bring him down. I just needed to figure out a way to do it, and I knew exactly where to start.

The library shone with black bookshelves that lined the walls, and towering piles of books dotted the floor. It needed more shelving and a better layout to house the tomes it already had, not to mention the new ones I'd be buying.

No, that wasn't right. I was going to set things sorted out here and then be on my way, preferably before the Asshole Shadow King returned.

One thing I knew for sure was that I needed to do some research. If there was any way to defeat the Shadow King and free Dominic, it was probably within these four walls. Dominic had had centuries to plan his revenge, and that was plenty of time to rustle up some evil literature and hoard anything that might be used against him. Sure, he'd missed the part about the Stone of Veritas, but he might have some other treasures in here. Most villains would have burned the books that contained information on how to defeat them, but if I knew Dominic—and I did—he'd kept it here as an extra little fuck-off to the fae world, which had betrayed him and hurt him to the quick.

Hours later, my fingers were dry from flipping pages, and my eyes glazing over. There was nothing here. No magical fix to free Dominic from the monster he'd become, no way to end the war and save his soul.

I closed the book and placed it on top of a pile on one of the tables. If Dominic had let these books remain, then they probably contained nothing of significant value. I sighed. Perhaps I didn't really know him at all.

Dominic

I laughed as I stood in the arena and sought the fae with the darkest heart. The heir of Mentium, they called him, one of the future rulers of the realms that had rejected me and tossed me aside. With my remaining power, I could destroy him, take him with me as I tumbled into Mortia's realm, leaving this life once and for all.

It would be so easy. A flick of the wrist. An incantation. A hurling of darkness that engulfed us both. A century ago, I would have done it. A decade ago, a year ago, a damn month ago I would have made that decision, channeling all my anger into reaping one more soul for the God of Death.

These fae were my mother, my cousins, the elders of my town, and all the fae who had deserted me in the worst possible way at the very moment I'd needed their support. The fae who'd turned the course of my life to the shadows and dark. The fae for whom I'd spent centuries planning my revenge.

But I didn't feel angry as I looked at their faces, even as they held me under the power of their accursed Stone of Veritas. No, I felt only...impatient. Impatient for the fight to end. For the battle to finish.

To get back to Lexi.

Sure, I could keep fighting the war, send spies to trail the

Veritas fragments and steal them using thieves through my darkways, then rebuild my army and strike again. But I wouldn't.

None of that was important.

The war didn't matter after all. I chuckled darkly, the shadows swallowing the sound, as I contemplated that my life's work was irrelevant. I'd spent five centuries planning this war, and it didn't fucking matter.

I could use the dregs of my magic to destroy the Mentium brat, but what was the point? He was harmless and had done nothing to me. He was just as much a victim as I was. The battle, the entire war suddenly felt pointless. Even worse, it felt wrong. As though I were aligning myself with the powerful fae who'd ostracized me instead of avenging myself on them.

Was I just as bad as them? The leaders of my village had merely denied me a future. But, looking around at the bodies on the red clay ground, I could see I had done worse. Much worse.

So, instead of choosing death, I chose life. I chose Lexi. I channeled my wisps of power into creating one final darkway, a pathway made of shadows and black magic that would take me home.

It turned out that revenge wasn't the strongest emotion after all.

In the darkway, my emotions swirled too tightly and the passage exploded into nothingness. I cursed and took some deep breaths so I could calm down enough to form another one, sweat forming on my brow as I used my last drop of magic.

I'd ruined my chances with Lexi, obviously. I'd murdered, kidnapped, built a terrifying army and set it on her family and friends. She had no reason to be mine, but I just needed to see it in her eyes so I could know for sure. Needed to meet her gaze one last time and read the truth there, read my fate in the emotion in her twinkling blues.

At my Shadow Fortress, I saw her.

Lexi.

She stood at the edge of the cliff in the pouring rain, over-looking the dark sea and the moonlight glinting off its choppy waves. Her long hair was blowing in the wind like whips of ink, her golden dress flowing out behind her, and she looked like a goddess among shadows. Even with the anger etched into her stance, she was still the most beautiful creature I had ever laid eyes on.

I stared blatantly, taking in every detail of her profile. The way her blue eyes sparkled even in the darkness, the slight curl at the corners of her lip that showed she was always on the brink of a smile, and the courage that radiated from her like fire from the sun.

But then she whirled around and saw me, and her expression changed. Disgust twisted her features as she took in my form—dressed in all black, my hair wild and tangled from constant battles, probably smelling of blood.

As much as I wanted to reach out and touch her, to take her in my arms and feel her warmth against me, I knew it was impossible. She would never let me near her again.

Through the teeming rain, the hatred in her eyes was sharp, cutting deeper than any blade ever could. My shoulders crept up around my ears, a tension that would never be relieved.

In that moment, I knew she would never love me, never forgive me, never give herself to me with her whole heart. Not while I still lived. Perhaps after I died, she would remember me fondly.

I chuckled darkly. That was all I wanted now, to be remembered well by the human woman Lexi.

But my life would be long, and hers short, so even that distant wish was hopeless.

She stared at me with disgust etched on her face, her wet hair blowing in the wind, her golden dress plastered to her body, not saying a word.

"You are still here," I said, stopping ten feet from her to give her the space she needed. I didn't deserve to be any closer. Had expected her to flee the instant I opened the gates and set her free, but here she was, as solid as a dream.

"I'm just about to leave," she said flatly, speaking loudly to be heard over the thrumming rain but not giving me anything but revulsion. No fear, of course, she was the only one who never looked at me with fear.

"Of course," I said, but my stupid heart still thudded to know she hadn't gone yet. Even so, the look on her face told me that hope was dead, and my gut twisted.

She crossed her arms over her chest. "Is the war over?"

"It will never be over. Not while I draw breath," I said, regret making my voice hoarse.

Her eyes narrowed at me. "Do you hate them so much?" she demanded. "Those other fae? The innocents who never lifted a finger against you except to defend themselves?"

I looked at her, my hands dangling uselessly by my sides as drops cascaded from them when they should be wrapped around her waist. "I feel nothing toward them," I said truthfully. "Not anymore."

"So why can't you stop the war?" she asked.

I shrugged, my shoulders heavy like they were weighted with concrete. "I may have started it, but I cannot end it. Not alone. Those I have injured will never stop fighting until I am dead." I took a deep breath, considering my next words carefully. "Revenge multiplies, it does not fade."

"You would know," she retorted sharply, and I knew I had earned the anger in her voice, the bitterness she couldn't restrain.

"Yes," I said simply.

Finally, some real emotion entered her voice, something other than cold anger. Her arms across her chest hugged her now, keeping her safe from me. "Why did you have to start all this in the first place?"

I searched her face for the perfect answer, the one thing I could say that would make her love me again. It was streaked with rain, waiting for an answer I couldn't give. In the end, I settled for the simple truth. "I was angry."

"So scream into a fucking pillow," she spat. "People piss me off, but you don't see me starting a genocide every time some asshole cuts me off on Main Street."

I didn't know where Main Street was, but her import was loud and clear.

I tried for a smile, but the corners of my mouth were as heavy as my shoulders. "I needed that advice a couple of hundred years ago," I said.

"Bet a thousand bucks someone mentioned that you shouldn't start arma-fucking-geddon somewhere along the way," she hissed. "But you thought you knew better than everyone else, you thought you had it all figured out and you ignored anything others suggested. Same damn problem every narcissist has."

If anyone else had said that to me, or anything one hundredth as insulting, my shadows would have eviscerated them instantly. But not Lexi. And not now. I was tired of violence, sick of being hated. All I wanted was a smile from my girl and a long rest, but she had nothing but vitriol and I didn't think I'd ever relax again. Not in this life, at least.

"Yes," I agreed. "You are right."

She didn't know what to do with my acquiescence, which was so unlike me. Usually I battled and debated until I'd convinced everyone in the room that I was right, or destroyed those I hadn't.

"Stop being so agreeable," she said, kicking the stone wall that looked over the sea, water splashing from her dress as she did. "You're an asshole. Show me who you really are. I'm sick of seeing your good side, while you go off torturing and killing everyone else, leaving me in damn limbo. I don't know how to feel about you if I can't feel angry."

"So get angry," I said. "Scream and shout and hit and kick me, tear my throat out, skewer me with your barbs. You have free rein, so go ahead and make the most of it. I will not hurt you back. I promise. I have never made that guarantee to anyone else."

She screamed in frustration. "You're being fucking nice. Stop it. Show me who you really are!"

My shadows swirled around her instantly, holding her immobile, her arms stilled by her side. I stalked closer and I whispered against her cheek, her soft skin caressing my lips, but I still didn't let myself touch her. I didn't deserve that.

I whispered just louder than the pattering rain. "I am a monster, Lexi. A murderer. Your worst fucking nightmare made flesh. So do yourself a favor and hate me."

The words sat between us like lead, and all I could hear over the pounding ocean and battering raindrops was the echo of hate-me hate-me hate-me, knowing that would be my legacy. I'd always enjoyed being disliked by others, I damn well reveled in it. But having Lexi hate me was unbearable. Better I had died during the battle.

My shadows released Lexi, but she didn't run away. She put out a tentative hand to my arm, wiping away some blood that was mixing with rain in rivulets down my sleeve. "Are you hurt?"

"I hurt some people," I said gruffly, flinching under her care. Her hand faltered but then resumed roaming my arm, looking for injuries, then moving across to my chest.

"My friends?" she asked.

My answer was instant, like a puppy trying to please. "No." She breathed out a sigh of relief.

I stood there, mute underneath her touch, a whole war inside me. I wanted to draw her closer and at the same time push her away. This was my torment.

"What happens next?" her voice was small, barely a whisper now. She had ceased her search and was instead gripping the folds of my wet tunic. She didn't face me but kept her gaze fixed on our shadowed figures cast on the cobblestone ground, her head turned away from the ocean.

"Stay with me," I answered, my deepest desire bursting out of me under the heat of her touch.

But the answering wince of disgust that blew across her face told me everything I needed to know. She would never forgive me. A million sins could not be erased with one apology, and I didn't have enough years left to atone for mine.

She looked up at me then, her heavenly blues searching my eyes. "Don't," she said simply. "I can't give you what you want, not in the way you want. And it kills me because there's a part of me that yearns for you too." She lifted her head, her gaze locking onto mine as if challenging me to look away. "But it's not enough," she continued, her hand stilling on my chest. "You've destroyed too much, hurt too many people for me to forget. And maybe one day, after this war ends..."

I didn't need to hear her words, because the truth was in her eyes. This was our last moment together, the snatches of time that would all too soon become a memory that accompanied me to my grave.

"If this is our last night together," I began simply, her solid hands on my chest the only things keeping me upright. "Then..."

She leaned up and kissed me, her lips gentle against mine, rainwater sluicing off her cheek. I pulled away, giving her the chance to change her mind, but she moved with me, her mouth insistent. We stayed like that for a while, melding together as my shadows wrapped around us. I didn't dare move, afraid to break the spell, afraid to lose her. Her mouth moved against mine, and the sweetness of the kiss turned heated as my shadows tugged her body flush against mine.

Her kiss was a silver dagger slowly pressed against my lips, drawing out every drop of desire and longing buried deep within me. Every breath I took in felt like I was consuming her essence, her kiss sweet and spicy, doing nothing to sate my need for her. Every brush of her tongue against mine made me yearn for her touch, for her warmth, for her. A silent plea screamed in the depths of my soul, begging, praying for this moment not to end.

Her hands had slipped up to encircle my neck, fingers tangling in the messy strands of my slick hair. Her other hand, resting just above the dip of my waist served as an anchor keeping us connected. My own hands on her waist were on fire where they met her wet dress, scorching the fabric beneath the heat of my touch.

A low growl reverberated through me as Lexi bit softly on my lower lip. It was a silent plea, echoing louder than any words she could have uttered. The sound died in my throat as I answered with a nip at her lips–a promise of things that could have been.

"Try to remember me fondly after I am gone," I murmured into her mouth, and the words ignited her like they were the dirtiest sort of pillow talk rather than a plea. She moaned into my mouth in reply and jumped up, wrapping her legs around my waist and she gripped my hair with fingers like vices.

My heart pounded as I took a half-step back and turned, pressing her against the cold stone wall, my shadows helping to support her weight. The sensations overwhelmed me–the heat of her mouth, rain falling on my back, ministrations of her fingers through my hair, and most of all, the raw vulnerability in her touches. It was intoxicating and terrifying all at once.

Time stood still as I held her in my arms, her lithe body pressed so close against mine that we shared the same rhythm of breath. We became a single entity, a fusion of desire and silent confessions. Her fingers against my scalp were sharp tugs of reality reminding me that this was not a dream–it was a memory being etched into the last pages of my existence.

"I'll always remember," she gasped out between kisses, her words a series of promises given with every breath she took.

"Promise me," I urged, breaking away from her lips to trail searing kisses down her slippery neck.

"I promise." Her words turned into a moan as I grazed my teeth along the sensitive skin at the base of her throat.

Each sound that escaped her lips was like a needle to my heart, stoking the flames of my desire and guilt alike.

The way we moved together was desperate, deliberate, divine.

As our kiss deepened, the world faded. The stormy waves of the sea, the rain pounding on an evening breeze, and even the dawning moon's glow ceased to matter. All that mattered was that we were here, together for what must be the last time.

My shadows rose around us in response to my tumultuous emotions, their smoky tendrils creating a cage around us, stopping the rain and giving us space, as if the shadows wanted to prolong this moment just as much as I did.

"One last time," she whispered, as she wriggled back to give herself room and reached for my belt, fumbling with the clasp. My cock sprang free, pressing against the heat of her core as I licked a tear from her cheek, the mix of emotions and sensations almost too much to bear.

Her fingers wrapped around me and I groaned. It wasn't enough. It would never be enough. She was my sanctuary and damnation in one beautiful, heartbreaking package. Every inch of her that I touched and claimed as mine only branded me deeper.

"Lexi," I breathed, my voice a husky whisper in the other-wise quiet night.

I gasped as she moved her hands expertly. I allowed my eyes to close, losing myself in her touch, anchoring myself in the reality of this moment.

"Are you sure?" I asked her, even as my own hands didn't stop their journey up the curve of her waist to cup her breast through the thin, wet fabric of her gold dress. Her hardened nipple pressed into my palm, and I swallowed hard as she looked up at me with those sparkling blue eyes. They held a challenge that dared me to question her certainty. But I was a monster, now we both knew it, instead of us both being in denial, so I had to be certain she wanted this.

"One last time," she repeated.

Her thumb rubbed over the tip of my arousal, and I bucked into her hand with a low growl. My hands roamed down her body to where I wanted to be, needed to be. The thin golden straps of her dress slipped easily off her shoulders, and as soon as it puddled on the cobblestones, I stepped back a pace and let my gaze rake over her glorious naked body, searing every inch of her into my memory.

I tugged my shirt off over my head as I stared at her body, then bare skin met bare skin, and my chest tightened.

Unable to resist, I leaned down to capture her mouth once again as her hands fumbled with my belt and pants, eventually leaving me as exposed as she was.

I lifted her, pressing her back against the wall, protecting the back of her head with my hand, pressing my fingers into her wet hair. Her legs instinctively wrapped around my waist again bringing our bodies flush. She gasped, breaking away from our kiss to throw back her head, exposing the long line of her neck. I descended on it, kissing and biting until small sounds of pleasure escaped her lips.

Her wetness met my fingers as they finally found their way between her legs.

"I love you," I murmured as her body responded to my touch, my cock throbbing from just being in her presence.

The whispered confession lingered in the air. Her lips quirked into a sad smile, but she didn't reply. She didn't need to. The knowledge was in the shadows under her eyes and in the lines around her mouth. The truth was in the feel of her skin against mine, warm yet brittle. She loved me too, but not as much as she hated me.

I let my shadows take her full weight, and plunged my fingers into her core, feeling her clench around them.

Her legs quivered on each side of my waist, arms curling helplessly around my neck, anchoring her to me. The swift thundering of my pulse was loud in my ears as I slid my fingers slowly out and then plunged back in. My knuckles brushed against my cock with every movement of my hand, and her legs squeezed my waist.

Her eyes fluttered shut, a soft moan falling from her lips and mingling with the gentle hush of the night. Her fingers curled tighter in my hair as she rocked against me, desperate for more. I gave it to her, my fingers playing her like a game of bridge.

The taste of her lips mixed with the saltiness of our shared tears was heady, wonderful, horrific. I relished in every shiver and sigh I drew from her as if they were mine.

"One last time," she said, though it was closer to a sob than a whisper as her fingers laced through mine and she guided my cock inside her wet pussy. The rest of the world faded from existence, and there was only her soft warmth around my length, her mouth beneath mine, her legs around my waist, and the heat and press of our bodies and frantic hands.

She climaxed with a loud cry and I followed immediately, tears streaming down my face as I came hard inside her.

This was the last time. There would be no other because the only way I could regain her love was after my death.

So I could no longer wait for it.

Lexi

Dominic left with no words, just one final, lingering kiss. It seemed right. After all, what could I say to the fae I loved and hated in equal measure, who had lifted me to new heights and plunged me into despair? Who had shown tenderness and cruelty beyond belief? Goodbye didn't quite cover it.

He released his cage of shadows, plunging us both into the pouring rain again, and I let him go, strolling to the castle while I pulled on my sopping golden dress and then stayed at my perch by the stone wall. His words bounced off the white caps and roared back at me in the rumble of the ocean. *Remember me fondly when I'm gone.* He'd said that twice, and he wasn't one to repeat himself.

He was going to do something stupid. And, considering all the imbecilic things he'd done, that was saying something.

For one long moment, I wavered on the edge of decision. We had said our goodbyes. We'd shared our final moments. I should stay outside, head straight to the boats, and sail home to my family.

But I couldn't fight down the panic that gripped me. Ice slid down my spine and melted onto the skin at the small of my back, and then my feet were pounding across the cobblestones. Instead of finding a boat, I followed him into the fortress, chasing his shadow and the occasional glimpse of the back of his head.

Nothing was more important than catching him and shaking some damn sense into him.

I chased him down a winding spiral staircase I'd never been down before, my wet feet slapping on the stone steps as my heart thundered in my ears. The fingers of my left hand skimmed the rough walls as I descended, and as I followed him into the bowels of the fortress, my entire body tingled with the weight of magic.

If he killed himself, I was going to fucking murder him.

But deep down, I knew that he was a man of his word. He might be a monster, or an ex-monster, but he wasn't a liar. And if he said he was going to do something, he would do it. No matter the consequences. My heart raced as dread coiled in my belly, and I pumped my legs even faster.

Finally, I caught up with him as he entered a circular room I'd never seen before. There was a lingering tang of salt on my tongue, and my mouth felt dry and tight, my throat clenched. A faelight hovered above a large round cushion the color of dried blood in the otherwise empty chamber.

Although I'd never been here, I knew at once where we were from his long descriptions. "This is where you cried yourself to sleep after your mother rejected you," I whispered.

Dominic looked up when I spoke, and the expression that crossed his face was heartbreaking. He lit up completely at the sight of me but was so steeped in sadness that I feared I was too late to change his mind.

"It's a replica," he said. "The first part of the fortress I built."

"So you could remember your past." I stood in the doorway,

and my words echoed off the stone walls. "There's still good in you, Dominic."

He shook his head, digging his fingernails into his palms. "Not enough."

"Promise me you'll never kill another fae," I said roughly, my feet rooted to the rough stone beneath me. I wanted to make things right between us, and that was the only way.

"I promise," Dominic said matter-of-factly, like he was stating a fact not trying to wheedle through my defenses. Water dripped from him, making a small puddle at his feet.

"Would you swear with that binding magic thingy?" I demanded, sounding a smidge less authoritative than I'd planned. I wiped a lock of wet hair out of my mouth and tucked it behind my ear.

"Instantly," he answered, still with that odd mix of sadness and adoration on his face.

I took a step into the room, my body automatically trying to close the distance between us as my soul yearned for his. He needed me. I made him a better fae. I'd stopped him from being a murderous monster, hadn't I? But what I also realized in that moment was that I needed him. The restless part of me that had always sought adventure and was never satisfied was finally quiet with him. He was the answer to the question I'd been asking myself my whole life.

"Or even hurt anyone," I said, soaking him in, knowing he was a good person, even if he wasn't technically a person. "Promise you'll be the sweetest, kindest fae you can be until you die."

"That's easy," he said, crossing the space between us in moments but holding off from touching me as though if he started, he wouldn't be able to stop. "I promise." His voice was steeped in sadness I didn't understand. This was me forgiving him, shouldn't he be whooping in delight?

"Then you don't have to die," I explained, joining the dots for him and trying to lift that weight from his brow. "We can be together, don't you see? We can live here and have little shadow babies and teach them how to f... No, not fight. We'll teach them how to grow flowers or something." Without noticing, I'd scooped up his damp hands into mine, and they were warm and comforting. I knew I could never let them go.

He stared at me for long moments, still seeped in heaviness. "Will you introduce me to your family?" he asked, and finally a touch of humor entered his voice.

I imagined taking him home to Dad, sitting him down on our brown leather sofa and handing him a cup of coffee. We'd share pleasantries about the weather and the house.

And what do you do for a living? Dad would ask.

Genocide, dark magic, general zombification, the usual, Dominic would answer.

Kayla would tut the biggest tut of her life, and Razelle would probably faint and then plot his murder in secret.

I squeezed Dominic's hands. "Well...we'll sort out the details later. We can tell them you're a plumber or something. It doesn't matter. Just don't kill yourself."

The blackness of his eyes still contained depths of sorrow that I didn't understand. We were making up, weren't we? "I did not think you would ever forgive me," he said. "You told me you would never see me again."

"Mmm, sorry about that. I mean, it's not as bad as murder, so I'm not that sorry. And that was before you pinky promised not to hurt anyone as long as you live." I squeezed his fingers as tight as I could.

"I am afraid I cheated on that promise," he said slowly.

"How?"

"Because the rest of my life will not be very long."

I threw his hands down, screaming in frustration. "You don't have to do this," I yelled, then anger boiled through me and I slapped him in the face, leaving a satisfying red mark on his pale face.

He held out a gentle hand and caressed my cheek, wet palm on wet skin, as though I was the one who'd been slapped. In his other hand, he held up an empty vial and said, "It is already done."

Heart pounding, I stared at the empty vial in his hand. What the actual fuck? He had poisoned himself?

"Why?" I cried out, my voice shaking. "Why would you do this?"

The corners of his mouth lifted into a small, melancholy smile. "Because I can only atone for my sins in death."

A lump form in my throat as tears streamed down my face. "No," I whispered. "You can't leave me like this."

"I am sorry," he said softly, leaning forward to wipe away my tears with his thumb.

This couldn't be happening. The man I loved, who had spent centuries planning and executing terrible acts, was now sacrificing himself for me.

"But...what about me?" I choked out.

Dominic's eyes darkened with sadness. "I am doing this for you. Right now, you imagine you can forgive me, but that cannot last. The years and decades to come will wear away at your forgiveness until there is nothing left in your heart but bitterness. I cannot do that to you. I cannot do it to myself."

My heart ached at his words, knowing that he had been

searching for love and acceptance his whole long life, and that I'd been the one to tear his last hope to shreds.

"I forgive you," I whispered, burying my face in his chest and clinging onto him tightly. "Please don't leave me." He wrapped his arms around me and held me close as I wept. "Will you be punished in hell?" I finally asked, speaking through the salty fabric of his shirt.

"Hell?" His arms were tight around me, and I felt stronger because of them.

"You know, where bad people spend eternity after they die," I mumbled. "Fire and brimstone and eternal torture and all that."

He managed a dry chuckle. "You humans have some funny ideas. There is no heaven and hell, there is only the kingdom of Mortia."

I racked my brain, trying to remember which fae thing that was. "The Father of Death," I said when I remembered.

"Right."

"And will he punish you for all the..." I couldn't quite bring myself to say the word 'murder', not to the man I loved, to the man who was sacrificing himself so I would think kindly of him after death.

His lips quirked up in a smile again and brushed a wet lock from my cheek. "The master of death does not revile it the way others do. He is quite relaxed about the taking of life, given that he does it so often himself. Besides, he and I made a deal long ago."

I remembered Dominic mentioning a deal with Mortia, but he always refused to give me any details, no matter how many times I asked.

"And what were the terms of the deal?" I demanded.

"I would send him many, shall we say, offerings—"

"Deaths. Murders." My voice found a hard edge.

"Quite. And in return, he would give me dominion over those souls when I reached his kingdom."

"So you'll be some kind of lord in the afterlife?"

"No, not a lord," Dominic's voice was barely a whisper, his eyes focusing on something unseen. "Mortia has no lords. I will be a caretaker, a shepherd for lost souls. It will be my duty to guide them to their final resting place."

My heart pounded at his words, the reality of the situation sinking in. He wasn't just leaving me, he was leaving this plane of existence altogether. We would never see each other again.

"But you'll have to control murderous spirits for all eternity? That's... that's..." I choked on the words.

"Better than causing more pain and suffering in the world," he said, his voice breaking.

The realization hit me like a punch to the gut. No matter what he did, Dominic could never escape his past. Even in death, he would be haunted by his deeds.

"But how can you guide others to peace when you couldn't find it yourself?" I asked hoarsely.

Dominic's gaze returned to me, his black eyes filled with sorrow and regret. "I have found peace, human. In you."

His words tore at my heart and I clung to him tighter, gripping fistfuls of his wet shirt. He wrapped his arms around me and I buried my face into the crook of his neck, inhaling deeply, trying to memorize his scent.

"Can I come?" Suddenly, the thought of my endless life without him was unbearable. He was the one who had taught me about my true nature. He was the one who had shown me that even a creature of shadow could find love and redemption. And that even a self-proclaimed strategic genius and battle-hardened warrior didn't always have to be ridiculous. Sometimes she could be taken seriously. Sometimes she could be regal.

He barked a laugh. "This is not a plus-one situation." He ran a warm hand down my back. "Besides, what about all the adventures you want to have?"

I considered that. How I'd spend my life wishing to see more, learn more, do more, and wanted nothing but to travel and take in wild sights. My entire personality was forged around a need for exploration, and I wasn't about to throw that away.

"Well," I countered, "death is the biggest adventure of all. I'm sure there's a shit ton of interesting stuff and people down there. Or up there," I corrected.

He kissed me tenderly on the forehead, his musk and mint enveloping me for a brief, sweet moment. "No," he said, his voice hitching. "This is for me only. You have a long life ahead of you, and I will not be the one to steal it. I have taken too many already. Besides, I promised I would never kill anyone again as long as I lived."

I pushed his chest, hard, tears streaming down my cheeks. "Wrong, asshole. You promised you'd never kill another fae. I'm human, so you can kill me."

He pulled me close, one corner of his mouth hitching up in an almost-smile. "Ah, you found a loophole."

"I'm a strategic genius, remember," I said, forgetting to be angry and nuzzling into his neck. "And you also promised never to hurt anyone. That includes humans."

"I will not hurt you," he said, pulling me so tight my lungs squeezed and my breaths became short, but I didn't want him to hold me any looser. I wanted him to hug me to death.

"You are hurting me," I managed to gurgle, and he instantly dropped his arms, horror etched onto his face, those cheekbones flashing under the dim light. "By not taking me with you," I clarified. "And that is breaking your promise. So you have to."

"Larper, I cannot do it. I will not be the one to steal your breaths, snatch away all of those heartbeats that you are due. I will not, and I cannot. I am sorry." We stood face to face, not touching, and I could see what it cost him not to pull me into his arms.

"Not good enough," I said.

"It has to be," he said sadly, and he collapsed onto the large round cushion in the room's center as the poison affected his muscles.

I bent down and slapped him hard, shoving him, watching his limp body shake under the onslaught of my attack. "Take me with you," I shouted, and tears flew off my chin with every hard shove. "If you don't bring me with you, I'll go upstairs and throw myself off the cliff, then I'll die anyway."

"No," he roared, his voice finding strength and his black eyes boring into me. "You would not be reunited with me. You would be thrown in with the mix, and probably would not even remember me. And I could spend eternity looking for you among the dead and never find you. That would be utterly pointless."

"I'll do it anyway," I hissed. "You aren't the only one who gets to be dramatic. I love you, Dominic. And I refuse to live without you."

His black eyes were as deep as the ocean, containing worlds within them, and they pierced me right down to my soul as he whispered, "Are you sure?"

I stood to lose everything. Dad, the twins, Lisa, Delph. The people who meant the most to me, and who I had spent my life longing to please, to amuse, to love. But I always wanted more. My existence had to be more than just Hulu and Friday night drinks.

And looking down at Dominic, his black hair plastered to his forehead, his cheekbones stark against his rapidly paling face, I knew that he was exactly what my life had been missing.

So sure, I stood to lose everything, but without Dominic it meant nothing.

I lay down beside him, curling into his damp body, draping his arm over me. "Do it," I said, inhaling his scent and living inside his warmth for a moment longer.

"Anything for you," he mumbled.

He wrapped his shadows around me, cocooning us both in darkness until the only thing I was aware of was his body tangled in mine and our souls entwined. Pins and needles prickled every inch of my skin, and I felt myself falling, not into the round cushion beneath me, but through time itself, folding and wrapping, twisting and turning, and I grabbed hold of the one thing that tied me to my soul: the feel of Dominic's warm hand in mine.

The world receded into nothing, and even our bodies disappeared, but I clung onto the connection between our minds and hearts and followed the tugging deep in my gut that bound me to him, now and forever, as we left our mortal bodies behind.

All was black, now and forever.

Ronan

THREE MONTHS LATER...

The air in Rosenia Forest felt heavy, each breath thick with the mingling scents of jasmine and damp earth. Shadows flickered like restless spirits among the ancient trees, their towering trunks watching our progress. We were headed for Gaia's Ultimate Test. Just the five heirs, Neela, Leif, Dion, Gabrelle, and me.

I had an awful idea of what the Test might be, but I didn't dare speak it aloud, I barely dared to think it. Every time the idea crept into the edges of my mind, I banished it, grasping for anything else to think of, to fill my mind with other things.

A lot had changed in the past three months. The Shadow King had died, and every one of his creatures had followed him to Hell in the same instant, ever the loyal servants. The Shadow Walkers had simply ceased to exist, dissipating into fine powdery ash and floating to the ground. The risen dead had fallen where they stood, their souls finally at peace and their bodies left for their loved ones to mourn and bury.

Nobody knew exactly how the Shadow King had died. Leif thought he'd struck the killing blow during the Battle of Verda, and when the King had disappeared into one of his shadows, he'd limped home before finally, painfully, succumbing to his wounds.

"I'm telling you, dude, he was a shish kebab and I was the skewer," Leif insisted.

"That's disgusting," Neela said.

"Sounds sexual," Dion added, making all of us groan at the image of Leif skewering the dark monster King.

"Well," Leif said, puffing out his chest, "I *am* the Prince of Lust, the King of Sex, the God of Bed."

Gabrelle snorted, somehow making it sound elegant. "So you cheated on Alara to fuck the Shadow King, did you, oh mighty God of Bed?"

Leif growled and slammed Gabrelle up against a tree. "I didn't cheat on Alara. She is my one and only true Queen, the Princess of Orgasms, the Mistress of Cum."

Neela moved aside a thick liana with a flick of her fingers, then stepped past it. "So romantic."

Leif growled again, "You wouldn't understand."

"No, Duke of Skewering, we could never understand how your brain works," Gabrelle agreed pleasantly. "And I thank Gaia every day for that."

Leif gave Gabrelle a playful shove. "Shut up, Beauty Queen."

Gabrelle laughed, no longer offended by her old nickname. In truth, she had moved so far past that nickname that it bore almost no resemblance to her. Sure, she was heavenly to look at, a true feast for the senses, but she was so much more than that. She was open with her emotions, free with her love and not shy of sharing her displeasure either, a powerful Lure who would make an excellent queen.

At the prospect of my friend becoming queen, my thoughts sobered again. Not because she was unworthy—she was far from that—but because of everything else it meant. As faelings, the other heirs and I used to joke and play at kings and queens, never taking it seriously because it always seemed so far away. Sebarah made a game of inventing ludicrous ways to kill his mother, Celeste, forcing us all to join in and giving us strict parameters.

"She has to die while she's walking the dog," he'd say.

"OK, she's walking the dog and she falls off a cliff and dies," I'd say.

"No, the dog has to be part of it. The dog chases a bird off a cliff and pulls her along."

"Okay."

"Or, the dog runs around her ankles and she trips, smashing her head against a rock."

"Oh, that's a good one. Or it runs around her neck and strangles her."

By this time, Seb would be jumping up and down, jiggling his shoulders in excitement. "Or the dog freaks out when it sees Dion naked and climbs up her body and sits on her face and suffocates her."

We'd all end up in fits of giggles, proposing more and more ludicrous ways she could die. It was funny and fun because it was all so abstract, so impossibly distant. None of this was supposed to happen until we were hundreds of years old, having lived long lives already, and our parents even longer ones. But now that the majority of the ruling monarchs were dead, the remainder had to die. Those were Gaia's rules, and She didn't budge on anything, least of all matters as important as the safety and security of the realm.

Everything was coming together in an awful, perfect confluence of events.

The heirs had all been nominated and confirmed. I squeezed Neela's hand as I thought of how close we'd come to not being here together, to either her or I not being a part of this. And though my heart still ached for Sebarah, at least my heart was complete, which it wouldn't be without Neela.

The heirs had all Ascended. Leif was a powerful wolf, Dion a skilled Magirus, Gabrelle an impressive Lure, and Neela was perhaps the strongest of us all, a Grower beyond compare. Even I had managed to Ascend into a half-decent Mentium.

We were all ready and able to face Gaia's Ultimate Test.

Then the monarchs had started dying. Seb and Neela's mom died five years ago, then Leif's mom was killed by the Shadow Walkers, and finally, Dion's dad died during the Battle of Borogon just three months ago.

Which meant the remaining monarchs had to die.

And now Gaia had called us heirs for her Ultimate Test. The moment all our training and classes had been leading to. The one we must pass or die.

Which brought me back to those shadow suspicions that lived in the outskirts of my mind, and which I tried to push aside and pretend didn't exist.

Because this awful, perfect confluence of events couldn't just be a coincidence.

And when I entered the glade where we'd had all our lessons and started all of Gaia's annual trials, it all looked so familiar. The rocks dotting the perimeter, the garlands of flowers and leaves hanging across the dappled sunlight, the scent of jasmine emanating from the mattress where Leif always lounged. Everything was exactly the same as always, apart from the one detail that made my heart sink.

My father and Gabrelle's mother were waiting for us. Alone.

The two remaining monarchs, here to witness the five heirs undergo our Ultimate Test. But I suspected their role was far more integral than that, and bile swarmed up my belly and burned my throat as I locked eyes with my father's dark gray ones and saw sadness and resignation swimming in their depths.

Glancing at Gabrelle, I saw the same horror on her face that I felt in my bones. She stared at her mother with fear and shock, clearly harboring the same dark, hidden thoughts as me.

Neela knew something was up with me, and she squeezed my hand, looking up at me, but I couldn't drag my gaze from my father.

Even Leif recognized that something was off. "Hey dudes," he said, nodding at the King and Queen of Verda who were, in a twisted way, his peers, since he had already sat upon the Caro Throne. But he refrained from immediately flopping onto the jasmine mattress in the center of the glade, which was his usual first move, clearly sensing darkness in the mood.

The seven of us intuitively formed a circle around the glade's perimeter, roughly equally spaced, standing. Neela was beside me, just out of arm's reach, and Dad was opposite. Dad stood beside Chantelle, who was across from Gabrelle on Neela's other side. Leif and Dion filled in the blanks, like transition pieces between the heirs and the monarchs.

A thunderclap exploded above us and lightning sparked across the clear blue sky, spelling out a missive from Gaia.

The Ultimate Test has begun.

"That's it?" Leif said, crossing his arms over his chest. "No instructions? Just an ominous sky message and all of us standing around creepily in a ring?" He chuckled. "What next? A bare-knuckle fight?" His chuckles grew quieter and farther apart until they sounded more like whimpers, with all of us staring at him until he got it. "Oh fuck," he said. "It really is."

"Not a bare-knuckle fight," Neela said, and I heard the understanding in her voice. "This is the changing of the guard."

"The young surpassing the old," Dad said, his tone gravelly and resigned. His eyes swung to me, locking me in their beam, kind and accepting, asking me to be brave and volunteer to be the first to complete the trial. But my throat was dry and my arms were dead weights beside me, and I had no intention of going first, or maybe of ever going at all.

"The moment that we once faced as young fae too," Gabrelle's mother added, her eyes shining with memory.

It was down to me and Gabrelle, and there was zero chance of me going first. My limbs were leaden, for a start, completely failing to obey any command from my brain, and my brain wasn't exactly on board either. I stared and stared at my dad, and I would damn well keep staring until I died rather than step into the ring.

Gabrelle's shoulders trembled as she stared at her mother, her hands twitching as if torn between reaching for comfort and striking the first blow. Finally, she straightened, her voice steady despite the tears pooling in her eyes, and she stepped forward. "I claim my right to rule."

Chantelle nodded with a small proud smile at her daughter's courage and stepped into the ring to face her.

"Is this why you were so cold?" Gabrelle asked. "To make this moment easier for me?" She spoke quietly, but every syllable carried to every ear in the glade.

Wind whispered through the leaves and carried jasmine on

the air while Chantelle considered her answer. "I was as my mother before me," she eventually said. "She taught me well."

"Too well," Gabrelle said.

Chantelle's head snapped up. "You mistake coldness for lack of emotion, daughter. You always have."

Gabrelle and her mother were both in profile from where I stood, and I saw my friend's nearest fingers twitch. "Do you have emotions, Mother?"

The queen laughed prettily, but it was a mirthless sound that made shivers run down my spine. "I certainly used to," she said, evading the answer like the perfect diplomat she was.

Gabrelle took a step forward, then stopped. "Did you ever love me, Mother?" she asked, her voice cracking and betraying the depths of feelings rushing through her.

"Of course," Chantelle said dismissively.

"For more than just my Beauty?"

Her mother paused, cocking her elegant head to one side as she considered the question. "Beauty is everything," she finally said.

"Beauty is nothing," Gabrelle spat, squaring her shoulders against her mother. "It is nothing but a lie, a deception, and a mask. There's nothing real about it."

Chantelle smiled placidly, refusing to be drawn into the debate, not showing a single atom of what lay beneath her own perfect mask. "But that is where all power stems from, Gabrelle, from reading others and keeping yourself blank, from appealing to others and refraining from temptation. That is power, that is strength, that is what it means to rule. So no, Gabrelle, I don't love you for more than your Beauty, for there is nothing more than that."

Gabrelle hissed out a breath.

I sensed in my friend a fierce yearning to make amends with her mother, to discover a hidden vein of love flowing deep within her, to reconcile all the distance and coldness that had always lain between them. But this was no fairytale with a happy ending, this was reality, harsh and brutal, and Chantelle showed no sign of any warmth of feeling, just a cold pride that her daughter was strong enough to face Gaia's Ultimate Test.

When my friend spoke again, every syllable cracked with grief. "I love you, Mother."

Chantelle stepped forward and wiped a tear from her daughter's face. This was it, the moment where she finally showed some damn emotion, the instant where her mask fell and she shared an embrace with her only child.

But instead of pulling Gabrelle into her arms, the queen just wiped the tear on her own pristine white pantsuit and then dropped her arms to her sides. "Now is the time for strength, daughter. Show your peers how strong you are, what a powerful queen you will be, and demonstrate to Gaia that you deserve the top ranking among them."

The older woman stepped back, increasing the distance to the younger one, and nodded. "I shouldn't need to tell you to go ahead," she said sternly, one final admonishment for her child.

Dion pulled a muffin from his pocket and held it out, clearing his throat. "It's laced with Evermoon," he said, offering the baked treat to Gabrelle. He must have baked that for today, suspecting what the task entailed just like I did. I wonder if he always pushed those thoughts aside whenever they clamored for his attention the same way I did, or if he faced them directly.

Gabrelle looked at Dion mutely, and I could tell she was

taking the time to compose herself, to ready herself for what she had to do. Deep breaths made her entire torso expand, and she wiped away another tear as she looked desperately to D for help. But she didn't take the muffin, she shook her head at him, before turning to me.

She and I had always been close. We had always been the top two heirs, ranked first and second, destined to rule together while Seb, Leif, and Dion cooked and rutted and told bad jokes. At least, that was how it was until Neela showed up and turned everything on its head, then Leif got his act together and decided to take his life seriously. But none of that washed away the bond between Gabrelle and me, and the pain in her dusty pink eyes was so visceral I could feel it in my own gut.

I pulled my sword from its scabbard and spun it, offering her the hilt. It was a small piece of aid, but it was all I could offer her now.

"Use your Lure," Chantelle said. "It will help your final ranking."

Of course, this was the Ultimate Test, the last hurdle Gaia would make us leap before she decided our final rankings, which would determine our order of precedence for our entire joint reign.

Gabrelle blinked at me one final time without accepting my sword, then turned back to her mother, planting her feet squarely and nodding once, decisively.

The two looked into each other's faces, somber determina-tion on both of them. Mother and daughter were so different, driven by different values and different goals, the older draped in finery and wrapping herself in the opinions of others, and the younger fierce and independent and loyal to her friends above all, but right now they had never seemed more alike.

Two females, brimming with strength and power, agreeing that this final act should reflect their family goal to rule as the highest-ranked monarch they could.

The dusty pink halo around Gabrelle's shoulders shimmered as the entire glade filled with the storm of her Lure, the power growing and swirling around every fae present until she had us all staring at her, awaiting her command. Usually, I could withstand her power, but I had never felt it as strongly as this, and I fell to my knees before her, dimly aware of the others around me doing likewise.

Gabrelle's shoulders trembled as she stared at her mother, her hands twitching as if torn between reaching for comfort and striking the first blow. The pink glow of her Lure flickered uncertainly, a visual echo of the battle raging inside her. Finally, she straightened, her spine steady despite the tears pooling in her eyes.

Chantelle held out one trembling hand to her daughter, a smile faltering on her lips. Then Gabrelle narrowed her power and focused it into a beam that she directed at her mother, leaving me gasping for a moment, exhaling while I recovered from the strength of her Lure. I clambered to my feet, as did the other heirs and monarchs, but Chantelle was prostrate before her daughter, lying on the tangled ivy and squashed jasmine, her pristine pant suit rumpled about her prone body.

Never had the passing of power from parent to child been more obvious. The mother, lying in the dirt at the feet of her daughter, already surpassed in strength and skill, just waiting for death to seize her flesh and bones as her daughter had already seized her dignity. Never had the passing of power from parent to child been uglier, and I felt nauseated at the sight of the proud queen muddied and ridiculous.

I could see what it cost Gabrelle, how the fierce lines etched in her face were the only things that kept her from falling apart. But this was Gaia's Ultimate Test, the moment we heirs had been training for all of our lives, countless hours spent in training with the bow or sword and learning our innate power, honing both until they were as much a part of us as our limbs.

And our parents had known this moment would come. They'd encouraged us to train and improve, aware that each time we did, every single improvement in our strength and power, was one step closer to their own deaths.

Nobody said a word. Beside me, Neela radiated tension, but I couldn't lift an arm to comfort her, couldn't tear my gaze away from a glob of mud on Chantelle's not-so-pristine white pants. I'd never seen a speck of dirt on Queen Allura, never noticed a pleat out of place or a dust mote that didn't obey her command.

Silently, I willed Gabrelle to end this moment, to put us all out of our misery. Glancing at Dad, whose face was ashen, his dark gray eyes locked on his friend lying among the leaves, I vowed not to subject him to shame or to extend his suffering, but I immediately suppressed the thought before I burst into tears and ran off into the bushes.

One moment at a time, one breath at a time, one thought at a time. I would face that when I had to, but now I would focus on Gabrelle and her mother.

"Do it," Gabrelle said, and Chantelle pushed up onto her elbows and looked up at her daughter with puppy dog eyes, happy to be of service, waiting for clarification on the command. "Kill yourself."

Gabrelle's mask fell for a moment and I glimpsed the horror beneath her steely facade, but then everything happened at one. Dion stepped forward to offer his poisoned muffin, but it was too late, Chantelle's frenzy to obey was too strong.

Chantelle moved with a deliberate calmness at first, her movements eerily controlled. But as she reached the rock where Gabrelle usually perched during our lessons, something in her snapped. Her head struck the stone with a sickening crack, and the sound echoed through the glade, each blow sharper and more desperate than the last. Blood streaked down her face, and her pristine suit became a grim canvas of red and white. Gabrelle's mask of control faltered, her lips trembling as she took a halting step forward but stopped herself.

Neela gasped, Leif whined, and Dion flinched. Dad and I did nothing but stare and stare until Chantelle fell into the dirt beside the rock, her brains and blood distributed in globules, her eyes staring vacantly at the sky.

Leif made to run forward, but Dion grabbed his elbow to hold him back. Shaking, Gabrelle stalked toward her mother, sent one final probe of Lure into the fallen woman's brain to check for activity, then turned her back and walked in a wobbly line to Leif, who pulled her into a hug that looked like he was supporting her weight and holding her up just as much as he was providing comfort.

A warm hand touched my elbow and I turned to find Dad behind me, his eyes filled with tears. He pulled me immediately into a hug, holding me tight for long moments, and when he tried to get free, I held tighter, never wanting to let him go.

"It's ok, son," he murmured into my ear. "It's ok."

I tried to answer but my tongue was too thick, so I pulled him even tighter, breathing in his woodsy cologne, trying to picture Mom's face when I went home and told her I'd killed her husband.

Eventually, Dad prized me off. "This moment comes for all rulers of Verda, Ronan. It happened to me, and to my mom, and to her father before her. It is Gaia's cycle. Now it's your turn."

"I don't want it," I said, finally managing to spit some syllables onto the forest floor between us.

I sensed Neela's eyes on us, but Dion and Leif were huddled around Gabrelle, who was shaking and sobbing. I was glad not to have an audience, at least.

"I've lived a long life, Ro," Dad said. "Long and complete, and I'm ready to move on."

Shaking my head, I vomited out some more words. "I can't do it, I won't."

Dad's tone hardened. "No fae wants to outlive his children, Ro. You must do it, or Gaia won't allow you to live. Take my life or I'll never forgive you. I will curse your name and strike you from our family."

A few wet chuckles dropped out of my mouth. Either I killed my own father, or he'd disown me. I'd made hard choices before. Without even knowing the implications, I'd sworn to Seb to keep his sister off the Floran Throne then, as soon as I'd met her, I'd given up my inheritance to get her onto it, and was prepared to give up my life.

But this was different. I was grown now, Ascended, and I knew the implications of today. The future of the realm rested on my shoulders.

"What about Mom?" I asked.

Dad smiled. "She and I have said our goodbyes. After this is over, go to her. Promise me you won't avoid her out of guilt."

I nodded. "Okay."

"Say it."

"I promise." I caught sight of Neela's face and drew strength from her, then I turned to face my father. "I love you, Dad."

"And I love you, Ro."

Summoning every ounce of my Mentium power, I felt it grow within me and crackle around me like electricity until I could no longer contain it, and I let it flow into my father's mind, filling him with happiness and joy, pouring memories of Mom and me into his conscious thoughts, and I watched until he beamed with joy, positively glowing with delight, before I slipped my sword from its scabbard and into his heart.

Gabrelle

ANOTHER THREE MONTHS LATER…

Every time Mother told me I was beautiful, I'd despised her a little more. "Beauty is your weapon," she'd say, brushing the dust-pink strands from my face. "You'll never win a battle without it." With each comment on my clothing, my hair, my skin, I'd shrunk further into myself and away from her. And I swore that if I ever had faelings, I would never comment on their looks.

But now, standing with my fellow heirs on a floating dais above the heart of Verda City, with our images magnified a thousand times and projected onto the flat white clouds, with the people of the city watching and cheering, I understood her.

Just a little.

Not the way she valued beauty above all else, but just the importance of presentation. The heirs and I were being presented by Gaia to all of the fae of Verda, as their rulers. We stood in a circle, our backs to one another, looking out over the spires and gold of the city as the floating dais spun in lazy circles. Crowds of fae lined the streets below, waving flags and flowers from every window in every building. The scent of bluebonnet and roses filled the air.

I glanced at Ronan to my left, whose deep blue robes lined with yellow changed his whole face, turning him from an impish boy into a man. A king. His black gaze held depths of responsibility that were hammered into him in the moment he took his father's life, and which would never leave him, I was sure. Gaia was the harshest of teachers, but effective. Something had switched inside Ronan when he plunged that steel into his dad's heart, and I expected it was permanent.

I wondered if the same look haunted my own face, a weight of solemn responsibility imbued into my skin. I glanced up at the image of my face reflected onto the clouds above and started at how alike I looked to Mother. I didn't have her coloring, but the poise and determination made me look regal. I looked like a damn queen, and for once I was proud to be my mother's daughter.

My dusty pink hair was swept up into a loose bun and studded with diamonds. My robes were orange and pink, reminiscent of my House insignia, a setting sun over a pink-and-orange ocean, and I realized how wrong Mother had it all. Our House was about natural beauty rather than skin-deep looks, about the fiery sun and churning ocean and the depths of nature, not the facade of masks and appearance.

I broke into a massive grin, my teeth white against the clouds, and let the joy of this moment settle through my body, allowing it to sit side-by-side with the responsibility that already owned me.

On my right, Leif howled, and a thousand wolves in the city howled back. He wore a gray cloak with white stitching that reflected the sun like the fangs on his House insignia.

He'd been through the loss of his mother years ago, and the sudden propulsion to maturity that resulted. He'd been a fucking wreck, actually, and only in finding his mate Alara had he come back to himself. I was jealous, in a strange way, that he was further through his mourning process than me, closer to that perfect goal of acceptance. Even though I'd never been close to Mother, I still felt like a monster as I remembered instructing her to kill herself and watching her slam her head into that rock over and over again.

Damn you, Gaia. Damn your horrific methods for making us rise to our roles as leaders. Damn you for making me take my mother's life.

And thank you, fucking thank you, for shaping me into the fae I need to be. Looking out over the fae of Verda, all staring up at us and cheering and roaring, I finally understand that being a queen isn't about out-performing the other heirs or even strength or skills or strategy. All it takes to be a good ruler is to know, with one hundred percent certainty, that you will do whatever it takes to protect your realm.

Gaia, that fucking awful, wonderful goddess, certainly made me prove that I would do anything. Ronan too. All of us, in our own way. D watched his father die during the Battle of Borogon, Leif struggled with his demons and his packs across the realm, and Neela had it hardest of all, coming face to face with the rest of us heirs who were determined to run her off or kill her.

So yes, we could all say with certainty that we would do anything for our realm.

A boom rang across the city and a pulse of color shot from each of us heirs into the sky. Mine was orange-pink, like the setting sun, a symbol of respect for nature first, and beauty second. To my right, Ronan's pulse of color was deep blue threaded through with yellow, showing the dual natures of mood. He, out of all of us, understood that with the happy comes the sad, with success comes defeat, and with joy comes despair. Only as rounded rulers could we hope to rule.

To my left, Leif's pulse was a fierce gray, the gray of thunderstorms and wet fur and majesty, flecked with bone-white arrows. I twisted around to glance at Neela's pale pink shot of color, reflecting the rose palace and the rose insignia of House Flora. We'd laughed a million times about how she was a feral tomcat, the opposite of a rose-colored princess, but now I understood that everything was about duality, and she was no exception. The perfect pink princess was exactly the fae who needed the feral underbelly.

Finally, Dion's shot of color was red with flashing silver knives shooting up to the point where all five beams of light intersected above our dais, meeting with a brilliant purple glow that expanded above us and spread out, covering the entire realm in a protective purple glow.

A collective gasp rose from the crowd. For a moment, I felt the weight of every gaze, every hope, every dream resting on our shoulders. It was terrifying and exhilarating all at once. My pulse raced, not with fear, but with a fierce determination: we would protect them.

A breeze kissed my cheek as the dais began lowering. The roars of the crowd grew louder as we approached the ground, and soon tiny winged faeries and streamers were whipping around our faces. An extra tiny faeling with teal wings and curly teal hair lost control in her excitement and somersaulted straight into my skirt, making me laugh and wave off her apologies.

When the dais finally settled onto the ground, every fae before us swept to their knees, an ever-expanding wave of kneeling that rolled away from us across thousands of gathered fae. Forefront among them was Thorne, and I'd never been gladder of his serious face and his support.

After the coronation party, where we'd all been uncharacteristically sensible and very grown up, Neela insisted that we all head to the Lakehouse together to decompress.

"But I'm tired," Leif whined, tugging Alara along behind him as he came up to nuzzle Neela's shoulder.

"We're all tired," Neela said, "but we need this. We've spent all day being regal, now we need to let down our hair. Together."

The rest of us didn't take much convincing. I was curious how the Lakehouse might have changed after our coronation. Maybe it would grow little crowns for us, or turn our individually bespoke couches and chairs into thrones. Or, since it was intended as a place for the heirs to spend time together and bond, maybe it wouldn't let us enter since we were no longer heirs.

We took the moonway from the Rose Palace since it was closest to the festivities in the city center. A soft citrus scent welcomed us as we emerged behind the Lakehouse, but my nerves crowded my stomach as we approached the furred door. I didn't think I could handle being rejected from this place right now, not after everything we'd been through to get here. Sensing my unease, Thorne squeezed my hand, and I remembered to breathe.

With a gentle push, the door opened, and we all released little sounds of happiness, bubbles of relief. Leif and Alara yipped like pups and rubbed themselves against the walls in the entryway, while Ronan laughed at them and Neela shoved through into the main room.

Everything was unchanged, perfect. The room welcomed us in, warm and inviting. The floor-to-ceiling glass wall overlooked the lake, which was placid and still, reflecting thousands of stars on its flat surface. Leif's large silver couch, which had expanded enough to fit Alara too, looked comfy and cozy beside Ronan and Neela's oversized black leather armchair. Dion's beanbag looked just as goofy and out-of-place as ever, and my elegant glass chaise longue still beckoned me like an old sweater.

Dion went straight to the kitchen, running his fingers across the counters and sighing contentedly.

"Whatcha cookin', Double D?" Neela asked, plopping onto Ronan's lap atop their black leather seat.

"That's King to you," Dion said with a smile.

With one arm slung around Ronan's neck, Neela leaned forward in a flowery bow. "My apologies. Whatcha cookin', King D?"

Ronan and Leif burst out laughing, releasing all the pent-up energy of the day.

"Man, I could do with some King D," Alara mused, and Leif pounced on her, wrestling her to the rug.

Thorne and I relaxed on my chaise longue, which had softened a lot these past few months. Where it used to be hard as glass, to remind me of my posture and pose, it now held my body like a warm maternal hug, soft and cozy.

With a flick of her fingers, Neela summoned flames in the fireplace, which danced around the room and chased the shadows away. It was already bright, but none of us liked shadows anymore.

I would never look at a patch of darkness again without double checking for fangs. None of us would.

The threat had passed with Lexi sacrificing herself in a way none of us truly understood, but we knew we were safe, and that all the Walkers and creatures had returned to dust. But, like so much of what we'd experienced lately, we had emerged warier and wiser, aware of how good we had it, and how bad it could get.

"Music," Neela declared.

"Music what, tomcat," Ronan asked, lazily twisting a strand of her spiky blue hair around his pinky.

"We need music, doofus," she said sweetly, popping a kiss on his nose before leaping to her feet. "Why the hell don't any of you assholes have music magic?" she demanded, looking between us with interrogation in her gaze. "You can summon fire and drench cities and make fae do your will, but you can't manifest a little jazz when we need it."

"You can do those things too, princess," I said, letting myself relax against Thorne as he sat beside me. I slumped so hard against him that I thought I might melt into his side, my face melding to his chest and sliding down into his armpit.

"But I can't make music," she said, sounding quite sad about it.

"Donnebysilly," I murmured, wondering if I really might fuse with Thorne's nipple.

Neela turned on me. "Was that a music incantation? Do you need a hand movement to go with it? Can you teach me?"

"Courseacannn," I replied, almost asleep.

Thorne's solid arm pulled me closer to his side, sending a wave of his cologne around me, and I sighed in happiness.

"You don't need magic to make music," he said, translating my murmured nonsense into something Neela could under-stand. "You just need a soul."

Ronan laughed. "That could be a problem," he muttered, earning a fake scowl from his beloved.

Neela folded her arms across her chest, poking one hip out far enough to take out someone's eye. "This isn't time for your weird truth mumbo jumbo," she said to Thorne, then muttered, "God, I've never missed iPhones more."

Instead of replying, Thorne opened his mouth and sang. A sweet, beautiful melody filled the room, brimming with his husky tone, and sending goosebumps along my arms. Thorne and I had connected over music, fought over that faeboe he'd thought I was stealing from him, and come to understand each other through beats and song. He was a talented musician, and since he'd moved to Verda and spent hours every day practicing, he'd flourished. I could listen to his voice for days, but I knew he wanted more than that.

He didn't want to perform, he wanted to connect.

Thorne's voice wrapped around us like a warm breeze, rich with a longing I knew all too well. Each note wove together our pain, our joy, our losses, and our triumphs.

Without moving from my perfect spot against his chest, I joined in, adding my mezzo-soprano to his bass and following his lead in harmonies and crescendos. A strange peace settled over me. For the first time in months, I wasn't just surviving— I was alive.

Neela scraped her jaw off the rug then after a moment of hesitation, she joined in, punctuating our tune with thigh slaps and whoops. Leif's pure wolf song rose to meet ours, a sweet tenor I'd only heard once or twice before.

Ronan's head was swaying to the music, and Dion leaned against the kitchen counter with a massive smile, tapping against the marble with his fingers.

Alara's voice was almost as sweet as Leif's and together, we made music. The new kings and queens and our chosen loves murmuring and dancing and howling and making sound.

We played in perfect harmony, responding to one another's strengths and weaknesses like we were born to it. The same way we would rule.

It wasn't the best music ever made, it was more like a mesh of ideas and emotions all swirling together, all of us releasing our feelings into the air and grinning like idiots, and I fucking loved it.

Lexi

"You do not have to go."

Dominic's hand was on my shoulder, a pressure so light I could barely sense and so heavy it was all I could feel. Mortia's realm was strange like that, both physical and absent all at once, like I imagined it would feel to dance on the moon.

I stood overlooking our domain. The God of death had upheld his end of the bargain and bestowed a kingship of sorts onto Dominic in return for the thousands of souls he had reaped. A valley fell away from our large estate, rolling green fields dotted with flowers that when glimpsed from the corner of your eye were brightly colored but, on closer inspection, were pale and transparent. Everything in Mortia's realm was a paradox, and although I was no longer startled by every dichotomy, I was far from used to it.

"It's my cousin's wedding," I replied without turning around. "I have to go."

"Parting the veil is difficult," Dominic said, and I could hear the tension and worry in his voice. "I will come with you."

I huffed out a laugh. "I'm not a hundred percent certain you'd be welcome."

"Oh."

"Just since you turned the last one into a slaughterhouse,

you know," I clarified. "It's nothing personal."

"That was not me per se, it was the Shadow Walkers."

"Who were acting on whose orders?"

"Not exactly orders, more like telepathic compulsion."

I turned to face him, crossing my arms over my chest, feeling that odd sense of touching and not-touching. "And whose evil telepathic compulsion were they acting on?"

Worry was etched on Dominic's face. His black hair had grown shaggy, his dark eyes held more depths than ever, and I knew the toll on him was heavy. Every day he encountered another fae he'd killed, either by his own hand or his command, and each one pained him. I had slowly come to realize that Mortia had gifted him this kingship as a punishment as much as a reward, and that he was condemned to endless days of regret.

But he deserved that. He and I both knew it, so we didn't dance around it. I didn't lie to him and say he needn't feel guilty, and he didn't grovel and ask forgiveness. Not from me, at least, although I'd caught him more than once offering boons to those he'd killed.

Dominic's mouth twisted and the tricksy light limned his cheekbones. "Fine, I shall stay here." He looked me up and down, taking in my fae denim jeans, off-the-shoulder black tee, and my long hair pulled back in a loose bun. "Why aren't you wearing your pajamas? I thought that was some human wedding custom."

I kicked out at him, but he swatted my boot away easily. "Last time, I was caught napping. Literally. She had the wedding in the middle of the night, for God's sake, was I supposed to wear a ballgown to bed?"

He smirked, his gaze focused on me like I was the only thing in existence. "Everybody else seemed to figure it out."

"Be prepared, they said. The wedding could be any time, they said."

"Time to get dressed now, they said, and you ignored all that excellent advice," he interjected, and I scowled at him just as profoundly as he deserved.

"Stupid bloody tradition. I mean, who gets married at three a.m.?" I grumbled.

"Stupid kings and queens," he answered, knowing it would irritate me,

"Don't call my family stupid. Attempting to kill them is one thing, but I won't have you insult them."

Dominic caught my wrists without a smile on his face, apparently immune to my wit. "Be careful up there, human."

We used the term "up" to refer to the mortal plane, but that wasn't accurate geographically or physically. Our world was an approximate map of the mortal plane, and I'd spent the months since we'd arrived figuring out which hills and dales down here corresponded with which forests and cities up there.

Traveling was tricky and, somehow, easier than ever. To go long distances, you had to both move your feet, duh, but also think your way to where you wanted to be. One of those body-mind duologies that Mortia loved so much—not that I'd met the guy. Magic had no bearing on it, thank God, or I supposed, thank Mortia. So that meant that I was just as powerful as any fae down here, and Dominic couldn't wield shadows any better than I could. In fact, I'd spent every spare minute practicing traveling around this place and figuring out how everything worked, so I was secretly getting waaay better than him. Suck on that, Shadow King.

"I'm badass, babe. You don't need to worry about me," I assured him, while pulling my wrists free of his grip and striking a power pose.

"Badass? You are just shy of completely incompetent," he muttered, so I swiftly punched him in the belly and got a lovely "ocf" out of him.

"I'm very shy of incompetent," I said, then I twirled my fingers and summoned some water out of the air—another one of Mortia's fun paradoxes, where you needed water to make fire, fire to make air, and air to make water—and drenched my beloved from shaggy black head to leather booted toe.

His gaze raked over every dry inch of me, and his jaw was open. "I am impressed," he purred, pulling me closer. "Where did you learn to do that?"

I shrugged, pushing his soggy chest away with my palm. "I'm magic."

"No you are not, Larper," he said, calling me the nickname he only used when he was teasing. "You are many things, but magic is not one of them."

"Oh, yes? Like what?"

"You are smart," he began, looking me up and down, then pulling me close again. "Cute. Sexy as hell." I looked around at our not-very-sexy surroundings with a fake frown and he amended his description to, "Fine, way sexier than hell. You are strategic, brave to the point of stupidity, and very, very not-magic."

"That list started out well, but it went kinda downhill. Plus, you forgot battle-hardened strategic genius. You need to work on your compliments."

He pressed a lip to mine to shut me up, then mumbled. "I said you were strategic."

I spoke into his mouth. "The battle-hardened and genius bits are very important."

He laughed and pulled away. "But not magic. So how did you pull water out of your behind?"

"Gross," I said, making a face. "It wasn't ass water."

He shrugged. "If it was your ass I would not mind."

"Still gross. Maybe grosser. Anyway, I've been paying attention to everything since we arrived. You've had powers for so long you take them for granted, but I'm studying like there's some kind of death exam coming up."

"Huh," he said, at a loss for words and looking all sorts of impressed. Man, I'd never felt prouder.

"So, if either of us can part the veil, it's me. And I'll be fine. I know where the wedding is, I know where that corresponds to down here, and I'm ready to leave. So kiss me goodbye and then watch me go."

Man, I sounded badass. The truth was I didn't know exactly how to part the veil, but I had a few ideas and a lot of motivation.

I expected another argument from the King of Debate, but instead, he pulled me to his water-soaked chest and kissed me like it was our first time. I drowned in that kiss, falling to the bottom of the ocean and losing myself among the currents and pulls of his lips and the cold press of his body against mine. Time stilled while we embraced, his lips and tongue firm and demanding as he devoured me from the inside.

When he pulled away, he grabbed my shoulders, looking intensely into my face. "Take fucking care," he growled, then he spun on his heel and strode away like he couldn't bear to watch me leave. I stayed still for long moments, recovering from the intensity of that kiss, then I squared my shoulders and got to work.

An hour later, I reached the field of cloying jasmine that corresponded to the Jewettim Falls in Caprice. Delph didn't want to marry at the site of her last attempted wedding's massacre, for some reason, and after much debate, they'd landed on Jewettim Falls. Apparently, that was where Delph had first heard Darzan compliment her, or something. I mean, that must have been one fucking kickass compliment. Maybe he could give Dominic some lessons.

I settled onto a log, focusing on the strands of air—thin, glimmering threads that dissolved into droplets as I tugged them free. My soft fae jeans clung to my legs, soaked with the strange water that trickled from the torn veil. After several hours work, I was exhausted but had a large enough hole in the air to step through.

When I passed through to the mortal realm, I felt an immediate tug, deep in my belly, pulling me back home to Mortia's land. That was where I belonged, and being here felt all kinds of wrong, so I knew I couldn't stay long.

But for now, I ignored that yanking urge and stayed put, amazed at how overwhelming the world was—the soft scent of flowers from the wedding decorations made the jasmine seem tame, and the pounding of water falling upward— upward?!—was deafening. Nauseating.

Colorful mist swirled around my hips and legs, and as the elegantly dressed guests walked through it, the mist moved around them creating beautiful shades and shapes, but everything was so bright I couldn't see without squinting.

Through narrowed eyes, I saw her. My amazing cousin with the kickass job title and the hunky husband. Delphinium. She wore a plain white dress with silver embroidery, a perfect marriage of human and Caprician traditions that disappeared into the luminescent mist, so I couldn't tell if it swept the ground. Her black hair was loose around her shoulders, making her look younger, more like the girl I knew back in Hebes, my fierce protector and loyal cousin. I missed her fit to bursting.

Darzan looked like her match today. At their last attempted wedding, he'd been dressed to highlight their differences, but now he wore a white suit with silver lapels and buttons, and his golden hair was longer than usual, a halo of liquid gold. He was still terrifying and intimidating, but I somehow missed him too.

I scanned the guests, looking for my sisters, but they weren't there. Delph had told me she forbade them from returning to Arathay, and it seemed they were far more obedient than me. Dad wasn't there either, although I didn't expect him to be because he was a homebody. But I got a pang of longing at seeing the Verdan heirs I'd befriended, swapping barbs and teasing one another, and it felt almost as good as seeing my family.

Delph was gentle and placid as she married the fae she loved, smiling up at his severe face, glowing under his silver gaze. Not me. I bawled like a baby with croup. It was clear that nobody could see or hear me, because the sounds coming from my heaving chest were something like an ox in labor, yet nobody batted an eyelid.

It wasn't just happiness that had tears dripping from my chin. But sadness too. I had hoped to say goodbye, to let the twins know I was okay, to share one final hug with somebody made of flesh and blood, somebody who would know I was missing and feel my absence as strongly as I felt theirs, but nobody knew I was here.

Delph and Darzan shared a kiss that sparked little bolts of energy around the space, lighting up the rising stream in the waterfalls. Everybody gasped, so I knew that was special, probably a sign of Gaia's approval. Caprice was, after all, the realm of Lightning.

At the end of the ceremony, Delph gave a beautiful speech. True to her generous self, it wasn't about her love or her future, or even her new husband. It was about rebuilding the realm and finding solace for the loss so many families had endured.

Then she mentioned me. A tear trickled down her cheek as she spoke of the brave cousin, Lexi Smith, who had ended the Shadow War, and at her final words, she looked directly at me with a gentle smile on her face, those glowing silver eyes piercing right through my not-body.

Then I was gone. The tug in my belly pulled taut, irresistible and as strong as gravity, and I was yanked back home. A great sense of relief washed over me at being in the realm where I belonged. Gone was the overwhelming realness of the mortal world, the clamor and odor and blinding brightness of reality, replaced by the serene pastures of home.

The quiet of Mortia's realm welcomed me back, its paradoxes grounding me more than the chaos of the mortal world ever could. At last, I could breathe. I filled my lungs with the sweet, sweet air that I already knew more intimately than I'd known nature during my life, and I turned my head toward home.

Here, I belonged. Despite missing my human family, I knew I was in the right place, and that my soul would be forever beside its twin.

A smile tickled my lips. Adventure awaited.

Leif

YET ANOTHER THREE MONTHS LATER...

"Why have I never heard of the Barbed City?" Alara asked.

We were headed to that far-flung place in the shit-ass south of Ourea for an Ascension. Most Ourean Ascension Rites took place in the capital, Bluff Peak, but the Barbed City had rules of their own and didn't play nicely with others, so apparently, we all had to hike down there for an extra Ascension Rite. Which suited me just fine, because it meant an extra party.

My mate's question barely sat in the air for a second before Ronan jumped in to answer.

"Because you're a country bumpkin z-class wolf from the middle of nowhere," he said smoothly. "You didn't have the education we kings and queens had, and you wouldn't know a royal event from a furball."

Ronan smirked at Neela, who rolled her eyes. He was just trying to rile me up. He definitely was dropping bait in my ocean and hoping I'd bite.

Well, I wouldn't. I could handle a tiny fake insult to my mate without completely overreacting. After all, we'd been mated for over two years and I was a mature king with all my shit in boxes. But when I looked at her beautiful pale face framed with orange hair that glowed like the sun, I thought I detected a slight frown, and I couldn't have anybody upsetting my female.

I pounced at Ronan and we both flew out of the moonway and onto the surrounding rocks, so black and shiny they might have been made from obsidian.

"Take that back, asshole," I growled, pinning him down by the neck and snapping my jaws in his face.

"That's so not scary when you're in fae form," Ronan gurgled, somehow grinning despite the ever-decreasing oxygen making it down his throat.

He was goading me, again, but I couldn't help it. Instantly, I changed into my huge silver wolf, shredding my clothes in the process, then snapped my teeth right over his face and growled low in the back of my throat. I let a big glob of saliva drip onto his cheek for good measure.

"Bleurgh, are you trying to make me die of disgust?" he croaked, and I figured I'd better remove my paws from his throat before I killed him.

He climbed to his feet with a cocky grin, and as soon as I turned back into my fae form, he punched me in the jaw.

I whirled on him, anger blazing inside me.

"Now we're even," he said. "One little punch in exchange for you almost killing me. That sounds fair to me."

"You insulted my mate," I growled.

Ronan turned to look at where our friends had paused, still inside the moonway. Because they were still, they looked perfectly normal from our perspective, but if they started walking, they'd blur and disappear from view within seconds.

Alara was grinning at me, her orange gown hugging her curves and making me want to bury myself inside it.

"You call her a country bumpkin all the time," Ronan protested.

"I can do whatever I want with her," I said, and an image of my mate cuffed to the dungeon wall and panting in desire had my cock hardening, which was very noticeable to everyone given that my fancy party clothes were in tatters on the black stone at my feet.

Gabrelle called out, all cool poise tinged with amusement. "Okay, boys, when you've finished playing, we have a royal function to make." She folded her arms across my chest as she looked me up and down. "And it looks like you'll be arriving in your full glory," she said.

That killed my boner. Anybody looking at me nude, other than Alara, had me instantly limp, and my dick went to sleep against my thigh when it heard Gabrelle's comment.

Neela scoffed. "It's hardly a royal function. We're only going for the party."

"And the food," Dion added. "The South of Ourea does a fermented peregrine stew I've always wanted to try. It's supposed to taste like flying over prehistoric forests."

Ronan and I made it back to the moonway—which we were only able to locate since our buddies were standing in it—then we resumed walking to the Barbed City.

"D, I'll make you a pea-grime stew if you give me your pants."

He turned to look at me. He smelled of poached pears and porridge and had pale eyes and hair, so he'd clearly had a good oaty breakfast. "You can't cook."

"I'll learn if you give me your pants."

"No."

I turned to where Thorne was walking behind me. "Give me

your pants, truth boy."

"Fuck off," he said without looking up from his conversation with Gabrelle.

"Yeah, that's fair," I mumbled.

Alara stopped walking, and I almost bumped into her. She began peeling off her miniskirt, and I got hard for her, of course. "OK, babe," I said, pulling her to me by the hips.

"Later, Alpha," she whispered, and hell if that didn't make my cock even harder. But when she proffered me her miniskirt and shrugged, I realized what was happening.

"You can't be serious," I grumbled.

She shrugged again, and her orange eyes glowed with mischief. "Up to you."

She dropped the skirt on the smooth black stone at our feet, then continued walking away, her black leggings keeping her decent.

I watched my friends all recede into the distance before I grumbled and bent to pick up Alara's ridiculous tiny orange circle miniskirt. After shimmying into it, thankful it had an elastic waist and plenty of give, I raced after my crew, with my dick and the circle skirt flopping in time.

* * *

The Queen of the Barbed City was a right bitch. Honestly, she could give the Shadow King a run for his money. Apparently, she grew up dirt poor, and that had made her 'ambitious', which was supposed to excuse everything. Well, if you put ambitious in a gown and handed it your balls on a platter with a shiny knife, you'd get the Queen. She looked like she wanted to spay me and would smile while she did. After the formal introductions, I steered well clear of her.

We skipped the actual Ascension and headed straight for the party, obviously. Technically, we didn't have to attend at all since we were the current rulers—we could have sent Ro's or D's mom but we wanted the excuse to blow off steam.

Gabrelle had made me and Alara swap outfits, so she wore the skimpy orange skirt and I rocked her skin-tight black leggings, which barely made it over my butt.

A live string quartet hovered up near the ceiling, and at the end of every song, they poured glitter over the crowd, so we were soon sparkling like unicorns.

Gabrelle sauntered through the fae, eyeing me up and down with a scowl. She wore a tailored purple dress with complicated cutouts where her smooth brown skin peeked out, looking exactly like she hadn't just rushed on foot from Verda City to get here on time. Not a dusty pink hair was out of place.

"I thought you were going to borrow some proper clothes," she said, handing me a glass of bubbling Fae Fizz.

I accepted the glass and took a long gulp before answering. "Doesn't sound like something I'd say."

She cocked out a hip. "When we arrived in this hellhole, the first thing you said was that you had to run a quick errand so you didn't make a fool of yourself at the party. I assumed you were finding more appropriate pants. And maybe a shirt."

I finished my glass and swapped it with the full one Gabrelle was holding. Nice of her to bring me two. "Don't you know me at all, babe? I'm wounded." I put one hand to my heart to show how very upset I was.

Her mouth hitched up at one side. "So what were you doing? What was so important you couldn't attend the pre-party speeches?"

"Anything. Literally anything was more important than listening to those snooze fests."

She absent-mindedly took a sip of the empty glass she was holding before realizing I'd already drunk it for her. "Leif, tell me what you those 'errands' were. You know this place is a political bonfire, and a tiny spark could set the whole thing exploding. One wrong word from you, and—"

"Again, wounded," I interrupted, grabbing a crumbed morsel from the nearest passing rhona, a lumbering creature that had a tray of delights attached to its back as it meandered placidly through the crowd. "None of my words are wrong."

"This is serious, Leif," she said. "The peace in the Barbed City is more fragile than anywhere else in all of Arathay. The noble Houses are beholden to the Queen through unbreakable oaths, but rumors abound of their dissatisfaction. We can't be seen to side with any party or talk too long or too loud with one of the heirs. If you spent the afternoon with one of them, I need to know about it."

In the good old days, Gabrelle would have kept her emotions hidden and remained calm at all times, but now her face was turning purple to match her dress and there was practically steam coming out of her ears. I kinda missed the good old days.

"Chill, babe, I was just borrowing this." I pulled out my tennis ball and chucked it in the air, watching it arc beautifully before snatching it out of the air.

Neela sidled up to us, rocking her sky-blue leather pants that perfectly matched her hair. "How do you always have a tennis ball, wolf?" she teased. "You don't even have a shirt."

"I prioritize," I answered seriously, bouncing the ball off the obsidian floor tiles, and Gabrelle snorted.

Neela stood on her tiptoes and waved at someone through the crowd, but she was so short it was like a normal-sized person wiggling their fingertips by their ears.

Hoping she was trying to get some of that roast boar I could smell, I wolf-whistled, and the entire room froze and turned to us, then Neela called out to Delphinium and Darzan, the Lightning dudes from Caprice. By the time they reached us, without any boar, the party had returned to normal volume, with winged faeries cavorting above us and the hovering band playing over the strains of conversation.

Neela pulled Delphinium into a hug, blowing some glitter off her shoulder as she spoke. "Congratulations, hon. You too," she said, turning to Darzan next and reaching up to try to get her tiny arms around him.

Never one to be left out of a snuggle, I nuzzled against Darzan, who was closest to me, letting his gold hair tickle my nose. "Congrats, bro. What for?"

"My wedding," he said, turning his freaky gaze on me, but it didn't feel like a blade to my throat when he looked at me like it used to, more like a warm hand on my back. Apparently, the feel of a War Wielder's gaze reflected your relationship with him, so I guess that meant Darzan and I were buddies.

"Oh yeah, how'd it go?" I asked, smiling at my official new pal. "No slaughters this time?"

Gabrelle hissed at me, her sharp intake of breath like a blade through the tension. Neela's smile faltered, her pale complexion turning ashen. But Darzan didn't flinch. His lips pressed into a thin line, and his eyes met mine, steady as steel. "Not this time," he said, his voice a quiet storm.

Their realm had paid dearly for the Shadow King's reign, losing hundreds of fae lives during the Shadow wedding and again during the Battle of Capricia. And Delph's cousin had made the ultimate sacrifice, giving up her own life to end the Shadow King once and for all.

I let my inner Alpha rise to the surface, stilling the jocular fun while I placed a hand firmly on Delph's shoulder. "I am sorry for your family's sacrifice, and grateful for it. The realms owe your family a great debt."

My words were quiet but they echoed through the small space between us, replacing the inconsequential party chatter with something important, if only just for a moment.

Delph looked up at me, her silver eyes shining. "Lexi was at the wedding. I don't know how she did it, and I know I'll never see her again, but she was there. And she looked, I don't know, complete. Whole. Happy. I didn't speak with her, but she glowed with contentment and purpose, and I just know she's doing ok." She placed her small hand over mine. "So thank you, but I don't think it was a sacrifice at all. Lexi would make the same decision every single time, I'm sure of it."

The party receded into the background as Gabrelle, Neela, and I looked at Delphinium's face, and what I found there gave me hope. She radiated acceptance and strength, and under her rule, Caprice would rebuild and flourish.

Determination flowed through me to find the same acceptance and strength for myself, for my wolves, and for all the fae of Verda. We had lost hundreds of lives, and the shifter communities were hit the hardest of all, but we would rise from the ashes more powerful and alive than ever.

Gabrelle pulled Delph into a tight hug, and tears streamed from her face. She was more than just an ice queen now. And I was more than just a joker with good hair and a spectacular body. I was also an Alpha, a King, and I took those responsibilities seriously.

And I knew, better than anybody, that sometimes the next best move was to reconnect, strengthen friendships, and help others to recover.

With that in mind, I threw back my head and howled. When I had the whole room's attention, I projected my voice as loudly as I could. "Who's ready to party?"

Every wolf in the room howled back at me, even though none except Alara were from Verda, and I swear a bunch of non-wolves joined in. Darzan let loose a deafening bellow of joy and power that had me shaking, and then the party really began.

Epilogue–Neela

The gleam of a gilded building caught the last rays of the sun as I walked along Picolo Street, reminding me of when I'd first arrived in Arathay and planned to peel the gold off the buildings to sell for food and board. I was a cold, hard girl with a cold, hard past, and the fae world was overwhelming to me.

I wonder what that girl would think of me now. Blond hair now blue, old jeans with holes in the knees swapped for black fae denim that moved and stretched with my body, the hunted feeling replaced by a sense of belonging and ownership. Would she think I was weak? I flexed my biceps as my boots thudded on the cobblestones, knowing I had never been stronger.

No, she would just think I was a lucky bitch for how my life turned out. Married to a dark, brooding God of a male, living in my very own palace, with memories of Mom and Dad and Seb that I could visit whenever I wanted to, Queen of the fucking fae.

"Massive muscles," Ronan commented mildly at my flex, then casually hardened his oversized arms right in front of my face.

"Show off," I murmured, but God he looked sexy when he did that, and I couldn't help but lean up and grab his arm, hugging it to my face.

A family of seven passed us, the faelings giggling and running in circles while their moms tried to rush them along. They traveled under their own hovering faelight, which was a habit many fae still held onto after the darkness of the Shadow King, and I watched them as they passed by a ruined storefront, a bundle of chaos and love.

"Getting clucky, tomcat?" Ronan asked.

I elbowed him. "Actually, I was thinking how we need to make the fae feel safe again. They shouldn't have to walk around in fear of being attacked."

"Give them time. It's only been a few months. They'll gradually relax their guard and things will go back to normal."

We reached the Ogre's Nose, where we were meeting the others, and the rusted sign of a cranky ogre with a massive schnoz creaked back and forth in the light breeze.

Ronan opened the door to go in, but I grabbed his arm to hold him back. "Normal isn't good enough," I said. "We need them to feel safe and we need to make sure nothing like this happens again. Maybe we can train an army or something."

"An army wouldn't have helped, tomcat. Not against the Walkers."

"Then we'll..." My mind searched frantically for another solution. We couldn't just sit around and leave our fae vulnerable to whatever madman attacked next. There had to be something we could do. "We'll start a university, get a bunch of researchers to figure out what other dark magic is out there that might leave us weak."

Ronan kissed my forehead. "You want to pay a bunch of fae to research dark magic? Cos that doesn't sound at all dangerous."

I hissed in frustration. He was right, that wasn't the solution, or at least not all of it. "There has to be something we can do. Protecting Verda wasn't just an obligation—it was a promise I'd made to myself, to this world, and to everyone who'd suffered under the Shadow King.

Ronan became serious. He took my hands and held them loosely in his own, and I could sense his pulse slowing as he looked at me. "We will figure something out, I promise. And whatever you decide, I will follow your lead. I am your husband and your friend and your lover and your biggest fan. Most of all I am your servant, and you are my Queen."

He dropped to one knee and bent his head.

I tugged at his hands. "Get up, babe, you're being ridiculous."

There was a time when I would have sacrificed puppies to see Ronan kneel before me, would have given up every day in my future for just one hour when I saw him brought to heel. But that was long past, and now I only wanted him to stand up and stop embarrassing me.

"Honestly, can you stand the hell up," I hissed, looking around in the hope that we didn't have any witnesses. It wasn't exactly seemly for King Ronan Mentium to be kneeling in the grimy alleyway.

Most fae had no idea that Gaia ranked the five monarchs so that if there was ever any disagreement about matters of state, the higher-ranked rulers took precedence. It prevented wars and had kept the peace for millennia and was, frankly, a good idea. But most fae didn't know that, so it would look very odd indeed for one king to be kneeling before a queen.

Ronan raised his eyes from the cobblestones then, his black gaze boring into me and his knee still firmly on the ground. "Gaia placed you as the highest-ranking royal, and you have my fealty. I will always defer to you."

"Except when I tell you to stand up, I suppose," I said drily, folding my arms across my chest and cocking out a hip.

He grinned then and, in one movement, stood to his full height and swung me over his shoulder like a sack of potatoes. "Or when I'm off the clock," he added, sauntering into the Ogre's Nose wearing a damn princess like a satchel.

Despite myself, I giggled. All the queening I'd been doing was exhausting, and sometimes it was nice to just feel like a normal couple.

The bar was as understated as always, with dark wood, booths tucked around the edges, something loud, soulful, and smooth playing from the enchanted ceiling, and barely enough light to see by. The air smelled of roasted spices and aged spirits.

Ronan deposited me onto a bar stool at a marble table between Leif and Dion, then took his place next to Gabrelle.

"Really?" Gabrelle asked, raising a perfectly manicured eyebrow. She wore a yellow jumpsuit that fitted her curves magnificently, and when she crossed one long leg over the other, all of us turned to look at her. "We're sitting in rank order?"

I snorted, then looked around. The rest of our crew, Alara, Thorne, and my good friend Liz, had made themselves scarce this evening, so it was just the five of us, perched on stools around a small round table. Me in my rockstar black jeans and boots, then Leif wearing low-slung silver pants that highlighted the silver in his hair and eyes and a white tee, smirking like the cat who got the cream. Or the dog who got second place in Gaia's ranking.

Next to Leif was Ronan, my black-eyed devil who wore all

black, of course, and had a smug expression on his face at having deliberately placed us around the table in rank order. "Just for tonight," he said. "The throne room will rearrange to this order, so we might as well get used to it."

Ronan had always expected to rank first or second, with Gabrelle in the other position, and since Gaia had announced our rankings yesterday, I'd looked for signs of disappointment or frustration, but he seemed happy enough. And he was sincere when he'd knelt down outside and sworn his devotion to me, so maybe he really was content. I think he liked being dominated more than he'd ever admit.

But I had no intention of making any decisions without him and the others. We were a team, and I would only use my ranking as an absolute last resort, which was possibly why Gaia had blessed me with it.

Sure, I was strong and fast and one of the most powerful Growers that Verda had ever seen, but each of my companions was equally impressive. Leif, my number two, was the Alpha of Alphas and had kept the shifter communities back from the brink of war during the Shadow King's reign of destruction. Both Ronan and Gabrelle had proven themselves worthy by passing Gaia's Ultimate Test and killing their own parents, which I wasn't sure I could have done. Never having known my parents, I couldn't imagine throwing away the chance, and I knew for a fact it was the hardest thing Ronan had ever done. And Dion could turn mud into heaven with just a sprinkling of seasoning and a splash of his Magirus magic.

Gabrelle sat beside Ronan, in position number four, wearing her yellow jumpsuit like a badge of honor, looking more playful and free than she usually did. She and Ro had a longstanding rivalry, and I searched her face for signs of disappointment at her ranking but found none.

Finally, there was Dion. He wore a tailored navy suit and had leaf-green hair and eyes today, which gave his Mediterranean face a boyish look despite the strong jaw and deep-set eyes.

"I guess the first round's on me," he said, waving over a serving fae and ordering two bottles of Fae Fizz.

An odd tension hung between us, and I felt as though I needed to say something. Make a speech. I cleared my throat, with no clue how to start, and four pairs of eyes landed on me. "I, uh, want you to know that…"

I trailed off. What could I say? That I didn't consider myself better than them? That I wouldn't abuse my privileged position? That I valued their opinions and views and would strive to always take them into account?

It all sounded so wanky and formal, and I didn't want our friendship to be ruined by this weird and frankly arbitrary structure imposed by Gaia.

So instead of spouting any queenly nonsense, I raised my glass and finished, "That I always said I'd beat you assholes, and now I finally have."

Gabrelle met my gaze and raised her own glass. "I'll drink to that," she declared, then knocked back her drink and burped.

"Beauty queen!" Dion admonished, and so she burped again, long and loud.

"I'll drink to *that*," Leif said, grinning from ear to ear and downing his glass in one.

The tone of the evening changed at that moment, from tense to fun, from how-should-I-behave to fuck-it-who-cares, and each of us relaxed. We drank and chatted into the night, forgetting about the dramas of our past and the hard work ahead of us in rebuilding our realm and fortifying our fae, and instead focused on the present. On the warmth of our surroundings. On the pleasure of good wine and food. On five good friends with nowhere they'd rather be.

* * *

Hi, I hope you enjoyed the epic ending to the Royal Fae of Arathay! I loved writing this series, and part of me will always live over there, probably beside one of those wine rivers in Verda waiting for a dark, brooding fae to come and fall in love with me.

If you're not ready to stop the fun, head over to my completed trilogy that follows the same couple. A Fallen Angel obsessively hunts a mortal woman who lives in the Undercity because she is the key to his return to heaven. But she is driven by wild revenge and won't fall easily. Enemies to lovers steamy fantasy romance at its best, with captivating characters in a spellbinding world.

Read Vestige now!

xx Zara